THE REDWING SAGA

BOOK SIX

REALMS

OF THE

DEAD

SHARON K. GILBERT

REALMS OF THE DEAD
BOOK SIX OF THE REDWING SAGA
BY SHARON K. GILBERT
WWW.THEREDWINGSAGA.COM

First Print Edition - October, 2019
Kindle Edition - October, 2019

ISBN-13: 978-0-9980967-6-6

AVENUE FICTION

514 ROSE AVENUE, CRANE, MO 65633

Published by Rose Avenue Fiction, LLC
514 Rose Avenue, Crane, MO 65633

TABLE OF CONTENTS

FROM THE AUTHOR

And so, we commence another adventure of the Stuart and Sinclair families. Adele Stuart plays a pivotal role in this one. I've grown to love her dearly, haven't you? When I first wrote her character back in 2016, I'd no idea just how she'd emerge over the course of the books, but she and Sinclair had a certain 'spark' even then, which started me to ponder how I might let that spark develop. You'll find the results of that long 'ponder' in this installment of our tale.

You may also begin to suspect that very few characters appear in these books without purpose and intent. A person mentioned only slightly in one book, might play a greater role in a future installment. And though it may seem that some plot points die away without expansion or explanation, if you could see inside my head (a very scary place) you'd find hundreds of threads connecting these plot points, and many require a very long time to spin out.

Thus far, Charles has been on a path to discovery, and in this volume, he finally remembers important truths about his past. He's about to discover the identity of the Dragon behind the obsidian mirror, or one of them, at least (HINT: there are seven). Also, the enigmatic Anatole Romanov reveals information more clearly (imagine that), and we meet one of his fellow warriors in the person of a very nondescript sort of fellow.

As always, the language style is nineteenth century, and the spelling British. Thank you once again, dear reader, for taking the time to wander the streets of Whitechapel and Westminster with me, as we plumb the depths of underground tunnels and explore the many turnings of the Branham maze.

Oh, and spoiler alert for Book Seven: the prologue of *King's Gambit* is from the year 1948, and you'll get to see a glimpse of what Charles and his remarkable family will one day accomplish for the Kingdom of God.

Sharon K. Gilbert
September 22, 2019

To my beloved husband, Derek,
who patiently loves me
with the boundless heart of
a Charles Sinclair
and the endless valour of
a Paul Stuart.

I love you, Captain.

"By the pricking of my thumbs,
Something wicked this way comes."
– Macbeth, Act IV, Scene i

"ALICE: How long is forever?
WHITE RABBIT: Sometimes, just one second."
– Alice's Adventures in Wonderland
by Lewis Carroll

No more let Life divide what
Death can join together.
– Adonais, Section LIII,
by Percy Bysshe Shelley

Wilt thou shew wonders to the dead?
Shall the dead arise and praise thee?
– Psalm 88:10 (KJV)

PROLOGUE

Walpurgisnacht – Tuesday, 30ᵗʰ April, 1889

"Come, Napper! There's no time for playing. We promised Auntie Tory we'd be home by dusk!"

Adele Marie Stuart stared at the unfamiliar path ahead, trying to determine where the imprudent pup had gone. One minute, Napper was running alongside her; then, upon seeing a flash of brown colour in a lush carpet of bluebells, the dog raced ahead, instantly disappearing into the woodland's thick underbrush.

Poor Della began to fret, wishing she'd controlled her horse more carefully. Tory had warned her never to leave the château's fenced meadow when riding, and Adele had tried to obey, but without warning, the Hanoverian mare leapt over the stone fence, taking her distraught rider into the nearby woods and along the unfamiliar path. If she could just find Napper, then she could lead the horse back to the meadow, with her aunt none the wiser.

IF, she could find the dog.

Dismounting the stubborn horse, Adele explored the mysterious woodland, known locally as *Bois de F*ée, or Faery Woods. Dolly Patterson-Smythe told riveting tales of these ancient trees. Tales of sprites and ghosts, who danced within dewy glades at night; and of handsome vagabonds, who lured unwary women into underground lairs, never to be seen again.

According to Dolly, the spirits of these verdant palaces had once ruled the area, but with the rise of Christianity, retreated into their invisible houses, until they'd become little more than myth. Then, in the latter half of the fourth century, the Brothers of St. Rosaline planted a church, converted most of the villagers, and slowly conquered the pagan forests. In 520 A.D., the industrious monks erected a magnificent stone abbey, financed by King Chlodio of the Franks in appreciation for God's divine aid in his long war against the Romans. And so, the land and the people prospered.

But then, in 536 A.D., cosmic warfare lit up the skies over modern-day Cumbria. Eight blazing stars (seven fiery dragons and one heavenly pursuer) fought a terrifying battle that lasted for many weeks. All Europe, and even parts of Asia, witnessed the monstrous display, and in the end, the seven defeated serpents crashed to the earth, scouring and forever scarring the landscapes of both England and France.

According to epic poems of the era, just after the Great Dragon War, the monks of St. Rosaline's abbey took in an orphaned Celtic baby named Artorius, delivered to them by three mysterious knights, who (it was said), vanished into the aether just after leaving the boy with the priests. Poets sang that the infant's arrival at the abbey roused the ancient faeries from their long slumber.

Records later discovered by a nineteenth century tailor, revealed division amongst the monks, regarding these newly risen sprites. Some thought them ministering angels, for their countenances were glorious to behold, and they waited upon the child as if he were a prince. Other brethren prayed against the supernatural visitors, and one diary even described them as seven feet in height with long hair and faces of unnatural beauty.

In the year 544, a childless knight named Clovis du Saint Clair, adopted the eight-year-old orphan as his son and heir, renaming him Arthur du Saint Clair. As the remarkable child grew, he showed high intelligence, and his great stature, raven hair, and sea-blue eyes were the envy of all men. Saint Clair was kingly and good and filled with mercy. At the age of twenty, this extraordinary young man left his adoptive father to fight for King Childebert I of Paris, becoming a fierce knight. Bards of the era sang of Sir Arthur's military exploits and prowess, naming him a 'child of the gods'.

At thirty years old, the young knight inherited his late father's fortune and married Clothilde du Ross, the only child of his commander, the 1st Duc du Ross. One year later, Sir Arthur's fair-haired wife bore him twin sons, and the eldest of these became the 2nd Duc du Ross.

One song, Dolly told Adele, claimed the Scottish House of Sinclair descended from this remarkable Celtic knight, but she'd never seen proof of it. Adele had listened to the tales with wide eyes, mentioning her Cousin Charles was tall with black hair and sea-blue eyes and asking if it might be a sign of something.

'Likely not,' Dolly had answered with a wink, 'but then how do we know?'

Young Adele Stuart considered these ghostly tales as she walked through the lonely woodland, whispering prayers as she went. Now and then, she felt certain she heard footsteps, but each time she turned, found no one there. The fourth time it happened, she thought she discerned a flash of movement to her right, but decided it must be her imagination playing tricks.

"Napper!" she called as she reached a sign that read *Privé – Ne Passe Pas*. "No trespassing," she sighed.

The woods belonged to the abbey, and hence to its new owner. But surely, no one would complain of a girl trying to find a lost dog, now would they?

Adele decided to ignore the sign and forge ahead.

Suddenly, the silence was broken by the sharp rustle of dry leaves. Della's sharp eyes caught a second flash of colour, grey this time, bouncing through the blanket of bluebells. Hoping she'd found her dog, she led the horse away from the main path and into the dense thicket, her black gabardine riding trousers picking up tiny blue petals as she passed.

"Napper, you must come!" she called again, cupping her mouth with kid-gloved hands. She led the headstrong horse along the leaf-strewn forest floor, careful of thorny brambles and thickets where snakes rousing from winter hibernation might emerge. Sir Richard, Dolly's banker husband, had mentioned seeing a deadly asp two days earlier and cautioned Adele to ride only on the bridle paths; to keep away from the unfriendly woods.

Oh, why didn't I listen?

It was the deep sense of melancholy that ate at her spirit. She kept thinking of home: the Sinclair household, which she now saw as her own, and of her cousins, Elizabeth and Charles. How she missed them! She had come to live with her Aunt Victoria Stuart following Christmas, but after only a few days, she'd begun to miss Charles and Elizabeth. She wondered if Beth could feel the babies move yet (Dolly Patterson-Smythe had told her all about that side of pregnancy), and if Bella's new puppies were healthy. France was certainly an interesting place to live, but even the excitement of the Paris Exposition, with its international exhibits and modern machinery, did little to ease the girl's overwhelming sense of loneliness; hence her decision to ride and the unfortunate escape into the woods.

The May fête was but five weeks away, and Della had hoped to sail back to England in time to celebrate with the Sinclairs, but Victoria had twisted her ankle again, which put all travel plans on hold. Goussainville's new physician, a somewhat sour-faced Englishman named Sir Aleister Palmore, insisted the spinster remain house-bound for at least six weeks. 'No travelling', he'd declared with authority. 'If you want to avoid a permanent limp, that ankle needs time to heal.'

Della had no wish for her aunt to limp, but the idea of missing the fête was simply torture! Disappointed, Adele decided to ride before supper. Dolly Patterson-Smythe once mentioned that Beth loved taking her horse into the thick woods that lay twixt the castle and the old abbey, and that the duchess would spend hours jumping fences and hedges, or just sitting by the peaceful *Miroir* river, so named because its crystal clear waters reflected light as if from a polished blue looking glass. Beth had never owned a dog whilst here, Dolly explained, but Victoria's unruly terrier Samson sometimes followed her into the haunted trees, and had once become seriously lost amongst a stand of wychelms. Thinking now of the tale, a shiver ran along Della's spine. She'd noticed a tightly packed stand of *those very trees*, shortly before Napper's disappearance, and she feared she may have lost the sweet animal forever.

"Napper!" she called again. "Napper, come—oh, please, come!"

The stubborn mare refused to proceed any further. Adele let loose of the reins to allow the animal to graze at her own pace. She stepped deeper into the woods, the musty smell of rotting leaves mixed with fragrant wild iris filling her senses.

"Napper!" she cried. "Come, girl! Come!"

But there was no answering bark, no tell-tale hint that a dog of any kind had passed. Della began to despair. Tears slid down the girl's fair cheeks, and her blue eyes scanned the clearing in desperation for any sign of the willful pet. Her Cousin Charles had given her several lessons on how to track a criminal through open spaces such as a public park, and he'd mentioned broken twigs, trampled ground, disturbed leaves, and bent grass. But everything here appeared serene and unbroken, as though newly born. Not a leaf out of place, not a limb snapped or bent. Surely, her sweet doggy had vanished into thin air!

She'd reached a narrow opening, formed from a stand of half-dead yews. Their sparse branches intertwined into a natural corridor of brown and spring green. The portal took her through a long passage that seemed rather like navigating a living tunnel. After several minutes, Adele emerged into an unexpected and thoroughly magical clearing. Here, the air smelled of honeysuckle, and the late afternoon sun dappled the forest floor with a bedazzling web of dancing shadow and light. The intensity of the glade's magnificent colours struck her eyes with an otherworldly brightness, and in this Puckish realm, the idea of faeries and woodland warlocks seemed overwhelmingly real.

The thought made Della afraid. She felt vulnerable and completely alone.

Then—another sound off to the right!

She turned, hoping to see the dog's black and white fur, but instead perceived that strange glimmer again, somewhat like an iridescent rainbow against the whispering trees. Adele waited for several minutes, her eyes on the colourful display, but it vanished without explanation. She sighed, turning round and round, praying for a sign, any sign of her missing dog.

Nothing. Not a single shred of hope.

Miserable and defeated, she decided to return home without Napper.

The opening to the yew corridor had vanished!

Thick clouds rolled overhead and obscured the sun. The faery glade was plunged into a sea of greys and blacks. Adele lost all sense of direction. Had she entered from behind, from her left, from her right? She had no idea at all.

"Della Marie, you're such a fool!" she exclaimed aloud, fighting back the sting of tears. A faint buzzing sound caught her ears from nearby. She looked up to see a swarm of honeybees near the top of a majestic elm, constructing a hive out of reach of enemies; badgers or even bears.

Bears? she thought, her heart thumping in her ears. The idea of large predators had never entered her mind until now, and Adele suddenly felt very afraid.

Then, another rustling sound, just a few feet ahead.

Adele froze, her heart pounding. *Is it a bear?* Had it killed her dog? Is that why Napper never responded?

Something shot through the air, heading straight towards her!

Della shut her eyes, expecting to be torn to shreds and wishing her Cousin Charles were there to protect her.

Something stopped with a thud, just two feet away from where she stood.

The terrified girl opened her eyes to find a large grey hare sitting at her feet, its startlingly blue eyes fixed upon her face. The impossible eyes stared at the human as if to question why she'd invaded his personal domain. The large rabbit inched closer to her riding boots, sniffing as though inspecting her. It hopped forward another step, mere inches away now; its long ears pointed straight up. It seemed to Adele that it sang to her, but she heard the voice *inside her mind*.

Della began to feel somewhat dreamy, as though entering a light trance. The hare's magical song told of knights and horses and ancient warfare; of monks and battles and a man with sea-blue eyes. She became lost in the hypnotic chorus, and her arms felt like wings. Her feet wanted to dance, and all reality faded into nothingness.

Then someone shouted, the sharp command breaking the mesmeric sensation. Adele's head swam with ghostly images, but she forced her way homeward, to the world of men. As her mind snapped back, she could hear a bird talking, the rude caws coming from high overhead. The enormous bird swept down towards the hive, snapping at the bees, greedily filling its beak with dozens of angry insects.

"He will be sorry he did that," a man's voice spoke from her left.

Adele spun round, shocked to see a stranger standing in the centre of the clearing. He was tall and well-built, with finely sewn black clothing, lined in gold silk. His gleaming hair fell across the broad shoulders in raven spirals. In one hand, he carried a carved walking stick, tipped in chased silver.

In the other, he held a black and white dog.

"Napper!" Della cried out in relief. She dashed towards the man. "You found her. Oh, she's all right, isn't she? I was ever so worried."

"She is yours?" asked the rescuer.

Adele nodded. "Yes. A Christmas present from a very dear aunt. I worried a snake might have bitten her, or perhaps a bear."

"Bears never hunt in my woods. They are afraid even to enter it," the man assured her, the strange accent thick with velvety overtones. "She is a most curious little dog, no? And tired, I think. My manservant found her near my home and gave her some water, but she's grown sleepy as we've walked together. Napper is her name? It is fitting."

Adele nodded once again. "It's actually Lady Napper Stuart-Sinclair, but I call her Napper to keep it simple. I'm Lady Adele Stuart."

"Not Stuart-Sinclair?" asked the stranger, offering a dazzling smile.

"No, but I'd pleased if it were," she told him honestly. "I feel rather like a Sinclair. Duke Charles Sinclair is my cousin, you see, but he's been more like a father in many ways. It's all very complicated."

"Yes, I can see that it is," he replied, the playful smile making him even more handsome. "And this 'more like a father' gentlemen is a duke, you say?"

"Oh, yes! He is the 1st Duke of Haimsbury, and before that the 11th Marquess of Haimsbury. He's also an earl many times over. Six or seven, I should think; and a viscount as well. He descends from both English and French houses. In fact, he is heir to all manner of royal families. Charles Sinclair is one of the most important men in all the world, but none of it's turned his head. Not even a smidge of a smidge! He is a lovely man, sir, and he calls me his little cousin, but sometimes, says I'm more like a daughter. Oh, do forgive me. I'm talking far too much. Aunt Victoria says I should never dominate a conversation, especially when speaking to a gentleman. Please, sir, who are you?"

He'd been smiling the entire time, his sapphire eyes glinting with mirth. The handsome stranger set Napper on the soft grass and offered a deep, formal bow, sweeping his right arm along the ground as a suitor might do for a princess.

"Dear lady, your humble servant is Prince Aretstikapha Araqiel Hunyadi von Siebenbürgen, and I am at your service." The prince stepped close and drew Adele's right hand to his lips, kissing her gloved palm. The whisper of warm breath upon her bare wrist sent a pleasant shiver down the adolescent's spine.

"I am delighted to make your acquaintance," he whispered, fixing her gaze.

The grey rabbit and greedy raven watched from the forked trunk of an old wychelm.

"Thank you," Adele managed to answer. "You are quite gallant, but I hope you'll forgive me. You have a very long name, you see. I wonder, could you say it once more, Your Highness?"

He laughed, the effect musical and disarming.

"You are not the first to ask, dear lady," he told her. "Many who live in these lands have much trouble with my name, but in my homeland, no one thinks it strange or difficult. My second name is easier to pronounce. Call me Araqiel, if you wish. Or Ara, which is easier still."

"Yes, Prince Ara is much easier. Thank you," she said, trying very hard to sound grown up and serious. "You must live nearby, if you found Napper at your home. She'd run off to chase after something in the bluebells—a rabbit or fox."

The sleepy puppy ignored the hare and bird, choosing instead to nestle into the mound of soft grass.

"I do not think her interested in rabbits or foxes just now, my young friend. Your dog chases Morpheus and the land of Nod."

Della yawned, suddenly somewhat sleepy herself. "Oh, do forgive me!" she said, her hand upon her mouth. "I suppose I'm a little tired. The land of Nod? As in the Bible, you mean? And Morpheus, I read about him recently. He's in one of Ovid's books, I think. Is he to do with sleep? If so, it's very fitting."

"There is an ancient myth in my country that says Morpheus was the great god of dreams, and he could appear to dreamers in many different forms," he told her. "In fact, his name refers to this shapeshifting ability, you see. But though he is able to imitate any animal or creature, Morpheus prefers to display himself as one of you—I mean, of course, as *one of us*. A human."

"Pronouns in other languages can be very tricky," the girl graciously observed. "Tell me sir, *do* you live nearby?" she asked again. "I live with my Aunt Victoria Stuart, and she's mentioned no princes in the vicinity; only bankers and businessmen."

"I am neither of those," he told her. "Victoria Stuart is your aunt? How fortuitous! I'd hoped to meet that great lady, for she is friend to the Patterson-Smythes, I think. Is that not so?"

"Oh, yes, it is. Auntie Tory and Dolly are the best of friends. And Dickie—that's Sir Richard Patterson-Smythe—well, he's one of those bankers I mentioned. Are you new here, sir?"

"Very newly arrived. An explorer emerging into the light after a very long winter in solitude and darkness, you might say. My estate is old but quite large, though I currently live in one of the gatehouses. I shall unpack all the many crates, containers, and cases—all my special treasures—once my carpenters complete the renovations and repairs to my home. It is of some history to the area, I understand. A centuries-old abbey."

"The abbey? Oh, everyone knows where that is!" she exclaimed. "We've driven past it many times on our way to Paris. Have you been to Paris yet, Prince Ara? It's a very pretty city, and the Great Exposition opens soon with exhibits and inventions from all over the world. My brother said he may come and take me. Paul often visits Paris. It's for his job, you see."

"And what job might that be, dear lady? Is your brother also a banker, as is Sir Richard? Or is he with this Exposition you mention?"

Adele paused, recalling her brother's strict admonition for secrecy regarding his activities. "Perhaps, I shouldn't say too much about Paul's work. It is somewhat clandestine."

"Clandestine? Forgive me, my young friend. I study your English with great enthusiasm for I hope to visit England soon, but this is a new word for me. Would you explain?"

She laughed, the frank admission granting the young woman a sense of security, for surely, if this handsome stranger asked her advice on the English language, then he couldn't be dangerous, could he? Most adults enjoyed appearing all-knowing to the younger generation. She found the honesty refreshing.

"Clandestine is a lovely word, isn't it?" she said happily. "It refers to secrets. I've overheard Paul use the word many times whilst speaking to my Cousin Charles. Oh, you'd so like him. Charles is one of the most amazing men on earth! And he's promised to visit us soon. When my aunt injured her ankle last week, I wrote to him, and he answered right away, promising to come as quickly as he could manage. Cousin Charles always keeps his promises. And when he does come, he may even take me back with him. I do so miss England. We're having the Branham fête, you know. In just eight days. Oh, you should come!"

"A fate? As in destiny or fortune? That sounds rather interesting."

"No, sir. It's spellt f-e-t-e. Based on the French word meaning feast or festival. It's the four-hundredth fête, and my Cousin Beth's planned all manner of medieval events with armoured horses, just like the knights rode. And there's even a tilt yard! We're to have a demonstration by jousting experts on how fifteenth century knights used lances and swords against one another. It will be the most interesting of all events, I'm sure."

"It sounds barbaric!" the prince laughed. "And I thought the English considered themselves more civilised than most others. Tell me, my friend, how is this a feast?"

"Oh, there will be a great deal of eating, but it's all about opening the estate to outsiders. Rather like a week-long party."

"And this cousin will take you away from here to attend these revels?"

"He promised he would, and as I say Cousin Charles never breaks a promise."

The prince's smile disappeared, and he seemed to grow sad. "Ah, then I am pleased for you, my new friend, but if this admirable gentleman takes you back to England, how are we to learn more about one another? I have very few friends here, you understand. I should hate to lose one so soon."

The rabbit whispered something to the raven, who then flew away into the high branches. The hare's head tilted curiously, and then it, too, bounded off in the same direction as the bird. With her attention fixed on the handsome prince, Della saw none of this. Napper slept through the entire exchange, but the shimmering rainbow formation that Della had sensed earlier reformed itself into a small, brown owl and followed the two plotting animals.

"I shouldn't like for you to be without friends," Adele said, a bashful smile causing her pretty dimples to deepen. "Perhaps, I could ask my aunt if you might visit. You'd like Tory, although she's not quite herself these days. As I said, she's twisted her ankle again, and so doesn't get out much now, which makes her somewhat cross. She's not really old, but I think she's not as agile as she used to be. My Uncle James says Tory used to be as active as I and just as boundlessly curious. But it's late, sir, and we really must be going."

Della turned to fetch the pup, but the Cavalier King Charles Spaniel had fallen fast asleep beneath the whispering trees.

"Napper! Here now, girl! Come!" The sleepy-eyed animal roused slightly, licking at her front paw. "Napper, do be sensible. You cannot sleep all night in the woods. We're never to stay out after dark, and we must find Queenie before we can go home."

"Allow me," offered the prince. He collected the pup and cradled it in his muscular arms. "Who is Queenie? Is that another dog?"

"No, she's my horse. A stubborn one at that. I left her to graze beyond that strange yew tunnel, but that may have been foolish. I pray she's not run off."

"Never fear, my young friend. We shall find your horse. Do not concern yourself. Come. My home is just beyond the glade. I see your Napper is worrying that front paw. She may have injured it. We'll have my sister examine her."

Della drew close to the prince's side, examining the puppy's left forepaw. "Oh, there's a thorn in it! Poor Napper. Your sister? Is she an animal doctor?"

"She is a healer. What you call a surgeon or physician, I think, but she often treats our dogs. You'll discover my sister's heart is tender, much like your own."

"What is her name, if I may ask?" Adele enquired as she walked alongside the long-legged prince.

"Princess Eluna Valerina Charlotte von Siebenbürgen. Another long name, no?"

"Yes, very long. My full name is Adele Marie Stuart. Much easier to remember. Does your sister call you Ara?"

"Indeed, she does."

"And what do you call her, if I may ask?"

He laughed. "Sometimes, Eluna, of course, but when I wish to be especially endearing, she is my little Elunetta. A bright light in any darkness, or so she has always seemed to me. We have known one another our entire lives. She is my twin, you see."

"Twins?" Della asked as they reached a broad stone path. "My cousin is about to become father to twins. A boy and a girl, or so we believe."

"Is this the same remarkable cousin who comes to visit you? This—what was his name again? Duke Charles?"

Adele nodded. "Yes, that's right. And I'm sure he'll come soon, as will the babies. In June, in fact. Twins must be very rare."

"Oh, yes, they are! And we form a bond that is unbreakable," he said, smiling.

They walked past low meadows dotted with colourful cranesbill, ragged robin, globe flower, adder's tongue, and magical lady's mantle. Beyond these, stood two rustic red barns filled with mounds of yellow hay. To the left, the high street of Goussainville village came into view: The slate roof and tall steeple of St. Rosaline's church; *L'Auberge Rouge de Goussainville*, the village's busy inn; the blacksmith's shop and mews; Dr. Palmore's office; the rural schoolhouse; and a collection of picturesque shops. To the right of the old Roman road, stood endless acres of pine and juniper trees, and somewhere beyond those, lay her aunt's château.

Just ahead, Adele could see the first sign of the abbey, where several men repaired the estate's stacked-stone fences.

"Everyone looks very busy," Adele said as she waved to one of the men. "Is it true the village children throw stones at the abbey windows? I imagine that's why you put up the no trespassing signs. I noticed the sign at the edge of the woods. I'm very sorry I broke your rules, Your Highness."

"Not at all, dear friend! I am delighted you chose to disobey, or rather your spaniel did. As to the children who play here, I've come to know many of them, and they no longer throw the stones. They mean no harm by it. Truly, I enjoy meeting young people, but it is only polite to seek the owner's permission before entering a home, don't you think? Free will is a very important law."

"I've not heard it put that way before, but asking permission is only being polite."

To access the abbey compound, the duo passed beneath an enormous ironwork entry. The black metal had been twisted and worked to resemble a flock of ravens in flight. And supporting this avian canopy, stood a massive pair of limestone pillars, their mighty heads crowned by snarling dragons, made from the same twisted iron.

Within the courtyard, a hive of activity greeted the young visitor: men and women busily hoeing furrows, planting crops, shaping iron near a bright forge, plucking chickens for that day's meal, weaving willow baskets, sawing ash into long planks, setting bricks in the walls, and glazing windows. Della counted thirty-three workers in all, each person focused on his or her task.

Everyone bowed or curtsied as the prince passed by, and Adele suddenly felt quite out of place beside her regal and most important host. "Perhaps, I'm intruding, Your Highness," she said. "Everyone looks quite busy. I should go find Queenie and ride back to the château. I'm sure Aunt Victoria is worried."

"Queenie is your horse, no?"

"That's right, sir," she answered. "Her name's actually Regina's Snow Queen, but I call her Queenie. She's somewhat tall for the Hanoverian breed, but ever so easy to ride—if she likes you, that is. I'm afraid she's still getting used to me. I think she prefers her owner, my Cousin Elizabeth. That's Duke Charles's wife. The one who'll be having the twins in June. Beth's a champion horsewoman."

"Ah, so I see," he laughed. "But why should you walk, my friend, when you can ride? Besides, the path through the woods can be confusing, particularly at this time of year. Let me fetch my coach and I shall return you and your horse to your aunt's home before nightfall. What is your home called?"

"Château Rothesay. Thank you, Your Highness, I hate to impose, but it is very kind of you. Poor Napper doesn't look inclined to walk with her injured paw, and she's rather too heavy for me to carry."

"We'll have my sister look at your dog, and I shall send one of my men to fetch your horse."

Adele pondered the offer. *Am I being foolish? Surely, such a handsome and gentlemanly prince isn't dangerous—is he?*

She smiled, not wishing to offend her host. "Thank you, but perhaps, I'd better return right away. It's already growing dark, Aunt Victoria must wonder where I've gone. Please, let your sister know that we'd love for her to visit the château; along with you, of course."

"You are thoughtful and quite correct," he told her. "As it happens, my sister won't awaken for an hour, meaning we'd need to wait. Eluna works at night, you see, and sleeps during the day."

"Where does she work?"

"*L'Hôpital de Charité.*"

"Oh, the charity hospital! Yes, we visited there shortly after we arrived here. My aunt had a meeting. She's on the hospital's board of governors."

"Indeed? Then, your aunt and I have much in common, for I have been asked to serve on that august board. But will you come inside one moment whilst I speak with my butler? Then, we will go to your home. I promise."

Adele wanted to answer yes, but a voice whispered into her thoughts, gentle but insistent: *Do not go in, Della. Go home.*

She could actually hear the voice, and there was something familiar about its sound and sweetness. A gentle breeze kissed her hand, and Della reached out, expecting to find invisible fingers waiting to take hers.

The prince's face shadowed into a mask of anger, and his smile disappeared. "The spirits of the forest whisper sometimes, my young friend. Do not listen to them. Please, come in, lest they speak again. I shall not keep you long. Come inside," he prompted seductively.

The brown owl flapped overhead, and Adele heard the voice whisper again, this time more clearly.

No. Don't go in, Della! You mustn't! Go home, Adele. Do not go into the abbey! It is dangerous!

The tall prince's face twitched into a frown, as though he, too, could hear the voice. His light eyes clouded with a menacing darkness. He took a step forward. Overhead, the raven circled, and every worker stopped—halted in place, obeying an unspoken command.

Della prayed silently, wishing her Cousin Charles were here to protect her. Suddenly, she felt completely alone and vulnerable. Why had she followed this stranger to his home? Was it because of his beautiful face? His soft words? Because Prince Araqiel returned Napper?

Is he trustworthy, or am I a fool?

Adele began to tremble. "May I have my dog back, sir? I don't wish to be a poor neighbour, but I'm sure my aunt is worried about me."

The raven landed on the ironwork gate, peering angrily at the owl. A white owl soon joined the brown one; both with icy eyes of crystal blue.

The prince glanced up at the two owls, the angry lines of his face softening. "Yes, of course, your aunt will worry," he agreed, the stormy eyes returning to normal. "But, please, my dear friend, you must not go on your own. I will not permit it. These woods can be very confusing and dangerous. You must let me escort you."

Adele prayed again, fearful of making a mistake. "Yes, you're right. Thank you, sir. But my aunt will send someone to fetch me, if I'm not back soon. They may already be looking in the woods."

"Then, your aunt is a wise woman, for these roads can be treacherous. Dangerous highwaymen lurk within the whispering trees, but also *serpents*, especially at this time of year."

"Why this time?" she asked innocently.

"Have English children forgotten the old tales? In my country, the last hours of April bring a thinning of the veil, and the dead walk amongst the living, whispering to them. It is a night when witches fly upon the cold winds, and the hidden ones dance within the moon's silvery shadow."

"The hidden ones?"

"Ah, the hidden ones are the powerful *zana*. I believe the French call them the *fee*, and the English call them faeries."

"But faeries are like butterflies, hardly something to fear."

He shook his head, the movement causing the long spirals of raven to twist like undulating snakes upon his shoulders. "Faeries are hardly butterflies. No, my friend, the *zana* can turn malevolent when mistreated or neglected. One must offer gifts to them—as appeasement. If they do not receive these offerings, they will emerge to seek vengeance."

"And that happens tonight?" she asked, gulping audibly.

"Oh, yes! The wolves will walk on two legs, and the dead will run beside them."

"But surely that's superstition," she told him, though her voice sounded fearful. "There's no such thing as faeries, ghosts, and witches. Are there?"

He laughed, as though he knew unshared secrets. "Be not so dismissive, my young friend. For when tonight's moon rises, she will bring a *fête* all her own. Feasting and festivities that echo ancient days, lighting the path for the *zana*—what you call faeries. But you need not fear them. I shall keep you safe from all that. Wait here for but a moment, and I shall fetch my coach and driver."

He left her on her own, passing into the stone gatehouse's great oak door. Adele clutched Napper close, glad for the animal's warmth. The men and women working in the courtyard returned to their tasks, but kept their heads down. No one spoke to her, and only now did she wonder why they remained silent.

Five minutes passed, and then ten. Fifteen. An eternity! The owls remained on their perch, occasionally speaking to one another, and once the white owl rose up and circled, returning to the smaller brown bird and resuming his watch.

Della feared the prince had forgotten her, and decided to find her way home alone, but then a magnificent landau drawn by a team of four black horses approached. A stout man in a large, soft-brimmed hat that shaded his eyes sat upon the driver's bench, next to a well-muscled black dog. The animal growled at Napper, its ears back, teeth bared.

"*Zatknis!*" the driver spat at the dog, stamping his large boot to emphasise the command to be quiet.

"Now, now, Bruno, that is no way to behave," said the prince as he emerged from the coach's rich interior. "You will frighten our guest."

He had changed clothing, dressed now in an 'English' evening suit of black wool, cut to emphasise his trim waist and broad shoulders. The gold waistcoat had a subtle pattern to it, covered in symbols Della couldn't quite make out, but she felt certain she'd seen them before.

In the new ensemble, Prince Araqiel seemed even more handsome than before, and Adele suddenly regretted her decision to leave.

"You remind me of someone," she said, unable to recall just who it was. "Another prince, perhaps."

"Is that so? How very strange," he laughed as he assisted her into the midnight black coach. "I pray you'll forgive the delay. My sister had awoken early and told me of a very sick individual at her hospital, a man with a strange ailment of the blood. So pale and listless! A great pity. I fear that in my desire to listen attentively to her tale, I allowed time to fall from me. Is that how you say it?"

"Sort of. I usually say time gets away from me," she told him, hoping he hadn't taken offence. "You're very nice, Prince Ara, and I know my aunt will be delighted to meet you. I'd have come inside with you, but Cousin Charles made me promise never to enter a strange home on my own. He worries, you see."

"And so he should. The world is a very dangerous place, my new friend. Very dangerous, indeed. You know, Lady Adele, I hope to meet this cousin of yours, for it is clear that he has earned your loyalty and respect. I should like to earn his respect as well. To begin, I promise to see you home safely."

"Thank you, sir," she said, holding Napper close.

Araqiel called to the driver in an obscure dialect and then shut the door, locking its silver handle.

"Now," he said, sitting close, "tell me more about this cousin who is about to have twin children. I find him very, *very* interesting."

CHAPTER ONE

2:10 pm – ICI Training Centre - Queen Anne House

Four hours before Adele met the mysterious Prince Araqiel in the woods near her aunt's home, the very man the Romanian aristocrat found so 'very interesting' had just thrown a hard, close-fisted punch at Della's brother, Paul Stuart. Both men were bare to the waist, dressed in linen trousers and soft leather shoes to allow for easy movement. Their nearly identical physiques were strong and well defined, glistening with sweat. The two cousins fought in a square arena, floored with lightly-padded, grey canvas. Ten tables of spectators surrounded the sparring men, shouting encouragement and advice.

"Watch his left foot, Charles!" a Scotsman called from the nearest table. "Paul, keep clear of that right hook!"

The technique the men demonstrated was called *savate*, and the cousins had been teaching it to the agency's thirty agents-in-training each afternoon for the past week. Known also as *boxe française*, the fighting style was born on the decks of French naval ships and used by sailors in Marseilles, who, if boarded by pirates, learned to grasp parts of the vessel to maintain balance whilst fighting. In such dire and unwieldy circumstances, using one's foot as a weapon made perfect sense.

After spending so much time in the darker venues of France's back streets, James Paul Robert Ian Stuart, the 12th Earl of Aubrey, had become a master at savate. He'd spent the past fortnight instructing his cousin in its many strategies and moves. Already a champion boxer, Charles proved a quick study. In fact, that particular afternoon, it seemed as though the young duke had learnt his lessons a little too well, for he'd already won two bouts and was about to win a third.

When a lightning-quick kick landed on Haimsbury's lower back, it nearly caused him to lose his footing. But the duke absorbed the blow and twisted to the right, forcing the earl's forward momentum to throw him off-balance. Aubrey recovered and responded with a nearly impossible, mid-air spin, slamming his left foot against Haimsbury's midsection, assuming this would win him the match. To the earl's shock, Sinclair absorbed the kick and then rolled to the side, forcing the airborne Aubrey to slam to the canvas with a great thud! With both on the mat, the two men grappled with one another, using traditional wrestling moves. In response, the training centre's audience took to their feet, cheering them on.

"Get 'em, Lord Aubrey!" a new agent shouted to the earl.

"Show 'im who's boss, Your Grace!" another called to Sinclair.

The men's skills were evenly matched, but Sinclair managed to reach round his cousin's shoulder and pull him into a head-lock with a knee at the earl's back. Stuart squirmed in every direction to free himself from the powerful hold, but his cousin's grip was too tight.

"I yield!" Aubrey shouted at last, his voice winded. "You win! I yield, Charles! I yield!"

Sinclair released the earl, his own face dripping with sweat. "Good, because I'm done!" the young duke grunted as his arms fell to his sides.

Exhausted, both men fell onto their backs, covered in sweat, blood, and bruises, laughing like a pair of school boys. The all male audience broke into cheers and applause, some already arguing over where each man had failed or succeeded.

James Stuart had watched his nephews from the sidelines of the training centre, a pair of cotton towels in his hands. The Scottish duke slapped Martin Kepelheim on the back as the tailor made a checkmark against an entry in a small leather notebook.

"That's ten pounds you owe me, Martin," crowed Drummond. "I told you Charles could best the earl three out of five. Sorry, Paul. Better luck next time," he told the younger cousin as the two men regained their feet.

"As his teacher, I'm quite happy with my student's progress. Well done, Cousin," Aubrey told his friend as he shook the victor's hand. "Very well done!"

"I owe any accomplishments to my instructor," Sinclair replied, panting heavily as limped towards his uncle. "Apparently, the earl's long hair has nothing to do with strength. Not this day, at least."

"Then explain why you're growing yours longer," the earl laughed.

"To please my wife," Haimsbury answered.

"Hair or no, enjoy your wins, for they'll soon be but a memory. I've only taught you the *basic* moves of savate, Charles," Aubrey added with a wry grin. "And I was holding back."

Drummond smiled proudly, handing towels to both men. "If you're holding back, then you fooled us, Paul. And it looks as though Charles predicts your moves before you even make them. You'll need to start using those advanced moves soon, if you're to beat this one."

The earl crossed through the thick ropes of the ring, laughing as he dropped into a wooden chair beside Sir Thomas Galton. "He doesn't predict my moves. I'm just being easy on him. It's his age, you know," he added, glancing at Haimsbury, who'd stopped a few feet short of the ropes to catch his breath. "Need a hand, old man?"

Charles wiped his eyes with the towel. "Four months' difference makes me an old man, does it?"

"Four and a half," the earl noted gleefully.

Kepelheim began to examine Sinclair's injuries. "Charles, you mustn't let your cousin hurt you too very badly."

"So my wife keeps telling me," said Sinclair. "James, did I hear mention of a bet? If Martin owes you ten, then you surely owe me a share of that. Need I point out that the earl is limping far more than I?"

"Charles cheats to make up for his advanced age," Aubrey claimed as he rested his feet on the table, wincing as the left calf muscle began to spasm. "He's spent a decade boxing with policemen in a no-rules league. I, on the other hand, have respect for Queensberry."

"Hardly!" Haimsbury exclaimed as Kepelheim applied pressure to a cut over the young duke's left cheekbone. "Ouch! Easy there, Martin!"

"Yes, I imagine the medicine does sting, but you don't want a scar. The duchess would never forgive me."

"Ignore His Grace's protests, Martin. He could use a scar or two," Aubrey told the tailor as Tom Galton checked him for bruises and similar injuries. "That so-called cut barely counts as a scratch. And my footwork is perfectly legal in France."

"Only if you're a felon," Sinclair countered, "but even if it is legal, its primary users are pirates and criminals. Which are you?"

"I suppose that depends on the day," the earl responded with a handsome grin. "You've certainly taken to it, though. That last *fouetté* was quite impressive, and you've learnt to counter my kicks with surprising finesse. Well done."

"I have a fine instructor," Sinclair told his friend. "What time is it?"

Kepelheim and Galton glanced at their watches.

"Two-seventeen," the former answered.

Galton disagreed. "I have two-twenty-one."

"Someone's watch is faulty. However, the two of you will have to debate which needs repair whilst we change," the earl told them, wincing as his left knee complained at bearing weight. "You know, Charles, it won't do for us to disable one another. Perhaps, we should make this a weekly demonstration, rather than a daily one."

"Afraid I'll best you again?" his cousin teased as they climbed down the marble and ironwork staircase that led from the ballroom to the first floor apartments. "But as I'm such an old man, I'll concede to a weekly match. We can schedule the next for late June or even July. From this moment forward, I am on holiday until my children are born."

"And a grand day that will be!" the earl exclaimed happily. "Are you still travelling to France this week?"

"Yes, in fact, I'm leaving for Branham this evening, and from there to Dover. The channel steamer boards at ten."

"This evening? I thought Beth planned to kick off the fête with a party this Saturday. Won't you miss it?"

"Actually, that's why I'm leaving today. If I'm to share hosting duties with my wife, then I need to take care of some business in Paris first."

"The Sûreté matter?"

The duke nodded. "I could speak with Goron any time, but I plan to bring Della back with me, but if I'm to leave in time to see Beth,

I'll need to hurry. I'd not planned to be so long with that last match. I still have half a dozen privy council boxes to get through first."

"It's because you're improving that they get longer," his cousin encouraged. "I wish I could go with you to see Adele, but someone has to keep an eye on our wives."

"How's Cordelia doing?" the duke asked as they reached a short flight of stairs and climbed up to the private apartments.

"Overall, much better, but she's a bit nervous today. Her mother's coming to visit this evening, and she always overstays her welcome. I've suggested Connie live in one of my hotels, since her son's kicked her out, but she prefers staying with us."

"What? He's kicked her out? Surely, not!"

"Well, perhaps not so dire as that, but William certainly makes his mother's life a misery. The insufferable baron fills the house with men of questionable motives, interested only in spending Will's money."

"What money? I've heard he's already gambled or whored away most of his inheritance," noted Charles as they walked.

"If not all of it, then most. I believe a trustee keeps control of the household account. Baron Wychwright plans to stand for his late father's Parliament seat in October, but I doubt he'll win. His reputation has suffered far too much. Even Constance finds him tiresome these days."

"I'm sorry, Paul. You have far more patience than I. Is Delia still having those awful nightmares?" he asked as they reached a broad corridor with doors to three apartments.

"Not as often as before, thank the Lord. Her mother still complains of heart palpitations, which makes Delia feel guilty for the slightest criticism. I've offered to pay for the best surgeons to examine her, but Connie refuses."

"Probably because she's malingering."

"I'm sure she is, but I may insist she see a doctor to rule it out. She thinks Gehlen's quite handsome, so I may ask him. Delia still wonders about her father's murderer, Charles. I'd like to assign more agents to his case, if it's all right with you. I think knowing the fiend's been caught would go a long way towards helping her endure all this."

"I've no problem with adding more agents to the case, especially as it may help us find Albert Wendaway amongst Redwing's nests. Choose whatever men you want. I'll speak with Major Smith at City Police when I return, if you like, but I doubt he knows any more than we do."

"What if Smith's withholding evidence?" the earl asked. "Honestly, Charles, I don't believe Wendaway could have done it without help. The late baron's murder has Redwing written all over it. The criminal signatures are too similar to Hemsfield and Anderson, but if Wendaway did kill Hemsfield, he had help. The man's too slight to hoist a two-hundred pound dead man up eighteen feet."

Charles stopped. "Calling Albert Wendaway slight is understatement. A sneeze could blow him away. He couldn't hoist one hundred pounds, let alone two. But you may be right about Smith. He has a reputation for dismissing Met Police as inferior. If he is withholding evidence, he'll regret it."

"You'd pull rank?" Aubrey asked.

"Of course, I would. It's the one advantage to being commissioner of an independent branch with very few rules and off-book funding," the duke said, smiling. "I now have the power to make life decidedly uncomfortable for the major if he chooses protectionism over cooperation."

Paul grinned. "Of course, your position as shadow crown prince doesn't hurt either. I wonder how many people are aware of that?"

"Very few, and I'm sure Smith isn't among that small number," Charles answered. "Which reminds me, Gerald Pennyweather's keeping track of business whilst I'm away, but would you have time to glance through any paperwork from Salisbury and wire me if you find anything urgent? The prime minister's aware of my trip to France, but there's a tricky negotiation ongoing regarding the Horn of Africa presently. Britain's bidding against France with the local Ottomans over strategic lands there."

"I'm well aware of those negotiations. In fact, I did most of the ground work," Paul answered. "Does this make me the shadow prince's shadow?"

"I imagine it does," Charles laughed.

They'd reached the master apartment, and the two cousins paused at the tall door.

"I'm really proud of you, Charles. You've made remarkable progress in a very short time," said Aubrey.

"Progress within governmental corridors or fighting with my feet?"

"Both," the Scotsman replied. "I pity the man who challenges you in either arena. I just pray the day never comes when you and I do more than spar."

"I can't imagine it, can you? Will you and Cordelia be attending the ball this weekend? I know she's planning on you both."

"Of course! My wife's quite looking forward to a long visit at the hall, but we may have to bring her mother along to Branham; though, I hope to entice her to remain in London and shop on my coin."

"Now, that sounds very dangerous," the duke laughed. "Seth Holloway will be at Branham during the fête. I suppose you could always unleash him on Connie, if she comes. He'd take her mind off shopping. Women seem to find those freckles charming."

Paul smiled. "Seth's charming now, is he? Didn't you once think he was after Elizabeth?"

The duke failed to smile in return. "I'm not convinced he isn't, but thus far, he's shown only friendship towards her."

"Is Beth aware of your continued doubts?"

"No," Charles answered, his right hand on the doorknob. "And I prefer to keep it that way."

"Not because of her health, I hope?"

"No, Beth's doing very well, though she tires easily. I'm told it's normal at this stage. But as a precaution, Gehlen's put her on semi-confinement. Are you heading back home, or will you stay and have luncheon with me?"

"It depends on what Mrs. Smith has prepared."

"I've no idea, but she was icing a chocolate torte this morning, when I stopped in for coffee."

"With the raspberry filling?" Charles nodded. "Well, then, I'd love to lunch with you, Cousin. What time do you leave for Branham?"

"Not before four."

"Good. That gives us some time to talk."

"Meet you in my office in half an hour? I need a quick bath first."

"As do I," the earl answered. "Half an hour, then."

Paul proceeded to the second master, just round the corner, and Charles entered the main apartment, where he ran a hot bath. Ten minutes later, he tied the sash on a velvet-trimmed dressing gown and stood before the steam-covered mirror. Wiping it with his right hand, the duke considered the contours of his face. He and the earl shared many features in common: cleft chin, decisive jawline, a distinct and deeply carved Cupid's bow to the upper lip, high cheekbones, large almond-shaped eyes, and arched brows. Their noses also had similar shapes, though Charles's was slightly wider at the bridge. But there, the similarities stopped, for Sinclair had black hair that curled, whilst Stuart had chestnut locks that fell in gentle waves to his shoulders. Their eyes varied as well. Sinclair's were a highly unusual mixture of Caribbean blue and turquoise, rimmed in thick black lashes. The earl's possessed chameleon characteristics, changing with his mood. When happy, they shone as clear and blue as a Highland lake; but when angry, they'd cloud into a greyish hue that sent a warning to everyone nearby.

Charles had known Paul Stuart for ten years, and he cherished the relationship; but their close friendship had nearly sundered over the love of a woman: Duchess Elizabeth Georgianna Stuart, who'd chosen Charles as husband. That he and Paul could emerge from the previous year's crucible as more than friends, close as any brothers, was a wonderful miracle.

He glanced down at the gold wedding band that circled the fourth finger of his left hand and smiled.

"I love you, little one," he whispered aloud as he left the bath to dress in the main bedchamber. Silk socks, supple leather boots, finely woven trousers in rich Merino wool, black braces, white silk shirt with starched collar, grey and crimson waistcoat, Haimsbury crested fob and gold watch, pin-striped cravat. Charles looked like any wealthy West End gentleman. However, unlike most, before donning the bespoke waistcoat, the duke fastened a leather holster round his chest, filling it with a specially-made Smith and Wesson revolver, a Christmas gift from his Scottish cousin. All these items had been selected by the duke's new valet, David Anderson, the former Mr. Thirteen, and secured in a leather portmanteau for his employer's convenience, along with two silk handkerchiefs and a pair of grey gloves.

Once downstairs, Charles said hello to Gerald Pennyweather, his PPS, or personal private secretary. "Anything new in the post?"

"All on your desk, my lord," answered Pennyweather. "And I let Mr. Kepelheim into your office. I hope that was all right, sir."

"Yes, of course. Ask Mr. Lester to send luncheon to the library, will you? Lord Aubrey and Mr. Kepelheim will be joining me, and possibly Duke James."

"Very good, sir."

Charles walked past the two morning rooms that served as the ICI reception area and all the way back to the northwest section of the main floor, where he entered the library, that now served as his office.

"Afternoon, Martin. I'm glad you stayed behind. I take it you're still trying to sort through that annoying code?"

The tailor sat at a round table, not far from a curved mahogany desk. He glanced up just as Sinclair took a seat in the upholstered desk chair, his face disappearing behind a stack of red, governmental boxes.

"It looks to me as though your tasks are no more satisfying than my own," the tailor said as he pushed away the troubling manuscript. "I know most of what's in those red boxes is secret, but if there's any way I might help, I should be happy for a break from these exasperating coded lines."

Charles set two of the boxes to one side, so he could see the tailor's face over the tower of work. "Do I hear a full stop in your voice, Martin?"

"You hear frustration with a dash of hunger, actually. I haven't the stamina you and Aubrey display. Unlike the pair of you, I require occasional nourishment and a few hours' sleep. But I'm sure a sandwich would go a long way towards restoring my good mood."

Haimsbury ran a long-fingered hand through his lengthening hair and yawned. "I may be able to withstand hours without a meal, but a good night's sleep would be a blessing. It's useless even trying whilst I'm in London. The truth is I miss my wife. Beth has a way of distracting me in the evenings. I'm useless on my own. How did I ever manage without her?"

"Poorly, I should think. As do we all without love and family. Shall I ring for Lester to improve our moods?"

"I've already asked him to serve us in here. The earl's coming down to join us, and James promised to stop in."

"Excellent. I imagine you're far hungrier than I, Charles. You and Aubrey worked off all your breakfast in those five matches. And may I say you've certainly learnt your craft well, and so very quickly! If only I could sort through this code with similar alacrity. I shall be glad to leave it behind for a week at Branham."

"As will I," Charles admitted, leaving the desk to join Martin at the table.

Kepelheim closed the book and placed it in a brown leather valise. "I may bring this to Kent with me, though. Young Holloway is most helpful with symbols. He's cracked a few of them already, though we've still no idea what message is written on those stone walls."

"But if you've deciphered some of the symbols, then can't you begin to piece together sentences, or at least words?"

"If there were obvious words, yes, but the symbols don't appear to be linked. Yes, I know that sounds mysterious, but then that room defies all translation! There are letters that look very like known languages, but they have diacritical markings that appear to alter the meaning. And most of the symbols are completely foreign! You've seen them, Charles. It's like trying to discern a pattern amongst a field of black."

"I've only been in there a few times, but I remember seeing letters that resembled Greek, Gaelic, and Latin amongst that shadowy field. Might it be the same message repeated in all languages?"

"That's what we assumed, but I'm no longer sure of that. And I'm not sure the writing is even stable."

Charles started to ask what the tailor meant, but was interrupted by his cousin.

"Did you and Galton reconcile your watches?" Aubrey asked Kepelheim as he sat at the carved oak table. "And where's that promised torte? I'm starved!"

"On its way," Charles told his famished cousin. "Martin was just explaining about the puzzle chamber at my home. He claims the writing is unstable, or I think that's what he implied."

"Is there no whisky in this house?" asked Aubrey as he poured a glass of water. "How can the writing be unstable? Surely, no one's gone in there and altered it. The room's always locked."

"Someone has altered it," Martin insisted. He withdrew the book from his case and opened it to a marked page. "But what's entirely improbable is my own copy keeps changing. See here? This symbol that looks like a lower case delta with a cross over the top?"

"Yes," answered the earl.

"It was a divided circle with a circumpunct yesterday. You'll notice also I've written this copy in ink, yet there's no crossing out or other sign of erasure. How is that possible?"

"I'd say it was always a delta with a cross, Martin," Aubrey told him. "With all the symbols in these pages, how can you be sure one's changed?"

"I'd love to think it's my memory that failed, Lord Aubrey, but this has happened many times since we began this project. Seth keeps a copy with him at Branham. I believe he's coming back to London for Lord Salisbury's party this evening, and I've asked him to bring his book along. We'll compare notes then. If his is altered, then we must look to a spiritual cause. And that leads us to greater problems."

"I still think you're misremembering," the earl argued. "Occam's razor, Martin. The simplest answer is usually the correct one."

"Oh, so this is where you're all hiding!" James Stuart called as he entered the library. "Are we having an informal meeting?"

"Martin's been telling us about his mystical changing book," the earl told his uncle. "Come, join us, James. Charles and I have earned our luncheon, but we're happy to share a morsel or two with those who only sit and watch."

"And I haven't earned mine? Is that your implication? Shall I take you back up to the ring and show you a Scottish trick or two, son?"

"No, thank you, sir," Aubrey laughed. "You've taught me those lessons far too many times when I was growing up."

"Very well, then," Drummond smiled. "I've just enough time to eat, and then I must be off to Scotland."

"Is that today?" asked Sinclair. "But you're coming back for Saturday's party, I hope?"

"Of course! I'd not miss our girl's opening ball for anything. I've the funeral tomorrow afternoon, and then the will reading the following morning. Shouldn't take more than three days."

"I'm very sorry about your friend, Uncle," Charles said. "I wish I could have met Lord Granddach."

"He longed to meet you as well, son. He was your great-uncle, of course. After my mother died, my father remarried Richard MacAllen's sister Charlotte, who gave birth to your mother Angela—and Paul's mother Abby, of course. I imagine you'll both be mentioned in the will. Are you sure you don't want to come with me?"

"I would go," Charles answered, "but I promised Adele I'd visit soon, and I have to meet Sûreté Chief Goron regarding ICI matters."

"Aye, the lovely Della Stuart. We've missed her pretty face since January. Paul? Will you come along?"

"I can't leave Cordelia, James. But give my best to Uncle Richard's friends and family. Are you fetching Baxter and his new bride whilst you're in Glasgow?"

"I am indeed!" Drummond declared happily. "Our newlyweds have spent three glorious weeks by the seaside, meaning our Baxter's likely ready to see Branham again."

"It was good of you to offer them your cottage, sir," noted Sinclair.

"Actually, it came into the family with the MacAllens. It was part of your Grandmother Charlotte's dowry. I should probably just give it to you, Charles. It's a grand place. We call it a cottage, but it's six bedrooms and two drawing rooms, plus a conservatory that overlooks the Firth of Clyde. Beth used to love going there during summer months. You should take her up there once the bairns are born."

"I may just do that, sir," Charles answered, smiling. "Ah, here's our repast."

Lester entered, pushing a large trolley, laden with an assortment of silver-domed dishes. The Queen Anne butler arranged the entire meal on a nearby table and removed the domed lids. "As per your orders, Duke James," he told Drummond. "It's set up as a buffet. Are you sure you wouldn't like us to serve you?"

"Nonsense, we're capable of serving ourselves, aren't we, son?" he asked Charles.

"He's right, Lester. You needn't worry about us. As with my uncle, I prefer to keep meals simple. You're doing a splendid job here, by the way. Thank you for helping to train Mr. Anderson as my valet. He's become indispensable."

"I'm pleased to say he remembered all the basics on his own, sir. It was merely a matter of instruction on newer methods, which reminds me, my lord, the electrics men asked if they might install those new telephone lines to both houses whilst you're at Branham."

"I don't see why not," Charles answered. "Uncle, have we vetted all the men involved?"

"Is this Ernest Lowell's outfit, Lester?"

"It is, sir. Yes."

"He's all right, Charles. Lowell comes from a multi-generational circle family. He never hires anyone who hasn't passed a rigorous investigation first. You can trust him in your homes."

"Then, tell Mr. Lowell he may install the telephones next week," Haimsbury told the butler. "Thank you, Lester."

The butler left, and the men began to fill their plates. Drummond offered a short prayer, and all four started on the roasted pork, buttered carrots, parsnips, and rosemary potatoes. As promised, a rich chocolate torte with raspberry filling awaited them for dessert, and the men enjoyed it with coffee, which Drummond spiked with a splash of '48 Reserve.

"Never could abide plain coffee," the Scotsman laughed. "So, now, Paul. You said this morning you had news. Is it business or pleasure?"

Paul took a sip of coffee. "It's not business, and it pleases me no end. We've not said anything for fear of complications, but Cordelia's expecting our first child in October."

Drummond's face widened into a massive grin. "A baby? Paul, that's wonderful news!"

"It certainly is!" Charles told his cousin. "It's the best news since learning I was going to be a father. Complications? What do you mean? Delia's all right, isn't she?"

"Gehlen thought he detected a small heart problem. Delia's heart, I mean. He suggested we consult with a specialist in Edinburgh. A man named MacCallum."

"That's why you and she took the train up last week," Charles observed. "And?"

"And Dr. MacCallum pronounced her fit and healthy, physically at least. Her mind still wanders now and then, but overall the pregnancy's proceeding normally, and she's very happy about it."

"Good heavens," Charles sighed happily. "But why did Gehlen mistakenly detect a heart problem? He's one of the finest doctors in the kingdom."

"He believes his instrument was at fault. Blood pressure devices are notorious for inaccurate readings, but MacCallum's designed one that uses mercury rather than the old water-based units. She spent an entire two days with MacCallum, and he's convinced Cordelia's healthy. No heart problems at all."

"That is very good news!" Drummond declared, taking to his feet. "Paul, your father would be pleased as punch."

"Yes, sir, he would. Are you leaving already?"

"I told my engineer I'd be at the station by four. Martin, will you be going to Salisbury's soiree this evening?"

"I will, Your Grace. I'm playing a selection of piano pieces for Lady Salisbury. She's a dear friend and loves to sing."

"Well, give her my best. Tell her I hope to see them both at the fête."

Kepelheim stood and collected his valise. "I wonder, might I share the coach with you, sir? I thought we could discuss our little project."

"Oh, yes, that," Drummond answered mysteriously.

"What project is that?" asked Aubrey.

"A new invention," Drummond answered. "And as with most innovations, it requires time and money. Come, Martin! You can catch me up on this code you're deciphering."

The tailor gathered up his coat and hat. "I fear the code eludes me, sir, but we'll sort it out." He looked to Sinclair. "Forget about what I said regarding my copy. I'm most likely mistaken about the changes. My eyes grow ever older, you know. Lord Aubrey, there are no words to express my joy at your good news. Please, offer my fondest wishes to your lady wife."

"You can tell her yourself tonight, Martin. Delia and I will be at Robert's party as well."

"Oh, then, we'll all celebrate together. Shall we, Your Grace?"

"See you Saturday, Charles! Give our girl a kiss from her old grandpa, will you?"

"I will, sir. See you Saturday, and I'll have Adele with me."

"Then the celebration begins, eh?"

The duke left with Kepelheim, shutting the library doors. Alone now, the two cousins returned to their chairs. Charles poured them both a glass of red wine. "This should probably be champagne, but we've none chilled, and I find it lacks definition at room temperature. However, this is Martin's favourite Bordeaux."

"And mine," Paul confessed.

"To you and Cordelia and the new life she now carries, Paul," said Charles as he raised his glass. "May this child be born well and healthy, and may this be the first of many."

They both drank, and the earl topped off their glasses. "It's strange to imagine holding a baby. Adele was already two years old, when I discovered she was my daughter, but an infant is another matter entirely."

"It's an indescribable feeling, Paul. As though life never had meaning without it. That moment you hold your own child changes a man." He took a sip of the wine, pondering for a moment as though struggling with a question. Finally, Charles set down his glass. "Look, Paul, forgive my asking, and it may sound impertinent, but when did you and Delia become intimate? Henry thought it could take months, if not years before she'd—well, you know what I mean. It's none of my business. I'm delighted, for you both, but what changed?"

Paul smiled, his blue eyes twinkling. "Delia changed. I never once placed any burden on her for intimacy, you understand. Not once, and I even offered to take separate rooms over the entirety of our wedding trip. But she sleeps better if I'm with her."

"It's because she trusts you."

He smiled again. "I'm blessed to have that trust, Charles. Over the first few days of the trip, Cordelia slowly grew more affectionate, and then, on the seventh night, whilst in Paris, all that changed. I'd gone out that morning to meet with one of our French agents. Remember, I'd heard from Deniau shortly after Christmas. He was concerned about a man who'd bought the abbey near Tory's château. Whilst I was away, Delia planned it all out. She ordered a special dinner brought to our rooms. And she even purchased a music player and several cylinder recordings of piano nocturnes. Chopin or Brahms. Honestly, I can't tell you what was actually playing, for we never made it past the soup. Charles, it was the single-most perfect night of my life. I never understood what you have with Beth until now. Don't mistake me. I still love our little duchess, but this is different. So very different! More profound than I ever thought possible. And now, a child is on the way. It really is a miracle!"

"God smiles on you, Cousin. When did you say the baby is due? October?"

"Yes. Late October. Apparently, our first night together was quite productive."

"Does Beth know?" asked Sinclair.

"Not yet, but I plan to tell her this weekend. I dare not imagine what Connie will do when she hears the news! She'll probably move in until the baby's old enough for Oxford."

"I pray it's a boy, Paul. Or two boys, eh? Who knows? Twins do run in our family. But this baby's all the more reason to tell Adele the truth. She'll want to know she's becoming an older sister."

"Or she'll resent any affection I show to a child who's publicly mine, Charles. If I admit to being her father, then she becomes an ill-gotten bastard, born of a harlot. I won't let her hear such taunts."

"No one would do that," his cousin argued.

"You're generous, Charles, but most in our set would, only they'd whisper it secretly from behind silk fans and tall hats. And those cruel whispers would eventually reach my daughter. I'll not put her through that."

"Then arm her with the truth. If she finds out elsewhere, it will hurt far worse."

"Who'd tell her? You? James? No, it's best she call me her brother, which is why I want you to become her guardian."

The duke sat back in surprise. "What? Why?"

"Della already spends most of her time with you and Beth when she's in England, and she looks to you with the same love and trust she once gave my father. Charles, I think Adele sees you as the perfect replacement for the man she lost, when Father died."

"Her father isn't dead, Paul. You're very much alive."

"But don't you see? Adele thinks him dead, which is just as hurtful. I've already had my solicitor draw up the papers, and I brought them with me, just in case," he said, withdrawing a leather pouch from a bag filled with exercise clothing. "Everything's in here. All you have to do is sign."

Sinclair sighed, taking the packet. "Very well, but only because I love her and want the best for her. However, if she ever asks me about her mother, I intend to tell her the truth."

Paul grew quiet for a moment. "Just promise me you'll be gentle. So long as she knows you love her, perhaps her heart can endure it."

"I'd never hurt her, Paul. You know that. All I want is Della's happiness."

"That's all I want. With you as guardian, she'll be safe and happy."

"Have you told Cordelia about Cozette?"

"No, and she'll never learn it from me. She's very sensitive, and her mind is still quite fragile. It could cause significant emotional damage if she were to learn I've been a father all these years. I'll do anything to protect her, Charles. Anything."

"I understand. Very well, I'll sign these, but you must agree to let me raise Della as my own without objections. Indeed, if you refuse to acknowledge her, then I may even adopt her."

Aubrey's lean face broke into a massive grin. "I'd hoped you might suggest that. I've signed papers for that as well. It's all in the envelope."

"Is this why you let me win three bouts upstairs?"

"Perhaps," the earl answered with a wink.

Charles glanced through the paperwork, drawn up by a prominent QC. "Sir Simon Blake? I've never heard of the man. Do you trust him to keep this secret?"

"He keeps a low profile, but Blake's worked for our Uncle James for over thirty years. I trust him with my life." The earl stood, his bag in his left hand. "I should go. Connie's arriving in an hour, and I don't want to leave Cordelia alone with her too long. They inevitably argue. Give my regards to Paris, Cousin. Enjoy your time with Della and leave London and all circle business to me."

"Try not to solve all our cases in my absence," the duke teased, shaking his cousin's hand. "And give Cordelia a fond hug from me. Tell her how very happy I am for you both."

The earl left, and the young duke crossed the narrow corridor that led into the library and through a series of interconnected parlours until he reached the west drawing room, where his secretary kept an office. He knocked on the half-open door. "Gerald?"

A voice replied from somewhere inside. "Oh! Do come in, my lord. I'm just dealing with a slight problem."

The duke opened the door and entered. A gold-trimmed desk dominated one end of the rectangular room, and an oval table sat near the windows. Both desk and table were crowded with box files and newspapers. The central fireplace burnt cheerfully, and above it hung one of the many portraits of Elizabeth Stuart Sinclair that decorated Queen Anne House. Charles loved this one in particular, for it was painted to commemorate Beth's recognition as Duchess of Branham. She'd been eleven years old at the time, and he'd only just met her. Even then, Charles knew their relationship was destined for something great.

Gerald Pennyweather was a tallish man of twenty-three years and two months, with copper hair and light grey eyes. A woman would call him boyishly handsome, yet Gerald hardly saw himself that way. Pennyweather's mother arranged debutante balls for England's most powerful peerage families, and the bookish youth had interacted with nearly a hundred coquettish ingenues since turning fifteen. Despite such advances from the distaff set, Pennyweather never once took the ladies' offers seriously. His self-opinion related only to matters of the mind, not any perceived 'handsomeness'. The result was that ladies thought him even more endearing, and he therefore avoided society occasions in favour of work.

"Forgive the mess, Your Grace, but I'm endeavouring to recategorise all your records, to make it easier to cross-reference cases, you see. Sergeant Thick delivered several more boxes from Scotland Yard this morning, and I want to incorporate the new ones with all your governmental files."

"Shouldn't the investigations be kept separate from the privy council matters?" asked Haimsbury.

"Ordinarily, I'd say yes, sir, but it seems to me that many of your criminal cases have bearing on decisions made by council members, and several relate to some of your red box legislation and letters. I thought if I made copies of these, then I could correlate one with the other. Does that make sense?"

"Yes, I think I understand, but why don't you hire someone to help with the copying?"

"Oh, no, sir!" exclaimed the lad. "We couldn't do that! Most of these documents are quite sensitive. Surely, you prefer very few eyes look upon them. No, I think I should make the copies, sir."

"Nonsense," Charles argued, stepping closer to his secretary. "Here now, if you won't do it, allow me to find someone reliable. I know of several, trustworthy policemen with marvellous skills in office work. You mentioned Sergeant Thick from the Yard?"

"Indeed, sir. He delivered the parcels. He seems a sensible enough fellow."

"Quite sensible, and I know him very well. Thick served as my secretary when I was a superintendent. I'll see if we might not second him to the ICI. He not only has fine penmanship, but he makes a fair cup of coffee. I'll send a note today."

Pennyweather blinked, the muscles of his mouth slowly relaxing. "Ah, well, that would be very helpful, sir. I really think this method will prove useful in the months and years to come, but you're right. It would take far too long for me to make all the copies alone. If I may suggest hiring two clerks, then?"

Sinclair laughed. "Let's make it three to be sure. I'll ask Thick to recommend two other policemen we may trust. For now, I shall leave the rest in your capable hands. I'm off to Victoria Station."

"Very good, sir, but before you go, a new box arrived for you from the War Office."

"Just put it on my desk with the others. Lord Aubrey promised to glance through them tomorrow."

"Very well, sir. Oh, a gentleman sent a calling card whilst you were in the training centre. He asks to schedule an appointment at your earliest convenience. I have the card here, somewhere," he muttered as he set the box of files on the table. "Ah, yes! In my left pocket." He handed a silver-edged card to Sinclair, which read:

Dr. Antonio Calabrese
Sanguis, Ltd.
Chicago, New York, London ·

On the reverse side, written in a strong hand, Charles found a personal message:

Staying at the Carlton, Suite 13.
I'd be pleased to meet, soonest. – A. C.

"You say this person *sent* the card, rather than deliver it personally?" he asked his secretary.

"Yes, sir. A commissionaire from the Carlton brought it by about two hours ago. Should I have informed you right away?"

"No, not at all. You did the right thing, Gerald. Send a message to the Carlton and arrange a meeting there for next Tuesday morning. No earlier than ten."

"Of course, my lord. I'll make all the arrangements. Enjoy your trip to Paris."

Sinclair left the busy office, and climbed into a Haimsbury coach. By five o'clock, the *Captain Nemo Special* was chugging towards Branham Hall. In the past few months, Charles had commissioned a private company to lay a rail spur from Branham Village to a newly built trio of sheds. He also hired a team of trusted carpenters to construct a depot and receiving station, just two miles from the hall. The station had a mews with room for two coaches, and the depot had a telegraph and one of Aubrey's wireless transceivers. A second rail spur ran from the new station to the Branham brewery, with a third splitting off towards the electrics plant, making delivery of grain and coal more efficient. It also cut travel time from London by more than half an hour.

As the *Captain Nemo* sped along the rails towards Kent, the duke worked at his onboard desk, making a list of tasks: Contact Commissioner Monro regarding seconding three sergeants, including Thick, as ICI clerks. Ask Martin what he might know about an American company called Sanguis, Ltd., (for the name was ringing loud alarms in the duke's brain). Buy Beth a gift in Paris, a new necklace perhaps or a set of diamond earrings. Something to wear at Saturday's ball.

Since the end of February, Charles had divided each week twixt London and Branham, working Tuesday through Thursday in the city, and then returning to Kent for long weekends each Thursday evening. The schedule gave him three full workdays at Whitehall and Queen Anne, with five precious nights and four luxurious days with his beautiful wife.

As the duke sorted through the items in his mobile desk, he came across a box file marked simply with the letters 'LM'. Opening it, he withdrew a stack of letters sent by Lorena MacKey. Charles had no wish to keep secrets from his wife, but Elizabeth maintained a deep and abiding jealousy where MacKey was concerned, and he wished to avoid any arguments. And so, he kept all her letters on the train.

Every two days, a new one arrived, addressed with a typewriter and posted from the central London office. He had no idea where she lived, but Lorena insisted she was well cared for and content. The most recent note arrived that morning at Queen Anne House, and he opened it, intending to add it to the growing file.

> Dearest Charles,
>
> I'm writing once again to let you know we're still safe. As I've told you previously, another Redwing traitor lives with me here, and we're learning more about God each day. Anatole has not visited us in many weeks. If you see him, please, tell him we need to speak to him.
>
> With the prince absent, I would ask one small favour of you. I hesitate to mention it, but my friend and I have no one else to consult. Do you remember Margaret Hansen of the Empress Hotel? She wants desperately to leave Redwing's web of deceit, but has no one to help. Might you offer assistance? She trusts you and Lord Aubrey. I believe she'd go with one of you, if you called on her. She's terrified to leave on her own.
>
> I beg you to visit her soon, Charles, for Redwing members are dying all across the world. Don't ask me how I know, but I have it on good authority that nearly two-dozen have been killed in three different countries.
>
> If you call on Margaret, let her know she can join us here. I'll give you our location only after I hear from you. As usual, please address your letters to Prince Anatole Romanov, c/o The Carlton Club. A trusted messenger will deliver it to me the same day.
>
> Thank you for your continued prayers, my dear friend. Because of you, I no longer fear Redwing, for I place my trust in God. Charles, I am convinced a major war is about to erupt twixt the red and black camps of the Enemy.

Please, be careful. Keep watch for shadows and deceptive women.

Forever grateful,
Lorena

He returned the heartfelt missive to its envelope and then filed it with all the others. He'd have Elbert Stanley call on Hansen, pretending to represent the police. If he felt the woman wanted to leave, then the duke intended to offer help.

Now, how to explain to his pregnant wife why the inner circle intended to assist a brothel-keeper.

CHAPTER TWO
3:07 pm – Branham Hall

One hour before Charles Sinclair boarded the *Captain Nemo Special*, a startling discovery was made at Branham Hall. It all began when a somewhat sleepy Stephen Blinkmire noticed five balls of fur, bouncing past his lawn chair. The ordinarily serene western park had been recently transformed by the arrival of a hundred exhibitors for the upcoming fête. The lawns and orderly flowerbeds had given way to a small city of tents made from golden canvas, topped with a variety of pennants indicating the original participants of 1489. The Field of Golden Cloth that Duchess Elizabeth had dreamt of only a few months earlier had become a dazzling reality.

Amongst this magnificent array of fifteenth century re-enactors and costumed performers, the family maintained a private compound where breakfasts were served and naps might be taken. So it was on that very afternoon that an eight-foot giant's slumber was rudely interrupted by the barking of five furry mouths. Rousing slowly, the giant's abnormally large feet hit the ground, pounding rhythmically upon the wet blades of grass just beyond the north park slope. The massive leather shoes battered the newly mown lawn, but the massive gentleman wearing that footwear displayed remarkable agility for such a grandly built frame. His red cheeks puffed as he ran, his eyes never leaving the prey before him: a line of wriggling puppies, four black, and one of a yellow so pale that it passed for creamy white.

"No, no!" the giant cried as he chased the undulating canine parade. "You mustn't go near the water! Not yet! You're too young! It isn't safe!"

Stephen quickened his pace to catch up with the playful siblings. The largest of the three-month old pups was Dart (short for d'Artagnan), already the leader of the sibling pack, a rambunctious scoundrel who loved water as much as he loved almond biscuits. Behind Dart ran Portia, Porthos, Athos, and Aramis (the white). Aramis had a timid nature, and he was by far the smallest of the litter, but Keenan Shaw, master of the hounds, insisted the unusually coloured Labrador would surpass even his father Briar in stature at maturity, for his paws far outstepped his current size. They were in fact, *massive*.

It was this inequality of design that so often caused the sweet-tempered pup to quite literally trip over his own feet; a phenomenon that now occurred, forming the precipitating factor in a chain of events that would lead to that aforementioned, very important discovery.

"Don't go in the water!" the giant shouted, his eyes fixed on Dart rather than his own feet.

The carefree puppies refused to obey, and so, the chain commenced.

Aramis's oversized back paws tangled with his front, causing his long body to curve into a c-shaped, bouncing ball.

The pup cried out in surprise.

Athos turned about at hearing his brother squeal, immediately followed by Portia and Porthos. These three siblings wheeled about so very quickly, that the subsequent ballet of comic errors took mere seconds to unfold.

None of the puppies anticipated the felling of a three-hundred pound 'tree' of flustered flesh.

Blinkmire had seen the knot of black-and-white fur forming before him, and then attempted an impossible pirouette towards the lake to avoid crashing into the wriggling, canine mass. Had Stephen been a smaller man, it's likely no harm would have been done at all, but size twenty-nine shoes require a certain amount of finesse to stop properly, especially in wet grass, and Blinkmire's right foot slid helplessly and most unhappily, into the thick mud at the edge of Queen's Lake.

The puppies heard the sound of splashing, and half a second after the waveforms struck their tympanic membranes, the resulting tsunami of water hit their puppy faces. All five were soaked in cool, spring water, as though the lake had invited them in.

By one minute past Aramis's initial foot-tangle, all five animals had leapt into the cold lake to join their fallen friend.

The facts were these.

Stephen Blinkmire had never actually learnt to swim, which is why he feared so much for the young pups. But the edge of Queen's Lake sloped very gently towards the deeper section of the thirty-five-foot lake, allowing even a somewhat panicked non-swimmer (and most certainly one who stood eight feet tall) to maintain secure footing on the muddy bottom. Stephen's thrashing lasted only a few seconds, ending when his large brown boots found that secure footing.

However, the spectacular and rather raucous event had caught the ears of nearby groundskeepers, Malcolm Peating and Tommy Powers, the team's chief. The two men had been finishing the trim on a specially designed boxwood knot garden, formed in the shape of the Haimsbury-Branham crest near the largest of the golden-cloth pavilions, the command centre to the four-hundredth Branham fête's city of painted tents. It took the men several minutes to reach the water, giving Blinkmire time to notice an unusual and very solid texture beneath his right hand.

"Here now, Mr. Blinkmire," called Peating as he reached the lake's edge. "Don't struggle, sir. It'll just make it worse. Them rains've stirred up the silt down there, I reckon, an' yer likely ta slip down in, if ya thrash about. Take my hand, sir."

"I'm not sure I can, Mr. Peating," answered the giant. "If I do, I may lose my balance. I'm poised rather precariously, you see. Upon a carved stone."

"There's no stones in this part o' the lake, sir," the junior gardener insisted. "Now, take my arm, sir. Please, afore ya sink in the mud."

Blinkmire did his best to reach, but even the slightest movement towards the extended hand proved unwieldy and awkward, for the eight-foot-tall gentleman was simultaneously endeavouring to maintain his balance *and* keep the dogs from paddling too far into the water.

"Don't go out there!" Stephen cried as he grabbed for Porthos's tail. "It's too deep!"

Naturally, the animals paid no heed, except for white-furred Aramis, who turned about and dog-paddled towards his friend. Bella and Briar were patrolling the crowded pavilions along with a pair of well-trained mastiffs, and all four adult canines now galloped towards the fracas with all speed.

The result: Blinkmire's face took another soaking as one-hundred-and-twenty-pound Briar leapt into the water, followed in succession by three other, very large dogs. Poor Stephen soon found himself inundated by swimming canines. Only the firmness of the mysterious stone beneath his right arm kept the floundering man afloat.

By now, nearly everyone working in the area had heard the commotion, and the scene became populated by diggers, carpenters, arborists, plumbers (busy installing a new fountain near the main tent), practising performers, exhibitors, armoured knights, squires, an array of footmen, and one very frantic hunchback.

"Dear me!" cried Count Riga as he rushed towards the lakeside. "Come, Bella! Briar! Mr. Blinkmire, are you all right? Oh, my dear Mr. Blinkmire, you're soaked to the skin!"

The Romanian count's spinal malformation made running a chore, but he managed, loping gingerly to protect his curved back. Following behind, ran John Kay the hall's head butler, who'd been enjoying a tea break near the south entrance when the ruckus occurred, and close behind Kay, ran a trio of uniformed maids; and lastly, a freckle-faced young man with a thick thatch of auburn hair.

"I'll get him!" the athletic redhead shouted to Riga, easily passing by everyone as he sprinted towards the lake. Without a second thought, Seth Holloway splashed into the cold water, instantly up to his boyish cheekbones in lake and puppies. "Here, take my hand, Mr. Blinkmire. I'll help you ashore."

The much shorter Cambridge don assisted the befuddled giant, and together, the two men scrambled onto the grass and mud of *terra firma*.

"I only pray the duchess didn't see that," the giant moaned as Seth led him from the lake and up the grassy slope to the seating area.

"I'm sure she'll see the humour in it," Holloway assured him as Stephen took a chair. "It's a new way to take a bath, I suppose. Are you all right? Shall I send for one of the doctors?"

"No, I'm only embarrassed," Blinkmire muttered, somewhat out of breath. "I was fearful for the puppies, you see. And then, despite my warnings, they leapt into the lake anyway. If it weren't for that large rock, I'd most surely have fallen over!" cried Blinkmire. "The duchess is still sleeping, I hope? I pray I've not awakened her."

The flustered giant's question received an immediate response, for a heavily pregnant woman appeared at the top of the hill. "It looks as though she is very much awake, old man," Holloway replied, hastening up the hill. "Beth, you shouldn't be out here. You know you're to keep off your feet today, and this grass is slippery."

Elizabeth Stuart Sinclair looked as though she'd swallowed a very large medicine ball, and even the soft draping of a chiffon blouse did little to conceal that fact. She took Seth's hand, leaning upon his arm as they descended the slope slowly.

"It's very difficult to nap with so much excitement just outside my windows, Lord Paynton. But why are you and Mr. Blinkmire soaked to the skin? Mr. Kay, fetch towels for our guests, won't you?" The butler called the order to the footmen, who rushed back up the hill to gather up towels and blankets.

"Thank you, Your Grace. It's most understanding of you," he said, glancing down as his suit. The coat, shirt, trousers, boots, even his face and hair; all dripped with water. The puppies swam to shore, each twisting its body to shake off the wet, resulting in an unwanted shower for nearly everyone, including Blinkmire, who took the brunt.

For some reason, the gentle giant began to laugh. "There's just no drying out, is there?" he exclaimed good-naturedly. "Do forgive me, everyone. Your Grace, I'm very sorry to draw you out here. You're all very kind to come to my aid. I'd hoped to avert a catastrophe, and instead caused one to happen—and with such ferocity! Viktor, I'm glad you didn't try to submerge yourself. Not only is the water freezing, it's rather dangerous in there. Very slippery, and there are stones near the shore. Oh, thank you, Mr. Powers. You're very kind," he told the chief gardener, who offered the dripping giant one of his garden towels.

"You're welcome, sir. It's not perfectly clean, mind you, but I only wiped my hands on it a time or two."

Elizabeth took a chair at a nearby table, easing herself into the creaking wicker. In the background behind her head, a team of carpenters, plumbers, and gardeners finished the final touches to the sea of golden tents. Above the gold, waved an army of colourful flags, marking each as belonging to Drummond, Haimsbury, Anjou, and several dozen other great houses from England, Scotland, and France. All were surrounded by magnificent fields of flowers and gravel footpaths. The entire Branham estate had undergone a major transformation since March, and now stood ready to greet the thousands of visitors who'd attend from all over the country, if not the world.

With Stephen recovering at the table, the adult dogs decided their assistance was no longer required and returned to patrolling the grounds. The five puppies clustered near the duchess, sniffing at her skirt pockets for treats.

Seth noticed and scolded the animals. "Dart, you naughty doggy. Down, Porthos! Down! Leave your mistress alone. No, Aramis, you may not jump onto my lap," he told the white pup. "Stay down, all of you, until you're dry."

"I'm not sure it matters, as you are already wet, Dr. Holloway," suggested Riga with a sly grin.

"Perhaps, not," laughed Seth, glancing down at his suit. "I'd already bathed for the day, but it looks like I'll need another one before tonight's party." He stood and whistled to the pack. "Come! Come, all of you! With me!"

All five puppies chased after the handsome professor like eager students to a spot near one of the cherry trees. He withdrew a wet rubber ball from his trouser pocket and tossed it towards the farthest pavilion, nearly two hundred yards away. "Fetch!" he shouted.

Every paw hit the earth, and the furry quintet bounded after the brightly coloured ball. Laughing at the scene, the viscount returned to his chair, his eyes on the duchess. "That is but a moment's distraction, I fear. They will certainly be back."

"Such is the way of puppies and perhaps children as well," she told the men. "We'll soon put the latter theory to the test, though. Mr. Blinkmire, how did you end up bathing in the lake?"

"Well, my lady, it was never my intent, but I suppose I had it coming. I tried to keep the puppies from any harm, you see. Aramis isn't a strong swimmer yet, and he invariably follows the others. It was a foolish thing to do, I suppose. However," he continued as he removed the soaked jacket and set it on the table, "I may have unwittingly come across several objects that don't belong. Mr. Powers, have you any idea what those large stones near the edge of the lake might be? The one beneath my hand felt finely carved, if you get my meaning. And there were several others, all of similar size. It felt rather like pieces of a broken statue."

"There's not likely to be any statues in the lake, Mr. Blink-mire," Powers insisted.

"Yes, but I'm sure of it," Blinkmire replied. "I may be sizeable, but my sense of touch is rarely mistaken."

The broad-shouldered gardener signalled towards his assistant and removed his work coat. "I'd planned to get wet later anyway to check that new fountain, so I set out my waders this morning. Shaw, go fetch 'em for me, will you? They're by the green and gold Aubrey tent. Over near the tilt yard."

"Might it be debris from the work crews?" suggested the duchess. "I'm sure there've been many bits of rock and timber discarded over the past few months. Perhaps, our recent storm dislodged something and cast it into the lake. Might that be it, Mr. Blinkmire?"

"I suppose it is possible, my lady, but this felt like a face."

"My lady, may we escort you back indoors?" asked Kay.

Seth took Beth's hand. "I'll see she gets back safely. You see to our Mr. Blinkmire."

The butler turned to the soaked giant. "Here now, sir, Lord Paynton is correct. Allow me to return you to the house. You'll catch your death sitting out here."

With the butler's aid, and accompanied by Riga, Blinkmire made his way up the path to the main gardens of Branham Park. Soon, he was soaking in a hot tub, and by half five, sat before a cheerful fire, warming his toes and sharing cinnamon spiced tea with Count Riga.

Seth Holloway interrupted to say goodbye. "I'm off to London, gentlemen. I trust you're feeling warmer, Mr. Blinkmire?"

"Warm as toast, sir. Is our duchess all right?"

"She is, and I've convinced her to retire early tonight—after she enjoys a short visit with the duke, of course. I plan to shop for more Prussian blue whilst in London. I've run out, I'm afraid, but I'm determined to finish the duchess's portrait before she gives birth."

"I'm sure the duke will find the painting pleasing," Riga observed. "From what I've seen thus far, sir, it's a masterpiece."

"I'm not sure about that," Seth replied, "but the project passes the time whilst I take my turn keeping watch over her welfare. Oh, the duke wired that he'll be arriving here around six, but can only stay until eight. It will be a short evening, I'm afraid."

"Then, he's leaving for Paris?" asked the count.

"He is, which means I'll be returning here first thing tomorrow. I hope you'll keep an eye on our duchess overnight."

"It is a most pleasant pastime," Riga observed with a smile. "I wonder, do you plan to call on Lord Salperton?"

"Yes, in fact, Henry and I are attending a soiree at Lord Salisbury's home tonight, but we'll both be here bright and early on the first train. With Gehlen in Scotland..."

"Dr. Gehlen is in Scotland?" asked Riga in a worried tone. "Duke James left for Glasgow this afternoon, and now you tell us Anthony Gehlen is also away?"

"I'm afraid so, but he promised to return as soon as he's buried his father. As the new Earl of Pencaitland, Gehlen has to wade through a lot of inheritance paperwork, I should think. It's a shame the two of them couldn't patch things up before Lord Edgar died."

"Fathers and sons are ever at odds," Riga sighed. "Why must it be an adversarial relationship?"

"Being a father doesn't come naturally to every man, Count," Holloway answered, thinking of his own, strained relationship with his father. "I suppose we must all try to mend fences whilst the opportunity is there. Shall I bring you back anything from London?"

"I could use a new set of strings for my cello, but otherwise, I am content," Riga said gently.

"Strings. I can do that," Holloway answered. "Mr. Blinkmire, about those stones. I don't know if anyone's told you, but you were right. Powers discovered what looks like a finely chiseled marble head near the shoreline, and there are other bits submerged nearby. He and his men plan to dredge the lake tomorrow morning for all the remains. It looks as though the recent storm may have disturbed the lake bottom and uncovered an unknown statue, after all. Until tomorrow, then!"

Seth left the two older men to enjoy the warmth of the cheerful fire. Stephen sighed, a strange look darkening his features. "Do you ever have premonitions, Viktor?" he asked the count.

"Sometimes," the other answered. "Have you experienced one?"

"I'm not sure. But whilst touching that strange stone head, I had an overwhelming sense of doom. I pray I'm wrong, but with so many thousands of people about to descend upon Branham, it seems a very strange time for an unexpected statue to surface. Or am I being too suspicious?"

"I've never known you to be suspicious, Stephen. But it does seem very strange indeed."

"If only Prince Anatole were here," the other whispered. "He'd know what to do about it all."

"Yes. Our prince has remained out of touch," whispered Riga. "He is a man of mystery."

"Not a man," countered Blinkmire, "but certainly mysterious. It's unsettling to think of a statue hidden beneath that lake. Like the vanguard to something quite evil. Let us pray I'm mistaken."

The two men gazed into the flames, both praying for peace.

CHAPTER THREE

7:31 pm – Aubrey House

Nearly three hours after Stephen Blinkmire scrubbed behind his large ears to remove the last vestiges of silt, and an hour and a half away by train in Westminster, a very frustrated Paul Stuart was dressing for the party at Lord Salisbury's home. He stood before a mirrored cedar closet, buttoning a pair of black woolen trousers, and in the background—coming from the bedchamber next door—he could hear his mother-in-law's strident voice. She was scolding her daughter for gaining weight, unaware of Cordelia's delicate condition, and Paul had heard enough. For fear of her cruel, elder brother's reaction to the idea of an Aubrey heir, Delia had begged him to keep the news from her family as long as possible, but if Connie intended to lecture his wife on eating habits, the earl would make sure the interference stopped.

Now.

Barefooted and wearing just the shirt and trousers, he crossed through the connecting bath and entered the countess's bedroom, not bothering to knock.

"Paul, please, we're dressing!" his beautiful bride exclaimed. "Mother is helping me select the right clothes for this evening's party."

"Yes, I gathered as much," he answered, unable to hide his annoyance. "Apparently, Connie thinks you put on too much weight during our wedding trip. Isn't that so?"

The dowager baroness's cold eyes rounded in shock. Up until now, her son-in-law had shown remarkable patience, kindness, and gentility; but it now seemed the rumours of the earl's volatility were true, and Constance had no intention of allowing the wealthy earl to control either her or her daughter.

"It is a mother's prerogative to offer advice," she replied haughtily. "I suggested Cordelia might have a seamstress let out her skirts until she can take off a few pounds. You were only away for nine weeks, Paul. To gain three inches on one's waist in so little time is..."

"Completely normal," he finished for her.

Delia began to shake her head in panic, her greyish blue eyes pleading with him not to reveal their secret. "I think he means it's normal for me. My sweet tooth always rules my head, I fear. And with all those delicious French and Italian pastries to tempt me, I simply overindulged. You're right, Mama. I shall have the skirts altered."

"Overindulgence is one thing, my dear, but gluttony is quite another!" Connie declared. "But not to worry. You'll soon take off those extra pounds with my help. I shall speak to your cook. It's Mrs. Lind, as I remember. I'll just let her know to prepare lighter dishes for you from now on. Bone broth and... "

"There's no need to do that," Paul interrupted. "I have already spoken to Mrs. Lind, Connie. I've told her that Delia requires a special diet for the next five months or so. A healthy, nutritious one, and her *doctor* will prescribe it."

"Doctor? Delia, my dear, are you ill?"

"Not exactly ill, Mama," the young woman dithered. "It's just that... I mean. You see..."

"My wife is with child, Connie. In five months or so, she'll give birth to our first son or daughter."

If Paul weren't so very angry, he might have laughed at the amusing avalanche of expressions that fell across his mother-in-law's face. Wychwright hemmed and hawed and finally gaped at them both, her mouth open as though the news were an impossibility—for in truth, the conceited woman had never imagined any man might find her daughter the least bit attractive.

"A baby?" she managed at last. "Delia, you're—I mean you're going to have...? But how is that possible? Are you sure? Have you been seen by someone?"

"Yes, we're sure, Mama," Delia answered defiantly, the shy girl's courage rising as Paul took her hand. "We've consulted with Dr. Gehlen several times now, but he suggested we wait until I was further along to announce. We'd planned to tell you..."

"A *baby!*" the woman exulted, clapping her hands together joyfully as though the whole thing were her own personal victory. "Oh, a baby! This is quite wonderful! My, yes, of course, you must have a special diet and the very best doctors. I could move in, if it would be helpful, my dear. You'll want to refurnish the old nursery, I should think. It's been a very long time since it housed a baby. Oh, a *baby!*" she sang as though the word itself had intrinsic value. "How wonderful!" Connie hugged her daughter with more affection than Delia could ever remember receiving.

"Thank you, Mama," she muttered, not sure how to react.

"I'll be with you all the way, my dear," the woman declared forcefully. "As for tonight, I'm sure there's something we can do with one of your dresses to make it work. Perhaps, we could tighten the corset a little."

Paul bit his tongue, not wishing to cause his wife any more distress than she already felt, but he had no intention of allowing Connie to assume control—not now, not ever. "That isn't necessary, Constance. I shall help my wife with her hooks and laces. I've grown accustomed to doing it."

"You?" asked the dowager baroness in shock. "Oh, no, it simply isn't done! You're..."

"Her husband. And a husband does have the right, you know," he reminded her.

"Yes, I suppose that's true, but she'll need a lady's maid, and a nurse, and a governess, a nanny—oh, and the finest doctors. Nothing but the best for my future grandchild!"

"Gehlen's the leading obstetrician in London, Connie, and Delia already has a lady's maid. A very good one. It just happens tonight is her evening off."

"Who? Is the girl reliable?"

"She was personally trained by Esther Alcorn, which means her education is the finest. Ada MacKenzie. As to any other new hires, we'll see to those once my wife is further along." He paused, an idea forming. "I rather like the idea of redecorating our nursery, and it's far too large a project for Cordelia. Why don't you ask my butler to show you where it is? Perhaps, you'd offer us advice?"

"Yes, yes, of course, I will. I'll go find Bailey right now and take a quick look. Oh, this is simply wonderful! A baby!" she said again, her greedy eyes gleaming.

The dowager baroness left the room at last, and Paul turned to his wife, his eyes growing soft. He kissed her lips sweetly. "I'm very sorry, darling. I had no right to blurt out the news like that, but I will not have your mother upsetting you about your weight. And for the record, even if you weren't with child, I'd have interfered. I shall always defend you."

"But Mama's right, Paul. I do eat too many sweets," she answered, her eyes sad and still.

Aubrey took her soft face into his hands and offered his best smile. "You are beautiful beyond compare, Cordelia Jane Stuart. Absolutely perfect in every way. I love every curve in your body. Surely, you realise that by now. I wouldn't change one thing about your figure. Not one."

"But my arms are too plump, and my waist has never been as trim as Elizabeth's. When I wore her gown on our wedding day, Mrs. Alcorn had to let out the seams, or else I'd have burst the bodice!"

He caressed her shoulders, slowly drifting into more intimate areas. "I love the way that dress fit you. You are a Titian wonder, and every artist in the world would line up to paint you, if I'd let them. But your perfect body is mine, and mine alone. I revel in its beauty, my love."

She began to giggle, as he kissed her throat. "But I shall grow evermore fat with each passing day, husband."

He gazed into her eyes. "Cordelia, I love you and will always love you. And as our child grows, I shall love your figure all the more. When I awake in the morning, my first thought is of you. All day, as I walk the noisy corridors of government, my mind drifts back to you. When I fall asleep in your arms each night, I dream of you. My darling, God created us for one another. I love you, *mo bhean*," he said, using the Gaelic for 'my wife'. Paul drew her close and kissed her soft lips, his hands wandering to her waist.

"Not now," she laughed. "We have to dress!"

"Do we? I could lock the apartment door to keep out unwanted intruders. We'll pretend there's no annoying party to attend, no world to worry us. It will be as it was on our wedding trip. Just the two of us, without responsibilities or distractions. As if only we exist."

He began to unlace her silk corset.

Cordelia giggled as he kissed her throat. "Really, Paul, we'll be late," she whispered halfheartedly.

"Yes, we will be late," he answered, his warm breath in her ear. Paul offered her an impish, conspiratorial grin, and then locked the apartment door. The Earl and Countess of Aubrey would indeed arrive at the party *very* late.

8:12 pm – Château Rothesay, near Paris

"Goodnight, Your Highness! Thank you again for returning our Adele to us!" Victoria Stuart called as she waved goodbye to their handsome, but very unusual new neighbour. As it happened, Sir Richard and Dolly Patterson-Smythe had been visiting when von Siebenbürgen arrived with Della in a magnificent coach and four. Stuart invited him in, and they all engaged in small talk over a selection of fruit, cheese, canapes, and wine. Then, as the moon's large face appeared in the drawing room window, the prince suddenly rose, offered apologies, and announced his intention to leave.

"Do forgive me, my new friends. I must speak with my sister before she departs for her night's work. I hope you understand," he told his hosts. He turned to the adolescent. "My very dear Lady Adele, it was a great pleasure to meet you this afternoon, despite the troubling circumstances that brought you into my woods. If ever you are near my home again, I pray you will come inside and spend a little time with us. My sister and I shall make you most welcome. Most welcome indeed!"

With the prince gone, the four adults sat round the creek stone fireplace, sharing old family stories and discussing French and English politics, whilst Adele wrote a letter to her brother. She'd just finished, when she overheard Victoria mention something quite wonderful.

Della turned round, her face alight. "Auntie Tory, did you just say Cousin Charles is coming tomorrow?"

"Yes, I did. Your cousin telegraphed me shortly before the prince brought you back, in fact. It seems, Charles has business in Paris and asked if he might take you with him."

"To Paris?"

"Yes, but not only Paris, my dear," Tory explained with a sly grin. "He hopes to take you back to England. Of course, you'll probably want to remain here and study with your tutor, but..."

"England!" the girl exclaimed, rushing into her aunt's arms. "Cousin Charles is taking me home? Oh, Auntie Tory, that is the best news I've heard in such a long time!"

"Is it? But I thought you liked living here," Dolly observed, winking at her friend. "I'd assumed you'd want to stay here until August at least. Didn't you, Dickie?"

"Don't ask me," the balding banker muttered, his nose in a newspaper. "I keep out of women's talk. But I'd thought you wanted to see the Exposition, Adele. We'd all planned to go on Thursday for the preview."

Dolly nibbled on a black current tart. "I'd forgotten about that, Dickie. Adele, it's invitation only, but Sir Richard was put on the list because his bank underwrote some of the cost for that hideous new tower—what is it called again?" she asked her husband.

"The Eiffel," he told her. "Named for the designer. It's the tallest man-made structure in the world. Even taller than the Great Pyramid. American and English builders are already scrambling to design one taller. Utter nonsense, if you ask me."

Adele was unimpressed. "I don't care about all that. Who needs exhibits, when there's the Branham fête to attend?" she asked happily. "Beth's promised medieval games and even knights in armour, just like in the faery stories. Besides, she's going to have her babies soon, in just over a month. I can't miss that." She stopped and stared at her aunt. "May I go back with him? Please? I'm very sorry if it sounds as though I'm ungrateful, but I've missed them all, you see."

"I understand perfectly," the maiden aunt said, kissing her niece's cheek. "I'm quite used to it, my dear. Beth loved coming to the château, and then invariably grew bored within a week and talked about leaving again. Holidays, birthdays, and of course the fête drew her back every year. But then, so did the thought of a certain Captain she missed." The Scotswoman paused, her dark eyes narrowing. "Della, it wouldn't be Winston Churchill's got you anxious for England, would it? I know you received a letter from him a few days ago. It's much too soon to form serious attachments, my dear. You must wait until you're sixteen, at least."

Adele laughed. "Winnie? A serious attachment? Oh, hardly! He's a friend, that's all." She gathered up her stationery and pens, placing them in a hinged, satin box. "But Cousin Charles is coming tomorrow?"

"So his telegram said," answered Victoria as a Parson Russell terrier scampered into the room and sat before his mistress, staring.

"Now?" the Scotswoman asked her dog. "Samson, you just went out. Come here and sit with me. I've got nibbles." The animal leapt onto his owner's lap, nosing at her nearby plate. "You're going to get very fat, you naughty doggy. Where's Napper?" she asked Della.

"Sleeping. I think our adventure wore her out. I am very sorry to have disobeyed, Aunt. Although, it was actually Queenie who did it. I merely followed as rider."

"You must learn to control your horses better, Adele," Stuart answered, handing Samson a bit of cheese. Sighing, she looked to her friend. "I suppose we ought to have a party whilst Charles is here. Tomorrow's May Day. Is there anything special going on in the village we might take him to?"

Patterson-Smythe was a handsome woman of fifty-one, and she'd arranged her silvering blonde hair into a swirling chignon. Her soft grey eyes crinkled at the corners as she laughed. "Tory, that is such a silly question! Hardly anything ever happens in that village. Especially lately. Ever since Prince Ara moved into the abbey, it seems the entire village's gone quiet as the grave."

"I wouldn't call it *that* quiet, Doll," argued her husband from overtop his newspaper. "Just different. There's a bonfire tonight in the village square. And aren't they having that festival tomorrow? You know, the one with the ash pole and all that nonsense."

"Yes, but that's hardly the sort of thing we can take Charles to, dear. It's all so very pagan. Honestly, for a village that claims to be one of the earliest Christian settlements in France, you'd think they'd have stopped all that long ago."

Her husband turned the page to read the financial columns. "It's not pagan, Dolly, it's tradition. There's a difference."

"Is there? If so, then I don't see it. When it comes to keeping old traditions, I'm generally in favour of them, but not that one, Dickie."

"Which one is that, Auntie Dolly?" asked the curious adolescent.

"The May pole!" Dolly exclaimed. "The men of the village chop down a huge tree and place it in the centre of the square. Then all the young girls dance round it, dressed in flowers and finery. It's a pretty little dance, mind you, but you'd think the priest would put a stop to it. I mean really! It invites darkness, not light. Of course, tonight, they're probably having that huge bonfire. I'm very glad the prince found you and brought you home, Della. Tonight of all nights, you wouldn't want to be alone in those haunted woods."

"Tonight? Why, Auntie Dolly? Is there something special about tonight?" she asked.

"My dear, it's Walpurgisnacht! I suppose you've heard it called Beltane."

"That's enough," her husband warned Dolly. "You shouldn't get into all that superstitious nonsense. You'll frighten the child."

"Yes, but Dickie, the Stuarts and Sinclairs deal with such non-sense every day. I mean, the inner circle has to battle against local beliefs like that. You know perfectly well they're more than just superstitions."

"I know no such thing. Or I prefer not to think about it. May we discuss something else? The Exposition, for example."

"What's Walpurgisnacht, Auntie Dolly? Is that a German word? Some sort of night, I suppose."

"Yes, but as I say, it's rather like Beltane back in Scotland. Some of the locals consider it the most important night of the whole year."

"Why?"

"Ghosts, my dear! The dead rise up and walk, because the veil twixt the worlds thins. Didn't you ever hear about it back at Briarcliff?"

"No. What is it?"

Tory lit a cigarette, finding the topic dull. "Come, Richard, let's you and I take a walk. We can discuss that hospital project of Beth's. She's still looking for donors, if you and Dolly wish to contribute."

The banker set aside his newspaper and took Victoria's arm. The two of them left through the open French doors, followed by Samson.

Dolly patted the empty spot next to her on the sofa. "Come here, darling girl. Come sit by Auntie Dolly. My husband has no patience for ghost stories, for he thinks it's all made up. But most of these old tales have roots in truth, you know, and as a Stuart family member, it's important you understand spiritual matters. Walpurgis-nacht is one of them."

Adele joined her friend on the green and white striped sofa, tucking her small feet beneath the soft skirts of her dress. She'd changed into a more suitable costume after Prince Araqiel brought her home, and Dolly gazed at the adolescent, suddenly seeing a preview of how the girl might look as a young woman. Adele had long chestnut hair with copper highlights that rippled along her back and arms, and her blue eyes had recently taken on the same hue as her cousin, Charles Sinclair. The lashes were dark brown, and her mouth blushed with a hint of pink. She stood tall and willowy, but already at nearly twelve, the feminine outline of womanhood had begun to shine.

"My darling, you are going to break hearts one day," Dolly whispered. "No wonder that prince is interested in you."

"He isn't interested in me," the adolescent argued. "He's very nice to me, it's true, but he asked a lot of questions about Cousin Charles. I think he's more interested in him."

"Did he? Perhaps, I'm wrong, then. What were we discussing?"

"Walpurgisnacht," Della reminded her friend. "What is it?"

"Ah, yes. Well, Walpurgisnacht is a tradition that began in the Harz Mountains. Have you studied those in your geography lessons?"

Adele nodded. "Yes, they're in Germany."

"Indeed, they are. It's an old Germanic belief that on the last night of April, witches ride to a great meeting in the halls of the highest mountain called the Brocken. Goethe's *Faust* is set there. Have you read it?"

She shook her head. "It's on my shelf, but I've not yet read it."

"Well, you should," the woman told her. "Walpurgisnacht is also called die Hexennacht, the night of the witches."

"But witches aren't real, any more than ghosts are," the girl proclaimed.

"Oh, my dear, they are real. You'd be surprised to learn how many witches there are. But they don't look like the faery stories describe them. They're not old and ugly, but look just like ordinary women. And some are very beautiful. According to legend, St. Walpurgis fought against these witches, which is why the night came to carry her name. On Walpurgisnacht, villagers all across Europe gather to light bonfires to keep out the evil ones; to stop the witches from conjuring up the dead."

"Fire keeps witches away?"

"Well, that's what people claim, but I think the bonfires actually attract them."

"Fire attracts witches?" asked Adele, her eyes wide.

"Yes, but also ghosts. I'm not saying the dead actually come back to life tonight, mind you. I really don't think they do, but demons can pretend to be our dead loved ones. I think that is the true source of these beliefs."

Adele grew thoughtful. "Are you saying demons are real, then?"

"Oh, yes. Of course they are! Ask your Cousin Charles, if you don't believe me. Your family's fought against evil like that for centuries."

"Do you think Prince Ara is evil, Auntie Dolly?" she asked in a whisper.

Patterson-Smythe nearly said no, but then a strange shiver ran through her spirit, for the girl seemed sincere. "Della, why would you ask me that? Has he done something to make you fear him?"

"No. It's just a feeling. I should go up to bed." She gathered her writing materials and school books, placing everything into a small basket. "I'll be very glad when Charles gets here. I'm never afraid when he's around."

"Why is that? Surely, your brother keeps you safe, too. Darling, why are you so attached to Charles?" asked Dolly as she held the girl's hands.

"I'm not sure. Paul's a very wonderful brother, and he does make me feel safe, but there's something special about Charles, don't you think? He reminds me a little of my father. Not only the way he looks, but the way he acts. The way he laughs. Georgie and Robby will be very lucky."

Dolly pulled the child close. "Darling, you're also very lucky. We all love you very much."

"Yes, I know. I just miss my father sometimes. Goodnight, Auntie Dolly. Please, have Tory wake me as soon as Charles gets here. Even if it's midnight. All right?"

"He isn't even boarding the ship until ten, darling. It may be afternoon before he arrives."

She sighed. "Such a very long wait." Della kissed her friend's cheek. "Come, Napper. Let's go to sleep now. The sooner we dream, the sooner Cousin Charles gets here."

The dog followed her into the corridor and up the back stairs. Patterson-Smythe remained in the drawing room, her eyes on the fire. Tory's dog Samson returned and jumped onto the sofa. Dolly absentmindedly stroked the terrier's ears. "You don't believe in ghosts, do you, Samson?"

The fire crackled, and it seemed the tongues of flame took on human shapes, like hundreds of dancing figures.

As Dolly fell asleep before the fire, a bonfire burnt brightly, several miles away. Beyond the castle's fenced gardens, far past the pleasant meadow, deep within the *Bois du Fee*, the faery woods; in the very centre of the magical glade where Adele met Prince Ara, a great fire blazed high into the night. And all round its hot flames, danced a thousand spectral creatures. High above, the silver moon observed the ancient rites, her dark eyes shining.

Also above the ghostly revellers, flew a large bat, winging its way through the haunted trees and into the bowels of the great abbey beyond. Once there, it changed its shape into a fly and entered the highest window through a broken pane, not yet repaired. The clever insect transformed once more, this time into a beautiful man, dressed in gold and black finery. The tall figure wound his way downwards, following the dusty steps once trod by St. Rosaline's monks; deep, deep into the earth, until he reached the very bowels of the once sacred building. He'd had a successful day and whistled a tune from *Faust* as he entered the cold crypt.

Here, hidden from prying eyes, stood fourteen rectangular boxes, decorated in runes and jewels and covered over with polished obsidian. Each box was specially designed for a singular inhabitant, and the runes told not only the story of the box's contents, but also its purpose. Presently, most were empty, waiting for the absent sleeper whose energy would ignite the runes and fuel a primordial ceremony.

He drew a chair beside one of the largest coffins, sitting close enough to touch the icy obsidian.

"Comfortable?" he asked the box's inhabitant. "I remember what it was like to be confined in the seven realms, old friend. I know it can be a challenge, Brother, but it needn't make you weak. How is it a mere five-thousand years beneath the stones left you so very vulnerable, Raziel? I do not complain, of course. As the humans so often say, your loss is my gain. It was a mistake to patronise Saraqael. Indeed, it was a mistake to release him! Sara cannot be trusted, and he is much more clever than you. But not clever enough for me," Araqiel added, glancing at a breathtaking box adorned in midnight blue quartz and moonstones. "I have a very special box awaiting him, you see, and I shall use it, once he helps me capture the fourteenth part—that all important key."

The box rattled, as though something inside it tried to escape. Ara tapped the lid, laughing. "Do not struggle against the chains, Brother! They are soft compared to those which encompassed me. Your plan to re-assemble your old book was laudable but imperfect. What would you gain by speaking The One's words, Raza? Eternal freedom? A return to our Golden Age? No, you would not, for the words themselves have no power without *The Voice*. The Other is The Voice, and it's a certainty that He will never side with us. Grandmother Chaos tried to slay Him. Father Kronos sought to undo Him and received exile in Tartarus for his efforts. Satan offered Him all the kingdoms of the earth. What fools these immortals be, eh? No, what our kind need is a way to reverse The Other's own reversals. A precisely fashioned set of spiritual complications. Wheels within wheels within mystical wheels, eh? The machine, Raza. The Great Machine! The one Kronos proposed long ago is still a possibility, and I am building it. An old friend has offered his assistance for a fee, but the cost is small. He asks only for an army of the dead. Such limited vision."

The sounds of chanting and violence filled the dank, cold air of the crypt, and Araqiel's face shone with pride. "The world dances to our tune, Brother. Soon, the rich and powerful, all the crowned heads will bow to us. To me."

The box rattled again, emitting a low growl. "Yes, yes, the prophecies of old say otherwise, but how is it The One is allowed to work all things together for good without challenge? My machine will work all things together for evil. Beautiful, tempting, seductive, glorious evil, Raziel. Our Chosen One begins to remember, old friend. He remembers his purpose and our voice. And he is on his way to me. The flames and the dance bring him here. Once I've assembled all the parts and switched on the device, I shall rise to the heights, and you my old rival, will wallow with the *wusuru* worms. I do hope you enjoy your new home, Raziel. Because you will live in it forever."

CHAPTER FOUR
6:47 pm – Branham Hall

"Darling, I'm home. Sorry to be late. We had trees across the line," Charles called into the apartment. "Beth?"

The duke could hear water running in the connecting bath, and so he crossed through. "Beth?" he asked again, peering into the steamy room.

The linen cupboard stood open, blocking the chamber's sole inhabitant. "Charles!" his wife exclaimed as she shut the painted door. She had just stepped out of the bath and wore only a silk and lace dressing gown, partially closed. Water was draining from the blue-and-white porcelain tub, which still held soapy water. Elizabeth's wet hair clung to her shoulders and back in long curling strands.

"I didn't know you'd be stopping. Hadn't you planned to go directly to Dover?"

He kissed her, his arms round her bare middle. "Why would I come this close to Branham and not stop to say goodbye to the most beautiful woman in all the kingdom? I've missed you."

"I've missed you as well." She rose up on tiptoe, kissing his bearded cheek. "I was just getting ready for bed."

"Already? It's not yet seven."

"Yes, I know, but I'm very tired. It's been a long day. I rose at five due to noise on the pavilion field. Our mastiffs took issue with one of the exhibitors. Powers has it all in hand."

Her story concerned the duke. "Why would the mastiffs bother them? Were they misbehaving?"

"So I understand. Both men are young. It happens sometimes, darling, but no one's hurt. How long can you stay?"

He gazed into her dark eyes, the smell of her raspberry and vanilla soap enticing. "Long enough. Shall I join you in bed?" he teased, opening her robe. The soap's heavy scent filled the room, and he drank it in as he kissed her lips.

"That would be so very nice," she whispered, "providing, our doctor hadn't forbidden it."

He sighed. "Ah, yes. I've managed without you since January, I suppose I can last seven more weeks."

"Seven?" she asked, pulling the robe closed. "If you mean until the twins are born, it's only five, Captain. Please, don't make me wait any longer. My poor feet couldn't take it!"

"Yes, it's five until your delivery, but seven until heaven," he whispered hopefully. "Isn't it?"

"Seven? Oh, wait, I see what you mean," she said, her dark eyes twinkling. "I miss being with you as well, Charles, but it may take a little longer than a fortnight afterward. I imagine it all depends on how quickly I recover."

"May I not at least sleep next to you when I'm here? I miss having you beside me at night, Beth. It's lonely enough when I'm in London, but I still don't understand why Anthony insists you sleep alone."

"You know the reason very well, Charles. I'm tossing about so much at night now. If our bed were wider, then there'd be room, but presently, these children of ours insist on taking their share."

"I could have a second bed installed, and we could at least be in the same room."

She stroked his bearded face. "Captain, it's not for much longer. Besides, I... *Oh!*" she cried out, reaching for her back.

"What? What is it?"

"A sharp kick! I think Robby's practising football against one of my ribs. Apparently, he wants to play for your old alma mater."

"He'll require room, if he's to score at Parker's Piece. And I doubt Georgie's giving any quarter," he laughed. "You're all wet, Beth. Shall I help with your hair? I could brush it dry."

"That would be lovely. Agatha's developed a friendship with Tom Delith. He's a shepherd at Anjou Farm. I gave her the night off to have supper with his family."

Charles took a brush and began stroking the wet curls. "When you say friendship, do you mean romance?"

The duchess nodded. "Of a sort. It's very early days, but she's of a marriageable age. I can't begrudge her love, now can I?"

"I'll take over as your maid, then, shall I?" he laughed, struggling when he reached a small tangle.

"When must you leave? Do you have time for tea first?" his wife asked from her chair.

"I have two hours at most, I'm afraid, but when I return, I shall be bringing back a surprise."

"What surprise it that, darling?" she asked, turning round.

"Adele."

Beth's eyes lit up. "Our darling Della? Oh, Charles, that's wonderful!" she exclaimed, standing and throwing her arms round his neck. "But I thought Tory couldn't travel."

"She can't, which is why I'm bringing our girl back with me. However, if I can convince our aunt to use a bath chair..."

"Which you won't."

"Ah, but if *I can*, then perhaps, her doctor will allow Victoria to come as well. This fête is the hall's four-hundredth anniversary, Beth, and I'd hate for Tory to miss it. Shall we ring for supper?"

"Yes, if you don't mind. I thought I'd eat up here tonight. There's a nightgown already set out at the end of the bed. Could you help me with it?"

The silk gown was cut full and opened to the waist. He slipped it over her head, and then tied the bodice. Gold ribbons and ruffles decorated the gown's high collar, and pin-tucking created fullness to allow plenty of room for the duchess's expanding waistline.

"You're such a vision," he whispered. "All my dreams come true. Really, you are, Beth. I am truly blessed."

The compliment caused her to laugh. "Why? Do you dream of plump women, Captain?"

He smiled. "Only if that woman is you, but you're hardly plump, Princess. You carry the future of our family. I dream of holding them. Our children. You have made me so very happy, little one. And soon, Paul will know that same happiness."

She held a tortoise shell comb, used to detangle wet hair. "Paul? Charles, are you saying Cordelia's pregnant?"

"I've spoiled their surprise. Sorry, darling!" He took the comb from her hands and started drawing it through her wet hair. "I love these curls."

"Don't change the subject. How long have you known?" she asked, taking back the comb.

"A few hours. He told me this afternoon after our savate demonstration. Beth, does this news upset you?"

"No, of course not. Only—well, it's a surprise, that's all. Forgive me, Charles. Of course, this is wonderful news. Honestly, I'm not sure why it's struck me so oddly. Why do I feel upset all of a sudden?"

He drew her close, his hands on her hips. "Perhaps, it's because Paul's fathered a child you thought would be yours."

"No, I don't think so," she insisted. "Does he seem happy about it?"

"Of course, he's happy. Why wouldn't he be?"

She pulled the comb through her hair, thoughtfully. "I'm not sure. Don't pay me any mind," she continued, forcing a little laugh. "Really, I'm pleased for him—for them both. Only I've never quite pictured Paul tied down by children. He's never really seemed the fatherly type. I pray I'm wrong."

"You are very wrong," the duke insisted, taking the comb from her once more and stroking the long curls to untangle them. "In fact, Paul's already mentioned the possibility of passing foreign assignments to someone else. Beth, he's changing. Cordelia's brought out a yearning for hearth and home in the earl. Which is yet another reason I want Adele here. She's his firstborn child, and she deserves to know about the baby." He grew quiet for a moment, his eyes on the comb. "Paul's asked me to become Adele's guardian, but I may hold off until the baby's born. Give him time to change his mind."

She turned round, stealing back the comb. "He asked you to become Adele's guardian? Why?"

"To protect her from gossip."

"Whose gossip? Charles, really, Adele deserves to know the truth! If she ever asks me about her parents, I intend to tell her, no matter what Paul may want."

Sinclair sighed. "Must we argue about it?"

"I'm not arguing," she insisted.

"May we not discuss it, then? I just want to enjoy being near you for an hour or two, before I have to leave again."

She turned back towards him, throwing her arms round his waist and pulling as close as her advanced pregnancy allowed. "Forgive me, Charles. I simply don't know what's wrong with me these days." She looked up, her eyes filling with tears. "You make a sacrifice just to spend a little time with me, and I spoil it by arguing. I love you, Charles."

"And I love you, little one," he whispered, sweetly kissing her forehead. "You've gone through a great many changes in the space of only a few months. It's understandable that you'd have an odd moment now and then. Shall we talk about something else? What about the nursery? Is it finished?"

This caused her to smile, and she wiped the tears from her eyes. "Very nearly done. We're waiting for the special cots to arrive from London. Oh, and Dr. Price has hired two village women as wet nurses. Mrs. Eileen MacCallum has a one-year-old daughter she's just weaning, and Mrs. Hazel Keller has a ten-month-old son. Hazel's husband died two months ago."

"I'm very sorry to hear that," Charles told her. "But is Price sure Keller can handle nursing two children at once?"

"Oh, yes. She really needs the money. Her husband was killed in East Africa, during the rebellion, and he left her in debt. I hope it's all right, but I paid off the outstanding debts for both families, and they'll all move here in early June."

"A family and a widow with a child? Surely, they won't sleep on the servants' floor? The men and women are separated, and it's too far from the babies."

"Of course not. I've opened two apartments in the east wing for them."

"Not that evil wing, Beth. I want every stone torn down and every trace of William Trent removed! In fact, I've already ordered it done as soon as we've moved back to London."

"No, darling. I've put them in the original east wing. And I agree with you about tearing out that awful monstrosity. I never understood why my great-grandfather had it built in the first place. These apartments are on the second floor."

"What about our babies? You don't intend for them to sleep alone?"

"No, Dr. Gehlen's hired a nurse from the London for us. And Mrs. Alcorn and Mrs. Wilsham will share duties as Nanny. They're all moving in after the fête, and the older children will attend school.

Mr. MacCallum is a skilled horseman. He'll join the mews and work for Clark."

"It sounds as though you have it all in hand. Darling, tell me the truth. Does it bother you that Paul's happy?"

"Why would it? Charles, I have only ever wanted his happiness. Please, forget my earlier reaction. My emotions are just peculiar lately. Dr. Gehlen said to expect it." She pressed against her left side. "Practise is over. Robby's moved now. I'm sorry, darling," she told him wearily. "I really must lie down for a minute. Do you mind?"

He kissed her cheek. "Not at all. You lie down and I'll ring for supper."

The duke pulled a long twisted cord made of red silk. The bell rope was connected to a sturdy wire that ran through the top rim of the servants' passageway and ended at the bell parlour. The hall's design included a narrow labyrinth of secret corridors, used for centuries to access the various bedchambers without disturbing guests. Built at a time when servants should work invisibly, the secret maze, as the Branham staff called it, was seldom used by anyone, except electrics men.

Elizabeth stretched out her five-foot, two-inch frame upon a flowered brocade sofa, and Charles sat beside her. "Shall I help braid your hair? Any proper lady's maid would."

Beth laughed, touching his strong hand. "No, it's still too wet for that. The fire will dry it. Charles, is this Paris trip for pleasure or business?"

"A little of both," he admitted. "The missing Cambridge student, Lionel Wentworth, was seen with a second man in Montmartre. This companion's description sounds a great deal like Sir Albert Wendaway. It's my hope to arrest them both."

Her expression darkened. "You will not expose Adele to criminals, Charles. I won't allow it."

"Do you think I would? I plan to incarcerate them with the Sûreté for the present and extradite them to England later. I'd never expose our darling girl to anyone dangerous."

"No, of course, you wouldn't. But Charles, do be careful," she said, her grip tense.

"I'm always careful, and this won't be my first arrest, darling. I've been at this for over a decade."

"Yes, I know, but it's been such a lovely few months. It rather feels like the enemy has retreated, but we both know that's not true."

"I promise to take care, but so must you. Will Seth be here through the week, or is he staying in London?"

"He didn't say, but I think Seth hopes to talk with Martin Kepelheim this evening at Salisbury's soiree. Something about your puzzle chamber. Have you found any new clues?"

"None. The room's still a complete mystery," he told her, massaging her small feet. "Oh, I met with our builder, Mr. Avery, and his men have completed the initial stages of your hospital project. The warehouses have all been cleaned, and the walls and windows repaired. There was serious smoke damage from the St. Katherine's fire last December, but the structures remain sound. They've begun putting up the dividing walls for the patient wards and offices. Avery anticipates walking us through the new layout in about two months."

"That's sooner than he'd originally thought. We should host a fundraising event, Charles. If Tory does come back with you, she and I could start working on that. Oh, do convince Dolly to come, too. She and Dickie rarely miss the fête, and this year's going to be such fun. And that reminds me. Your armour arrived yesterday."

"My what?" he asked her, his right brow arching.

"Your fifteenth-century armour, darling. Remember, Mr. Jamieson measured you for it? Paul has also agreed to participate. I tried to lure Seth and Henry into joining in the display, but both claimed poor athleticism."

"Beth, what on earth are you talking about?"

"The jousts!" she exclaimed. "Darling, you said you'd take part. Don't you remember? We discussed it in this very house, not long ago. Paul had just returned from his wedding trip, and he and Delia were staying here for the weekend. I told you both we'd installed a tilt yard in the north gardens, and a professional team were coming in from France. They perform at fairs and the like. It's theatre, not a genuine contest. I asked if you'd take part, and you said yes."

"I'm not sure I did, Beth, but..."

"You *did*, Charles. Do you think I would ask you to do anything dangerous? You need only wear the suit whilst on horseback. It's purely for show. Darling, the first Duke Henry won the lists at the fête in 1489, and I thought it would be nice if you and Paul re-enacted it."

"We're to joust? Beth, I'm not sure about this. I ride well enough, but I've never done so wearing a suit of armour."

"Not a real joust, Charles. All the two of you need do is ride several passes back and forth, unarmed. I insisted that you carry no weapons, not even frangible lances."

"Frangible?"

"The type that break easily. Do you think I'd endanger the father of my children?"

"Must their father dress up at all?" Seeing her face, he relented. "Very well, I'll do it, but only to make you smile again." He drew her hand up and kissed the palm. "Fair lady, we unworthy cousins will do our best to provide you an afternoon's entertainment."

Elizabeth slapped his wrist. "You tease me now!"

"No, little one. Forgive me. I'm just a great fool in love with the mother of my children."

"Charles, if you're worried that it's dangerous, then, I shall inform M'sieur Brodeur. He's the director of the reenactment."

"No, I'll do it, but I make no guarantee as to my prowess. You say the armour's already here?"

"Kay has it," she answered. "And your valet, our brave David Anderson, has been training with Brodeur on how to dress a knight. You'll look splendid, Charles! In fact, your longer hair fits the time period quite well."

"And my beard?" he asked. "Does that still please my queen?"

"Yes, even the beard. I rather miss kissing your bare face, however, the beard does suit you."

"And what fifteenth-century dress will you be wearing?"

She began to braid her hair against her left shoulder, and Charles helped her to sit up. "Thank you, Captain. I shall wear the same style of costume Duke Henry's young wife, the Lady Rosalind wore. Oddly enough, she was also pregnant at the time—with their last child."

"Rosalind. She was the Marquess of Anjou's daughter, right?"

"She was, yes. You've a very good memory."

A knock sounded, and Charles answered the door. "Oh, Kay. We're just talking. Come in."

The tall butler bowed to the duke and duchess. "I'm to say your supper will be delivered shortly, and Mr. Blinkmire wonders if you'd have time to speak, Your Grace," he added, looking at Haimsbury.

"Yes, certainly," the duke replied. "I'll be down momentarily. Where is he?"

"The red drawing room, sir."

Kay left, and Charles kissed his wife's hand. "I shan't be long, fair lady."

"I look forward to it, Sir Charles. Wake me if I've drifted off when you come back, will you? For now, if you'd bring me that small red book?" she asked, pointing to her dressing table.

He fetched the novel, noticing its cover. "*Der Schimmelreiter?*"

"I'm practising my German. You promised to take me on a tour of Europe after the children are born, remember?"

"I remember. What's it about?"

"The novel? The title means grey horse. You might like it, Charles. The main character, a man named Hauke, is a mathematician, and he moves to a rural village in Holland, where he notices the dykes aren't functioning correctly, and so he redesigns them. The people are grateful, and he's elected burgermeister."

"And the grey horse?"

"Herr Hauke owns a magnificent horse which seems to bring him luck, but some of the villagers believe the animal is actually a ghost, for it appeared at the same time that a legendary horse skeleton vanished from a nearby island."

"Ghost horses?" he asked, an odd tingling sensation running along his hands. Charles hadn't felt that strange electric charge in a very long time—not since Boxing Day, when a terrifying Dragon had tried to pull him through a portal inside the hedge maze. Charles had never told Elizabeth about the experience, and everyone involved agreed to keep the secret. Since that day, the Sinclair family had lived in peace. Now, the idea of a ghostly stallion reminded him of something else; a glimmer of memory from his childhood.

A suit of armour. A fire sword? Horses?

No, something else.

"Charles? Darling, you're far away."

"Sorry. I think I'm in need of food, but first I'll go speak with Blinkmire."

"You're very sweet to come here just to say hello to us," she whispered.

"I couldn't leave for France without a kiss," he said, leaning in to take one. "I miss you, Mrs. Sinclair."

"And I miss you, Captain. Oh, I hope we can all be together this weekend! Father said he'd be done in Scotland by Saturday. Paul and Delia are coming, aren't they?"

"So he said. Now, the sooner I dash downstairs and say hello to the others, the sooner I can return."

He left her, the electric tingle still running through his hands.

Ghost horses and armour. Dragons in the mist. He could almost hear the clanging of heavy swords, the shouts of dying men. Charles shrugged it off. It was but a childish worry.

CHAPTER FIVE
7:28 pm – St. Sophia Cathedral, London

Father Georgio Georgiadis Lambelet was dealing with yet another crisis, and the aged priest felt torn twixt two choices. On the one hand, he could stand his ground and insist his charges remain inside the protective confines of the Greek Orthodox church's compound, or he could relent and allow the persistent young women to leave for an hour—just this once. Ever since Christmas night, he'd watched over the ladies for Prince Anatole Romanov, teaching them the basic tenets of the faith, answering their innocent, though sometimes quite difficult questions, seeing to their physical needs as well as spiritual, and baptising both as newborn believers in Christ.

Now, the ladies sought permission to pay a call on a desperate friend in the East End, who'd written to plead for help. How could he deny them so honourable a request?

"We promise to return as soon as we've seen her, Father Georgio," Lorena MacKey told the sixty-two-year-old priest. "And if she'll come, then we'll bring her back with us. We've been praying for her for a very long time, sir. She'll not visit us here, you see. Meg fears retribution."

"Retribution? From whom?" the cleric asked as he hung up his red and gold *phelonion*, an outer vestment similar to a long cape. "God would never strike against a sincere heart. Never!"

"Not God," Violet Stuart, formerly called Susanna Morgan, explained patiently. "But there are evil men who keep watch and might seize Meg as a traitor to the cause that Lorena and I once supported. Sir, you know what these men can do—what they'd do to her! Please, Father, we implore you! Meg Hansen's letter indicates a contrite heart, but she lacks the faith to come here on her own."

"Might not Prince Anatole fetch her to us?" he reasoned aloud. "Surely, that would be safer for all."

"We'd ask him, but he's not visited since we arrived here last December. Have you seen him, sir?" Lorena asked anxiously. "Is he in London?"

The priest's heavily lined face frowned in a single movement, as though every muscle grew slack all at once. "No. I have not. To be frank, I begin to fear for him. The prince has enemies who'd see him removed from this world."

"But how is that possible?" Violet exclaimed. "How could Anatole be hurt? He's an immortal."

"I don't know if he can be killed, but his kind can be injured. He may have been taken captive. Do you remember the lessons we studied of Daniel's prayer?" he asked the women as he led them from the vestry and out into the moonlit cloister walk. "It took three weeks for the angel Gabriel to reply. But during those tense weeks, Daniel continued to pray for an answer, unaware of the conflict twixt God's holy messenger and a fallen one. You see, the enemy knew Gabriel brought important information for Daniel; information of the Lord's final plans for mankind, and so took him captive. Daniel, chapter ten, tells us this enemy was the powerful Prince of Persia, also an otherworldly being. Michael the Archangel helped Gabriel to escape.

"Now, we cannot know whether those three weeks of human reckoning equal the same within that otherworldly theatre of battle," he continued. "Three human weeks might flow as months or even years in supernatural streams! And we might also assume that Michael battled against the Persian prince the entire time Gabriel spoke with Daniel, for Gabriel informs Daniel that he must return to fight against this supernatural Persian ruler, and that the Prince of Greece would soon join the battle."

Both women grew uneasy, and Lorena asked, "Are you saying Anatole is vulnerable? That it might be a long time before we see him again—if ever?"

"We cannot know for sure, and we must therefore pray for him," the priest whispered as he stopped at the entrance to the compound's chapel. "Praying for God's supernatural warriors may sound unusual, ladies, but we see through a glass darkly. As though the complex brightness of God's full truth is too much for human eyes to behold.

"Now, as we stand outside the chapel, I suggest you take half an hour to seek God's guidance regarding this matter. I find Psalm thirty-seven of great comfort during times of decision. Spend a little time with God, my dear sisters, and tomorrow He will provide the answer. Surely, your friend can wait another day, can she not? Pray now, and afterwards, join me for supper in the rectory. Mrs. Sotiropoulos has made her famous mutton stew."

Lorena nearly spoke up, but Violet held her back. "Thank you, Father Georgio. As always, we're grateful for your counsel. We'll seek the Lord's answer and ask Him to protect you and everyone here at St. Sophia."

The priest departed, and the former Susanna Morgan drew her friend into the chapel's cool interior. She kept watch in the doorway and waited until Lambelet turned the corner to the rectory before speaking. Then she shut the arched wooden door.

"If Anatole is delayed or injured by another of his kind, then we must pray for him," began the American. "But if what Meg says about my father's true..."

"Everyone thinks you're dead, Violet. The woman known as Susanna Morgan is but an entry in H-Division's files. Nothing more."

"If only that were true!" the American worried. "I tell you, if my father's in England, he won't rest until he's found me. And the great Antonio Calabrese doesn't take prisoners, Lorena. If I don't obey him from now on, he'll skin me alive!"

MacKey shuddered. "Would he hurt Meg?"

"Probably. Calabrese stops at nothing to get what he wants. He's the one made me a prostitute in the first place. He sent me to England to ensnare Clive Urquhart. My father hates Clive almost as much as I do; something to do with a woman long ago. Clive thinks himself powerful, but he's a squashed bug compared to my father. If he thinks Meg is keeping secrets, then he'll kill her, after he tortures her—the Sicilian way. Is there anyone you can trust to go to the Empress for us?"

"Yes, but I'm not sure he's in London."

"Do you mean Haimsbury?" Violet asked. "Are you still writing to him?"

"Yes, every other day, but I don't always hear back. I told him it isn't necessary, but he sometimes answers. His last letter said he might travel to Paris soon."

"Will he stay at a hotel? You could send a letter there."

"I think he's staying in his aunt's home. I can't send anything there."

"Why not? If the address is typed, who'd know it's from you?"

Lorena bit her lower lip, pondering the idea. "No, I won't risk it. Besides, Charles has done enough for me. Could we write to Lord Aubrey?"

Violet shook her head, the long dark locks constrained into a sedate chignon. "No. He's married now, remember? How can I ask a newlywed to endanger himself for me? For us? Lorena, neither of us treated Paul well—before we found Christ, I mean. You cast a spell on him in Scotland, and I tried again and again to lure him into my bed, just to please Clive Urquhart. Oh, how I detest that fat little man!"

"We're supposed to pray for the Redwing members, remember? Father Georgio says it will help us to heal. And Anatole said the same thing. It's why he insisted you try to talk to Clive last Christmas."

"I know, and it was the hardest thing I've ever done!" the American whispered. "I bless God's tender mercy that Clive wasn't home. Anatole said it was my willingness to talk to him that mattered, not whether I achieved it or not. But had I seen him, I'd probably be in prison now, for I'm not sure I could have kept from scratching out his evil eyes!" Violet exclaimed.

Lorena took her friend's hands. "I understand. If we cannot find another to help, then it's up to us. We'll have to find our own way to help Margaret, because we cannot leave her to the mercy of Redwing, Violet. Not if your father is on the warpath."

The echo of boots on the flagstone floor caught their ears, and the women moved from the doorway and into the orderly rows of carved oak pews. A shadow shifted near the front of the altar. A dark figure wearing a cowl over his head.

"Hello. Father Georgio suggested we come here and pray. We won't be long. Is that you, Mr. Andropoulis?" Lorena asked, praying the intruder was one of the seminary students and not a Redwing messenger.

"No," answered a deep voice.

The women stared at one another, and Violet stepped forward slightly, summoning up the courage to protect her friend if necessary. "Who are you? Are you a student?"

"No."

"We are covered by Christ," Violet declared. "If you've come to hurt us..."

"I come to help," the shadow proclaimed. "I am a friend, Daughters of Eve."

Lorena took Violet's hand. "Who are you? We don't know you, sir. What is your name?"

"I am Shelumiel, servant of the One, the Most High God, Creator of all. You are to come with me. Your time here is done. The being you call Prince Anatole now fights against the rebel Prince of France. I have been commissioned to take you to a new refuge, on his behalf."

"How do we know you're telling us the truth?" Lorena challenged the stranger. "You could be from Redwing."

Shelumiel removed the heavy cowl. His entire face was alight with so glorious a shimmer that the women fell to their knees in fear. Though neither saw him move; suddenly, the gleaming messenger stood beside them, his bright hands upon their faces, one pressed to each woman's cheek.

"Fear not, beloved of God. The One has heard your prayer and will provide an answer. Come with me, for your time here is done. My brother Zerachiel will deliver word to Father Georgio."

Before another heartbeat, the women vanished along with the messenger, leaving only vibrating air where they'd formerly knelt.

The chapel fell silent, and a sleek black rat emerged from a far corner. The creature scurried through a hole in the south wall, where it transformed into a large bat. The night creature flew out into the warm air, rising up through an unseen portal, where it vanished into the mirror realm called 'sen-sen'.

With the blink of an eye, the bat arrived at an abbey near the sleepy village of Goussainville, France. Transforming into a man, he knocked on the gatehouse door.

"Who is it?" a voice asked gruffly in French. "What do you want?"

"I wish to speak with the prince," the false human replied. "Tell him Flint is here."

The doorman muttered several French obscenities and left. A few moments later, the heavy wooden door creaked slowly open, and the gatekeeper stepped into the chilling darkness. The gatehouse was old and musty. The visitor passed by several large urns, filled with hundreds of scented spring blossoms. The demon with a hundred names turned up his nose. He preferred the smells of death and putrefaction.

Albus Flint waited in the darkness, his black eyes still. Finally, he could sense movement above, just at the top of an old stone staircase.

"What is it now?" a deep voice called from the shadows above.

"I bring news from London. The hated One begins his next move. Shelumiel has arrived, and he's brought Zerachiel with him. The forces strengthen, my lord. Perhaps, it is time to begin the next phase."

The tall figure snapped his fingers and immediately the torchieres along the walls burst with flickering flames. "I've no idea why my sister prefers darkness," he said languidly, as he descended the steps. Prince Araqiel wore a red silk robe that trailed behind as he walked, flowing like a river of blood. His cold blue eyes flashed as he strode purposefully towards his guest.

"What are we to do?" asked the thin caller. "If Shelumiel is despatched, then our plans must be known!"

"So?" asked the prince. "Do you think this news disturbs me? On the contrary, it means the One fears me. And well he should fear me, for I am about to undo all his wretched work. Come, old friend. Join us on this witches' night. My sister and I are about to indulge our palates in the fiery heat of youth. A street urchin no one will miss, for its parents had already sold it to a procurement house—a house which I now own. A little bit of silver can buy most anything, my friend. A traitor's kiss or a meal. Come, Uriens. Join us and we'll make plans."

"Do not call me that!" the demon lawyer complained. "It is a hated name, and I no longer use it. Not now."

"Hast thou shed all thy feathers, my pretty bird of death? Very well, then. I shall call you Albus. Dost that make thee happy, Worm?"

"Yes, but you may cease the Elizabethan language. Your attempt at English humour needs improvement."

Araqiel laughed as he put an arm round the lawyer's shoulders. "Were I not in such good humour, I might pluck thy worthless feathers and boil thee in oil, Upstart Crow. But come, now, join our celebration feast. It is a night for witches and warlocks and devilish wonders. A night for making plans. A night for revels."

The former Stone Realms gatekeeper followed his host into a dimly lit parlour. A tall woman, clad only in a scarlet robe, wiped blood from her mouth. She beckoned him closer.

"You look hungry, Albus. Please, join us. I've left enough to feed a crow."

A large table made from carved ash dominated the candlelit room, and Flint could see the ghastly meal, each wrist and ankle tied with heavy ropes; already half-drained of blood and the heart still. The lawyer winced. He preferred rats and bats, but human would do in a pinch.

"Thank you," he said, bowing in subservience to the cruel woman who'd once been his captor. "My lady is most generous."

High above the hideous banquet room, a human shivered in a tower chamber, realising he could be next if he failed to do everything his master ordered. The cowering human's name was Lionel Archibald Wentworth, and he fell asleep weeping great tears of regret—and wondering if God's forgiveness might extend even to those who lived in Hell.

CHAPTER SIX

8:41 pm - Lasberington House, Hanover Square

Seth Holloway kept fiddling with his tie, glowering with utter dismay into the floor-length cheval mirror. "I've never been able to properly work the knot on these," he told a dark-haired man to his right. "You'd think with all the dances I've attended since turning eighteen, I'd have mastered the skill by now, but truly, Henry, I'm hopeless!"

"Here, let me," said MacAlpin, rising from his chair. "The secret's in how you arrange the two ends at the beginning, you see. Honestly, I didn't master it until a few years ago. My nurse taught me. Dear Mrs. Winstead can do just about anything. I wonder how I ever managed without her, and I pray I never need find out. There now," he said, finishing the task. "You're the picture of British manhood. Every young lady there tonight will make sure you're top of her dance card."

"You sound like my mother," laughed the auburn-haired viscount. "She's beginning to hint that I should marry soon. She'd always hoped I'd convince Elizabeth to become my wife, but we both know how that turned out. Talking of family, how's your father doing?"

"Better since he spent a little time down here. I'm still amazed the queen managed to convince the old bear to come out of his den, but he actually enjoyed his visit. I find myself missing him, which surprises me. Oh, by the way, I think there might be an impromptu meeting. You might want to bring along your notebook."

"Martin already warned me about that," he said, patting the pocket of his overcoat. "It's all in here. Tomorrow's the first of May, Henry! Can you believe how quickly time's passed? If I'm to return to teaching this fall, I'll need to start planning a curriculum, but I hate taking time away from our projects. I'm torn, to be honest. The vice-master's suggested I might qualify for a full professorship which could eventually lead to the Stanton Chair, but there are heavy strings attached."

"What sort of strings?" asked Salperton.

"I'm not sure, but to quote Vice-Master Boswell, 'a department chair is loyal to Trinity first and foremost.'"

"Loyal? What the devil does he mean by that? Look, here, Seth, if this required loyalty means keeping quiet about any Cambridge connexion to the deaths in Kent last Christmas, then you may want to reconsider. Aubrey told me yesterday that six more students were reported missing in Normandy in January, and they vanished at almost the exact same time as the Kent deaths."

"Six? Are they all Cambridge students?"

"Three are. The others are from Oxford."

Seth grew quiet. "Three and three. Just like our team. Were these men part of a Blackstone project? I remember overhearing Trinity's master, Henry Butler, speaking to one of the other dons about it. Apparently, Blackstone wanted six men in total from our college. Three men went to Branham, and the rest to France. Why on earth would they be digging in Normandy?"

"No idea, old boy, but more to the point, why are all six men now missing?"

"Seven with Wentworth's disappearance," Seth reminded his friend.

"True. Ah, but this French tale gets stranger yet. Aubrey told me there was a localised earthquake the same night the men vanished. Authorities there believe the men fell into a crevasse."

"What?" asked Holloway in shock. "Is the circle investigating it?"

Henry had been sipping a small cognac and he placed his empty glass on the marble-topped table. "Yes. I think it's one of the reasons Charles left for France this evening. He has a friend who's head of the Sûreté, and he plans to confer with him. You know, Seth, it occurs to me that you're perfect for the circle! Forget Trinity and its demands for loyalty. Pledge yourself to a fellowship that makes a real difference! If you join fulltime, you could leave off teaching entirely and explore archaeological digs on the duke's coin."

"Which duke might that be?" asked the younger man as he added a gold Rotherhams watch to the white waistcoat.

"Haimsbury, I should think. He is the head of it all, though James still manages family matters, of course. He's our clan chief, you might say."

"Did I tell you my father's returning to England?"

"Really? When?" asked Henry.

"I'm not sure. I finally received a reply to my letters last week. He's been residing all this time with some foreign prince. He and mother promised to explain it all, but he's loath to put much into writing. Typical for my father. The great Lord Salter trusts very few people, and always assumes his letters are read by outsiders."

"Who's to say they're not?" laughed Salperton as he straightened his own tie. "I say, old chum, we're not so bad. My face might not have the Grecian lines of a Charles Sinclair, but I've a jolly good sense of humour, and my chin's not terribly out of sync with my face. And you, my friend and lodger, have the boyish charm of a Chopin! No wonder my maids keep giggling whenever you walk past. Who knows, Seth? Tonight, we two might just meet our future brides."

9:58 pm – Dover

"Good evening, Your Grace. Welcome aboard."

Charles Sinclair stepped through a phalanx of uniformed naval officers, shaking hands with each and making small talk. He knew Captain Sievers from previous crossings and asked after the man's family.

"Another son, sir," the captain replied. "This makes three now. And I hear your child's soon to make an appearance, my lord."

"Five weeks more, so we believe. And it's to be twins, Captain Sievers. Our doctor's confirmed two heartbeats."

"Is that so? Then, it's a double blessing, Your Grace. What takes you to France this time, sir? Police business again?"

"That and a visit to my aunt's home. I'll likely see you again in a few days. I'm bringing my young cousin back. You'll remember, I brought her over in January."

"Ah, yes, sir. The Lady Adele. A delightful child."

"If only she would remain a child," Charles said wistfully. "She'll be twelve soon. They grow so very quickly. Do I have my usual cabin?"

"You do, my lord. The royal suite. Briggs!" he called to a lean lieutenant. "Escort His Grace to the royal suite."

The young man saluted. "Right away, Captain. This way, Your Grace."

Charles followed the first officer to a spacious cabin with two rooms and an en suite bath. The officer set down the duke's bags. "Do you need anything else, sir?"

"Not just now, Lieutenant, except for food. I had a small meal before I left Branham, but I'd eat again if it's available."

"Of course, my lord. Cocktails and finger foods are served all night in the lounge, but I can ask our cook to prepare something heartier. Sandwiches or soup?"

"Both would be most welcome. I'm famished. Must be the sea air."

The young man smiled. "It's been known to have that effect, my lord. Will you be eating in your rooms, sir, or enjoying the lounge?"

"No, it's a lovely night. I'll eat on the decks, if that's possible"

"Of course, sir. It could take an hour, given we're full up with passengers."

"An hour's perfect. Gives me time for a quick nap."

"Which deck, sir?"

"I'll find a spot on the starboard side," the duke responded.

"Very good, sir," the first mate said. "Wine?"

"Oh, yes, thank you. Have your steward choose what he thinks is best."

"I'll do that, sir. I'll have the meal brought to you in an hour."

The young man shut the door as he left, and Charles unpacked a portable writing desk. He removed the personal journal Beth had given him and placed it on the bedside table as a reminder to write when he awoke. He placed his pocket watch beside the journal, the latch open to allow him to see the time. Finally, with his coat draped on a nearby chair, the exhausted duke lay back and shut his eyes, falling into an uneasy dream of ghostly grey horses and a terrified Lorena MacKey.

CHAPTER SEVEN
9:59 pm – 20 Arlington St., Salisbury House

As Charles boarded the ship at Dover, several members of his inner circle gathered in Westminster for the first party of the season. "Prime Minister, my lords and ladies, may I present the Viscounts Salperton and Paynton," announced a splendidly attired butler to a room filled with chattering guests. A brace of footmen took the young peers' overcoats and hats, whilst a trio of coquettish debutantes cast sparkling eyes upon the handsome newcomers. The stylish mansion stood a stone's throw from Buckingham Palace, making it a simple matter for the prime minister to pay his daily call on the queen. The four-storey Georgian home had recently been updated with gasoliers in each of the four state rooms, and gas fireplaces kept visiting dignitaries warm whilst arguing over foreign policy and the latest Parliamentary business.

The 3rd Marquess of Salisbury had never cared for the official residence on Downing Street, complaining that its rooms were cramped and cold. Instead, he'd purchased this house ten years earlier as his London headquarters. The sturdily built prime minister was speaking with a well-dressed gentleman in his late twenties, but hearing the announcement, excused himself and crossed the room to greet his newest guests.

"How very nice to see you again, gentlemen. I hope you're both hungry. My wife's put on a massive spread, and her sister's invited half the debutantes of London. Really, one would think Georgina worked as a peerage matchmaker, she's put in so much effort. I do hope you'll enjoy yourselves."

Henry shook the prime minister's hand, noticing several pretty young ladies glancing in his direction. "It's always a pleasure to be here, sir, and you'll never hear me complain about a party with such lovely ladies as enhancement."

"Enhancement? I'd call it an enticement, old boy!" the portly marquess joked.

"Ah, but very pleasant enticements," Seth added, noticing one young lady in particular with nut-brown eyes and auburn hair.

"Any idea when Aubrey will arrive? Or Haimsbury?" asked Salisbury. "I do hope they're coming. I've business to discuss."

"I believe the duke's bound for France this evening, Prime Minister," Holloway told him. "Last minute trip. Aubrey? Now, there's a man who's tough to pin down, but then he's a newlywed. I imagine marriage alters a man's habits."

"My wife has certainly altered mine, young man! And as the father of seven children, I can tell you that family does alter one, but in a very pleasant way. Most pleasant. What business takes Haimsbury to France? Not crime, I hope. London's had its fill."

Seth glanced at Salperton, realising he had no right to discuss inner circle affairs in public. "I'm not sure, sir," he stuttered.

Henry jumped in to rescue his friend. "Ah, well, I believe it's family business, Prime Minister. Lady Victoria's turned her ankle, you see, and Charles has gone there to shepherd Adele Stuart back to England. She's Aubrey's sister, if you'll recall. Della's been living there since January, and the duke is returning her for the Branham fête."

"Ah, yes, the fête! My wife and I plan to attend, if I can get away. She loves the steam-powered carousel, as did our children when they were younger. Have you met my eldest son, gentlemen? Allow me to introduce him. James Gascoyne-Cecil, the Viscount Cranborne," he said, indicating the young man to his left. "James, these fine gentlemen are Dr. Henry MacAlpin, he's the Viscount Salperton—in his own right, mind you. Inherited from your grandfather, I think, is that right, Henry?" Salperton nodded. "And this redhaired scamp of a professor is Dr. Seth Holloway, the Viscount Paynton. Eldest son of Lord Salter, you know."

The prime minister's son shook their hands. "Henry and I are well acquainted, Father."

Salperton smiled, a bit embarrassed. "Yes, we've spoken often, and it's always a pleasure, Lord Cranborne. How is Lady Cicely?" he asked. "I do hope she's no longer troubled by nightmares."

"My wife is much improved, thanks to you, Salperton. I was never much of a believer in alienist methods, but you certainly helped with my good lady's melancholia. Dreadful malady. She's bright as a penny now!" He turned to Seth. "Lord Paynton, I believe I've seen you before. Didn't we share a train ride last summer?"

Seth managed a smile, for he'd begun to wish he hadn't come to the party. Crowds of strangers made him feel rather out of place. "Did we? I fear I've a dreadful memory for faces, Lord Cranborne."

"As do I, actually," the other man answered, "but those copper locks are hard to forget. I imagine ladies love it, though."

Seth prayed his cheeks hadn't crimsoned to match his hair. "I'm sure I wouldn't know, but it's kind of you to remember me."

"You were with your father," Cranborne continued. "I've known Salter since I was a pup. I seem to recall he was angry, but then your father's often complaining about this or that."

Seth's cheeks grew even warmer. "Yes, my father often uses rail journeys to enforce his opinion upon fellow passengers. Trains make for a captive audience, I suppose."

Cranborne laughed to put Holloway at ease. "Ah, well, fathers," he said, nudging Salisbury. "They try to rein us in, but we strain at the bit, eh what? But we sons inevitably fall into line, don't we? Mine drew me into politics, and yours into—now, what is it Lord Salter does again? Scientific sort of stuff, isn't it? Engineering? No, wait, it's antiquities or some such."

"Antiquarianism, actually. But archaeology is the new term for it," Seth replied, happy to discuss his passion. "Father's doing well enough, I suppose. He's not written much, but I did finally hear from him last week."

"As did I!" Salisbury interrupted, his cheeks pulling at his wiry beard. "Don't take his lack of correspondence to heart, young man. Salter's always been somewhat stilted in his views, but he means well. I heard from your father this past week. He's due to return to London in a fortnight, but I imagine we'll be sending him and your mother off again soon. Or rather the PEF will."

"Yes, he mentioned that possibility in his letter, sir. If the destination is Egypt, then I'm not surprised. Lord Aubrey told me there's been a spot of trouble there, relating to the new canal. If you need a translator, I'm always available."

"But don't you teach at Trinity? Have you the time? The matter could take months to untangle."

"I'm on sabbatical from teaching at present. I've undertaken a private assignment for Duke Charles."

"Ah, well, then I mustn't pull you away from that. I'd not wish to make an enemy of our new duke," the prime minister jested. "But let's not discuss government work tonight, gentlemen. My wife arranged this soiree to get us all out of the winter doldrums. London's been too solemn of late, or at least we Parliamentarians have been. There are card games ongoing in several of the salons, if you're interested. Also, we've a small orchestra playing upstairs. This house has no ballroom, but the upper gallery is quite spacious. You'll find most of the young ladies are up there. Oh, and that tailor fellow is here! I believe he's playing the piano in our music room. It pleases my wife, you know. Kepelheim's always been her favourite."

The prime minister took a filled wine glass from a passing footman just as the butler announced the arrival of two more guests. "Ah, here's Lord Aubrey at last! Now, we may discuss foreign matters with better insight."

"Oh, no, you don't!" Salisbury's wife exclaimed as she joined her husband. "You'll not lure Lord Aubrey into any government talk, Robert. Not this evening. As a newlywed, he's still on a sabbatical of his own, and I'll not have you trying to coerce the earl back to field work so soon."

"I'm afraid your good lady has commanded it, sir," warned Salperton. "When women speak, we foolish men must obey. Mustn't we?"

"No truer words were ever spoken," the prime minister agreed with a smile. "Our wives must always have the final word, eh?"

"Evening, everyone. Do we talk of wives or politics?" asked Paul Stuart asked as he and Cordelia joined the group.

"Both," replied Salisbury.

"May I offer an opinion, then?" asked Aubrey. "Oh, good evening, Henry. Seth. It's lovely to see you, Lady Salisbury," he told Georgina, offering a friendly kiss to her cheek.

"Your opinion, Lord Aubrey?" asked the prime minister. "I pray it soothes my wife's heart, for political talk seems only to rouse her ire."

"Is that so?" laughed the earl. "Then may I say that our wives should always be considered the centre of life? After all, where would we men be without them?"

"Very well said," Georgina applauded. "And I'm very pleased to meet you at last, Lady Aubrey. Ignore my husband. I'm the real power behind his administration, or at least, he makes me think I am. Welcome to our home, my dear."

"Thank you, Lady Salisbury."

"No, no, you must call me Georgina. I've known your husband for all his life, and I think half mine! May I call you Cordelia? I do love that gown. Apricot is truly your colour. Is it from a London designer?"

With Paul's help, Delia had finally chosen to wear a stylish, off-the-shoulder gown accented at the throat by double-stranded pearls with an empire waist that disguised her thickening waistline.

"That is kind of you, Georgina," she answered bashfully. "Of course, most of my friends call me Delia."

"Delia it is, then. And the gown? I very much doubt any of our London seamstresses made it, unless of course, Mr. Kepelheim had a hand in its design. Martin generally makes menswear, but when he worked for House of Worth, I bought everything he made. Such elegant gowns! Did he make it by chance? If so, then I must have him make one for me."

Delia smiled, not knowing if the woman should be taken at face value. Her husband came to the rescue.

"Martin had nothing to do with it, Gina," Paul said. "Not this time. He's far too busy designing clothing for my cousin. Actually, I bought this gown at a shop in Venice. *Barozzi's*," he added, emphasising the name. "I'm sure your husband's heard of them."

The prime minister's smile disappeared. "Might that be Vincenzo Barozzi, Lord Aubrey? And was his service satisfactory?"

"Most gratifying, but alas, he's closed shop."

Salisbury stroked his beard thoughtfully, and Paul switched topics. "I wonder, have you seen my mother-in-law, the Dowager Baroness Wychwright? She left before we did, but I don't see her here."

"Constance? Well, yes," Lady Salisbury told the earl. "I believe she arrived half an hour ago. She mentioned the music room, I think. She might still be in there. Shall Delia and I go see if we might locate her?"

"Do you mind, darling?" Paul asked his wife. "We'll wait here."

"Get used to it, my dear," Georgina whispered to the young countess. "They want to talk politics. My husband's parties invariably become meeting places. Go ahead, gentlemen. We abandoned wives will enjoy ourselves elsewhere. Do you play or sing?" she asked the younger woman.

"I play a little," Cordelia answered. "But my singing is better."

"My singing's quite awful! I shall play and you can sing. How is that?" The two women left, threading their way through a crowd of gossiping politicians, towards the pleasant sound of a grand piano.

The prime minister stroked his grizzled beard, set the empty glass on a tray, and took another serving of wine from the footman. "Let's do this in the library, shall we? Salperton, why don't you and Paynton come as well?"

Paul turned to his two young friends. "As of this moment, gentlemen, you've signed on with the Foreign Office. But as you both work with the ICI, we'll call it one of our cases."

The men convened in a small library. Salisbury offered the three men a cigar. Only Paul took one, and he clipped the end and lit it, drawing deeply before releasing the silvery smoke with a smile. "Very nice. These are from the Americas, aren't they? Cuba, if I'm not mistaken."

"I should have known you'd guess," Salisbury grinned. "I have several boxes, if you're interested. Now, tell me about Barozzi. Why is his shop shut?"

"I'm not sure, but my best guess is that he's jumped ship." Paul turned to the other men. "Henry, you and Seth know that I serve England overseas. Please, say nothing to Delia, but whilst on our wedding trip, I visited several of our espionage contacts. She knows a little of what I do, but I prefer she not realise the extent of the danger I often face."

"Of course," Henry promised, sitting back with a glass of wine. "Who's this Barozzi person? I take it he's not a dressmaker."

"No. I bought the gown elsewhere," Paul replied, tapping the cigar against a silver dish. "Vincenzo Barozzi is the third son of a prominent family in Venice. His father, Adolfo Barozzi, is one of five Italian leaders of Redwing."

Henry gasped, but Holloway showed no surprise. "Actually, I'm aware of that family," he told the others. "My father sometimes stays with the Barozzis when in Venice, and I met him once. He was with another man. Taller. As tall as you, Paul. A fierce, dangerous looking fellow who seldom smiled. Carried a walking stick made of Indian rosewood with a silver wolf's head handle. His name was Trent."

"William Trent?" Aubrey exclaimed, staring at the professor in shock. "You met William Trent in Venice?"

"We are talking about the baronet who married Duchess Patricia, correct?" asked Holloway.

"Yes. Did you know him well?" the earl asked.

"Not really, but my father knew him quite well. They spent time together in Venice as well as Austria. Once I started at Cambridge, my parents travelled without me, but he'd refer to Trent sometimes in his letters. The man seemed quite mysterious."

"Do you know his origins?" Salperton enquired. "It's just no one I've spoken to seems to know much about him."

"Nor do I, but I can tell you what little I know," Seth replied.

"Please!" the earl urged his friend. "How did you first meet him?"

"It was in this man Barozzi's home," Seth answered as the prime minister handed him a glass of brandy. "Oh, thank you, sir. Trent was there to talk with two others. They had several artefacts they wanted my father to evaluate. Let me see if I can remember. There was a small statuette of an Akkadian goddess. Ishhara, I believe. Also, a cylinder seal showing Marduk, and a large obsidian mirror."

"A mirror?" Paul echoed. "Hand or floor?"

"Floor, which is extremely rare in antiquities, but Father declared it genuine."

"How tall was it?" the earl asked.

"Quite tall. Taller than you, certainly. I was amazed by it, for it's so very rare to find unbroken sheets of volcanic glass. The frame was rosewood and carved with figures. Trent said he'd found it at an auction up near Carlisle, but the design wasn't English. In fact, my father thought the mirror dated back to the Bronze Age."

"And it appeared to be an ordinary mirror, otherwise?"

"Yes, but then I wasn't permitted to touch it. Paul, are you implying this mirror is similar to the one in the duke's puzzle room?"

"It sounds similar. What else did you learn about Trent?"

Seth sipped the brandy. "Not much. He was travelling with a man and a woman. An American businessman and a Milanese woman. A very odd type. Pale as milk. Always dressed in black."

"Contessa di Specchio?" asked the earl.

"No, though I met the countess several times during our travels. Di Specchio knew practically everyone in government. No, this woman's name was Irish, I believe."

"Irish?" echoed the earl. "Curious. The Christian or surname?"

Holloway shook his head as he gazed into the glass. "Calling her forename 'Christian' might be a stretch. The woman had a distinctly pagan manner. I doubt she was ever christened, *per se*. Wait, she used to joke about how people could remember her name. How did it go again? Yes, that's it! 'It's like Stop with a e', she'd say with a little laugh, but I never understood the humour."

Aubrey nearly dropped his glass. "Stopes? Are you saying you met Moira Stopes?"

"Moira, yes, that's it! She and Trent were quite close. Intimates, if you get my meaning. But how is it you know either of those women, Paul? Neither frequented Branham during Trent's time that I'm aware."

"More to point, how is it your father ran with these people, Seth?" asked the earl suspiciously.

"Ran with them?" shouted Holloway. "Look, Paul, my father didn't run with anyone. He and I may not always get on, but he's a good and decent man. If he met them, then there had to be a reason."

"And there most certainly was," the prime minister interrupted. "Salter ran with such rabble on my orders, Paul. As a scholarly man who speaks the digger's language, Lord Salter may hide amongst groups closed even to you. Your abilities to blend and disguise yourself are legendary, but some plans require a more open deception with an amiable, fatherly type."

Seth laughed. "I'd never call George Holloway fatherly!"

"Perhaps, not to you, son," Salisbury observed, "but his manner to outsiders gives that impression, and for the record, your father is very proud of you. Whenever we speak, he brags upon you constantly."

"Really?" Seth whispered, his blue eyes filled with amazement.

"Really. Now, as to Barozzi," Robert continued, "we'd suspected him of treason for some time, but couldn't prove it. Lord

Paynton, your father spent many weeks with Barozzi, meeting all manner of individuals and then sounding him out afterward. Salter left Venice convinced Barozzi was still true to England but posing as a turn-coat to obtain information. That's why I sent Aubrey to test the man again."

"And he failed that test," Paul declared, setting the cigar down. "There's no doubt he's been a cuckoo in our nest all along, which is a great loss to England, because the man's a mechanical genius. If what I heard is correct, then he's building a massive machine for someone. I saw the plans, and I believe this machine has to do with us. The inner circle, I mean. Is Martin still here?"

"In the music room, I imagine," Salisbury answered. "Shall I send for him?"

"Yes, I think we should."

The prime minister pulled a bell rope, summoning a servant. A silver-haired footman responded a moment later.

"My lord?"

"Fetch Mr. Kepelheim from the music salon, will you, Carstairs? And see to it we're not disturbed once he joins us."

The servant departed, and the prime minister poured brandies for four. "I'm aware that Martin prefers cognac, but we ran out an hour ago. Paul, how much does Duke Charles know about our American problem?"

"Only a little. He's been inundated with crimes to solve since he and Beth married. We talk privately now and then, but generally, we have only the time to react. Proactive steps require planning and patience, if that's where you're headed. Do tell me you're not sending me off to Chicago again, Robert!"

"Not yet, but that day is rapidly approaching. Presently, I'm keeping my eyes on Paris. The Exposition there will draw record crowds, all of them influential, some royal. However, I've just learnt that the city of Chicago is planning a major world exposition of its own, ostensibly to celebrate the four-hundredth anniversary of Columbus's discovery."

"Ostensibly?" asked Henry, who'd been sipping the brandy. "Why use that word, sir? Surely, it's a legitimate decision. 1892 will mark four hundred years since Christopher Columbus discovered the Americas. I'll not get into historical accuracy, but it's the official story. Four hundred years is a great milestone. Duchess Elizabeth certainly thinks so, as she's marking the four-hundredth Branham fête with a large celebration."

"That is true, but our little duchess isn't using the Branham Fête as cover for something more sinister," noted the earl. "Robert, you said the fair will be held in '93. Why not '92?"

"A very good question," Salisbury answered, his cigar smouldering in his thick fingers. "I've asked the city's newly elected mayor about the date. Mr. Clegier implied a lack of preparation time as the cause for the delay. I find it puzzling to be sure. But as with Paris, Chicago's exposition will draw industrialists, financiers, artists, actors, publishers, writers, inventors, monarchs, and other world leaders to their city. Paris is already seeing record numbers in their hotels, and the fair doesn't open for several more days. Gentlemen, it isn't the crowds that concern me, though they allow anarchists to infiltrate more readily. I'm concerned about the secret meetings that will take place right beneath our noses, camouflaged by these crowds. Generally, our guard dogs bark whenever danger draws close, but it's difficult to discern the wolves amongst the fold when one's meadows are crowded with so many foreign sheep."

"Which foreigners concern you, sir?" asked Holloway.

"All of them," Salisbury sighed as he flicked ash onto the rug. "I do not speak of nations only, sir, but also of domains. Ah, here's Kepelheim."

The tailor entered, carrying a small book of poems in his right hand. "I've been reading to the ladies," he told his friends. "*Khubla Khan* by our old friend Mr. Coleridge. A most unsettling poem, don't you think? The tragic references to so great a chasm within sight of the magnificent palace of Xanadu is universal. More's the pity that Coleridge never completed it. But of course, that was not my only reading. One must include Shelley, Byron, and Keats. A sonnet from the bard now and then, of course. It's a shame Lord Aubrey's no longer angling for a bride, for Lady Salisbury's salons are awash with delightful little fishes!"

"Is it now? Did you land any of those little fishes, Martin?" asked the earl with a wink.

"Ah, well, my good friend Mrs. Calhoun was amongst that select audience, as I'm sure you know. She and I made plans for tomorrow, and the dear lady may come to the fête with me, if she can break away from London. Now, how may I be of service to the august leader of our country?"

Salisbury handed the tailor a glass of brandy. "I'm not sure about the august part. If you want the truth, Duke Charles carries more weight than I do these days. Pity he's not here. He'd planned to come, when I spoke to him last week."

"Ah, well, that was before our aunt turned her ankle, and my sister's letter arrived," the earl explained. "He'll be back by Friday. You spoke a moment ago of guard dogs failing to bark at wolves hidden in plain sight. Just what do you think Chicago's Redwing chapter is planning, Robert? And how do we stop it?"

"I'm not sure it can be stopped," the prime minister replied darkly, "but a man's arrived in England who may offer insight."

"Excuse me," Martin interrupted, "but why are we discussing wolves at all?"

"It's to do with the Paris Exposition," Aubrey told the tailor. "You remember Her Majesty's Golden Jubilee celebration in '87. Fifty crowned heads, bringing their entourages, cooks, servants, drivers, coaches, clothing, jewells, and religious practices with them. Westminster hotels were full to bursting, and nearly every great house as well. The streets were alive with reporters, tourists, and anarchists, making it almost impossible to sift truth from lie. Our men must have stopped two-dozen assassination plots."

Kepelheim sipped the cognac. "Oh, quite good! De Luze?"

"One of my last bottles," answered Salisbury. "The comparison to our queen's Golden Jubilee is fair but pales to what may happen in Paris. We invited fifty European royals. Paris has invited the world! And so the appearance of Antonio Calabrese in England must signify either alliance or war within Redwing's ranks."

"Who is Antonio Calabrese?" asked Seth. "Italian, I suppose?"

"Sicilian, but lives in Chicago," Robert replied. "A very powerful industrialist with influence amongst politicians on both sides of the Atlantic. He brags that he's bought every judge twixt Chicago and Vienna. This is not his first crossing, either. Calabrese spent several days in Paris last December, where he met with Redwing members from Austria, Germany, France, and England. And if I'm right, there's to be another meeting during this Exposition. That's where your inner circle comes in, gentlemen. I spoke of alliance or war earlier, but I begin to doubt an alliance is possible. In fact, I fear

Germany's chapter is about to mount an assault on the remains of William Trent's Round Table."

"You know about that, sir?" asked Holloway. "The Round Table and the Lords of the Black Stone, Redwing's German chapter?"

Robert Gascoyne-Cecil's grey eyes twinkled as he set the half-smoked Cuban cigar into a small bowl. "Of course, I know, young man. I also know about the missing bodies, the truth behind that hallucination tale you chaps put about, and I may know something you of the circle do not."

"What is that?" Paul asked.

"That this American plans to unleash something beyond all imagining upon London. And this new assault will make Ripper and this Dybbuk creature's crimes seem like a parlour game."

CHAPTER EIGHT

Midnight - The RMS Newton, somewhere on the channel

Charles Sinclair stood at the railing, gazing into the grey waters of the English channel. He could hear the chugging of the steamer's engine and screw, propelling the sleek ship through the choppy sea. He quietly marvelled at the progress mankind had made in so few years. Only recently, had schooners yielded to steam power. Air ships like the Queen of the Meadow gave mankind wings, and according to James Stuart, inner circle scientists predicted a future where air and sea-going vessels would draw their power from massive engines fueled by petroleum derivatives. Could commercial air travel be far behind? It seemed man had no limits.

"The moon is lovely tonight," a woman's voice called from his elbow.

Charles turned, finding a tall individual with dark hair and clear skin. She looked no older than twenty-five. Her cheeks glowed with expert touches of subtle artifice: powder, rouge, kohl lining round the chocolate eyes. She appeared tense, though her opening line sounded casual enough.

"I'm afraid the sea's a bit rough," he told her. "Not exactly a night for strolling the decks."

"Then, why are you here?" she asked boldly.

He offered a friendly smile. "Thinking. My cabin's large enough, but I'm not one for confined spaces. Somehow, they stifle my brain."

The woman laughed, the movement of her ruby mouth fluid and lovely. "I take it your brain is engaged all the time. Forgive me, have we met?" she asked.

"I don't believe so. Perhaps, you saw me when I boarded at Dover."

"No, we arrived late. Everyone else was already on board. Still, I'm certain I've seen your face. Wait, I have it! You're that policeman, aren't you? The one with the titles. Charles Sinclair, 1st Duke of Haimsbury. You're famous."

"Hardly," he protested. "If my picture decorates newspapers, it's nothing to do with me but my activities. The price one pays for government work."

"No, your story has been repeated like it's a modern faery tale. The young heir to a great title and vast fortune is presumed dead, but nearly thirty years later is found working at Scotland Yard. And now you are a duke! Far more than a government worker."

"Perhaps, but I'd be pleased to see my name disappear from the headlines. I prefer anonymity."

"I fear you'll never have that again, Your Grace," she told him. "I am Angiolina Calabrese."

He shook her hand. "Calabrese? I've recently come across that name. You mentioned 'we' when you spoke of arriving. Are you, by any chance, related to Antonio Calabrese?"

"Why, yes!" she exclaimed, her eyes dancing erotically. "He is my father. Forgive me, this must seem contrived; our meeting this way, I mean. I know my father had hoped to speak with you."

"Yes, I received his card asking for an appointment, but I hadn't the time. I asked my secretary to arrange a time next week."

"We received your note," she told him. "And because of it, Father decided to pay a quick visit to a fellow businessman in Paris. Really, we had no idea you'd be on this steamer, Your Grace, but my father will be overjoyed to learn it."

He gazed at her, appreciating the classic Mediterranean beauty: dark eyes and lashes, a straight nose, full lips, and curves to entice any man.

Save him. Charles could love only one woman.

"Just what is your father's business?" he asked. "His card said Sanguis, Ltd. Is that an English company? I wonder, for your accent is hardly American."

She laughed, a husky, velvety sort of laugh that could influence fawning gentlemen of any age into spending all their money on furs and gems. But Angiolina Calabrese's accent sounded far too polished for a mere harlot or madam. It rang of Westminster, finishing schools, grand balls, and landed gentry.

"No, I'm not American, but I can see the confusion. My father travels a great deal for his business. He met my mother in '65, at a party in Mayfair. Mother was his third wife, you understand. Father's been married six or seven times. They divorced when I was two, but he's always kept in touch. Birthdays and Christmas gifts. Letters each month. Mother died when I was twelve, leaving me rather well off. After their divorce, she married into money and was widowed shortly after. When she died, it all passed to me."

"Money cannot replace a mother. I'm very sorry for your loss."

"Don't be," she answered, her face towards the moon, the night breeze blowing her loose hair. "Mother and I never got along. Father sent his condolences, of course, as well as the odd cheque or bit of bauble. And then, suddenly, last month, he called at my home, claiming he was looking for a second daughter; an American, who'd come to London four years ago. I'd no idea I had a half-sister! The police told Father she was dead, murdered by some fiend in the East End. I was utterly shocked, Your Grace. Completely undone. I'd no idea about any siblings. Mother never said a word, and Father's letters mentioned no other children. To find out I had a sister, but then hear she was murdered! It was all too much, you know?"

"Yes, I see how it would be."

"That was in December. We had a memorial service for her at a small church in the City—St. Etheldreda's near Wormwood. Do you know it?"

"Etheldreda's?" he asked, thinking of the hellish Redwing headquarters on number 33 of that street. "It's Catholic, isn't it?"

"Yes. Father's Sicilian, and apparently my sister was raised in the old faith. My mother and stepfather preferred Church of England, I've no particular favourite. I'm agnostic, I suppose. After the service, I shared a meal with Father, and then he sailed back to America. I'd assumed we'd not see each other again for years, but then, about three weeks ago, he sent a telegram. All it said was 'She's Alive'. Four days ago, he showed up at my door, claiming he had proof the body named as hers was that of someone else. Your Grace, I don't know if my sister is alive, but if she is, then I intend to find her. Though I've never met her, she's my own blood. Blood is important, don't you think?" she asked, an odd look on her face.

"Miss Calabrese, may I ask your sister's name?" That irritating tingle buzzed across the nape of his neck and along his fingers. Charles held his breath, certain her answer would prove important.

Which it did.

"Cassandra," the woman told him, tears pooling on her dark lower lashes. "I'm sorry to be so emotional, Your Grace, but my father's not the kindest man in the world. I'm ashamed to say he sent her away to England when she was very young. And he must share some of the blame for whatever happened to her."

"Cassandra Calabrese," Charles repeated, the name echoing in his memory with very dark associations. Why was that? Something Ed Reid had told him. "May I ask why you thought your sister died in the East? As you may know, my former occupation was Scotland Yard detective, and I was in charge of many investigations in the East. Your sister's name isn't familiar. Did she use any others?"

"I believe she used several aliases," Angiolina told him. "Regina Malmont, Doretta Samuels, and Susanna Morgan."

Morgan! the duke thought, taking care not to reveal his mind. The tingle across Sinclair's neck and hands began to scream as each nerve responded to the shocking revelation. Susanna Morgan. The very woman Paul Stuart had tried to help; the woman he'd probably fallen in love with—Susanna Morgan's true name was Cassandra Calabrese. Reid had mentioned it briefly, when he told Charles the body named as Susanna's had to be that of another woman.

This entire meeting suddenly felt contrived. He turned to examine the woman's face more carefully, searching for 'tells' that marked a liar.

She wore no gloves, and her nimble fingers clutched at the metal railing, indicative of internal anguish—or a skillful actress. A large black stone set in rubies adorned the fourth finger of her right hand, and though her left had no companion rings, a bangled bracelet sparkled with linked rubies amidst chains rimmed in diamonds. Calabrese had access to wealth, either her own or that of impressionable men. Her face could easily inspire a poet or sculptor. Something about her porcelain complexion seemed otherworldly, and her mouth reminded him of someone else. Or was it the shape of her ears? He struggled to draw the connexion, but that tingling wouldn't stop.

"May I ask, Miss Calabrese, who was your mother?"

She took a moment to reply, gazing out at the waves. "Phoebe. I suppose you might call her a ladder climber. Society's ladder, I mean. Her father was a baronet. I assume he died long ago. Mother never spoke of him. He was a bit of a black sheep. She often said I took after my grandfather."

"His name?"

"No one you'd know, but my father knew him quite well, I understand. His name comes up at certain meetings I've attended recently. There's a prince whose to meet us in Paris. I've heard him speak of my grandfather as well."

"You look familiar to me. That's why I ask."

She smiled, again that gaze so utterly disarming that Sinclair began to wonder if her perfume weren't an intoxicant. It reminded him of Serena di Specchio's ability to pull him into trances. Charles wondered if all this were one of his 'waking visions'.

"His name was Sir William Trent," she answered, her manner offering no hint as to motive.

Don't let her see the shock on your face, he told himself. *Remain calm.*

"Trent, you say?" he asked, the monosyllabic word feeling poisonous to his tongue.

"Yes. I've no idea where he is now. Most likely dead. I have photos from mother's childhood, and even then, he looked fifty or more. Why?"

"As I said, only the sense of familiarity."

"I've lost nearly all my family, Your Grace. Learning I had a sister, but hearing she'd died the same day was so difficult. If there's any chance she lives, then I intend to find her."

He touched her forearm, a test to measure her intent. She failed, for in that instant, Angiolina threw herself into his arms, her hands tightening round his waist. As Charles held her, thoughts of Beth filled his mind, wondering what she would say if she were here.

"Forgive me," she said, stepping back, her posture apologetic, almost subservient. The mysterious woman wiped at her eyes, and he offered his handkerchief; one of a dozen monogrammed silk squares he'd received as a Christmas gift from Elizabeth.

"It's very late. Shall I walk you back to your cabin?"

She shook her head. "No, thank you. You've been very kind to listen, and I'm sure you have other things on your mind tonight."

"Not much," he said. "My wife, of course. I miss her every minute. There is no one like my Beth."

"Ah, yes. The Duchess Elizabeth of Branham. I remember seeing her photograph alongside yours. Your wife is a very beautiful woman."

He smiled. "Yes, she is. Miss Calabrese, if I can offer any help in your search, you've but to ask it. In fact, I wonder if your father hadn't meant to seek my professional help in locating your sister. Is that why he asked to see me?"

"I believe so, but Father's so busy. I have nothing but time on my hands."

"Is he going to Paris for the Exposition?"

"Yes. Sanguis is a chemical concern, and he's meeting with a group of investors, who underwrite some of Father's newest discoveries. I'm not to say what they are, though honestly I don't understand any of it. I've no head for chemistry."

"Neither do I," he laughed. "I prefer numbers; particularly ones that add up."

"As any policeman would, I suppose."

"Where are you staying?" he asked, that persistent tingle buzzing along his hands.

"We've rooms booked at the *Hôtel Terminus*. It's brand new, just at the entrance to the Exposition grounds. We were lucky to get them. I hear they're full."

"Yes, I was told the same, but the manager is an old friend to my cousin and put me in the royal suite."

She laughed. "Then what I read in the papers must be true! Is it England's next king who offered me his handkerchief?"

"Not at all. Those rumours are nothing but sideshow. It's my cousin's influence, not mine. The earl owns part interest in the *Terminus*. Look, I have a meeting tomorrow morning with Chief Goron of the Sûreté. I could ask him to keep watch for your sister. Have you a photograph?"

"Yes," Angiolina told him, "but all the copies are in my state room. I could fetch them after you walk me back."

He considered the possible outcomes to such a gamble. "Certainly, but I'll remind you that my wife owns my heart."

She smiled. "You are a remarkable man, then, Your Grace. Why don't I leave the photo for you at the *Terminus?* Then, we won't risk that heart."

She blew him a kiss and turned to go. Sinclair watched her leave, the subtle swaying of her hips beneath the taffeta evening dress seemed almost like a dangerous dance. Suddenly, he wanted to be with his wife, to hear her musical voice in his ear, to feel her warm breath upon his cheek; hear her laughter; see her smile; to lie in her comforting arms and let the weight of the world pass away.

Charles remained at the railing for a little while longer, watching the white-capped grey waves rush past the ship. The round moon seemed to watch him, and that familiar tingle crept along his nerves as though whispering secrets from long ago. He felt weary and utterly alone.

CHAPTER NINE

1:31 am – 20 Arlington Street, Salisbury Home

As Charles Sinclair retired to bed, the revels on Arlington Street had at last begun to wind down. Most guests had long since left for home or other night venues, winnowing the numbers down to the usual stragglers, who gathered together in a single salon to trade gossip and tell stories. The Egypt Problem dominated many of these, and the moulded walls and marble fireplaces echoed with shouts of Empire, France, Suez, and El Khebir. Despite every attempt to drag Aubrey into these drawing room debates, the earl's attentions remained fixed upon his wife.

His mother-in-law, however, had set her attention on attracting a new husband, for rather than dress as a recent widow should, Constance Wychwright had worn a scandalously bright, off-the-shoulder dress. Connie explained it to her shocked daughter, by saying the scarlet gown was all she had available, as she lacked a lady's maid to iron anything more suitable. Paul said nothing to contradict the flimsy excuse, despite the fact the woman had a dozen or more pressed and perfect widow's weeds she might have chosen, hanging in her ample closet. It was obvious to anyone what mischief his mother-in-law was planning, but choosing diplomacy over war, the earl kept his thoughts to himself and promised to hire Constance a personal maid the very next day.

As politics waned, other topics were floated amongst the mixed company. A few mentioned Ripper, others talked of the Dybbuk or the so-called 'White Lady' ghost. Then the Earl of Brackamore suddenly brought up, of all things, the recent murders in Kent. Brackamore sat on the governing committee for Russia at the War Office, and he believed the Lion Hall Murders, as Whitehall insiders now called them, were somehow connected to political anarchism.

"The Okhrana must be involved!" the apoplectic earl declared as the remaining revellers relaxed near the drawing room fire.

"I doubt the Okhrana has cells in Kent, Lord Brackamore," Martin Kepelheim observed from a corner of the room.

"That statement reveals how very little you know, Mr. Kepelheim, but then I'd not expect a tailor to keep abreast of security matters. Those anarchist vermin scuttle about everywhere in our kingdom, and Kent is a very important county, sir! What if those fiends had taken hold at Branham, eh? What then? And now the duchess insists on opening her home to them! Why isn't Haimsbury keeping a lid on it?"

Kepelheim crossed the room and took a new position closer to the demonstrative earl. "The fête is a four-hundred-year-old tradition, and I can assure you that every precaution is taken during the event. But can you explain, my lord, how these murders are of any benefit to anarchists? Surely, you're not saying Colonel Collinwood or Peter Patterson were targeted by spies? Or worse, that they themselves were involved with espionage?"

"Of course, they were!" Brackamore bellowed. "Any fool could see it!"

"Why?" the tailor prompted. "Yes, there have been times when our Oxbridge elite are recruited by foreign provocateurs, but poor Patterson was but an average student; not the type to be courted by Russian agents. And the colonel never served in Russia that I'm aware."

"Their reason is anarchy, sir! Pure and simple. These Russians require no other excuse to sow discord in our kingdom. Anarchy is their *raison d'etre*, and brutality is their hallmark!"

Delia turned to her husband, asking simply, "Paul, why would Russians want to murder anyone in England? We're not at war with them, are we?"

"No, darling, we're not," he answered, kissing her soft hand. "However, there are tensions developing over disputed territory once controlled by the Ottoman Empire. Both Russia and England have eyes on those prizes." He turned to address the strident War Office minister, his arm round his wife protectively. "Lord Brackamore, I agree with your description of the Okhrana's activities here, but I have personally investigated the murders in Kent, and the evidence leads to other perpetrators. Both the Intelligence Branch and the ICI are following every lead. None takes us to Russia."

"Ah, but have you spoken with their ambassador?" Brackamore argued, his round grey eyes nearly bulging from their pale sockets. "I meet with Baron de Staal daily, sir, and he intimates that a Russian connexion does exist. He claims a rogue element within the Okhrana have begun a scorched earth policy in England, and Kent is just the ignition of that conflagration."

"Technically, a scorched earth policy is employed by defenders not offenders, Lord Brackamore, but I see your point. Might de Staal be intentionally misdirecting your gaze? The man does play all sides."

Harrumphing loudly, the pompous politician tipped back his entire glass of bourbon in one swallow. "Yes, well, I suppose you'd know, would you? Lord Aubrey, I do not deny your talents in the field. They are well known at Whitehall, but your expertise is on foreign soil, not England's green and pleasant land. Perhaps, you should leave domestic matters to those of us who serve faithfully at home."

"I never thought of you as a domestic, Ethan. Is that a new branch of the Home Office?"

Everyone laughed at this, and Cordelia, who understood practically nothing of the conversation, dared to interrupt. "Gentlemen, I have no head for politics, and it wearies me to try. Perhaps, the other ladies in the room feel the same. I wonder, might we choose an activity that includes everyone? Why don't we play cards? There are thirteen of us, but I'd be happy to sit out. I'm not very good at them anyway, but I do enjoy watching."

Paul kissed her hand, his eyes soft as he appreciated her beauty and subtle persuasion. "My wife is very wise, ladies and gentlemen. Politics are divisive and dull. Lord Salisbury, are you up for a game? Ladies, do you prefer whist or backgammon?"

"Why don't we dance?" asked a coquettish ingenue sitting near the fireplace. Her name was Hermione Alderson, and she was a distant cousin to Lady Salisbury, now living with the prime minister and his family. "The foyer's certainly large enough. There would only be a few couples anyway. Lord Paynton, might you enjoy a dance?" she asked the bashful viscount.

"Ah, well, I'm not sure there's any music," Seth managed to reply.

Kepelheim cleared his throat. "Sadly, Miss Alderson, the orchestra departed long ago."

"How about a tale, then?" suggested Cordelia. "My husband tells me Mr. Kepelheim is one of the best storytellers in England. Would you offer us a story, please, Martin?"

"Martin's a consummate teller of tales, but first, let's all fill our glasses." The earl stood and began pouring drinks for everyone. Once he'd refilled his own, Paul returned to his chair, kissing his wife fondly. "You'll make a wonderful hostess, Delia. Shall we plan the next party at our home?"

"I'd love that, husband," she whispered. "Thank you."

Connie Wychwright said very little, for she was busy plotting how best to reach the next rung on London society's tall ladder. Her troublesome eldest son's name had been removed from many a hostess's list, for the baron had fallen out of favour with the conservative party. *Let him rot*, she thought darkly. Will Wychwright had spurned all her suggestions to improve his lot, and he'd spent nearly all his inheritance, making him a liability rather than an asset. Lord Brackamore, however, was a wealthy widower, and a possible candidate to become the next chancellor. And he'd cast several appreciative glances in Connie's direction.

"Do tell us a story, Mr. Kepelheim," the dowager baroness cooed in her sweetest voice. "But avoid anything Russian. We'd not want to entice these Okhrana devils, now would we?"

Brackamore laughed heartily at this, and he actually winked at Connie. *He's taken the bait*, she thought to herself. *Now to set the hook.* "Do forgive me, my friends. I feel a sudden chill. Lord Salisbury, would it be possible to turn up the fire?"

"I'll get it, Robert," answered Aubrey, starting to stand, but Brackamore jumped up and reached the control switch first.

"Allow me, sir," said the older man with a somewhat simpering smile aimed directly at the charming widow. After raising the gas level to the fire, the unwitting fish even offered the scheming dowager baroness his own dress coat. "I wonder if this might help until the fire warms the room?" said the hapless trout as he drew the coat round Connie Wychwright's shoulders. "We cannot have a lady chilled, now can we?"

Aubrey stared at Brackamore, dumbfounded. He saw through his mother-in-law's scheme, of course, but decided to let the foolish fish chew on the sharp lure. If the widowed earl found the overly powdered woman's bait tasty, then he deserved being landed by so obvious an angler.

With his audience settled in and warming themselves, Martin took a prominent place before the fire, a glass of sherry in his hand. The dancing flames painted his round cheeks with flickering light. "My lords and ladies, allow me to offer a tale I first heard when I was just a boy. As some of you may know, I had the great honour to grow up near our lovely Lady Aubrey. Broadmoor Hall, the Wychwright home in Windermere, is but a two-hour drive from another grand and regal home, which dominates a tall hill in Eden Valley. That verdant valley is a fertile ground for ghosts and ghouls, and I heard many such stories whilst growing up there. The following is one such tale, and I promise you that everything in this story is true. All of it. From beginning to end. I shan't reveal the name of the family, for they are well known, but the events occurred just this way."

He took another sip of sherry, wiping his silver moustache before beginning. "The root of these events occurred long before I was born; in the sixth century, to be precise. History is somewhat scant regarding those early, post-Roman years in England, but as the Romans withdrew, their presence left a vacuum into which many new leaders arose. Many of these leaders were wealthy Romanised citizens, whilst others came from oppressed and enslaved tribes who wished to remove all traces of the much-hated foreigners. It's no wonder then, that warfare soon erupted throughout the various regions of our island.

"Of course, the structure of our realm was quite different then. England did not exist. Regional fiefdoms rose up and fell, but over time, settled into recognised kingdoms. There was the kingdom of Kent, of course, ruled over by the descendants of the great Norse warriors, Horsa and Hengist. And there were Wessex, Sussex, Saxony, East Anglia, and Mercia to name but a few. During this time, the beautiful Eden Valley pasturelands fell under the control of the Rheged clans. Here, the children and great-grandchildren of Coel Hen, renowned in song as Old King Cole, established themselves. One of the greatest of these was King Uthred, who ruled around the time of the first Dragon Wars."

Cordelia shuddered, pulling close to her husband. Paul placed his arm round his wife, whispering, "Take heart, *mo bhean*. I am your shield. Nothing will reach you that does not go through me first. Always remember that."

The young wife smiled as he kissed her cheek. Martin took note of the girl's pale countenance and offered his own assurance. "My dear friends, if anyone here finds such tales disquieting, remember where we now sit: within the safety of a warm drawing room, inside an elegant house, within the great metropolis of London."

A bat flapped at the window, and Connie Wychwright jumped, the action intentionally exaggerated.

"Oh, what is that!" she squealed, pulling Brackamore's borrowed coat closer round her ample bosom.

The widower rushed to her side and drew a chair close, that he might sit beside her. He took her hand. "Only a bat, my dear. Nothing but a bat."

Paul suppressed a grin. "What are the Dragon Wars?" he asked the storyteller, his wife's hand clutched in his.

"Ah, well, that tale must wait for another night, but there is an old legend that the Eden River Valley was not naturally formed, but is the result of the first of these wars. During the late fifth century, songs, diaries, letters, and paintings from all across Europe and parts of the Orient tell of three great dragons that fought for control of the heavens. These monstrous entities flew at one another for weeks and weeks, filling the skies with fire and smoke. A monk writing near what is now Paris recorded the battle in fine detail. I've read those accounts and have a copy. Brother Julien witnessed two Dragon Wars and wrote of what he saw. He claims the first battle was not three dragons vying for power, but two seeking to restrain the third. He described the two as 'holy ones', radiant beings with multiple sets of wings, and they brandished weapons unlike any he'd ever seen. The third appeared similar, but with darker hues. Julien believed the third dragon was a fallen angel, and that the two defenders were sent by God. Later, a second war erupted, more furious than the first, but it all ended on what Julien called 'the night of two moons.'"

"How can there be two moons?" asked Constance.

"It sounds implausible, I know, but that is how it is described in these old accounts."

"How did the wars finally end, Mr. Kepelheim?" asked Cordelia.

"The first great war ended with the defeat of the fallen one," he replied, finishing his drink. Lady Salisbury refilled the tailor's glass, and he bowed. "Thank you, dear lady. It's thirsty work. Now, I mentioned that the Eden Valley's existence is said to date back to this first war. If the tales are true, then the defeated dragon crashed into the region we call Cumbria and ploughed a great trough into the earth with its massive body, forming the valley and the river all at once. I cannot say if this is true, for I've read other histories that contradict it. But King Uthred built a great castle at the very site where the defeated dragon fell, and he took the name Pendragon, which means dragon's head."

"Uthred Pendragon?" asked Delia. "Is he the same as Uther?"

Martin smiled. "You will soon see, dear lady," he answered. "Now, it is said that Uthred had a beautiful daughter, who fell in love with a great knight. Uthred met this fierce warrior on the banks of the Eden River. The lad had no family; indeed, it was as if he'd arisen out of the aether, but all who met him loved the man. His countenance was like brass, eyes as blue as sapphire, and his swordsmanship without equal. He unseated all comers in both battle and the lists, and soon became Uthred's champion. Sometime before the Great Darkness fell, that period we modernists innocently call the 'Dark Ages', before those days commenced, Uthred fell upon the battlefield. Without a son and heir, Uthred named his great champion the next king. And so, our fearless knight buried his beloved sovereign, married the daughter, and established a new kingdom, finally uniting the warring factions of England's tribal lands beneath a single banner. That king's name was Artorius, who settled in Pendragon Castle before building his own grand palace at the top of the hill. We know this king as Arthur."

"But I thought Arthur was a myth," Lady Salisbury interrupted. "You said this tale was true, Martin."

"So I did, dear lady, and I do not retract that statement. Many of the poets and songwriters have mistaken or intentionally obscured names and dates, but I have seen the evidence with my own eyes. A valiant knight named Artorius did indeed arise in the Eden Valley, and he reigned over a kingdom of united tribes. But only for a season. Soon after his palace was complete, many of the subject kings began to grumble, claiming Artorius was not a blood heir, and therefore had no claim to the throne. War inevitably erupted, soaking the soil and filling the river with blood. After dozens of battles, Artorius fell, but it was not another knight who unseated our hero, but *a woman*. A devious devilish woman, who entered his household and cast a witch's spell upon him. She became defacto ruler of the kingdom for a short season, but Artorius eventually realised the truth and banished her from court. This witch cursed the land and the king, predicting his defeat in battle and prophesying that the dragons would return twice more to the earth: first at the moment of Artorius's death, and the second, when he arose to rule again.

"Now, my tale may sound like fiction, but I've seen the originals of letters and diaries written by monks and pagans alike, and the basic facts remain the same. Artorius's kingdom divided, and his heart fell into ruin. Enemies attacked the palace on the hill, and his precious wife was sent to a convent for safekeeping. It seemed as if the Biblical apocalypse had arrived, for war raged everywhere—brother against brother, and entire villages were burnt to the ground.

"But then, as the witch had prophesied, the dragons returned. This second dragon war commenced on a midsummer evening. The stars shone as usual that night, and two warring battalions had just set up their tents and pavilions: Artorius on one side, and seven tribes and their kings on the other. As the moon rose, seven great stars left their natural courses and turned towards the earth, followed by an eighth—this one much larger. It is said that this eighth star appeared to be at war with the other seven, for it pursued them. The thunder of their voices, their fiery breath, and blinding weapons overwhelmed the senses of the soldiers and lit up the sky for miles and miles around. Every knight had rushed from his tent to watch the hellish display, kneeling in prayer, certain the Apocalypse had come. The seven great monsters flew against the one, again and again and again, sparking lightning so bright, the entire battlefield was bathed in silver; until at last, the mighty defender grew big and bright as the moon, unleashing a fury beyond imagination against the rebellious seven. He then hurled these rebel angels into seven different directions, no doubt leaving great scars upon the earth wherever they fell."

The tailor paused, taking a sip of his drink to add dramatic effect.

"And then what?" asked Cordelia breathlessly.

"Then, believing their actions condemned by God—for the vision of seven rebels overwhelmed by one was surely a vision of their own rebellion—the seven rebel human kings put aside their differences, forming a union and pledging to unite beneath the banner of King Artorius. But the great king had disappeared. Vanished sometime during the aerial battle."

"Where did he go?" the young countess asked, squeezing her husband's hand.

"My dear Lady Aubrey, no one knows!" the tailor told her. "Some say he was translated to heaven. Others that he was taken to Hell. Still others believe he was rescued by a trio of faery maidens and whisked away to an island of the dead, where he awaits his return to England—the day when we are once again beset by Dragons."

"But what of his wife? What happened to her?"

"The lovely Queen Gwynedd lived on, they say. And she gave birth to a son, the very night the seven dragons were hurled to the earth. That son was taken to safety by loyal knights, and left with monks near a village in what is now modern France. The beautiful queen died shortly after, and it is her diary that I've only recently discovered."

Paul stared at his friend. "I've heard you tell parts of this before, but you're saying all this is true?"

Kepelheim nodded. "On my honour as a member of your esteemed family's circle, my lord, it is all true."

"And this diary? Where did you find it?" he asked the tailor.

"In a great house known to many of us, though I shan't name it."

Seth Holloway had listened quietly, certain most of the tale was invention. With Aubrey convinced of its authenticity, he began to wonder how it connected to the inner circle.

"Might I study the diary, Mr. Kepelheim?"

"Of course. I'd be pleased to share it with another history aficionado, Lord Paynton, and I've recently uncovered more evidence of that same tale elsewhere, in France, and I'd be happy to have your opinion."

"But what about the baby?" asked Lady Salisbury.

"Ah, well, it is said the boy had adventures of his own, and that his descendants have become influential peers and princes. Who knows? Perhaps, one day, one of them will rule as king."

"King of England?" asked Delia. "Surely, that would mean the boy's descendent is the Prince of Wales!"

"Or perhaps, the boy influences the world in other ways," Martin replied. "Perhaps, one day, his shadow will sweep across the world."

"You mean, when the dragons return?" suggested Holloway darkly.

"That is precisely what I mean," the tailor whispered. "And I fear that day approaches."

CHAPTER TEN
Aubrey House

The Salisbury gathering broke up shortly after Martin's story finished, and Paul offered to share a coach with his mother-in-law. Not entirely to the earl's surprise, Brackamore offered to 'see the lady home'. Paul waited up to make sure Connie did indeed arrive back at Aubrey House, and then the bone-weary earl bid his scheming mother-in-law goodnight and climbed into bed beside his sweet wife. It was long past four when he finally fell asleep.

Less than one hour later, a loud knock roused Aubrey from that happy slumber.

"Sir!" called his butler anxiously. "Sir! Please, my lord! Please, you must awake, sir!"

The earl slowly blinked, trying to clear his head, for he'd only just entered deep sleep. "Yes?" he called into the darkened room.

"Please, my lord! It's urgent!"

Bailey rarely knocked at such an early hour, so the earl left the bed and put on a dressing gown. Once he reached the door, Paul opened it a crack. "The countess and I had a very late night, Bailey. I do hope is important."

The servant also wore a dressing gown, which was thoroughly out of character for the prim and proper butler, and his wiry, silver hair needed a good combing. "Forgive me, my lord, but Mr. Kepelheim is here and begs you to come down. He will not take no for an answer. I asked him to call again later, but he insists the problem cannot wait. He must go to Branham immediately!"

Suddenly, Paul was stone-cold awake. "Did something happen to the duchess?"

"I don't know, my lord. He did not say."

Leaving Cordelia sleeping, Paul hastened into the corridor and down the back staircase, a faster route than winding through the home's first-floor state rooms. In less than a minute, he reached the tiled foyer.

"What's happened?" he asked the tailor. "Is it Beth?"

"Forgive me, my friend, for it's obvious I've disturbed your sleep. No, it isn't the duchess. I've just received a message that requires I borrow one of your trains at once."

"What? A train? It's five in the morning, Martin. Is Beth injured? Ill?"

"I believe the duchess is well, and I pray this matter doesn't touch her, but it's quite possible it will eventually."

"Out with it, Martin!"

"Yes, yes, of course. Do you remember Sir Simon Pembroke? The baronet who lives near Branham Village?"

"Of course, I remember him. Why? Martin, what's this all about?"

Kepelheim withdrew an envelope from the inner pocket of his jacket and handed it to Aubrey. "A courier delivered this to my home last evening after I left for Salisbury's home. My manservant, Evans, placed it on my bureau, but I didn't retire immediately. I spent some time reading in my drawing room first. As a result, I found this note only half an hour ago, when I began to change for bed. It's very strange, for the letter's written to Charles, yet it came to me, care of my home address. The reason is implied within. Read it, Paul, please."

Aubrey took the letter into the morning room, where his butler had already lit a fire. He plopped into a leather chair and read the letter to himself:

Dear Duke Charles,

Forgive the presumptive communication, Your Grace, but I've had a most unusual encounter that requires an experienced, investigative hand. A 'circular' hand, if you get my meaning, sir.

As you'll recall, when you and Aubrey visited here last December, I'd hoped to show you the sarcophagus discovered at Castle Anjou, but instead fell upon poor old Collie's body. I know you're investigating the colonel's death as well as that of the Cambridge student, Peter Patterson, but I believe I've just discovered the key to identifying their murderer. No, the killer isn't that boy Wentworth that all the papers keep naming. Sir, I really must speak to you in person, but severe gout keeps me from travelling. I wonder if you'd consider calling on me tomorrow? If you cannot, perhaps, Aubrey might come? I pray Mr. Kepelheim transfers this to you, for we've had a series of odd happenings here, and it's my belief someone is watching the house. Therefore, I fear my man might be followed, and I hope to misdirect the devil's steps.

If I do not hear back by tomorrow, I'll assume the missive misfired or was apprehended by this nefarious man's agent. I pray you'll come, Your Grace, for I suspect this involves you in some way. It's a feeling, but I cannot shake it. I am not one for hyperbole, so when I tell you this is a matter of life and death, you must assume I am in earnest.

With very great respect,
Sir Simon Pembroke, 2nd Baronet

"He thinks he's in danger? That he's being watched?" asked Aubrey as he folded the letter back into its container. "By whom?"

"As you can see, he makes no reference that will reveal his mind, other than to imply he has information of very great import," the tailor replied. "Pembroke is a man of true colours, Paul, but if our enemies can enter his home and murder Colonel Collinwood without observation, it is therefore reasonable to assume they can reach Sir Simon just as easily and kill him. Now, I know that you have three trains in London presently. Might I use one to hasten to Kent and offer assistance? I dare not leave it any later. Truly, I fear for Pembroke's life, and as he lives so near our dear one, I fear for her as well."

"You're not going alone, Martin."

"I'd never dream of pulling you from your lovely bride, Paul. I'm perfectly able to make the journey on my own, but the earliest commercial passage to Branham leaves at ten. If Sir Simon thinks himself in danger, then it's imperative to talk with him as soon as possible. I've wired a reply, saying I'd meet him for breakfast. No later than nine."

"Martin, I can't have you riding into possible danger without escort. I'll go with you."

"Paul, I'm a capable shot, and..."

"No, I won't allow it, and that is final. With Charles away, I'm in charge of the group. It's my decision. I'll go with you."

Awakened by her husband's departure, Lady Aubrey entered the morning room. She wore a blue and cream, striped dressing gown, trimmed in lace, and her blonde hair was braided against her left shoulder.

"Go? Go where, Paul?" she asked. "Are you leaving?"

The earl went to her and kissed her cheek. "I'm sorry we woke you, dearest. I'm afraid something's happened in Branham."

"Oh, no! Is Elizabeth all right?"

"She's well, or so we believe, but it sounds as if there might be trouble. You remember that I'm trained to handle any and all danger?"

"Yes, but I'd prefer you didn't," she whispered.

"Darling, danger and I are old friends. I'll be just fine, but I cannot let Martin go alone. With Charles away, it falls to me to go with him."

"Why? Why are all of you so very secretive about things? Paul, I don't want you to go!"

Lady Constance Wychwright entered the morning room.

"It seems everyone's up very early, considering how late our night went. What's this about Paul leaving?"

"I'm afraid it's business, Connie. A matter of some urgency in Kent."

Aubrey fully expected the dowager baroness to take her daughter's side, but instead the widow supported the earl. "Ah, I see. Well, then, if it's business, you must go," Connie said sweetly. "I'll look after Cordelia in your absence. Is there anything we can do to help?"

Stunned, the earl looked at his mother-in-law, trying to decide what giggling sprite had taken her place during the night.

"Thank you, Connie. The best help would be to enjoy the day as you would otherwise," he answered. "Sleep a little longer if you can.

Later on, perhaps, the two of you could visit Madam du Monde's dress shop and select fabrics and styles for my wife's new wardrobe. Or you could look at new furnishings for the nursery, but also for any other rooms in need of improvement. This house hasn't been redecorated for twenty years."

"But I prefer to do all that with you," Delia told him, pouting.

"And I will help when I return. I promise," he assured her with a kiss.

"But aren't we going to Branham on Friday evening? If I'm to be there for the fête and ball, why can't I come with you today?"

"Because I don't plan to stay, darling. I'll likely be back this afternoon. At least, it's my hope."

"Very well. If you insist, but you must promise to take care."

The young countess tried to put on a brave face, but to her husband, she looked like a frightened child, and it broke Paul's tender heart. "Martin, would you and Connie mind giving us a bit of privacy?"

The tailor took Wychwright's arm. "Not at all. Did I hear mention of nursery plans?" he asked the widow. "Redecorating can be such a chore, but I've a friend, who does wonders with these old houses. Her name is Mrs. Calhoun, and she is a marvel at updating the dullest of bedchambers!"

Once they'd gone, Paul shut the door and turned to his wife. "What can I say to make this better? I'll do anything to see you smile."

"Then, stay here."

"If I could, I would. My darling, my work is such that there will be times when business demands I leave you for a short while, but I will always—*always* return to you. And whilst away, my thoughts dwell only on you. As I say, it's likely we'll return by afternoon, but I'll send you a telegram as soon as I know more. I promise."

"Very well. But I shall spend lots of your money to make up for it."

He laughed. "Delia, even if you redecorated this entire house ten times, you'd scarcely make a dent in my annual income. The government pays me very well, and the Aubrey estate and its holdings have left us obscenely comfortable. My own investments augment that even further. Now, choose whatever you want and fill your closets with lots of new clothes. Just remember, I love you with all my heart. Any time we're parted is agony to me."

She kissed him, stroking the rough beard of his dimpled cheek. "You need to shave. I prefer kissing your smooth skin. The beard tickles."

"Does it? Then, I'll shave as soon as possible. Now, go enjoy the time with your mother. Who knows? This might help to heal the rift twixt the two of you."

"I very much doubt it," Cordelia mumbled. "I mean, I'll try."

He drew her chin upwards and kissed her passionately, his arms tight around her waist. "I'll dream of these soft lips," he told her. "Keep them warm for me. And rest as much as you can, darling. Sit when you're in the shops and let your mother do the work." Aubrey smoothed her golden locks, kissing her forehead. "How I shall miss you! I promise, if it seems the matter will take more than a day, I'll let you know."

"Very well. But promise to be careful."

"I am always careful, dear one, and you can tell our growing son or daughter that. Now, come upstairs and help me pack."

CHAPTER ELEVEN

8:38 am - Château Rothesay, near Goussainville

"Bonjour, M'sieur. Comment puis-je vous aider?"

Charles Sinclair's French and German were adequate to the basic requirements of continental travel, but hardly proficient with a sleep-deprived brain. He was exhausted from having spent the past twenty-two hours on four trains, a channel ship, and a very dusty coach, but most of all he wanted to see Adele.

"Yes, you may help me, especially, if you speak English," he answered hopefully.

The lean butler smiled, answering in a British accent. "Of course, sir. How may I serve you today?"

"Wonderful! I'm Duke Charles, and I believe my aunt is expecting me, though perhaps not this early."

A look of surprise passed quickly along the middle-aged man's pleasant features. "Duke Charles? Oh, do forgive me, Your Grace," he apologised as he opened the door wider. "You're quite correct. We'd not expected you until this afternoon at the earliest. We've had a bit of excitement, and our household is on alert, you might say. I've been given orders to screen everyone who calls, just to make sure each is friendly."

He took the duke's hat, coat, and gloves, signalling to a young footman to commence bringing in the bags. "Take His Grace's luggage to the Carrick, Mr. Rice. My lord, if you are weary after your journey, I can have him draw you a bath. The Carrick Suite's tub is quite large."

"No bath, thank you. Later, but not yet. Now, tell me about this bit of excitement you mentioned. Why is the household on alert?"

"The Lady Victoria and the Patterson-Smiths hosted a visitor last evening, sir. When he'd departed, Lady Adele retired to her rooms. Shortly after, we heard Lady Della scream, sir. Such a terrified cry! She thought she'd seen a prowler, or so we believe, Your Grace. Lady Adele described this shadow as a *thing*, sir, which she saw lingering beneath her window. My men and I scoured the area, and we found no intruder. But there were prints beneath Lady Adele's window. A large animal's, in fact. Rather like a bear's, my lord. As you can imagine, Lady Victoria is acquainted with such strange occurrences, for we experienced them on several occasions whilst Duchess Elizabeth resided here. As such, Lady Victoria now insists only those on her list may be admitted."

"I'm glad I'm on the list."

"You are at the very top, Your Grace. Breakfast, sir?"

"Yes, actually. I'm famished," Haimsbury answered as his aunt appeared on the staircase.

"Charles, what a lovely surprise, my dear. We'd not expected you until much later today." Tory was dressed in riding trousers with a boot on her right foot, but only a thick bandage on the left. She leaned heavily upon the rail as she descended in a series of quick hops.

Sinclair rushed up and gave her his arm. "You shouldn't be climbing," he scolded her. "Whatever were you doing upstairs?"

"Living, my dear. One cannot avoid stairs in a four-storey home, now can one? How was the drive in from Paris? You did come from Paris, I take it?"

"No, there were no tickets left for the line to Paris. It seems all the trains are crowded with tourists."

"Surely, they'd have given the Duke of Haimsbury a seat, my dear! Did you ask?"

"No. I made no fuss, but our circle friend André Deniau met me in Calais and suggested we hire a special to Lille, and then another from there to Creil. There, we met another circle member. A clever chap named François Cretiens. He and Deniau drove me here from Creil in an unmarked coach. It was all very secretive, but mostly enjoyable. The countryside is beautiful, but I confess, the roads are not."

"Yes, I'm afraid our country roads are nothing but rutted washboards, fit only for scrambling eggs in a basket. If one had a basket of eggs on such a journey. Did you? Of course, not. Russell, have one of your footmen take the duke's cases up to the Carrick Suite."

"Already done, my lady," the tall butler said with a slight grin.

"Oh, good. Well done. You'll like that suite, Charles," she told her nephew. "It's very masculine with all that oak panelling and hunting scenes men so love. My brother always uses it whenever he visits. He's in Scotland now, so I hear. Is that right?"

Charles started to respond, but Victoria continued as if no answer were required.

"Poor old Richie MacAllen," she prattled as they walked. "Such a pity to see the old guard dying off. But that is life, I suppose. My dear nephew, you look worn through! I'm very sorry about the line to Paris. It's because of this Exposition, you know. Nearly everyone is crowding into the city because of it. And that includes the bad with the good. Crossing the channel has always been tedious, but now it's become decidedly dangerous. I'm very pleased you made it in one piece. How is Beth?"

Charles smiled as his garrulous and very opinionated aunt finally took a breath, allowing him a brief opening to reply. "She's well, and it's a joy to see you again, Tory, though I'm very sorry you're injured. Shouldn't you be in a wheeled chair of some kind?"

"Nonsense. That new physician Palmore is being obstinate with his medical advice, therefore, I am being a recalcitrant patient. He'll soon tire of me."

"Regardless, let me help you to a chair. Will it be the morning room, or were you about to enjoy breakfast?"

"Neither, actually. I'd just come down from fetching my eyeglasses. They're always disappearing, but I can't read without them now. Age brings insight but poor eyesight," she quipped. "I'd planned to spend the morning on the south lawn and catch up with the newspapers—though, they're probably all filled with these horrible Portmanteau Murders. I'm sure you've heard of them."

"No, actually. What are they?" he asked, but she appeared not to hear him.

"We'll take breakfast on the lawn, I think, Russell," she told the butler. "The sun's simply glorious this morning, Charles, and Della promised to do some watercolour painting. She's become quite an artist since January. Perhaps, she'll paint you," she chattered as she led him through the massive entryway.

"What murders, Tory?" he asked again, her arm through his.

"Oh, nothing to worry you, Charles. Leave all that to the Sûreté and the Prefecture. No, it's that strange bear that worries me. We've never had them before; well, not that I can recall. Perhaps, it belongs to one of those Travellers."

"Gypsies?"

"Yes. They've begun to gather near the woods. They keep bears, I've heard. Did Russell tell you we found bear tracks beneath Della's window last night? I'm sure whatever—whomever—she believes stood there was caused by her imagination."

"You think she imagined it?"

"I think Adele saw something, but not what she described. Though, one wonders, why she'd describe a bear in such a way."

"What way?"

"Really, I do think she dreamt most of it, but after yesterday's events, I find it all very odd."

"What happened yesterday, Tory?" he asked as they walked through a medieval armoury and into a wide gallery.

"It's to do with that new neighbour of ours. A very strange man. We've a lovely little veranda out here, Charles. Just through here."

They'd entered the Rothesay Conservatory, a spacious sunlit room, dotted with pleasant wicker chairs, three tables, and several large floor cushions. A brown-and-white terrier slept upon one of these, whilst a tricolour spaniel snored on the other.

"Napper seems to enjoy French country life," whispered the duke as they passed by the spaniel.

"Yes, but she had quite an adventure yesterday. Poor thing's hardly roused since. Let's not wake them."

They tiptoed past the sleeping animals, careful not to speak further, and emerged into a flagstone sitting area that ran the length of the faery-tale castle. The morning sun dappled the lawn with every green imaginable, and along the flowered hills beyond, stood an army of horse stables, sheepfolds, granaries, and barns. Charles could see several dozen horses of all shapes and sizes, grazing in a neighbouring meadow; a flock of sheep in another; and far to the west, the tall pine trees of a dense woodland.

A pair of strutting peacocks and one peahen strolled past them, not more than ten yards away. The male birds fanned their magnificent tails proudly, hoping to impress the hen. She turned away, not the least bit interested.

"Is it what you expected?" asked Victoria. "We're not terribly large, but the estate is easy to manage and self-sustaining."

"It's a beautiful place, Tory. It looks like a Dupré or Renoir landscape, come to life. Adele must love it here," he told his aunt as he helped her to sit.

"She does, but she misses you terribly, Charles. That sweet child has adopted you as her new father, you know. It's reminiscent of when Beth lived here, for I hear your name spoken daily, only this time it's 'Cousin Charles' rather than 'Captain'."

"I'm honoured to be so remembered," he said wistfully. "In truth, I've missed her just as much."

"Ah, but she sees it from a girl's point of view, Nephew. Poor thing waits anxiously for each post's arrival, and when your daily letter finally does come, she reads it again and again, and then rushes to pen one to you in return."

"I've read hers many times over as well. Della's French is beyond my own now. Beth's had to translate a few lines for me now and then, particularly when Della quotes from a book. I'd not realised *Alice's Adventures in Wonderland* was available in French."

"Oh, I imagine it's in most languages now. Carroll's work is quite popular, though I've no idea why. Our Adele devours books just like Beth did, and she lives for the post, as I said."

Tory laughed as another thought came into her head. "However, there is one other correspondent whose letters *might* mean a bit more than yours do, Nephew, though, in an entirely context."

"Beth's, I should imagine," Charles observed.

"No, not Beth's, though Della loves hearing from her, of course. I mean the ones from Henry MacAlpin. The viscount writes weekly, and Della invariably grows quite dreamy for several days after each arrives."

"Ah, yes, I'd noticed that," Charles admitted.

"Had you? But do you appreciate what it means, Charles?" she asked perceptively.

"Yes, but it will pass, Tory. I've spoken with Beth about Della's infatuation with Henry, and she agrees it will most likely fade with time."

"Beth's infatuation with you never faded, my dear."

He smiled. "No, and I'm grateful for that miracle every day, Aunt. However, in Adele's case, it's likely to fade. She's nearly twelve, which means she's experiencing adult emotions without the benefit of adult experience, but we mustn't interfere. If we try to dissuade her, the attachment will only grow. Surely, you must know that."

Victoria found his parental advice amusing. "And how did I learn that, my dear? By making that very mistake! Dolly's the one encouraged Elizabeth in her singular attachment, but even she agreed any contact must come from you before Beth wrote. Actually, I'm glad Henry writes. His letters always cheer Della, and the girl needs cheering. Despite her love of French literature and music, Adele has no one else her age for company. Her friend Winston Churchill sends letters, though not regularly. His parents have returned from America, and he's back at Harrow, which makes him quite busy, I imagine. Oh, and did I mention he and his Great Aunt Maisie are coming to the fête next week, assuming Beth is still having it. Is she? Having it, I mean?"

"If over a hundred hammering carpenters and ditch-digging plumbers mean the fête is on, then yes, she's having it. We remained in London for most of the construction, due to the noise, but went down for Easter."

"Yes, she wrote and said you were leaving her there. She never explained. I presume you had criminals to catch in London."

"That much is true, but Beth experienced some rather unsettling contractions just after Easter services."

"Oh, my! No one told me about that!"

"We didn't wish to worry you, dear," he said, taking her hand. "Gehlen was there with us and sent to London for a colleague named John Braxton Hicks. He works at St. Mary's. Braxton Hicks seemed to think the contractions normal for that stage of a twin pregnancy, but agreed Beth must remain at Branham until she delivers in June. I've been using my new train to go back and forth twixt London and the hall ever since. Three days in the city, followed by four with my wife. It's worked thus far, but I shall be very glad when we can bring our children back to Haimsbury House and live together as a family."

"And Beth agreed to all that?"

He smiled. "She did. Your niece complies with all the doctors' instructions. She's allowed short walks on the lawn, so long as she isn't alone, and moderate hours in a chair, but Gehlen insists she rest often. Which, I'm very happy to say, she does."

"That is remarkable! No other has ever been able to control my niece's inclinations, Charles. But why doesn't Beth have the babies in London? Surely, it's closer to her doctors."

"She wants the next duke or duchess to be born at Branham, but we're prepared. We've installed a vast array of medical supplies, according to Anthony Gehlen's list and hired Olivia Reston away from the London. Reston keeps a close eye on my wife now. Oh, and Price has found us two young women to serve as wet nurses. I think we're just about ready to meet my son and daughter."

"My dear, it all sounds quite lovely. And what of Beth's Castle Company? How are they doing?"

"As you probably noticed, Count Riga and Mr. Blinkmire fell in love with Branham, and so Beth's invited them to live at the hall permanently. Both men appear to have found refuge in the never-ending libraries and serenity of the gardens."

"And the other men? And Ida? What of them?"

"Ida's married to Elbert Stanley now."

"They've married?" echoed Victoria in surprise. "I had noticed they seemed to be growing close. How lovely, Charles. Did you attend the wedding?"

"Beth and I would have, but they eloped to Brighton in March," he explained. "We'd no idea they planned to wed, or at least I didn't. If they'd told me, I'd have arranged a formal ceremony."

"Perhaps, they preferred to keep it quiet. Elbert Stanley is a very sweet and unassuming man, and Ida is somewhat shy."

"I'm sure you're right. As a wedding gift, we bought them a lovely house in a pleasant section of Stepney, and Ida's training as a nurse at the London. She wants to help with Elizabeth's new hospital when it's finished. And Stanley's now a Detective Inspector with the Intelligence Branch, which gives him a healthy salary for his new bride. I've made him our liaison to H-Division."

"And Baxter? Have he and Alcorn married yet?"

"Six weeks ago," he replied. "They'd planned to wait until May, but Esther asked if they might arrange it for earlier, so they'd not miss the fête. They've been enjoying the brisk sea air near James's castle ever since."

"At the Crovie cottage? How delightful! It all sounds quite like a very happy ending, doesn't it? If only life always gave us such treats."

"What treats are those?" asked Dolly Patterson-Smythe as she entered the patio through the conservatory doors. She wore riding trousers and boots, and her silvering blonde hair was tied in a wind-blown chignon. She'd just ridden over from her estate, three miles to the north. "If it isn't Charles Sinclair! I hadn't expected to find you here this morning," she exclaimed as he kissed her cheek. "My, but you look fit and regal as always. My dear, you are the most handsome man I have ever seen. Bar none. Oh, and it's a shame you weren't here last evening, you'd have given that peacock prince quite a contest!"

"What prince is that? Tory, is this the guest you mentioned earlier?"

Victoria sighed. "I suppose it's bound to come out eventually. I'd not wanted to burden you with it so soon after your arrival, Charles, but this man's presence reminds me of that other one—what's his name again, Dolly?"

"Prince Alexei Grigor," answered the baronet's wife. "He works with both the English and French governments."

"Yes, that's it," Tory said, nodding. "Alexei! That smug Romanian prince who took Beth from the ballroom last November. You remember, surely, Charles. The night before your wedding."

"How could I forget?" the duke answered, and he intended to say more, but was interrupted when Russell and a footman appeared, pushing a trolley laden with breakfast.

"Shall we serve now, Lady Victoria?"

"Oh, yes," Tory told Russell. "Charles, is it all right?"

"I'm starved," he said, his mind working back to Grigor and his supernatural hold on Beth.

The butler continued. "Your Grace, had we known you were arriving this morning, Cook would have prepared a full buffet with many hot and savoury offerings, but for now, we can offer you cold foods. Fruit, juices, pastries, fresh bread, marmalade, and butter. Tea and coffee, of course. I have asked Cook to prepare meats and eggs, which should be available soon."

"Oh, this looks like a great deal of food already," Tory insisted. "Wait an hour, and we'll see if we still need the hot items, Russell, though the idea is most welcome. Please, tell Cook she can reuse the egg and meat dishes for luncheon, if she likes."

"Mrs. Paschal never wastes a crumb, as you know, my lady. Shall I pour?"

"Oh, no, Dolly and I can manage it. Thank you, Russell. Are these yesterday's or today's papers?"

"A mixture, my lady. As you'll see."

"Then I think we're well taken care of. Please, let Lady Della know where we are when she awakens."

"I will, my lady. Just ring if you need anything."

"Della's still asleep?" Charles asked as the men left.

"I think our Adele was reading a book very late into the night, for I noticed her light burning," Tory explained. "She so reminds me of Beth. Always losing herself in a romance novel. Or else running off on a horse into the woods as she did yesterday. That's how she came upon this strange prince, you see. He's purchased land nearby and is doing it up. Apparently, he found Adele and her dog wandering alone near the turning for the river. That river is very dangerous, Charles, and there are sections with swift currents and very sharp rocks. People have died in those waters! I've told her not to go there, but the girl never listens."

"Was no one with her?"

"You ask that as if I can control a young lady with ideas! Wait until your Georgianna grows up, my dear. You'll see. Beth was the same. She'd gallivant off on her horse without telling a soul where she planned to go. Of course, we had inner circle men following her most of the time, but even Elizabeth sometimes slipped the net and grew lost in those woods. They can be quite dangerous."

"Della's in her room?" he asked, suddenly worried. With tales of bears, Gypsies, deadly streams, and now mysterious woods, he needed to see her for himself.

"Yes, but let her sleep a little longer, Charles. She had a difficult day."

"I'd rather make sure she's all right, if you don't mind, Tory. Where's her suite?"

"Well, if you insist, ask Russell to show you, or one of the parlour maids. We don't have nearly as many servants as you, of course, but it's enough that I forget names, particularly if they're new. We've already lost several of our young ladies to Prince Ara. I think he charms them, if you ask me. Seems he's hiring half the village lately. And all to renovate that haunted abbey."

"He's bought an *abbey?*" he asked. The very word had dark associations to Sinclair, reminding him of the blood-soaked transformation chamber beneath the ruins of St. Arilda's near Branham.

"Yes. The locals call it *le lieu fantôme.*"

"The ghost place?" he echoed, his fingers beginning to tingle in that all too familiar manner. "That isn't reassuring."

"It's just a name, Charles, and no one believes those old stories," Victoria told him.

"Oh, but I believe them!" Dolly interjected as she spread raspberry jam on a chocolate-filled croissant. "St. Rosaline's has a very dark reputation, Charles. I suppose, the monks were all right, but after they abandoned the place, it became a haunt for all manner of creatures. I've experienced some very strange things whilst walking through those woods. It's why Dickie and I always go round it now. Oh, these are really good, Tory! You must get our cook the recipe."

"I'm sure Mrs. Paschal will be happy to send it back with you, but you mustn't give Charles the wrong impression. Rational people don't believe those old legends," Victoria said, casting a disapproving eye at Dolly. "I suppose that sort of ruin is bound to have a ghost story or two, but all that will likely change now. Even the villagers approve of this new prince. Unlike most of the begging royalty that've come streaming out of the Carpathians in the past two decades, this one seems to have a great deal of money. He's certainly sparing no expense to renovate the abbey. Russell goes into Goussainville frequently, and he tells me even the local priest is impressed. Of course, their congregation have suffered two tragedies of late. A brother and sister, both found dead not far from the river. A man camping nearby was arrested. You see, it's humans who cause most of the evil in this world. We cannot always lay the blame on ghosts and demons."

"Who investigated their deaths?" asked Sinclair, the tingling increasing and slowly moving from fingers to forearms.

"A policeman from Sarcelles called here to ask if we knew the children or had seen anyone loitering about. I can't remember his name. Obviously French, of course. I'm sure Russell kept his card. We'd seen no one, but Dolly, didn't you and Dickie lose several sheep?"

"Yes, but we often do when the Travellers are making their way through. They're drawn to this area, probably because of all the open land."

"And this new prince you met is Romanian? As are the Gypsies. Might they be drawn to him as well?"

"I suppose so. Charles, you sound like you're conducting a police interview. Are you troubled by this person?"

"Only doing my job, Tory. I'm your protector, and I take my job seriously. What's this prince's name?" he asked her.

"Oh, it's one of those Romanian tongue-twisters," Tory began. "Aretshee... Arutsuh... Oh, I can't remember. Dolly, can you? You and Dickie know him far better than I."

"It's Aretstikapha Araqiel von Siebenbürgen," Dolly answered, pouring a cup of coffee. "Dickie's bank helped him with the purchase, Charles. Ara's certainly a handsome man, though very odd. But then most European royalty are odd, don't you think?"

"Distressingly odd?" asked the former policeman.

"Odd in the usual way, I suppose," Dolly answered, adding cream to her cup. "Coffee, Charles?"

"No, I want to see Adele first."

"I can't say that surprises me. You have a natural gift of parenting," his aunt told him. "Go see her and when you come back down, we'll talk further. I'm so very glad you're visiting."

"As am I," he said, kissing her cheek.

"Prince Ara will certainly be pleased to learn you're here," said Dolly. "He's expressed a keen interest in meeting you."

"An interest in me? Why?" he asked, pausing at the entrance to the house.

"Oh, everyone's interested in you, darling!" laughed Dolly. "Go on up, Charles. But hurry, before Tory and I eat all these lovely croissants."

Charles left to find Adele, learning her apartment occupied two floors of the northeastern turret. Victoria refused to install gas at the château, believing it spoilt the natural ambience of the old castle. The duke therefore climbed up a candlelit passage that took him through an old staircase that curved round and round, upwards like a spiral. The anticlockwise steps reminded Charles of his childhood—

something he'd long ago forgotten, save in nightmares, but even now the memory lay in darkness.

What was it? A journey into an old attic space? A forest of disused boxes and toys that held a secret? A figural clock with a mounted king—and a... A Dragon?

Pausing at the top of the staircase, Charles had a momentary flash of crystal clear memory that transported him back in time to the singular, life-defining moment when he'd discovered the obsidian mirror at Rose House.

Dawn of his fifth birthday. The day his father died.

Hello, boy. Shall we play?

A shiver of ice ran along the nerves of his arms and back, and Sinclair felt as though his entire body had shrunk to that of a five-year-old. Two fiery eyes stared at him from within a swirling black surface. An ancient mirror.

The hideous voice bid him enter.

Come, boy. Come and play. This is where you belong! You will rule just as your ancestor did! You need only cross through the glass and claim your crown!

The duke leaned heavily against the cool stone of the tower stairway, his heart hammering like a crazed blacksmith upon an anvil. This caused a ringing in his ears, and he clapped his hands against the sides of his head to stop the dreadful sound; to force the clanging noise to end—the grating, snarling, *tempting* voice to cease!

He could feel himself pulled closer to the waiting portal. Feel the Dragon's hot breath upon his face. The cold surface of the mirror—and then, *he felt his hand pass though it, followed by his arm... his foot... and then... and then...*

"Cousin Charles?" a small voice spoke from somewhere in another time and place. He felt a warm sensation on his cold fingertips, and pressure along the wrist, as though someone had taken his hand. The Dragon? Had he crossed over into the mirror world?

"Charles? Cousin Charles?" the small voice asked plaintively. Then its tone altered into frank worry, calling out in a whisper, "*Father?*"

Those two syllables cut through all the noise, all the fear, all the dark memories, and the duke's eyes popped open to reality. The brightness of Adele's sweet face banished the forbidding darkness of the Dragon's realm, but the unexpected rush of relief nearly caused him to collapse. Falling to his knees before her, the distraught duke tried to cover his weakness by embracing her, but the boundless love within her slender arms caused him to weep, as though he were the child, and she the adult.

"Hello, little one," he managed to whisper as she wiped his bearded cheeks. "How I've missed you."

Della covered his face with kisses, and Charles lifted her up, using the wall to steady himself as he regained his feet. It seemed that her strength transferred to him, almost like the passing of fire. He was reminded of that same sensation with Georgianna in the terrifying Stone Realms, when she had revived him.

"Are you all right?" asked Adele, completely unaware of the spiritual attack her dearest friend had just faced. "I thought I heard someone coming up the stairs, and then a voice inside my head whispered your name. I never imagined it was really you, though. We'd not expected you until later, or even tomorrow. Oh, I'm so very glad you're here!"

She showered him with more kisses, and Sinclair relished every one. Finally, the duke set her down and kissed her soft cheek. "Thank you, Della. Thank you so much. You mean more to me than you'll ever know, darling. It is often the women in my life who lead me through darkness, and you've just done that. Thank you."

"Have I? You're very pale. Are you ill?"

"No, darling, just tired."

"Then, you must rest," she declared. "Have you eaten?"

"Not yet. Breakfast is laid downstairs, though. Tory mentioned your plans to watercolour this morning."

"Yes, but I may do it tomorrow, now you're here. I'm so very glad you've come early! I've missed you so much!"

"And I've missed you, little one. Oh, but wait! Wait just a minute. Let me see," he said with a proud smile. "Has my little cousin grown taller? It seems to me that you scarcely reached my elbow when you left England, yet now you're rapidly approaching my shoulder. How is that? Does French air agree with you, or have you been drinking from some faery spring?"

Adele began to laugh, her voice like tinkling bells. "Oh, no! I've merely grown as all young ladies must, Cousin Charles. But I could stop, if you think I should."

"I should never stand in the way of a young lady's duties. If you must grow, then you must grow. But truly, are you taller?" he asked seriously. "Has Tory measured you lately? I'm sure you're taller by an inch or more."

"I have grown an inch and *a half* since my last measurement, which was done by Madam du Monde when she made my dress for your wedding," she declared proudly, taking his hand as they walked. "Tory keeps a diary with all my vital information. She says I'm in a growing spurt, but when I reach her height, I must stop."

"An inch and half in only five months? Sounds painful."

"I think it happens while I'm sleeping, but I can sometimes feel sharp pains in my shins. It's my bones stretching, so Dolly says."

He smiled. "Yes, I remember those pains. I grew very quickly, too. I was always the tallest in my age group at school, and I grew six inches in just fourteen months when I was about your age. Height runs in our family. I wonder how tall you'll be?" he mused as she led him towards her apartment.

"Much taller than Aunt Victoria, I think. Perhaps, as tall as Dolly. She's almost six feet tall. Come in!"

They entered her apartment through a panelled white door, beyond which stood a three-room suite painted in stripes of cream and pink, with pale yellow roses as accents. The bed had an arched canopy with gossamer drapes at the corners, and a brass and crystal chandelier hung from the coffered ceiling. Two walls held pedimented bookcases, their shelves filled with recent novels in several languages, French and English histories, botany and animal studies, books on military campaigns, and a section crammed with biographies. A set of matched bookends, iron cast in the shape of rampant lions, contained Della's current school books, which she showed to her guest proudly.

"I promised Auntie Tory that I'd keep to my lessons whilst here, and a tutor comes each Friday to mark my books. I'm working on Latin and Greek, and my history's on the Punic and Gallic wars. Rather boring, actually, but it helps with my classics. Also, I'm reading German faery tales in the original language and a little poetry as well as several novels written in French. That was my idea. I told M'sieur Roubolet that fiction would be a very good way to expand one's vocabulary. See? I've begun reading Jules Verne, just like Cousin Beth. You can tell her I've bought her a new copy of *Vingt Mille Lieues sous les Mers,* since her old one disappeared. I always think of you as Captain Nemo when I read it. Though I don't think you look lonely. Not really."

"No? Perhaps, that's because I have you and Beth in my life now, Della. And it's very thoughtful of you to buy the book for Elizabeth. I'm impressed with the scope of your studies, but why no mathematics?"

She laughed. "M'sieur Roubolet's not very proficient at maths, though he tries. I thought I might work with you. I'm doing algebraic equations on my own just now. They're rather easy, actually. I hoped you might help me to advance to something more difficult, perhaps calculus."

"Now you're speaking my language, little one. We'll spend an entire day in the reassuring world of numbers, shall we? Oh, Della, it is so good to see you!" he exclaimed, lifting her up into his arms once more. "You're growing so quickly, it will be difficult to do this soon. In fact, you may not want me to carry you at all. I hope I'm not being condescending, darling, but I so love it when you giggle like that."

Della laughed and laughed, happier than she'd been in many weeks. "You are staying a long time, I hope?"

"I am here for two days, and then you and I—and perhaps Tory, if we can persuade her—are all going back to England. Is that all right?"

"Oh, it is very all right!" she exclaimed, hugging him tightly. "And may I stay with you and Beth again? Paul's married now, you know, and he'll want time alone."

"You may stay with us for all your life, if you want. Now, I have to work a little whilst here. A bit of business in Paris, but you can join me, if you wish. I'm to visit a colleague at the Sûreté tomorrow morning."

"Is it involving a crime?" she asked.

"Yes, and I could use a good detective. Are you available?"

"Of course, Commissioner. I shall be Dr. Watson to your Holmes."

"Perhaps, it will be the other way round," he laughed. "Now, let's join Tory and Dolly on the lawn, and you can tell me all about Parisian life."

Approximately fifteen miles to the west, as the raven flies, a voluptuous woman rose from her bed, her red hair mussed. She wore nothing at all and took no care to don a robe, despite the fact that she wasn't alone. She turned back to the large, four-poster bed, squinting unhappily as the mid-morning sun stuck her pupils. In response, she pulled the heavy drapes shut.

"How I hate that insolent ball of fire, but I cannot avoid his rays today, I fear. For today, is the one we've longed for, Brother. Our prey has arrived," she told the sleeper. "Time to rise. Get up, get up!"

Prince Araqiel's left eye slowly opened, and his arms moved slightly as he sluggishly came to life. The muscled chest began to expand with a deep breath, followed by a lengthy sigh. "Ah!" he exhaled with satisfaction. "What a lovely night. Must it end, my dear? I so enjoy this ritual of sleeping; drifting into a pleasant oblivion as one rides upon a sea of possibilities! It is a beautiful gift wasted on humans. I wonder if the children of Adam realise just how lucky they are to experience it?"

"They require it, Ara. Unlike you, who uses it as an escape," the woman answered, tugging at the satin quilts. "Now, get up and let us prepare. Did you not hear me? *He is here.* I can feel his presence, can't you?"

"Must you always shut the drapes?" complained the handsome sleeper. "I am forever waking in a darkened room. Not everyone hates the sun, my dear. Some of us actually draw energy from its powerful rays."

"I refuse to play your games, Ara. Rise. Our king is here."

"Who?" he asked lazily. "I thought I was your king, my green-eyed sister."

"I refer to our human king, as you well know. The perfect blood. Charles Sinclair has come to our ground. Our land, where we have the power! He's fallen into our web like a tasty little fly, so let us wrap him up before he sails back to England."

"You're always in such a rush. Why is that? I spent many long years inside the lower realms. You know very well how much I detested those chattering birds, particularly that meddlesome gatekeeper. Why did you let him out? He's done nothing to advance our plans, indeed he nearly cost us access to Branham with all his little games. Now do go away, Eluna. I should like to sleep another day or two."

She moved back to the bed, leaning over to kiss him on the mouth, her copper tresses spilling across his bare chest. "It's you who loves the sunlight, my brother, so arise and greet it! Besides, today is the first of May. It is your favourite, no? There is much to enjoy in this world of human civilisation, sweet one, but sleep is not one of them. One cannot feed or plan or plot whilst asleep. You waste time in such idle pursuits."

"You may not plot or plan or dream in the land of Nod, but I do, sweet sister. As I float upon a changing sea, I discern much more than you know."

"What I know is that we must call on Lady Victoria before our king leaves. You entice the girl, whilst I take our chosen one."

Grudgingly, the prince sat up in the enormous bed, his long hair falling in gleaming ringlets over broad, muscled shoulders. "There is no rush."

"But he may leave tonight!"

"He will not. Sinclair will remain at least two days. I have foreseen it in these useless dreams of mine. Lunetta, your desire for a hasty victory will be your downfall. Hasty plans are doomed to failure."

"You act as if we have all eternity, Ara. I assure you, we do not. Am I not the one who's lived here since the great deluge? The one who's walked amongst these besuited apes?"

He laughed at her comparison of men to monkeys. "Besuited apes! Now, that is amusing. But I see your point, beloved. Have you forgotten that 'twas I who wandered the lower realms without light? All on my own, without you to shine upon me? Alone in a living darkness?"

"Of course, I know that, Ara, which is why you crave the sun. Didn't I release Uriens to help you escape? Come now, let us dress and make ready."

"Must we rush? Another month will not matter. We can sail to England and take the king there," he whispered huskily. "What is it about Sinclair that so incites your senses? I begin to think there is more to your plans than overturning the old order. Have you fallen in love with this boy?"

"He is no longer a boy, Ara. Charles Sinclair has grown into a rather splendid man."

"If you say so. But what charms can a human offer that I cannot? Am I not adequate to the task?" He pulled away the quilted coverlet, revealing himself to her, his body demonstrating enflamed desire with no equivocation.

"Stop showing off," she complained, covering him up again. "I'm not comparing you to Charles Sinclair. No one compares to you in that category, my love, but it's vital that we ensnare his soul, is it not? That requires time, meaning we must begin now."

"Your plan assumes his soul can be ensnared."

"Do you doubt it? Sinclair is the chosen one! His blood is the result of millennia of work! There is no alternate plan, my darling. We must ensnare him, else you and I will lose our places in the council. Do you want your younger brethren to rule over you? Ara, my darling," she said, sitting beside him, "I would erase all that happened to you, all those years hidden below, and I can do it—WE can do it—but only if we follow the plan. The machine can unmake the past, but it requires him to ignite it."

"Ah, yes, the machine. Tell me, Lunette, is this my plan or yours? It was so very long ago, I sometimes forget," he asked her slyly.

"It is *yours*, my love," came her careful reply.

"Mine? Why then do I sense someone else's guiding hand behind your actions. One attached to a scheming heart? Must I imprison Saraqael before his time? Is it he who would take my place? Sleep in my bed?"

"Sara is nothing, and no other guides my hand," she said, kissing his palm. "We need the boy. Only you can bring him to us."

"It may not be as easy as you think. The boy is bright, and he has determined friends. Particularly that great giant who broke my claw. That hurt, I'll have you know."

"Yes, sweet one, I know it hurt," she said, kissing his fingers, "but you had healed by nightfall. And Sinclair is bright, because we designed him that way. We needn't worry about his annoying band of friends here, Ara. You take the girl. Leave the man to me."

"But he *was* left to you, and you failed miserably. Remember? Why you even mixed an aphrodisiac into his champagne, but still Sinclair spurned your advances. I may have been confined to the Stone Realms, but I saw your failures through the *asaru* stones, Sister. You were never out of my sight. I saw each of your attempts to entice Sinclair, but he refused you time and time again, didn't he? Even when you threatened to tell his wife you'd conceived his child!" the prince laughed. "Did you really expect him to believe that lie?"

"Many other men would have," she answered.

"Yes, many would. In fact, most would, but this Sinclair is different. He took his marriage vows seriously. Though he'd fallen out of love with that Amelia creature, he still refused to cheat on her. How, then, will you entice him into your bed whilst he's married to this enchanting duchess; the woman of his dreams, eh? She is indeed a beauty. I used to watch her through the stones, and when she wandered the realms, I often walked beside her. I can see why Trent lusted after her. I should very much like to take her myself."

"Stop it!" she scolded him. "That feeble human has nothing to offer Charles that I cannot."

"Really? You offer only failure."

"Not this time," she crowed. "This time, I know his type, and I shall use a more tempting skin. I've already tried it, and he responded slightly. Just a small change here and there, and I shall test his will again."

"And how many tests do you plan to try?"

She threw a vase at him, which he skillfully caught with his left hand.

"I hate you sometimes!" she shouted.

"Yes, I'm aware of that," he laughed, setting the vase on a table. "Which skin is this that nearly enticed him? Show me."

"No."

"Don't pout," he told her, pulling her close. "Show me your new body."

"Very well." Her material form grew indistinct and liquefied into a cloud of nebulous smoke, and as it took shape again, the red hair turned dark, the eyes shifted from green to deep brown, and the body contorted until it settled into a new silhouette with more rounded assets and longer legs

"Well? Do you like the new me?" she asked, teasing his nose with a lock of the thick tresses.

"Lovely. It's been a long time since you used raven hair. But why this pattern? Is it known to him?"

"It is similar to that of his wife. I saw the desire in his eyes when we spoke on the ship."

"You are a vision, Eluna, but must I repeat myself? If Sinclair would not betray a wife he did not love, then he will never betray this one. Other human men will line up to please you, buy your furs and jewells, but not this one."

"Perhaps, I imitate his precious duchess completely, then," Eluna said, transforming into a perfect copy of Elizabeth.

Araqiel's eyes ran over her new body, finding it tempting indeed. "If this is how she looks in life, I can see why he's bonded to her."

The prince placed his arms round the nude facsimile. "Come, join me in dreams once more."

She slapped him hard, immediately snapping back to her usual look. "You are a devil!"

"As are you."

"He'll come to me begging, and then you'll regret your insults, Ara!"

"Perhaps," he answered, returning to the bed. "But time is our enemy. It is at the heart of all. I seem to recall this Gévaudan having a rather fine voice. Perhaps, you could return to the stage as a different singer. Does he appreciate music?"

"A little. Charles did enjoy my singing when I was Antoinette. He kissed me once, you know. Our king has a very supple mouth. Like kissing the softest velvet or a dewy rose."

Araqiel laughed. "Only you would describe a human in such terms, Eluna Valerina! You are too romantic about these evolved apes. Very well, let's visit this paragon of manhood. Tell me, do I call you Eluna today, or is there another name you prefer?"

"Perhaps, I reveal my true name to him, Brother. Would you like me to speak it? Remember what happened the last time that name was voiced."

He pulled her to him with great force, biting her lower lip and drawing blood; then he kissed her mouth passionately. "You will speak nothing that I do not allow, and you will do as I say, Eluna. Nothing more, nothing less. This territory may have been yours for a few years..."

"Centuries," she corrected, wiping the warm blood from her mouth. "It has been mine for centuries."

"Regardless, it is *my* land now that I am awake. And once we have entrapped this king, I shall return the world to its former glory. The beginning from the end, the end from the beginning. Past, present, and future reshaped to suit *my* needs. The Crucible of Time will be reset, my Sister-Wife, and once Sinclair's blood has served its purpose and powered the machine, you may use his body as you wish."

"Gladly," she whispered, biting his ear lobe. "Now, dress, but take care to look more English than Romanian. That is the mistake Raziel and Saraqael made. Where is the little troublemaker, by the way?"

"Which?" he laughed as he rang for one of the servants.

"Saraqael, of course. I know where Raza is. Assuming you've not freed him, of course."

"Why would 1 do that? I so enjoy his company," the prince smiled. "Our brother is quite attentive in his obsidian prison. He hangs upon my every word. As for Sara, my gargoyles tell me he's flitted off to Russia. Apparently, he's become enamoured with some spiritualist named Helena Blavatsky, and together they're visiting a Russian mystic. Gregory Rasputin. I think it a waste of time, but Sara's convinced this youth will play a role in the future war to come. If there is a future, of course. Now, my dear, let us put on finery to please our very important Englishman and then make our way to Château Rothesay."

"No, no, Paris, my love."

"Paris? But he is at Victoria Stuart's home, is he not?"

"Yes, but tomorrow morning he goes to Paris, a city of infinite possibilities, and one that dances to my tune. He's reserved a suite at the *Hotel Terminus*. The royal suite, in fact. Shall we have a bet?"

Ara smiled, his dragon eyes glinting red. "You lost the last time we bet, Eluna. Are you sure you wish to do this?"

"Yes," she boldly declared.

"And the wager?"

"That I am asleep in that suite's bed by midnight tomorrow."

"Or what? I've no need of money, if that is your stake."

She laughed at the word 'stake'. "How funny you would use that word, my brother! If only you knew the legends about stakes and our kind."

"Is it incorrect? I am still learning this awkward English tongue. May we not speak the old language?"

"No, you must speak English as if born to it. Let me think. If I fail in my task, then I promise to let you sleep for one month, and I shan't wake you."

He smiled, the lips sliding into a crooked grin. "Is that so? An entire month? A full rotation of my glorious Luna? Very well. I accept, but with one addition. If you fail, then you agree to participate in my plan, no matter what I ask."

She hesitated, assessing a thousand possible reasons why he might make such a condition. *What is he plotting?* "Very well. I shall sleep in one of his bedchambers by tomorrow midnight."

"With him in your bed," Ara added.

"That was not the bet!"

"Oh, but it is," he ordered her, twisting her left wrist. "Say it!"

"Yes, of course!" she cried out. "With him in my bed."

He kissed the wrist, erasing her pain. "Good. Now, leave me. I wish to bathe."

She departed the chamber, passing the uniformed valet, who bowed obsequiously. Eluna continued down, down, down the carved stone steps until she reached the lowest crypt. She needed no torch to see, for Eluna's bright eyes saw perfectly well in darkness. The dank room held many large rectangular boxes, but the most spectacularly decorated dominated a large room near the back of the labyrinth.

Eluna had shaken off the dark hair and eyes, returning to her usual form. She laughed as she sat beside the coffin. "Raza, can you hear?" she asked the box.

A minor shaking of the obsidian was her answer.

"Good. Our plan is working, my love. Ara thinks me his obedient kitten, but the ancient lioness will soon feed upon his flesh. Sleep but a little, and I shall free you. Ara thinks his machine will trap Sinclair, but he is wrong. The machine will trap *him*."

The box emitted a moaning sound, and she stroked the sides, weeping into the bejewelled wood and volcanic glass. "My poor, poor Raziel! My beloved scribe. Writer of poems and king of mountains. Sleep but a little more, and I shall free you. And then, you may seek vengeance upon Araqiel and his Dragon brothers. And as a reward, I shall bathe you with silver, my love. And together, we will bring the world of men crashing down to ruin."

CHAPTER TWELVE
9:10 am - Pembroke House – Branham

"Do come in, won't you, Lord Aubrey? Mrs. K., will you bring us a tray of refreshments, please? Tea for me. Branham Blend, if we have any left. Aubrey, what works for you?" he asked the earl.

"Coffee, if it's no trouble."

"Oh, Branham Blend tea sounds quite nice, thank you!" Martin Kepelheim told their host.

"I've been outdoors this morning," the baronet explained as he led them through a wide hallway, and towards an open set of French doors. "It's a lovely spring day, and I thought I'd read a book whilst awaiting your arrival, you see. When a chap retires, he has to fill the time with something, and reading keeps the brain cells active. Do have a seat, won't you? Ketchum will bring everything out in a moment."

They'd emerged onto the north lawn of the manor house. Eastward, the fifty-acre estate rambled towards the edge of town and Henry's Woods. Twixt the house and Branham Village, rose tall towers of tumbledown limestone, perched high upon what looked like a manmade hill or motte. The visitors chose comfortable chairs round the table, close to their host.

Paul pointed towards the ruin. "You're practically in Queen Eleanor's backyard, Simon."

"So I am!" laughed the jocular baronet. "As I told you at Christmas, there's a warren of ancient tunnels that runs from my rose garden all the way into Eleanor's old fortress. Well, into what's left of it, that is. I imagine it was a magnificent château once. Our second King Henry spared no expense to please his French queen back then. Oh, he was enamoured with her, as were most men. Eleanor was a beauty! Have you seen the portraits? I've always thought she resembled the late Duchess Patricia. Long, slender throat, high cheekbones, pale eyes, and mounds of thick blonde tresses. But her beauty was only half her power, for she controlled the Aquitaine, which was the key to controlling France. I expect the castle Henry built her was magnificent once. You can make out the ruins of a pair of French turrets, there at the two corners. There are even blue slate roofing tiles, that hang on for dear life whenever the east winds pick up. I sometimes find them in my yard after a storm. The place is home to nothing but bats and badgers now. More's the pity." Pembroke grew silent, almost as if he'd become lost in reverie.

"Your letter sounded urgent, Simon," prompted the earl.

"Oh, yes, the letter! My old noggin's not what it once was," he said, tapping his head. "I'm so glad you received it. Do forgive me for summoning you without preamble, gentlemen. It isn't my way to force myself into people's lives; particularly lives as busy as yours, but I didn't know what else to do, you see."

"Do about what?" asked the earl.

"I don't mean to be secretive, Lord Aubrey, but allow me to explain once Ketchum's brought out the refreshments. Both she and her husband have worked for me over fifteen years, but I'd prefer even they didn't overhear what I have to tell you. Call me mad, but it sometimes seems that my old house has very large ears, which is why I thought we might speak out here. Something about the sunshine makes this matter seem less dark, if you get my meaning."

Kepelheim's eyes were upon the gardens, alive with early spring colour. Tender red leaves had sprouted on the rose bushes, along with the inevitable thorns. Hedges had taken on shimmers of rustling green, and beneath these lurked handfuls of bashful violets and cheerful crocuses. Long lines of brightly coloured tulips drew the eye towards the original springhouse, used now as a garden folly. And beside the crumbling structure, sang a cheerful chorus of delicate snowdrops, blue anemone, and yellow daffodils; each blossom waving its delicate petals in the morning breeze as if to say hello.

Paul noticed very little of the garden, for his mind was focused on the baronet's mention of a need for secrecy. "You speak troublesome words for such a beautiful day, Simon. Why would you suggest your house has ears? If you think yourself watched, are you sure the staff are trustworthy?"

"As trustworthy as the sun itself, sir. Indeed, moreso! I'd expect the sun to fail rising and the globe to stop spinning before Mrs. K. would betray me. She's loyal as my old hunting dog, though you mustn't let her hear that comparison. And her husband is doubly faithful. No, they're right as rain and just as welcome."

"Then what makes you think you're watched?"

"Because I am!" he exclaimed, his plump cheeks grown red. He leaned in to whisper to the men, his voice tense. "There are certain things which I've never spoken aloud to anyone. Things I've discovered in writing. I'll explain in a moment." He looked up, his voice louder. "Ah, here's our repast, and it looks quite delicious!"

The two servants had joined them on the lawn, each carrying a large wooden tray. The woman, who served as both housekeeper and cook, began unloading items to the table.

"Coffee's in here, sirs, and Mr. K's got the tea. It's the last of the Branham Blend, Sir Simon. We'll need to ask Mrs. Stephens at the hall to mix us up some more. Oh, and I've put your morning pills on your saucer," she told Pembroke. "Now, there's cream and milk along with sugar. And we've biscuits, jam tarts, and those little cakes you like. Fruit and cheese, o' course. I can make fry-ups as well, if anyone's still hungry. The cheese is Stilton, sir. I hope that's all right; it's all we have at present."

"Stilton's always welcome, my dear Mrs. K. And there's no need for anything hot to eat. Not yet. Thank you, both. Now, if you'll allow us to chat alone, we'd appreciate it. I'll ring the bell if we need anything else."

"Very good, sir." Both Ketchums left, shutting the French doors.

The three men sat at a square table, covered in a white linen cloth, and Aubrey poured tea and coffee for the older men. "Beth used to make me do this when we'd play tea party," he laughed. "She insisted I learn to pour properly. It's somewhat humbling to have a child teach you a trade."

"Our little duchess knows how to do all things well," Martin agreed. "And she's a willing teacher."

"I hope I was a willing student."

Paul returned to his chair, stirring one cube of sugar and a splash of cream into his coffee. Martin added four cubes of sugar and milk to his cup of tea and selected several biscuits along with a slice of orange cake to start the day.

"You do everything with finesse and elegant mastery, Lord Aubrey," the tailor told his friend. And whilst I enjoy sitting out here with the colour of the meadows and field all round, perhaps we might hear why you sent so puzzling a letter to Duke Charles, but posted it to me."

"Ah, yes, that," replied Pembroke with a little grunt. "Damn this gout! Makes a man want to scream! But the letter. I'd never have sent it unless circumstances were dire, you understand. Haimsbury's a very busy man, and though we're neighbours, I respect his time and talents. You see, it's because of the visit."

"Our visit in December?" asked Aubrey.

"No, not that one. The other one. The visit I received two days ago. Most puzzling man I've ever met! And I think I may know his name, though he never gave it to me. He matched a description of a very odd fellow connected to that Blackstone Exploration Society poor old Collie worked with. I'm not implying the society itself had anything to do with Collie's death, mind you, but this man had a very disagreeable air about him. And he practically threatened me!"

The two visitors exchanged wary glances. Martin leaned forward slightly as he stirred his tea. "Can you describe him to us?"

"Easily, and I imagine Mrs. K. would add her own colourful descriptors, if you ask her. Thin to the point of emaciation, a face like a corpse, dressed all in black, and with the most somnolently punctuated voice I've ever heard. It was as though he trained in theatre somewhere and wanted to place me into one of those Mesmer trances. A very queer fellow!"

"He gave no name at all?" asked the earl.

"None, but he left me a book. He said it belonged to Collie and wanted to return it. Honestly, I've been to Africa, South America, China, even Greenland, but nothing else has ever so utterly chilled me as that man's expression!"

"What exactly did he say to you, Sir Simon?" enquired Martin.

"I've not the best memory, not any longer, but that conversation is fixed upon my brain cells as though chiseled in stone. Here's what occurred, and I advise you to speak with Mrs. K. as well, for she spoke with the man briefly at the door. Twas, oh, two in the afternoon, I think, when she called me from my library. I'd been napping as it happens. I often do in the afternoons. It's ageing, you know. You're far too young to understand, Aubrey, but Martin might. Now,

I confess I was a bit out of sorts, when the man first came into the room; still getting my bearings, you might say. However, it took no time at all to realise what a peculiar fellow he was! He asked if this were the house where Colonel Collinwood stayed last year, and I affirmed as much. And then he asked whether or not Collie had received any post to this address. As it happened he often did; some from old friends, others from a distant relative. A nephew, I think. But he also received letters postmarked Vienna, and these always caused him to start drinking heavily. Collie wasn't a drunkard, of course. Hardly, but the man did have a tendency to embibe rather too much when melancholy. Due to the war, I should think. I didn't mention these Austrian letters to my caller, for I assumed they were from an old flame of Collie's, for it was a woman's hand on the envelope. Flowery sort of writing, I mean, with flourishes and all that. I did tell this gentleman about Collinwood's other missives, without revealing these last ones. But the fellow didn't believe me. He actually called me a liar!"

"He said that?" asked Aubrey. "He used the word liar?"

"Well, no, not that precise word. Let me see if I can recall his phrase—I think it was something like, 'Might your memory be misleading you?' or some such twaddle. And he sneered when he said it! The fellow actually, *sneered!* But here it goes very oddly, sirs. If his visit weren't peculiar enough already, this scarecrow of a man asked me if Collie had stored any items in the house. He asked after a box. I assumed he meant the large casket we'd taken down to the cellar."

"The one that disappeared?" asked the earl.

"Yes. Have you found it, by any chance?"

"Not a sign," Aubrey replied. "Simon, are you saying this strange man wanted to know about that sarcophagus?"

"Yes, that's the word! Collie called it that as well. Sarcophagus. A box for eating bodies. Rather disquieting thought. Well, I replied that none of Collie's possessions remained in the house, for I didn't trust the fellow, you see. And I'd no intention of mentioning the sarcophagus. For all I knew, he'd stolen it and killed my friend as well as poor Peterson. Then, he asked if Collie left anything in his rooms. Had he secreted anything at all? A trinket from the digs? A statue perhaps? Parts of a statue? This last question—about the statue, I mean—had a sort of hidden insinuation to it, and I instantly knew this was why the man stood before me. He was looking for a statue! Well, I said no, for at that moment, I knew nothing of any statue. The man stared at me for a very long time—seemed like eternity, if you must know, and I nearly fainted from fright!—but when he'd finished, he tipped his peculiarly tall stovepipe hat and left the same way he'd come. But here it gets even stranger," whispered the plump baronet. "As soon as he left my study, I dashed after to see what sort of coach he'd taken. Whether hired or perhaps from Branham's mews. I prayed it wasn't the last, but I knew the duchess had allowed that infernal Blackstone lot to dig beneath the hall's grounds, so it was a possibility."

"And was it a Branham coach?" asked the earl.

"It was not. Nor was it a hired coach, for my friends, there was no coach there. As you know, the drive to my home is long and wide, and you can see departing coaches for many minutes before they return to the main road. But I saw no horses, no coach, not stick nor sign of humanity that didn't belong. In less than a minute, this man had simply vanished into the aether!"

The three men sat in silence, and Pembroke took his pill, washing it down with half a cup of tea. He nibbled nervously on a slice of cake, his eyes on the ruins of Queen Eleanor's castle. Overhead, a flock of ravens circled slowly, as though watching the trio. And within the garden, a badger stared from near the old spring house, its unnaturally human eyes fixed upon the earl.

"You were right to alert us, Simon. It is a very strange story," Kepelheim said at last, breaking the uncomfortable silence. "Have you spoken with Constable Tower about it?"

"No, sir. Tower's a fine young man but wet behind the ears, if you get my meaning. He'd not know how to deal with this. It's more up your street, Aubrey. Yours and your cousin's. I take it, the duke is unavailable?"

"He's in France at present, visiting our aunt and my sister. Or that's the pleasant side of his trip. He's also meeting with the local authorities about the deaths here last Christmas. The Sûreté have reported seeing a man answering Lionel Wentworth's description in Paris. I offered to go, but the duke insisted on handling it personally."

"And he's well?"

"Yes, he's quite well. It's kind of you to ask."

Pembroke gulped loudly, and the badger stepped closer, its black nose in the air, wide-set ears twitching.

"It isn't that I ask to be polite," replied the baronet, wiping his face with a white kerchief. "I ask, sir, because of the book that fellow left here. Why he insisted on doing so is mysterious, but perhaps, he intended it as a warning."

"A warning for whom?" asked Aubrey.

"Oh, it's obvious when you examine it closely! I must say, when I noticed it, I thought my old heart would finally give out."

Martin's eyes rounded. "And that would be the world's loss, my friend. I wonder, may we see the book?"

"Oh, yes! It's in the library, locked in my safe. But I'll be pickled if I can read it. It's in some language unknown to me with letters that defy translation. However, there a few words that appear over and over, and they are in English, sir. As though these have no translation into this other language. When you see the book, it will chill you just as it chilled me. Wait here a moment, and I'll get it for you."

The baronet left to fetch the mysterious book, stumbling on the bandaged foot and nearly pulling the table cloth with him as he stood, for it had somehow attached itself to his watch chain. With Kepelheim's help, the chain was disengaged without damage, and Sir Simon trundled off to the library, muttering the entire way.

Paul kept an eye on the badger, but his manner was deceptively carefree. He stretched out in his chair, yawning. "Do we stay at Branham tonight, or return to London?"

"I think we should stay, my friend," replied the tailor, who found the earl's question odd. Paul rarely engaged in casual conversation. Nearly every movement and word had meaning.

"Branham would be quite relaxing," he told the earl. "Might we stay a day or two and stroll through the pavilions before the crowds descend? We both brought a few items in a bag, but I could send to my valet for more—as could you, if you had a valet, that is," he added, smiling.

The ravens flew lower, their lazy circle made up of thirty-three birds. The badger glanced up at the avian formation, standing on his hind legs and signalling with his paws.

Paul gave no reply, and Martin continued. "Perhaps, Lady Aubrey could join us? I'm sure Cordelia would enjoy a long visit with

Elizabeth, and I'd love to play a round of chess with Riga. What do you say?"

Aubrey poured a second cup of coffee. "I think it's a marvellous idea. Delia needs time away from London, and I may be able to convince her mother to stay behind and decorate Aubrey House."

"Or continue her pursuit of Lord Brackamore, eh?" Martin teased. "I'm sure she thought herself clever, but Constance Wychwright's methods were almost as loud as her dress."

Stuart sighed. "Such is the price of love, Martin. When you marry the woman of your dreams, her nightmare family comes with the bargain." He leaned close, whispering to Kepelheim, his head turned away from the badger. "Keep your voice low. We're being watched."

"Ah, that explains it, then."

"We'll talk more freely after we leave, but I do think staying at Branham is a good idea. If Flint came here, then it's possible he and other members of that infernal Blackstone group keep watch on Beth. This visit strikes me as intentional. Like a dare—or a lure."

"The visit from Albus Flint, you mean?"

"You got that, too? Simon's description fits Flint perfectly. I've never really trusted that walking corpse. And turning up this close to the fête feels contrived. I'm not happy about this, Martin. Not happy at all."

"No, neither am I, which is why we should send for all our troops and circle round our duchess. You know, Paul, I'd like to see these tunnels, if you think I'd fit. I've reviewed all of Seth Holloway's sketches, but nothing substitutes for personal inspection."

"It's quite close down there, Martin. Are you sure you can handle it?"

"Oh, yes. It wouldn't be my first trip into the lower levels of Redwing's madmen."

"I pray it isn't your last."

"As do I."

The baronet returned, his face flushed and moist, and he puffed as he walked. "Here now," he said, sitting once more, careful to keep his watch chain away from the table cloth. "It appears to belong to the Blackstone group. There on the cover, you can see their strange monogram. I've never been able to fathom it, but I noticed the same burnished image on Collie's journal. He kept all his private notes in it."

The earl took the book. It was made from black leather, approximately one-inch thick, and filled with pages made of vellum, overwritten in black ink. The cover was stamped with the image of two golden trees, one upon the other. The bottom tree's branches pointed downwards and were covered in red fruit, whilst the top tree's branches reached into the sky and were bare and dead looking. A horizontal line divided the upper and lower trees. Circling these twin trees, was a golden snake, eating its own tail, and written upon the snake's body were a series of Roman numerals.

"What does it mean?" asked Pembroke.

"You saw this same image on the other books? Collinwood had one?"

"Oh, yes, and the Oxford men as well. They would sit and compare notes each evening over drinks. I always left them to it, for it was none of my business. Now, I jolly well wish I'd listened!"

Martin shook his head uneasily. "This symbol is used by *Die Herren von Schwarzenstein*, Lord Aubrey. It represents their warped view of the world. They see the lower world as Eden, and the upper as dead."

"Die Herren von Schwarzenstein? Lords of the Black Stone?" asked the earl. "I remember my father mentioning it a few times. Didn't you infiltrate that group some years ago?"

"I did, and I nearly paid for it with my life. May we keep this, Sir Simon?"

"Please, do! I've no wish to have the thing in my house, if you must know. And I also have Collie's letters. The ones I refused to mention to this devilish man. His name's Flint, by the way. Albus Flint."

"We'd assumed as much," Aubrey answered, "but how did you deduce that, Simon?"

"It was Mrs. K., actually. She gets about the village more than I, and she'd heard Danny Stephens over at The Abbot's Ghost public house mention the man. Apparently, he passed through there a few times and left quite an impression on our landlord."

"I met Flint just the once," Aubrey explained, "but he leaves a permanent impression on one's memory. The duchess has dealt with him several times. She has little good to say about him, but we'd assumed his organisation legitimate. Sadly, it's all turned out very badly. Another hard lesson learnt. Yes, we'll take anything left here by Colonel Collinwood, if you're willing to trust us with it."

"Oh, thank you! I really don't want them here. I'd already boxed everything up in hopes you'd be willing to do that," the baronet said, standing once more.

The strangely-eyed badger glanced up at the ravens again, who left their circular formation and began to split up; some heading towards London, others towards the sea.

Within the hour, Aubrey and Kepelheim had stored three boxes of material in their coach, along with the black book. As they entered the interior to leave for Branham, Martin removed the leather volume from the topmost box.

"You know, Pembroke mentioned finding words in here, written in English. I got the impression it was these caused him to write to Charles, but in our haste we forgot to ask him what those words were."

"Open it," urged Aubrey as the carriage moved eastward towards Branham village.

Martin unwound the leather tie which kept the book shut. It made a cracking sound as he turned back the cover. The pages had an aged look to the vellum, as though very old, but the skin was supple. "I wonder if this is sheep vellum? It has an unusual, velvety texture. Oh, I see what Simon meant."

Paul sat forward. "What?"

Martin turned the book round so the earl could see the writing. Amongst a collection of unintelligible symbols, written in red ink, over and over, were the words 'Sinclair', 'Paris', and 'Machine'.

CHAPTER THIRTEEN

7:39 pm – Millbank House, Goussainville

"Won't you sit?" asked Dolly Patterson-Smythe of her two guests. "Dickie's taking Charles on a tour of the grounds, and Adele's searching for music to play. That's why we're in here. It's the only room with a piano, aside from the ballroom, of course, but that room needs a good cleaning. It's been months since we had a ball. Do sit, Your Highnesses. It was so good of you to accept my last-minute invitation. I'd remembered you indicated a desire to meet Duke Charles. As it turns out, he wants to meet you, too. Isn't it lovely how life works out?"

Araqiel wore elegant evening clothes, looking like any other European gentleman: black wool trousers and cutaway coat, white waistcoat, and a white silk tie, which he'd wrapped several times before tying it—a Romanian touch in defiance of his sister.

Eluna had reverted to her normal appearance, green eyes and auburn hair. A ruby gown decorated with tiny winks of diamond dust drew every eye her way, and she'd brazenly worn no gloves. Her copper hair was swept into curls at the crown of her head, making her seem even taller, rivalling Dolly's five feet, eleven inches.

"Oh, you both look simply dazzling!" Dolly told her. Patterson-Smythe had chosen a sleeveless gold and black gown with an empire waist, which played up her wheat-coloured hair, and elbow length gloves covered her arms. "Your hands are beautiful," she told Eluna. "Hands always tell the truth about a woman, don't you think? Yours are so soft looking. May I touch them?" she asked.

The princess put out her arm. "But of course."

Dolly removed her own gloves and tossed them onto a chair. "I've never cared for wearing gloves anyway. You're so smart!" She stroked the back of the princess's right hand. "Oh, my, your skin's like the softest velvet. However do you keep your hands so soft?"

"Blood," the woman replied without batting an eye.

Dolly's face paled. "Did you say blood?"

Eluna laughed. "That is right, no?" She turned to her brother, asking a question in Romanian. He laughed and offered their hostess an explanation.

"My sister means milk, my dear friend. Not blood. Her English is still growing. Every day, we try to add new words and phrases. In Romania, we speak of the blood of many things and creatures. Eluna has called milk 'the life blood of cows' since a child. I explained it to her."

They all took seats along the windows of the music room, but Ara helped Dolly to hers first. Adele entered the room, and he immediately stood, bowing and then kissing her palm.

"Ah, my dear friend! The beautiful Lady Adele of Briarcliff Castle. Shall we hear you play this evening?"

Della smiled, thrilled at his endearments and gallantry. He treated her as a young woman, not a child.

"Yes, Highness, and I'm delighted to share some of my favourite music. One is a piece I struggled for months to master. I hope it reminds you of your homeland."

"I am sure your hands will play it perfectly," he said, bowing once more.

Charles and Dickie Patterson-Smythe entered then, and the latter reached for von Siebenbürgen's hand, shaking it firmly. "Good to see you again, Your Highness. As you can see, we've made a few changes to our home. Millbank's been in the family for years and needed an update. I'll show you the new reflecting pool later. It's always prettiest when the moon's out, I think."

Eluna stepped close and kissed the banker's cheek. "It is kind of you to invite us, Sir Richard. And I, too, love the moon upon the waters. A union of light and the primordial mother, no? The moon is much older than the sun. It is—how you say...?" she asked her brother returning to a long string of Romanian.

"I believe the word you search for is progenitor," he told her. "Is that right, my old friend, Sir Richard?"

"The moon's a progenitor? Not sure," the banker answered. "Do you mean its the sun's parent? Is that an old Romanian myth?"

Victoria had entered the room now, and all the men bowed. "Myths?" she asked. "Did I hear you mention myths, Dickie? Charles, will you help me to that green chair by the fire? All that walking about has left me quite exhausted!"

"You should be in a wheeled chair," he reminded her. "I can bring one back from Paris."

"We'll discuss that later. Now, tell us, what myths are we discussing?"

"Let's all find chairs, shall we?" asked Sir Richard. "We'll be casual this evening. It's our cook's night off, but she made us a lovely spread of cold meats and cheeses to tide us over. She always takes Wednesdays off, as we rarely have company mid-week. I do hope it's all right."

"Perfectly all right," the prince assured his host, still standing. "You are Duke Charles, I take it?"

"Oh, allow me," Patterson-Smythe interrupted. "I'd forgotten you'd never met. Prince Araqiel, this is Duke Charles of Haimsbury. Duke, may I introduce His Highness, Prince Aretstikapha Araqiel Hunyadi von Siebenbürgen. Did I get that right, Highness?"

"Perfect," the prince said with a bright smile as he shook Sinclair's hand. "Duke Charles, it is a very great honour. I've read much of you in the French and English press. I understand your background is in police work. Tell me, how does a policeman become a duke? Or is it the other way round?"

"Shall we sir?" Dickie suggested again. The men took chairs near Tory and Eluna, whilst Adele arranged music on the piano-forte's filigreed stand. Sinclair sat closest to her, the better to keep watch. He had signed the adoption papers that very day, after discussing it with Tory, and he wondered when would be the best time to tell her.

"Your police work?" the prince reminded him. "How did you find yourself investigating crime, Your Grace?"

"Ah, yes, that," the duke muttered disarmingly.

He had to be careful not to reveal too much, but say enough to keep this newcomer talking. Araqiel bore a resemblance to Raziel and Samael, and Charles wondered if this so-called 'prince' were another supernatural creature. If so, he had no intention of allowing this intruder to influence his new daughter, but he had to discover just what the prince wanted. To do so, required bait. If not Adele, then he'd have to provide it.

Perhaps, he could use the sister's obvious interest in him.

"One might say it found me, actually. I'll not get into my long history, but I studied mathematics at Cambridge. An acquaintance thought my way of examining the world was a good fit for police work, and he was right. I entered as a constable for the Met just after leaving Trinity."

"Trinity?" asked the prince. "I thought you said Cambridge?"

Sinclair smiled, wondering inwardly if the prince were pretending ignorance of English traditions. "Cambridge is a university with many colleges within it. Trinity is an old school, established by King Henry VIII in 1546. Actually, the old king very nearly scrubbed the universities from the face of the earth, along with Catholic churches and abbeys, but Queen Catherine Parr convinced him to make his own mark on them instead. So he combined several existing colleges into Trinity."

"Ah, I see. These colleges are religious?"

"Not as religious as they once were, no, but we still hold to certain traditions. The name, of course, refers to the triune God. The Almighty, who created all beings, including those beings we call angels."

Von Siebenbürgen's impassive face flinched for half a second. "The Almighty," he answered. "It is a suggestive title, no? Is this Creator actually all powerful? I wonder sometimes. Look how much evil this world holds. How war races across your continents like ants upon a hill. My sister and I have seen these wars up close, in our own lands. Russian troops ran like water upon our mountains, shooting their guns and exploding our homes with their dynamite. Forgive me, if I find it difficult to believe in this omnipotent being."

Charles took a moment to answer, and he sensed the others were waiting, perhaps hoping he would say nothing to offend the wealthy prince. Sinclair noticed Eluna's eyes never left his face, and something about her manner struck him as familiar. The way she held her chin? Or was it her posture?

"Belief is unnecessary to reality, Your Highness. I may not believe in Romania, for I've never seen it; yet here you are. Existence is an absolute, a constant, not a relative or unknown factor."

Von Siebenbürgen smiled, his sapphire eyes glittering. "I would contend that all we experience, all we take for granted as fact, is but an illusion. How say your mathematics to that? Must all numbers add up to the same, over and over? Or might there be alternative answers? Even alternative realms?"

"You begin to sound like a spiritualist, Prince."

Eluna jumped into the conversation, leaning towards her twin. "Spiritualism is an exciting prospect, is it not, Duke? You appear to believe in a Creator God, but didn't that same God evict humans from their rightful place? Adam was meant to be the ruler of Eden, yet he was unceremoniously thrown into a harsh and unyielding world. No, I would say it was the spiritual realm which lies just beyond this one that kept Adam alive during those early years. These angels you mentioned. Why shouldn't today's modern men and women seek advice from those same spirits?"

"Because we are commanded not to do so, Princess. That is why."

She waved her hand in protest. "Which means this selfish and uncaring Creator, whom you follow so blindly, evicts you again! Why, it is my belief that with spiritual tutelage, even the dead could rise again."

Adele had made her way to Charles's chair, and she took his hand. "Must we engage in philosophical debate, Cousin Charles? Perhaps, a song would allow everyone to smile again."

Sinclair kissed her hand, reminded of life's true joys: family and friends. "You're right, little one. And it is your wisdom which must rule this evening. Do play for us, and we foolish adults will listen as you teach us."

She laughed. "You always make me feel very important. Thank you."

"And you make me feel as if I can do anything," he told her. "What have you chosen to play first?"

She returned to the piano-forte and sat upon the padded bench. "I thought to honour our guests, I would play music from their homeland. I do hope this music won't cause you any harm, Cousin Charles, for one selection is the song I'd asked you to help me play last year at Uncle James's castle."

Sinclair recalled the spell which Lorena MacKey had cast upon him that night, reminding him of her previous alliance with Redwing. He prayed she'd truly changed. Her letters seemed contrite, but witches can lie so easily.

He glanced at Princess Eluna. *Is she a witch or something more? Something older?*

"What song is that?" he asked, pretending not to remember.

"The Gypsy number," she told him. "The *czárdás*. It's called *Czárdás Macabre*, and it's by Mr. Franz Liszt. I confess my playing could use improvement on some parts, but I think my left hand is finally keeping up with my right. Shall I?"

Dolly clapped her hands eagerly. "Oh, yes, please! I've heard you practising this, Della, and you have mastered it. Prince Ara, you and your sister will be surprised. Play, Della. We'll all listen, and then after your concert, we'll eat."

Adele took a deep breath, inwardly a bit nervous, but she noticed Charles beaming with pride, and she found her courage rising at so simple a thing as his love. She smiled, thinking of what he'd told her earlier. He had a surprise for her, and he'd tell her all about it when they returned home to the château. What might that surprise be?

She placed her long-fingered hands upon the ivory and ebony keyboard and commenced the first passages of the difficult piece. The notes of Liszt's impressionistic dance evoked mystery and a whirling sense of Dervish delight. The Romanians listened attentively, and Araqiel fixed his gaze upon her in a way similar to how a young man might, when admiring a fair lady—or perhaps, more accurately, the way a predator might gaze upon his prey. Either way, Charles formed a very negative impression about this so-called prince, and he thanked God for bringing him to France at this critical time. Della was in danger, and he had no intention of allowing anyone to bring her harm.

The concert continued with three more selections, each as difficult as the first, and when the final chord rang within the great room's coffered ceiling, Charles was the first to rise to his feet, shouting *Brava!* and *Well done!*

Adele took several bows and then crossed the room to offer a personal curtsy to the Romanian royals. "I hope it pleased you, Your Highnesses."

The prince took her hand once again and kissed its palm. "No other musician has ever moved me so, my dear friend. Thank you for sharing your talent with us. Now, as our hostess Lady Dolly has commanded we eat, then may I escort you to the table?"

The *almost* twelve-year-old looked to Sinclair. "Is it all right?"

He nodded to be polite, but then followed by offering to escort Princess Eluna. As they adjourned to the nearby drawing room, where a buffet feast had been laid, Charles recalled the first time he'd shared a meal with the Stuart clan. It had been at Duke James's London home, and it was he who took the hand of eleven-year-old Elizabeth. The idea that this prince might be assuming the same, protective role as he did with Beth sent waves of worry throughout his spirit. He'd taken the young duchess's hand in the same way, and later he'd married her.

Was Araqiel making a play for the child that Charles now called daughter?

Not on my watch, he thought darkly. If he had to find a way to slay this rebel prince, then he'd do it. No one would harm his family.

No one.

CHAPTER FOURTEEN
2nd May, 1889 - Préfecture de Police, Île de la Cité, Paris

Charles stared out the tall window at the city below. The building that housed the Parisian equivalent to London's Metropolitan Police dominated one corner of the *Place Louis Lépine*, next door to the *Hôtel-Dieu* hospital, at *One Rue de Lutéce*. The palatial Police Prefecture building offered enviable views of both banks of the Seine, as well as Notre Dame Cathedral, providing a breathtaking panorama of the city's leading landmarks. Most of the resident police officers spoke passable English, but Sinclair appreciated Adele's ability to navigate the language's subtleties without a misstep. She'd aided the duke in a somewhat tense exchange with a uniformed doorman, a *gardien* named Gaston, who insisted he knew of no division called Criminal Forensics, and that Sûreté Chief Marie-François Goron worked from an entirely different location. Charles had politely said he knew as much, but was expected at this address. He then showed his ICI warrant card as well as his CID card, which listed him as Commissioner of Intelligence for England's Home Office. Still, the stubborn man refused to allow the duke and his friend to enter.

Then, Adele sweetly asked if she and her father might tour the facility, for the Prefecture was quite famous in England, and she wished to write about it for her school work. The man, as it turned out, had a daughter Adele's age, and he softened considerably at her simple request, suggesting she speak with the head of Paris investigations, Prefect Henri-August Lozé. And so, thanks to the child whom he had just adopted, Charles now waited in said prefect's spacious office, as Adele sat nearby.

"Pacing won't make him arrive any more quickly," the girl told him plainly.

"Will it not?" he asked, turning and offering her a smile. "I suppose your brother's pacing habit has transferred to me. That was very quick thinking downstairs. You're very clever, little one."

"Cleverness is an inherited trait," she answered proudly. "Meaning, I take after my new father, right?"

He nodded. "Very right."

"Is this visit about a murder? I read about three very similar murders in the papers. One man and two women, each found chopped up inside a leather portmanteau. It's all very grisly."

"So it sounds. It's not about those exactly, but regarding a related crime, and also something to do with Branham. Do you remember how Lord Paynton arrived at the hall last Christmas? How he'd been seriously wounded in the tunnels beneath the grounds?"

"Of course, I do," she told him without hesitation. "Seth is rather handsome and very nice, don't you think?"

He laughed, leaving the sunlit window to sit beside her. "Is he? I'd not noticed. Are fathers supposed to notice?"

"Perhaps, not," she informed him seriously. "Only ladies and mothers notice, I suppose. Mr. Holloway is doing better, I hope? Beth—I mean Mother—talks about him in her letters sometimes. May I call her Mother?"

"Of course, and I know she'll love hearing it. You are happy, I hope?"

"If happiness means feeling like I'm walking on clouds, then yes," she laughed. "Honestly, it's like a wonderful dream. I hope I don't awaken and learn it's all imagination."

"No chance of that. Tell me, though, what does your mother say in her letters? About Mr. Holloway, I mean?" he asked, hoping his jealousy didn't show.

"Only that he's painting her portrait. But it's supposed to be a surprise for your birthday. Never mind. Pretend I didn't say it. Do you like him, Father?"

"Of course, though I've not really spent much time with him. He and Dr. MacAlpin have become good friends, and he's helping Martin with that puzzle room of mine."

"Dr. Holloway or Dr. MacAlpin?"

"Well, both in a way."

"I don't understand. Are you saying Dr. Holloway's what brings you to Paris?"

"No, dear," he said, bending down and tweaking her petite nose, "*you're* what brings me to Paris, but whilst here I'd like to find whoever hurt Holloway and also murdered Peter Patterson, the Cambridge student. We think it might be the third man from Cambridge, Lionel Wentworth. Chief Goron says Wentworth was seen in Paris last week and suggested I meet him here."

She puzzled over this, finally saying, "And you worry about us because of it, I suppose?"

He took her hands. "Of course, I do. If Tory could travel, I'd have insisted you both return to England at once, but as she cannot, I've come to fetch you."

"Because you prefer to watch over us yourself. Yes, I know, and I love you for it. It's what makes you such a good father."

She had just kissed his cheek again, when the door opened to two men: One was uniformed, tall and clean-shaven with glasses and smelled of pipe tobacco. His slightly shorter companion was dressed in a double-breasted suit and sported a thick waxed moustache and beard, which covered most of his face. The short man reached out to shake the duke's hand.

"Welcome to Paris, Your Grace," he said in a thick accent. "I am Henri-August Lozé. Goron told me of your plan to visit us, but we thought you would come tomorrow. Forgive Gardien Gaston. He is told to discourage all foreign visitors. With the Exposition beginning this week, we are flooded with them."

"We took no offence, Prefect Luzé. It's good of you to make time for us. Chief Goron, it's a pleasure to see you again. Gentlemen, allow me to introduce my delightful young cousin, and newly adopted daughter, Lady Adele Stuart. Her brother is Lord Aubrey. Adele is my assistant today."

Both men bowed, and Goron kissed her hand. "A very great pleasure, Lady Adele. Your new father is a most excellent investigator, and we pray you and he will offer us solutions to our many puzzles. It's been what, ten years since we last met, Duke Charles?"

"It was ten in February," Haimsbury told the inspector. "You joined our investigation as a raw recruit, as I recall, Chief Goron. New to the force, but both Morehouse and I found your approach and insights inspiring—and on once occasion, somewhat shaming! I'm delighted to see the Sûreté agrees with that estimation and made you its chief."

"*Merci, mon ami*, but we never solved those crimes, eh? A pity."

"No, we did not," Charles recalled, the memories of those very strange few days rolling back into his brain: The peculiar party on the outskirts of Paris, Antoinette Gévaudan's overt and persistent attempts to seduce him into adultery; then, someone drugging him— perhaps she, perhaps an accomplice—his confusion the following morning and poor memory, followed by an abrupt return to England the next day. Bob Morehouse had never really explained his reasons for abandoning the partnership with French authorities, but his last confession, written the night of his murder, implied a long connexion to Redwing. Perhaps, he'd been under their control even then.

Seeing the passing flash of dismay on his visitor's face, Goron offered condolences. "Forgive me, my friend. Truly, we mourn with you over the loss of Chief Superintendent Morehouse. A very great man, whose death came too soon."

"Yes, thank you," was all Charles could manage. He noticed Adele took his hand, somehow sensing his need for comfort. He glanced down and offered her a grateful smile.

Goron moved back to current crime. "My friend, is it possible these new murders are related to the old deaths? With the upcoming Exposition, our city is filled with strangers from all countries, all walks of life. And we find ourselves facing a new rash of murderous attacks. Not every three days as before, but random—though with certain similarities to those in '79."

The chief turned to Della, saying, "My lady, in a nearby office is a large map which details a mysterious string of disappearances that began five years ago and continue to defy all explanation. I am told you have a gift for interpretation of evidence. I should like your opinion on this map and how these events might fit together. If a pattern emerges, no? My assistant, Major Dufour, will show you, if you wish to help."

Adele laughed. "I'd be pleased to help, Chief Goron, but I suspect you actually wish to discuss crime on your own. Would you come down, please, Father?" she whispered to Sinclair, crooking her index finger. He bent low, and she whispered into his ear, "I don't mind, but you must promise to catch me up on everything later, all right, Holmes? I love you," she added, and then kissed him.

The adolescent left to find the major, and Goron shut the door. "She is a precious one," he told Sinclair. "It is no wonder you adopt her, eh? Do sit, Your Grace. Would you care for tea? Espresso? *Café au lait?*"

"We ate earlier and had coffee with croissants after checking into our hotel. I'm fine, thank you."

"A hotel? But your family's château is less than an hour's drive," noted Luzé.

"Yes, but there are many important items on my list today that must be done in Paris. And I've promised to take Della to see the Louvre, and tonight we're attending *La Traviata* at the *Théâtre de Champs-Élysées* at nine."

"Ah, with the talented Mademoiselle Adelina Patti as Violetta, no? Get there early if you wish to find a good seat, Your Grace. Hers is the greatest voice of our age," declared Prefect Luzé. "The city bustles with thousands of visitors and exhibitors, and nearly all love opera, my friend. Though the Exposition does not open until the sixth, we are already full to the brim of the cup! Some are drawn to our night life, I fear, which so often brings them to our door. But now I leave you and Goron to talk, sir. My office is yours so long as you require it. Chief, let my secretary know if you require anything."

The prefect bowed and left, and Goron took the chair behind the large desk. "Please, sit, my friend. Now, we may talk freely."

"Yes," replied the duke as he took the chair opposite. "You wired that Wentworth has been seen."

"So he has. Many times, and always in the company of individuals involved with our criminal ranks. I speak of Redwing, of course."

Charles blinked. "You know about them?"

"*Oui*, but only last year, have I learnt this. When I took over as chief of the Sûreté, I found many notes, left by my predecessor, which I've had to confirm with him in private. These flitting birds bring much evil to us, I think."

"Very much evil, François. You mentioned spying on Wentworth in Montmartre, and that he is seldom there alone. Who keeps him company?"

"He runs with questionable businessmen, known to flock with the Redwing crows. Criminal bankers. Those who roost amongst the crowded streets of Montmartre, but also reside in the finest noble houses. A great prince is the latest to attract his notice."

"A prince?"

"*Oui*. That is so. From Romania, or perhaps it is Transylvania. Tall, long dark hair."

"Is his name Alexei Grigor, or do you speak of von Siebenbürgen?"

"It might be either. Grigor appears in my files often, along with a son. Prince Rasarit."

"Have you seen or heard from either Grigor prince lately? Has Rasarit appeared in company with Wentworth?"

"We have no news of the son for many months. But the Exposition brings carrion crows from all nations, my friend. Americans, Russians, Germans, even high-rolling gamblers from Arabia and Turkey. Alexei Grigor met with nearly thirty influential men, only a few months ago. In December. Since that meeting, we've had an increase in murders. Three have the same design."

"The portmanteau bodies?" Charles asked.

"*Oui*. Not all the remains have been found. Only the head and hands are in the bags."

"Where are the bags discovered?"

"All near or along the *rive gauche*. The south side of the Seine. These are similar to your embankment killings, I think."

"They might be, but I'd appreciate seeing your files."

"Of course. I have made copies for you, but also copies of something else my predecessor left me. It is the real reason I had to speak with you in private. I wish to tell you a story which I do not think you will like, my friend. It involves you and your cousin, the Lord Aubrey. You might say I inherited—how you say?—a 'hot potato', and I have waited until a day when we might discuss it face to face. Man to man."

Charles appeared puzzled. "Are you telling me your telegram was a ruse to discuss this inherited problem?"

"Not completely, but I think this problem is somehow connected to these Redwing sightings as well."

"But they also connect to my cousin? Why? How?"

"I hope I am wrong, but I think, this is news that your new daughter should not hear, for it involves Lord Aubrey and the Lady Adele's birth mother."

CHAPTER FIFTEEN
2nd May - 10:03 am - Glasgow

The offices of Finlayson & Fleming had stood proudly on the corner of Maxwell and Hamilton Streets, Glasgow, for over a hundred years. Angus Fleming had taken over the practice from his father ten years earlier, and Rufus Finlayson from his the year after that. It was the latter man who now sat at the head of an oak conference table, peering over metal spectacles at Patrick MacAllen, the grandson of the late Major General Richard Patrick Andrew MacAllen II, 8th Earl of Granddach. On the opposite side of the table sat James Stuart, 10th Duke of Drummond, and both men looked now to the lawyer as they waited.

"Lord Granddach," Finlayson began, addressing the younger man and heir to the title, "the will your late grandfather left is quite straightforward."

"Good!" declared MacAllen impatiently.

"If I may, sir?" the lawyer scolded him gently. "I am required to read all the bequests. As I said, the legal language is typical, naming you as heir, bequeathing all entailed lands, titles, and deeds to you, sir." MacAllen started to interrupt again, but sensing it, Finlayson plunged in first. "*Of course*," he cautioned his audience, "the entail requires that all lands and attached monies remain the property of the Granddach Trust, but that is usual in these matters."

"They don't belong to me?"

"Titles and entailed lands never truly belong to the heir, my lord. If I may continue? Good. I must inform you, sir, there is one small proviso to your grandfather's will. It states that you must marry and produce a male heir within five years of taking the title, otherwise, your grandfather states that all titles and lands, as well as associated monies and trusts, revert to the secondary beneficiary, which would be, as of this date, I believe, your nephew, Your Grace," he said, looking to Drummond, "which I assume means the Earl of Aubrey. Is that correct?"

The duke shook his head. "No longer, Mr. Finlayson. Now, the closer relative is my elder nephew, Duke Charles of Haimsbury. Paul is third cousin to the MacAllens, but Charles is first cousin, and he's older by four-and-a-half months. I'm sure you recall the matter, Mr. Finlayson. I believe your partner handled some of the paperwork for my man, Ian Fitzgerald of Dunwaddy Street."

The lawyer nodded, his head bobbing like a woodpecker's.

"Yes, yes, of course. How could I forget, sir? It was not that long ago either, and of course, the marquess is now a duke. Wonderful news, finding your nephew again. Quite wonderful. Lord Granddach, is this stipulation clear to you? It is all spellt out at length in the will, of course, and you are free to have it overlooked by any legal representative of your choosing. We shall remit copies to you both, of course."

Patrick MacAllen looked as though he could spit nails. "You are telling me that I must marry and have a son before this blasted will is in full effect?"

"No, no, not at all, sir! That would hardly seem fair, now would it? No, as of this moment, you are the recognised and legal title holder, and as I said, you have access to the estate and grounds at your pleasure. However, since the entail requires that all lands and titles remain in family hands, your grandfather merely includes this proviso. Surely, you will marry and have children soon, will you not? You are, if I may say so, a handsome man with a good government job. I'm sure eligible peerage ladies will flock to your side, if you seek them out. So, there it is. Now, Your Grace, I also have a letter for you from your old war comrade, and he asked that I hand it to you personally."

The lawyer produced an unsealed blue envelope, typewritten on the outside. "You will see your name here, sir, and inside is a second, sealed envelope which contains instructions from the late earl. If you would sign here in acknowledgment of receipt?" The duke signed a short form and put the envelope into his coat pocket.

The lawyer nodded with satisfaction, his spectacles rattling as he did so and nearly spilling off his thin nose. "Now, if neither of you has any questions—oh, wait! Dear me, I very nearly forgot. There is the small matter of the dowry."

Patrick's face was all attention. "Dowry?"

"Yes, yes, well, your grandfather wanted to make certain that you had the odd bit of cash as needed, and much of the estate's bank deposits reside in your grandmother's dowry, you see. It amounts to a sizeable sum. The late earl deposited half in a London bank and invested the balance after he married your grandmother. The deposit accrues interest each year, and the investment account's done very well in the intervening years," he said, glancing through his precariously placed spectacles at a detailed balance sheet. "Yes, yes, the deposit account balance currently stands at just over half a million pounds, the interest of which will be dispersed into the trust's management account. The investment portion has continued to rise, its current total is—and this was as of last September, when the annual audit was completed—just under two million pounds."

The new earl's face broke out into a great grin, and he fairly bounced in his chair. "The total's two-and-a-half million? Now, that is a surprise. Good old Grandpa. He always could pick a winner, when it came to horses."

"I am glad the news pleases you, Lord Granddach, but to be clear, as the dowry comes under the entail, proceeds from investment do as well. When you marry and produce an heir—within the required five years, of course—then my instructions are to release the entire amount to you at that time. However, until such time, you may draw against the bank interest."

"Draw? Do you mean I have to borrow it?"

"Yes, sir, but one might see it as borrowing against your own future income. Of course, all financial decisions regarding the accounts will be administered by the estate's trustee."

Patrick glowered at the little lawyer, and a discerning man might actually see metaphorical smoke rising out of the new earl's ears. "Do you mean to say that I must beg some mealy-mouthed little lawyer for my monthly allowance? That is preposterous!"

"Well, uh, no, sir. In fact, your grandfather named someone outside our offices as trustee. It is the duke, sir," he said, nodding towards Drummond.

James Stuart's face lit up. "Is that so, Mr. Finlayson? Well, now, isn't that a pretty kettle o' fish?"

The lawyer's head bobbed even more rapidly now. "It is, sir, it is. If you will sign here, accepting the position, then we may dispense with further legalities."

The duke signed, his dark eyes bright. "Well, Patrick, this is quite a surprise to us both. I'll be leaving in an hour to return to London, but since you live and work there as well, I imagine I'll be seeing you often in the coming weeks." Standing, the duke shook the lawyer's hand. "Thank you, Mr. Finlayson. Offer my thanks to your partner, Mr. Fleming, as well. I pray his gout improves soon. Patrick, enjoy your new title."

The disappointed earl managed a bleak smile, but quickly turned to the lawyer as soon as the duke had left. "How do I break this will?"

The lawyer's small grey eyes blinked behind the thick lenses. "Break it, sir? No, I—well, I'm afraid it cannot be broken. It is a fair and ordinary will. Why should you wish to break it as its terms are favourable?"

"No reason. Whom do I see about the accounting?"

"Ah, well, that would be Mr. Parkinson, sir. Jacob Parkinson. His main offices are in Edinburgh, but he keeps a second office in London, on Tachbrook Street, Westminster. Near Vauxhall Bridge Road."

"Good. Very good," the earl said, taking a copy of the will in hand. "Excellent! Thank you, Finlayson. I'll be in touch."

"Yes, thank you, sir," the lawyer said, his hand aching from the young man's enthusiastic pumping. "A very happy day to you, sir."

As Drummond reached his coach, a burly man in a fine suit and grey homburg hat met him, handing the peer an umbrella. "It looks like rain, my lord," the larger man observed. "Did all go as you expected?"

The duke stepped into the coach, sitting across from a buxom woman with a pleasant face and dressed in green silk. The large gentleman followed, taking the empty spot beside the woman.

"I'll say it was a meeting filled with surprises, Mr. Baxter. As it happens, the late earl's grandson received a bit of bad news. He's apparently taking it out on his manservant, I see," Drummond added, pointing at the second large coach beside the curb, where Patrick MacAllen was berating another man. "Did you and he happen to strike up a conversation whilst I was inside?"

"Oh, they did, sir, and they talked a streak," the newly married Mrs. Baxter told the duke. "I'm not sure that young man's a servant, though, sir. He showed Neil a bit o' paper that looked like some sort o' warrant card."

Cornelius Baxter and Esther Alcorn had originally planned to marry in early May, but as the Branham fête drew nearer, it became clear to all that a quiet ceremony before Easter might prove easier to arrange. And so, on the eighth of April, the Stuart and Sinclair families celebrated two things: Duchess Elizabeth Sinclair's twenty-first birthday, and the marriage of Cornelius Treadwell Baxter to his lifelong friend and fellow servant, Esther Alice Alcorn. Duke Charles had offered to send the newlyweds anywhere they wished to go: France, Spain, Germany, even America. They need only name the destination.

Humbled by so grand a gesture, Esther responded with a small request. She wanted to see her childhood home again, the fishing village of Crovie near Castle Drummond. Though she'd left the village as a girl, Esther had fond memories of the seaside, and besides both her parents had been laid to rest there in St. Andrew's cemetery.

So it was, that Charles provided a wedding gift of five hundred pounds, which his uncle doubled. Duke James also provided the couple the use of his new private train, *The Royal Highlander*, and granted them full access to Drummond Lodge as their very own honeymoon cottage.

After learning of his friend's death, Drummond had wired the train's engineer to return to London and fetch him, bringing a bittersweet ending to the Baxter's honeymoon. Drummond and Granddach had served in dozens of Crimean military campaigns and sat at the same negotiating tables after the war. James's father had married MacAllen's elder sister Charlotte; the two men had practically grown up together, and it bothered James that Patrick MacAllen seemed to care so little about his grandfather. He did, in fact, seem thoroughly put out that he hadn't received a spendable compensation.

"I think you may be right about our new earl's servant, Mrs. Baxter," Drummond told Esther. "Patrick's rumoured to be the next head of Special Branch, but if he's already using police assets as personal body guards or worse as spies, then heads will roll, and I'll be the one to roll them!" He twirled his moustache thoughtfully as the coach pulled away. "So, Inspector Baxter, just what did this non-servant have to say?"

"I fear my wife is correct regarding the man's occupation, sir. He is, in fact, a certain Sergeant Garner. When I mentioned my involvement with the Intelligence Branch, the fellow grew somewhat less talkative. Prior to that, not realising I was with you, sir, the sergeant had much to say regarding Mr. MacAllen's influence in London. Sergeant Garner seemed to think the young gentleman inserts himself into many of the current investigations in which Duke Charles is involved. He did, in fact, mention the duke by name—several times, sir."

"Did he now? In what context?" asked Drummond as their coach moved forward.

"The fire last year at St. Katherine's docks for one. It seems Special Branch are calling it arson by a foreign power, and this Garner mentioned something else most curious, sir. He let drop the name Sir Clive Urquhart, a builder who dared to call on my lady last summer and seek funds from her. It seems this builder has filed a missing-person report on a woman, and he's named Lord Aubrey as a contact. The woman's father is a rich American, and has recently arrived in England to look for her."

"He's named Paul? What has my nephew to do with this missing American? And why would Clive Urquhart file the report?"

"Well, sir, according to Garner, Sir Clive named himself as the missing woman's sponsor. That she was the daughter of a friend, and he looked upon her with the affections of an uncle."

Drummond's face grew concerned. "Yes, I can just imagine what sort of affections that horrid little builder felt for a vulnerable young woman. So, did Sergeant Garner say if MacAllen found the girl? Did he give you a name?"

"No, sir, he did not, but he's taken the case to Commissioner Monro and asked him to summon Lord Aubrey for questioning. According to Garner, the commissioner has refused to do this, but now that Mr. MacAllen is the Earl of Granddach, his demands may be better received. The sergeant implied MacAllen intends to contact the Home Secretary personally and demand Aubrey be arrested."

"He'll regret that action, Mr. Baxter, or my name's not Stuart! Mark my words, this will turn ugly very quickly. Did you happen to get the missing woman's name?"

"Calabrese, sir. Cassandra Calabrese."

CHAPTER SIXTEEN
11:14 am - Whitechapel

Margaret Hansen checked a heart-shaped watch, she kept pinned to her skirts. She'd asked Ida to meet her at eleven o'clock, and it was nearly quarter past. What if the girl changed her mind? What if she informed the police? What if? What if? What if?

Meg pulled a black lace shawl up over her head, trying to disappear. She sat in the back of the Brown Bear Pub, praying no one would recognise her. She'd written to Ida as a last resort. Though she had no wish to endanger the former prostitute, Margaret felt certain her only chance to remain alive lay in finding a secure place to hide. Redwing members were dying weekly now, and many of their bodies had disappeared. She'd heard other things about the missing bodies; dark things, that they were being used in some sort of twisted ritual by the trickster Watcher, Saraqael. Others claimed the bodies were the vanguard of an army of corpses. Still others, that they provided ingredients for a hideous cannibal banquet.

Margaret had no wish to become part of such a devious scheme. But despite being careful, Margaret felt certain her days on this earth were numbered. Several times, she'd written to Lorena and Susanna, who now called herself Violet Stuart, asking if either woman might offer help, but their silence either meant they had none to offer, or else they had no wish to—or worse, that they, too, were dead. If she could only reach Charles Sinclair, Meg felt sure the duke would believe her. He'd always proven kind and a good listener, when he'd lived near her hotel. She feared putting anything else into writing. This time, she had to depend on a verbal message. A bridge of sorts, and Hansen prayed Ida would provide that bridge.

A tall woman had just entered the pub, her attire simple but chic. The strawberry blonde hair that had once enticed Hansen's clientele was now arranged in a simple chignon. A veiled hat covered the top half of Ida's face, and her hands were gloved demurely. Seeing Margaret, the well-dressed newcomer crossed to meet her. "I'm so sorry I'm late. I had trouble getting a cab."

"I wondered if you'd come at all, but I'm very glad you did," Hansen told Ida Ross Stanley. "You look so healthy now, Ida. I've never seen you looking so well."

Taking a chair opposite the brothel keeper, Ida offered a bright smile. "It's Elbert who's made the difference. He and the Haimsbury family, I mean. Bert and I lived in the duchess's dower house for a long while, and we married in March. Since then, Duke Charles makes sure we want for nothing. He even gave us a lovely little house not far from here. And I'm studying nursing, Mrs. Hansen. You know, Prince Anatole once told me that my future was bright. I had no idea what he meant by that, but now I can see it. Mrs. Hansen, you could have a bright future, also. I pray your letter means you want to get away from those awful men!"

"I want to, but I'm not sure I can," the older woman confessed, her hands shaking. "There's so much more binding me than ever burdened you, but if the duke would be willing to help me, then I'd tell him everything I know. Every detail about Redwing's plans. Have you any idea how to reach him? I dare not send him a letter. What would his servants think? Or his wife?"

"I'm sure the duchess would help you, too, Mrs. Hansen. She's ever so nice."

"She'd not want to help the likes of me," Margaret said, her hands twisting together. "Is the duke in London?"

"Elbert mentioned a trip to France, but I believe the duke's coming back for the Branham fête this Saturday. Elbert and I are going. Perhaps, you could go with us. Mrs. Hansen, the only way to leave the past behind is to take the first step on a new path. I know how difficult it is, but please, do it, before it's too late!"

Meg grew thoughtful, her eyes constantly sweeping the room for familiar faces from Redwing's membership. "Have you seen Lorena MacKey or Susanna Morgan?"

"I've not seen Morgan, but I overheard Prince Anatole speaking about MacKey once with Mr. Vasily."

"Anatole. He's another of those princes. I'm not sure they're to be trusted, Ida."

"I've only met Prince Anatole. Are there others?"

"Three that I know. Alexei Grigor, his son Rasarit, and Aleksandr Koshmar. I'm not even sure if any of them is actually human," Meg whispered tensely. "Oh, I've made such a mess of my life! If only I'd made different choices as a girl, but money seemed so easy to earn back then. A few hours on my back, a few lies; and in return, rich men gave me fancy dresses, perfumes, furs, and jewells. Just shut your eyes and let it happen." Her hands shook as she continued. "But later, when you get older, it's the rich men that shut their eyes, so they don't have to behold sagging skin and an imperfect body. And soon, even that stops, and they demand someone younger, prettier, or less expensive."

"Not all men are like that, Mrs. Hansen. My Elbert's not."

"I remember Mr. Stanley," she said, brightening for a moment. "A lovely man, and he always was a gentleman. He used to live at number twelve, but never once did he call on us as a customer. And he even tried to reform a few of my girls." Hansen passed a note to Ida. "I've written an address on this. Get it to the duke if you can. It's where I'll be until next Wednesday. I'm not going back to the Empress. Urquhart's lost control of Redwing, and I expect he'll be the next to die and then vanish. It's just a short step from him to me. Clive is part owner of the Empress, you see. His American backer is the other owner, and I hear he's come to England now. Oh, Ida, I'm terrified!"

Ida touched her friend's hand. "So was I, Mrs. Hansen, but you're not alone. You have many friends who want to help. Won't you come stay with us? We can watch after you until Duke Charles returns."

"No, I won't put you in danger. Just give Charles the note, please. That's all I ask, but," she added, emotion choking her voice, "if you would pray for me, that would be nice."

"Of course, we will! Elbert and I shall pray the Lord sends you help, Meg. But you must pray, too."

"He'd never hear me."

"Oh, but he would! He does!"

Hansen stood, touching the younger woman's face. "He certainly helped you, and I'm glad. I'm sorry for what Trent did to you for all those years, Ida. I never knew the true extent of it until just before he died. Remember to give the duke this note for me. I'll be at that address through next Wednesday."

"I promise. Talk to God, Meg. He's listening."

"I'll try. Thank you, Ida. If it's God's will, I'll see you again."

Hansen slipped quietly out the pub's side door and into the clattering sounds of Leman Street, her shawl shadowing her face.

Ida paid Hansen's bill and then walked the half block to the police station, where she met her husband. By four that afternoon, Elbert Stanley would be on a train.

CHAPTER SEVENTEEN
Prefecture de Police – Paris

"How can this information possibly involve Adele, François?" asked Sinclair.

Goron lit a brown cigarette. "I wish it did not, but there is no doubt. Allow me to explain," he said in his thick French accent. "When I assumed my duty as chief, I found many raveled threads, you might say. Twisted bits of yarn that seemed disconnect, you know?"

"Yes, I understand, but that's hardly unusual. The previous occupant often leaves unsolved cases for his successor."

Goron rose and walked to a portrait of Emperor Napoleon which hung on the wall to his left and then removed it. Behind the oil painting, stood a small dial safe, about one foot high and just as wide. He entered the combination. The open door revealed a lock box, which Goron removed. He secured the safe door, returned the painting to its prominent position, and then handed the box to Sinclair.

"Lozé was kind enough to let me keep this here. I give it to you. This is the key. Keep it and the box hidden, my friend, until you decide what to do with these troubling threads."

Charles unlocked the mysterious metal container. Within, he discovered file after file of criminal cases, most written or typed in French, but a few scribbles were in English. The investigating officers included names of over three dozen men; some from the Sûreté, others from the Stuart inner circle. He immediately recognised three names of circle agents: Sir Percy Smythe-Daniels, André Deniau, and Sir Thomas Galton. Haimsbury's French was sufficient to translate most of what he saw, and it seemed nearly every file contained a repetition of the same name, again and again: Cozette du Barroux, Adele's mother.

"What are these?" he asked Goron. "Why do I see familiar names listed? Some of these men work within my organisation."

"And the woman?" he asked, puffing the brown cigarette. "This du Barroux?"

"You've already surmised who she is, or else you'd not have given me these. I assume the answers are in these files."

"Speak to Deniau about them. He is one of your own men, no?"

"Yes, but..."

"But now you wonder if he can be trusted, eh?"

"I didn't say so. Why do you ask me about du Barroux?"

Goron paused. He'd worked with Sinclair only briefly in '79, but since the detective's rise to peerage and marriage, the newly titled duke's name and photograph had dominated front pages of Europe's press for months. Only when the most heinous crime occurred, or a major scandal erupt, did Sinclair and his beautiful duchess leave the headlines. As a result, Goron felt as though he knew Charles Sinclair rather well, and he'd developed a familiar attachment, whose root formed in '79, and blossomed further since '88. He wanted to help Sinclair, but doing so could put them both in serious danger.

"Well?" prompted the duke.

Sighing, Goron lit a second cigarette. "Do you smoke?"

"No," answered Sinclair. The seasoned investigator could read his friend's face, and what he saw there was *dread* not fear. "Just say it, François. It always helps to speak bad news quickly."

"Very well, but allow me to approach this bad news with delicacy. These files come from a secret branch within the Sûreté, which investigates spies."

"Are you saying Cozette du Barroux was a spy?"

"*Oui.* She was, but not a willing one. At least, I do not think so. Your new position as Commissioner of Intelligence makes you the head of an English spy agency, no? And you privately run a company called Inner Circle Intelligence. *Inner Circle,*" he repeated with great emphasis. "What if I told you that there is a similar group in France? A branch of this inner circle, which investigates crimes my men cannot touch?"

"I'd say I already knew that."

Goron laughed. "*Mais oui, mon ami,* but when you and Morehouse came here in '79, neither you nor I had any idea about such things."

"True," the duke answered. "And your point?"

"Do you know the other names in these files, my lord Duke?"

Charles flipped through the densely worded reports, slowly translating the entries. Other names stood out: Prince Anatole Romanov and Rasarit Grigor, but also—written over and over again—Paul Stuart, listed prior to March, 1885 as the Visconte Marlbury. "Why is Lord Aubrey's name here? Did your men follow him?"

"We never interfered with the earl's business, no matter what name or face he used, but we knew he came here as a spy. The brave officer who kept all these logs, Chief Pierre Camus, is now dead of old age, a blessed way to go, I think. I spoke with him before he died. He told me of something he called 'the war of the three birds'. One is black, one red, and the last is white. These three wage war upon the earth, and their battles sometimes leave scars in our beloved France. Camus called Lord Aubrey a white bird that circles. The red are diggers, and the black breathe fire. My friend often spoke in riddles, but after reading these reports, one might say my eyes, they are open."

He paused and turned his head, pointing out the tall window towards Notre Dame's twin spires. "She is beautiful, no? See how the light winks at us through the rose window. It is a glimmer of colour unlike any other."

"Yes, it's a magnificent building, François, but..."

"I do not wander in my mind, friend Charles. I tell you a truth. These two evil birds, the black and the red, they would break that window and kill that beautiful light. God's light. Read these pages carefully, for they contain information vital to your fight. All I ask is that you read the files, *mon ami*. Do with them as you will. Also, my friend gave me the name of a man who lives in London. They met here in Paris many years ago, and he worked with Camus. I've written the man's name so you do not forget. It is on the inside of the white file. He is a priest. Georgio Georgiadis Lambelet. Camus called him a keeper of truth."

Goron's secretary knocked, and the chief called our in French. "*Entrer!*"

"*Madame Pleyel est ici pour vous voir, m'sieur,*" the man replied.

"*Merci, Henri. Demandez-lui d'attendre. Cinq minutes.*"

The door shut, the assistant gone off to speak with the waiting heiress. "I beg your forgiveness, my friend, but I must interview a stubborn woman about the loss of her dog. Madam Pleyel. She is benefactress to many charities, and as such she require, how you say, the gloves of kid?"

Sinclair managed a smile, despite the questions in his heart. "Yes, that's how we say it, François. Thank you for these. You are a true friend."

"It is nothing," the policeman said, a crooked smile lifting his heavy moustache at the corners. "But let me quickly tell you of this man Wentworth. He has been seen in places where birds roost. The man is sprouting black wings, my friend. Be wary of your footsteps here, for these birds keep watch."

"I understand. Where was Wentworth seen?"

"Montmartre, in the company of a well-dressed gentleman. It is said these two are often accompanied by a beautiful woman with red hair. They frequent the *maisons closes*—what you call the brothels—as well as certain music halls. Flesh and blood are the product in such places."

"François, do you know which *maison close* housed Miss du Barroux?"

"A very upscale one. *Le Chabanais*. It is near the Louvre. 12 rue Chabanais. Alexandrine Joannet operates this place. She call herself Madame Kelly."

"Kelly? That's an odd choice for a Frenchwoman."

"Not so odd, for the woman is not French, but Irish. Be wary if you go there, my friend Duke. It is a place where the rich meet the powerful to talk business, and many foreign diplomats frequent those rooms; meaning it is a roost for black and red birds."

"Unlike you, François, I carry a revolver at all times."

Goron laughed, his round face lifting with relief. "Ah! Your rank and name may change, *m'sieur*, but this fact remains. You are always a cautious man, no?"

"Very cautious," the duke said as he shook his colleague's hand. "I'll read through these files once Adele and I complete our evening at the opera. If my French fails, I may seek your help. I cannot ask Adele."

"She must never know what is in those pages, my friend. Be sure to keep them locked—or if you prefer—burn them. They are yours to do with as you will."

Charles collected Adele from the map room, and the two of them took a hansom cab back to the hotel, where they shared luncheon before hiring a private carriage for their trip to the Louvre. As they neared the famous museum, they passed a four-storey Empire-style building made of white limestone decorated with scrolled iron railings at the windows. *12 rue Chabanais*. He reached for Adele's hand. How could he tell her that this was the very house where she'd been conceived?

Aubrey House, London

"Shall we lunch at the Royale today, Delia? Or do you prefer we call on Lord Brackamore's designer friend. You know, the one who paints murals. I thought we might consult on a pastoral scene for the baby's nursery."

Cordelia Stuart had no wish to go anywhere, for she'd felt ill since dawn. "No, Mama. I'd like to stay home. You may speak with the decorators, if you wish. Or painters, or anyone. I'm not up to it."

"You're ill again? I wonder if that's normal. Perhaps, I should send for a doctor."

"No, I remember Elizabeth being nauseous much of the time, and now I know how she felt. Please, don't pour me any more tea!"

Constance Wychwright set down the gold-embellished teapot. "You cannot go without a breakfast, Cordelia. You're nourishing the earl's child with every bite you take. Remember that. Oh, good morning, Bailey," she said as the butler arrived in the morning room with a tray of letters and newspapers. "Is the *Gazette* amongst those?"

"It is, my lady. Also, there is a telegram for Lady Aubrey."

"For me? I never receive telegrams. Are you certain it isn't addressed to the earl?"

"No, ma'am. It is from the earl."

He handed her the envelope. Delia withdrew the slip of paper, printed on a teletype machine:

DELIA: SALPERTON COMING TO COLLECT YOU AT FOUR. HE WILL DRIVE YOU TO VICTORIA. TAKE SCOTTISH KNIGHT TO BRANHAM. I WILL MEET YOU AT SIX. PACK FOR A

FORTNIGHT. MISS YOU EVERY MINUTE. ALL
MY LOVE. - PAUL.

"What is it?" her mother asked, stirring three cubes of sugar
into a cup of tea.

"We'll need to pack," Cordelia replied.

"Pack? Whatever for? I've made plans for the entire week!"

"Paul is bringing us to Branham right away. He doesn't say
why, just that Lord Salperton is picking us up at four. He says to
pack for a fortnight. Bailey, would you ask Ada to begin packing
my cases?"

The butler bowed. "At once, my lady."

If Connie Wychwright were a dog, she'd have growled. A sudden trip to the country sounded perfectly awful. She'd hoped to shop
for new clothes today, and Lord Brackamore had promised to escort
her to the theatre Friday evening.

"But Cordelia, what of our meeting with the decorators?
Shouldn't we wait a day or two before leaving? Lord Brackamore
said he hoped to take me—well, I suppose he meant *us*—to the theatre on Friday evening. Surely, the earl doesn't require us before the
weekend? The fête doesn't open until Saturday."

"He leaves no room for argument, Mama. I shan't expect you to
join me. Feel free to remain here if you wish. I'm sure Paul wouldn't
mind. If you are staying, the employment service Duke James uses
wants to send over four candidates for your lady's maid position.
Bailey has their contact information. Hire whichever you like. I'll
be taking Ada with me."

"Oh, yes, I'd forgotten about that. Do you trust me to begin the
renovations to the nursery on my own?"

"Of course, Mama," the girl said, kissing her mother's cheek.
"Now, I really must bathe. Are you staying or coming with me?"

Constance feared a cooling of her friendship with Brackamore,
especially as she'd noticed several other widows casting glances his
way at Salisbury's home. "No, I believe I'll remain. In fact, I shan't
be coming at all, if that's all right. I've never been fond of these
country fêtes. We had them back in Windermere, and they always
seemed provincial, I thought. More a treat for the villagers than
their peerage hosts. May I use the earl's account for any purchases
I need to make?"

"Of course. Paul's added your name to all his accounts, but remember it is his money you spend, Mama. Paul's very generous, but, please, don't overindulge. I shouldn't want to abuse my husband's good will."

"Oh, neither would I, my dear! Neither would I. Very well, I shall send word to the decorators to meet me here tomorrow. Had you a color scheme in mind?"

"The Aubrey colours are green and gold, but beyond that I suppose something that would work for a boy or a girl."

"I'll make the primary shades neutral then, shall I? Yellow is always cheerful."

"Yes, that sounds quite nice. Thank you, Mama. I'm really not up to all this decorating. It's a relief to leave it with you."

"Never fear. I'll take care of everything, Delia. Every last detail."

Cordelia left her mother to read the morning news, and climbed the back stairs to the master apartment. She didn't really trust her mother, but could see no other option than to leave her here, free to spend her husband's money. At least, decorating would keep the busybody widow from mischief. Or so, Cordelia hoped. It was much better than dwelling on the disturbing notion that her mother might have orchestrated Sir Albert Wendaway's attempted rape and assault against her own daughter. Or worse, that she may have collaborated in Sir Richard Haversham's plan to do the same thing.

Delia had finally managed to put those horrible acts behind her, thanks to Paul's constant support and devotion. She would do anything for her husband. Anything. And if he wanted her in Branham that afternoon; then, she'd move heaven and earth to make it happen.

CHAPTER EIGHTEEN
5:03 pm - Branham Hall

"Have our young viscounts arrived?" asked Kepelheim as he entered the hall's red drawing room. "Good afternoon, Riga. I hear you and Mr. Blinkmire had some excitement yesterday."

"The excitement was all Stephen's," the count replied from his corner chair. "And the Lords Salperton and Paynton are due within the hour. They're travelling on the same train as the lovely Lady Aubrey. It will certainly be a pleasure to have dear Cordelia gracing these corridors again. Not to slight our hostess, you understand. The duchess outshines all other women, that much is true, but there's something about Lady Cordelia that appeals to my poet's soul, I think. A sadness behind her fair eyes that makes those rare smiles all the more dramatic and uplifting."

"Yes, I know what you mean, Viktor," Stephen Blinkmire told the group. "As to my excitement, Mr. Kepelheim, I merely pray it provided insightful information."

"Insightful?" asked Aubrey as he took a chair near the window. "How does an unexpected splash in the lake provide insight, Mr. Blinkmire?"

"Oh, it isn't the aquatic adventure on its own, my lord, but the results of it. The discovery of a new statue. Apparently, it's quite old, by the looks of it. Perhaps, even before the Anjous settled here. It's all very exciting, and we're all waiting for Dr. Holloway's assessment."

Duchess Elizabeth entered the room, and all the men stood. Paul took her hand and kissed it. "You look radiant, Beth. You really do. How are my young cousins doing this afternoon?" he asked, touching her round stomach.

"They are both very active. Perhaps, they know you're here, and Robby is eager to learn how to spy from his Uncle Paul."

"Uncle Paul?" he laughed.

"It's how he always referred to you, when I spoke with him in that very distressing stone world last year. Georgie calls you Uncle as well, according to Charles. So, gentlemen, what are we discussing on such a lovely day?"

"Statues," replied Kepelheim. "Mr. Blinkmire says his misadventure led to the discovery of a new one."

"Oh that. I've only seen the head, but Powers says he's found ten pieces thus far. All are stored in the green shed near the stables. I'm sure Seth will want to have a look, when he arrives. He'll know if the pieces are from one or more statues, and if they have historical value. As the pieces were in the lake, it's possible someone threw them in on purpose, though I cannot imagine why. If the head's any reference, then it's certainly a sizeable figure. Powers estimated a total height of nearly nine feet."

"My! Well, certainly not a life-size portrayal then," Riga observed. "At least, we hope not. Can you guess the era? Does it look Roman?"

"Actually, it does rather," she told him. "If you're interested, I'm sure Seth would be pleased to have you go with him later, Count Riga." She turned to her cousin. "Paul, is it true you've sent for Cordelia?" Though Elizabeth knew already of the young woman's pregnancy, she'd said nothing of it to Aubrey, waiting for him to break the news in his own time.

"Her mother's visiting, and I didn't want to leave her alone too long. Is Gehlen coming to the fête?"

"I'm afraid he's delayed in Scotland. Legal matters regarding Pencaitland Manor, but he hopes to finish and be here on Monday. Oh, and I received a telegram from Michael and Andrea Emerson. They're in London and hope to be here tomorrow."

"Andrea Emerson?" asked Kepelheim. "Are you saying our Miss Jenkins is now Mrs. Emerson?"

"She is, but as Laurence Emerson has now passed away, Andrea's more properly called Lady Stillworth."

"Then Michael is now the Viscount Stillworth and heir to the earldom?" asked Martin.

"Yes. There's been so much death lately, hasn't there? First, Laurence Emerson, then Anthony's father passing so suddenly, and now Grandfather's childhood friend, Lord Granddach. Poor Grandpa's been to funeral after funeral these past few weeks."

"It is often how it goes," Kepelheim remarked sadly. "In our youth, we attend school with our friends. Perhaps, serve in the military together. Then, we attend one another's weddings, congratulate them on the birth of children, then grandchildren, and finally offer sympathies as we all begin to die. It is the cycle of life, I suppose."

"Yes, but a rather maudlin subject for so pretty a day," Beth added, trying to sound cheerful. "Shall we all adjourn to the lawn for tea?"

"An excellent suggestion, Princess," Paul declared, taking his cousin's arm. "Let's stroll through the golden tents whilst we may do so in peace. Come Saturday, the hoards will descend upon us."

The earl led the way with the duchess on his right arm, followed by the tailor, Riga, and Blinkmire. As the group reached the edge of the pavilions, Stephen's furry friends rushed up to greet their gigantic companion, and Aubrey scolded their leader, d'Artagnan. "Dart, you are a tail-wagging troublemaker, just like your father was when he was a pup! Powers, could you gather up our scampering canines, lest they trip our little duchess?"

Thomas Powers had been putting the finishing touches to the a jasmine-covered lychgate, and he called to the pups. "Come now! Come!" he shouted. The animals stared, sitting beside the tea table. The gardener whistled. "Come! Do us a favour now, and come to old Powers!" He whistled again, three sharp commands he often used with the sheepdogs, and the entire pack ran towards the gardener, allowing the humans to eat in peace.

Paul turned back to Riga, his hand holding Beth's. "Find chairs, everyone. I'm going to take our Princess on a short walk. Back in a few minutes."

Kepelheim, Riga, and Blinkmire chose comfortable chairs at a cloth-covered table, inside the largest of the golden pavilions. "It's certainly cooler in the shade, isn't it? It's grown surprisingly warm for early May. I wonder if summer will be hot. Last summer was quite cool."

Riga poured himself a cup of tea and another for Blinkmire. "I read that last summer, the average temperature in London was nearly fifteen degrees below normal. Some blame the weather for causing Jack the Ripper's foul deeds."

"I've read that theory as well, but it makes no sense," the tailor observed, stirring sugar into his tea. "But then many things seem nonsensical as I age. Sometimes, it feels as though the entirety of reality has become skewed. I wonder what our earl is up to?"

"Must he be up to something?" asked Riga. "I think Lord Aubrey merely wishes to spend a few minutes in the good lady's company. They are lifelong friends, are they not?"

"Yes, of course," Kepelheim agreed. "I expect he has news to give her."

"What news is that?" asked Blinkmire as he buttered a warm apple scone.

"Private news, I should think. But as we three have a moment to talk privately, I wonder, Count Riga, did you write to your friend in Budapest? The policeman?"

"Ah, yes, I'm glad you ask, Mr. Kepelheim. It was on my list of things to do today. Not write, you understand. I'd already done that, and Captain Matteçscu returned my letter only yesterday. He and my daughter were very close, you see. As children."

"You have a daughter?" asked Kepelheim. "I had no idea."

"My Louisa died six years ago. In childbirth. Both she and the boy are with our Saviour now. After I fled Romania, I changed my name. The Russians still look for me. I'd been arrested and condemned to death, but Prince Anatole rescued me with the help of Captain Matteçscu. The Okhrana think me long dead. My true name is Rigaleçscu. I am but one of thousands of refugees who fled the Carpathians in the '60s. I fear East London is filled with many such exiles."

"Yes, it is so," Blinkmire agreed. "Kepelheim? Is that German?"

"Yes, it is, only I was born in England. My great-grandparents came from Württemberg. I think of myself as English, though. It's all I've known. However, I did learn to speak German as a boy. My father served with the inner circle, you see, and I was expected to follow in his footsteps. Most of us inherited our positions."

"And Lord Aubrey, also?"

"Yes, which is why the earl takes his job so seriously."

"And part of that job is to protect our little duchess, I take it?" Riga asked the tailor. "Even now that both of them are married?"

Martin's hand paused as he stirred the tea. "Ah, yes, that. I am merely an old man whose opinion means little, but I believe our earl struggles with his new duties. Not only to his bride, although it's clear he loves the Lady Cordelia sincerely; but with his relationship to the duchess. Once, he was her sole protector, the keeper of the castle gates, you might say."

"But another now holds that key," Riga suggested.

"Yes," Kepelheim agreed, "but he will adjust. I think our young earl sees himself as an errant knight still—only now, he serves two ladies. But I would never question his motives, for they are pure."

Riga grew philosophical. "A gatekeeper must discern friend from foe. The earl's eyes are ever watchful. I think the duchess is in good hands."

"Which leads us back to my reason for asking you to contact Captain Matteçscu," Kepelheim continued. "Did he offer any insight into these alleged Romanian princes? And does anything from their histories lead us to their plans? It has been far too quiet of late. I fear something dreadful looms on the horizon."

"My friend seemed unwilling to share much in written form, but he did mention Raziel Grigor in connexion with a number of mysterious deaths, beginning in 1862. Bloodless corpses and rumours of cannibalism, but such crimes litter the Carpathians like blood-soaked stones, reaching all the way back into antiquity."

Blinkmire waved his hands, eager to speak. "Yes, but how would Grigor be involved? Forgive me for interrupting, for it's possible my dull mind simply isn't adding up the facts, but isn't Prince Alexei Grigor the same as the demonic being called Raziel? Surely, he emerged into our world in 1871. Is that not so, Mr. Kepelheim? When the Mt. Hermon stone was unpacked at the British Museum?"

"Your mind is hardly dull, Blinkmire. It's sharp as always, for you're right," Kepelheim replied, selecting a slice of lemon cake and adding it to his plate. "Grigor is supposed to have emerged from that stone and killed the curator who uncrated it. I wonder, Riga, is it possible this identity as the Romanian Prince Alexei is an entirely false history? That Grigor somehow manipulates our facts? Or might it be simpler? Might an actual *human being* named Prince Alexei have existed in the past, and he indulged in pagan rites of incubation to summon forth a demon?"

"Incubation?" asked Blinkmire. "I don't think I like the sound of that! Does it mean what I think it does?"

"It is an ancient practice amongst high-level Luciferians and pagans. Their ultimate power comes from inviting a spirit to dwell inside them. The human is then set-aside or perhaps combined with the co-habiting demon or fallen angel. I've read of blood sacrifices and transformational chambers that indicate an ultimate goal of incubation or habitation."

"Like the very chambers beneath our feet," Riga said tensely. All the men paused, as though each now realised the truth of Branham's location and occult purpose.

"And might a large group of people meeting with a singular goal provide an energy source for these rites?" asked Blinkmire. "My friends, are these country fêtes more than just carnivals?"

Everyone grew still and quiet, and it seemed that the constant buzzing of insects had stopped. The air thickened with tension. Kepelheim glanced over at the earl and duchess, who stood together near the folly.

A great dread crept into the tailor's ageing bones, and he noticed the duchess was crying and leaning heavily against the earl for support.

"God help us," Riga whispered. "What Hell awaits?"

"Yes, Charles told me about the baby," Beth informed the earl, wiping her red-rimmed eyes. "I've no idea why the news makes me cry, Paul. Perhaps it's hearing you say it that makes the difference. But believe me when I say I'm happy for you—for both of you, I mean. My emotions are simply unpredictable these days. Please, don't take my reaction to heart. Really, darling, I am happy for you!"

"I know you are," he whispered lovingly, using his handkerchief to dry her tears. "If I'm honest, I'm still unsure how to feel about it myself. After you chose Charles over me, I assumed I'd continue working in other lands as a British agent. This all happened so quickly! I never imagined being married to anyone but you, yet here I am, and with a child on the way. Our lives have certainly changed a great deal since last summer, haven't they, Princess?"

"Yes, they have," she whispered. "Will you tell Delia the truth about Adele?"

"How can I? Delia's much too fragile to learn such news. If I tell her about Cozette, then I'll have to be honest with Adele. I'm not ready for that, Beth. I'm not sure I ever can be. It's why I've asked Charles to adopt her."

Beth's eyes rounded in surprise. "You've done what? Paul, do you really plan to give away your own child? Would you do that with Cordelia's baby?"

"Of course, not. That's an awful thing to suggest!"

"And why isn't it awful to suggest giving away your daughter?" she asked.

"It's hardly the same, and I'm shocked you'd call it that. I'm only thinking of Adele, if you must know. Do you think for one minute she'd rejoice to learn she's the illegitimate accident of a harlot and a lying spy? Imagine how it would make her feel to learn I could have saved her mother, but didn't."

"Paul, I don't think Della would see it that way. She knows you better than that. We all do."

"I'm not the man you imagine me to be, Elizabeth. Not when I'm working. I'm much colder as that other person."

"What does that mean? Paul, your heart is the same regardless of what name you use or disguise you might wear. Please, before you make an irretrievable error, reconsider this!"

"Charles makes a better father to her than I ever could."

"Why? Because she reminds you of Cozette?"

Paul froze, unable to answer. "That's a terrible thing to say."

"Is it? Or have I neared the mark? I think as Adele grows, she's looking more and more like her mother. She certainly doesn't have your eyes. In fact, oddly enough, they're more like Charles's now. I imagine Cozette had such eyes."

"They were similar," he muttered, turning away.

"And now that you're married to Cordelia, the last thing you want is to be reminded of that affair. Do you think that mistake makes you less of a man? I certainly don't."

"You'd never understand, Elizabeth. You've never had to live a lie for months at a time."

"Haven't I? Do you think it was easy to live here with William Trent as my stepfather? To watch my mother fawn over him as though that dreadful man walked on water? And each time I wrote to you, each letter I sent, disappeared into the postman's bag as though dropping into oblivion. You rarely wrote back. And yet, despite your long silences, you seemed surprised when I fell in love with someone else! Really, Paul, I sometimes wonder if you aren't pretending to be another man here at home, and that your *true* self is England's spy!"

He stared at her, his lean face pale. "Shall I find a collection of china plates for you to throw at me, Your Grace, or will you be content to slap my face?"

She turned away, her eyes on the woodland beyond the great field of golden cloth. She'd begun to cry, and he reached for her hand, taking the trembling fingers into his, grateful when she didn't pull away.

"Beth, I'm so sorry. That was thoughtless and cruel. Darling, it's been a very long time since we've argued this way. We used to do it nearly every week. Why is that?"

She answered without turning, her voice small, almost like a child's. "I don't know. Perhaps, it's due to some deep emotional connexion that is easily strained. As though the slightest pull on that thread disturbs our hearts."

"I love you, Princess," he whispered, his arms round her shoulders.

She turned into his embrace, pulling as close as her pregnancy allowed. "I'm so sorry! Those were thoughtless words, and I didn't mean any of them. My feelings for you will never change, Paul. Not ever!" she told him. "I love you with all my heart and soul. And it is been difficult to see you married to another—and now, with a child on the way. I know I should be pleased, but why do I feel such disappointment?"

He kissed her cheek, tasting salty tears. "Now you know how I felt when you told me you'd conceived Charles's baby."

She swallowed hard, the truth stinging. "Yes, I suppose I do."

He stroked her hair as he spoke. "I've always pictured my son or daughter with dark eyes like yours, but I'm to blame for how it's turned out. I realise that, darling. I should have written to you more often and shown greater affection. I assumed you knew how I felt." He bit his lower lip. "If I had, you might be carrying my children now."

The idea of alternate versions of her present; how decisions made one moment, influenced life for years to come and even determined future generations, struck her with great force, and Beth pushed away, suddenly filled with confusion.

I love Charles. Why am I doing this?

"What time is Delia arriving?" she asked, trying to distance herself from the warring thoughts.

Paul lowered his arms and took a step backward, reminding himself that Cordelia was his first priority, not Beth. "I'm to meet the train at six. Are you sure about having us stay here for the next few weeks? We won't be under foot?"

"Under foot? Not at all," she whispered, though her voice sounded strained. "Charles and I are delighted to have you stay here, for as long as you wish. And I promise not to throw any china either. I love you, Lord Aubrey. No matter whose ring I wear, I still see you as my knight in shining armour."

He managed a smile. "Saturday afternoon, I'll have to wear that armour for real, won't I? Have you told your husband about the tilt yard?"

"I mentioned it," she sniffed, slowly regaining composure. "He's no happier than you, it seems, but it is for charity, Paul. To help pay for the new hospital. The event's ticket price is steep, which means the stands will be filled with peers and rich businessmen, who've also paid to attend that evening's ball. All the leading newspapers are sending reporters and photographers. Two are coming all the way from America. One from New York, another from Chicago."

"Chicago? That's a long way to come to watch two amateurs play about in clinking armour," he said as they walked back together. "I hope I don't disappoint, darling. I've never ridden with a lance before."

"There'll be no lance. It's all just playacting. I wouldn't put either of you in a position to be hurt. Do you really think I'd ask that of you?"

"It's a knight's honour to take a fall for his Princess."

"Not my knights," she whispered, "and certainly not at a charity demonstration. No, all you and Charles have to do is look handsome and ride past one another."

"Then, I for one, shall ask for a mercy pass," he joked.

"No need for that. As I said, it's all for show. No weapons. You need only look handsome. You should have no problem with that, Lord Aubrey."

"I'll do my best, Princess," he promised. "I hope you understand about the baby and about Adele, Beth. I've been worried about your reaction ever since Gehlen broke the news. Considering my poor conduct with you and Charles, I didn't know what to expect."

"You and I are as close as ever, Paul. We shall always be the best of friends."

He squeezed her hand and kissed it. "I'll always love you, Elizabeth. Nothing will ever change that."

"But Cordelia's earned your affections as husband. I can see it in your eyes whenever you speak her name. And I'm glad of it, Paul. Really, I am."

"I keep thinking about what Georgie told Seth Holloway."

"When?" she asked as they neared the main pavilion.

"When he was in that strange dreamscape—rather like the stone world you and Charles inhabited during his coma. He met Georgie there."

"Seth saw her? Really? He's never mentioned it to me."

"Hasn't he? I'd assumed Charles might tell you. It was during Henry's hypnosis session at Christmas, remember? You came running upstairs when Seth screamed."

"I'd almost forgotten about that awful night," she admitted. "We've had such beautiful days and weeks since. Peaceful and serene. Except for all the construction noise, of course. He really saw my daughter?"

"He did, and it made Charles weep to hear it. She'd given Seth messages for some of us. She even referred to me as 'Uncle Paul'."

"Robby called you that as well!" Beth told him, her voice sounding happy at last. "He said you and Charles are more like brothers than cousins, and so they'd always called you that."

"Did he? You've not really told me much about your vision of Robby. What else stands out? Did he mention if I had children?"

"No, I don't believe he did. As you might guess, he was tall, just like Charles. And looked somewhat muscular for only ten and a half. As though he'd already begun some sort of training."

"Most likely I'll put him through his paces," Paul laughed. "Did he mention anything else about me?"

She grew quiet for a moment. "He did, but I'm not sure if I remember it correctly."

"What?"

"He said they'd all been praying for Delia."

"He said the name Delia?"

"I'm really not sure now. He may have said they were praying for your wife. Paul, does it matter?"

"Yes, it does," he insisted. "Georgie told Seth they were all praying for Delia, because of the baby. Her words. Because of the baby. Now, what might that mean? Beth, do you think something might happen to our child?"

"Darling, it could mean anything, and they were talking about life in 1899. Surely, it means something far different. Please, don't borrow trouble. Besides, you've always said these visions Charles and I experienced were nothing more than dreams. I'm sure this baby will be healthy and grow into a fine young man or lady."

"Yes, you're right. I shouldn't borrow trouble. Come, let's go have tea, and then you can show me this statue Blinkmire's dunking uncovered."

The two cousins returned to the grand marquee to enjoy the afternoon meal, but a tiny seed of doubt had entered the earl's thoughts, and suddenly he felt even more protective of Cordelia.

And their future child.

CHAPTER NINETEEN
9:03 pm - Théâtre de Champs-Élysées

Adele had never felt so happy. The day in Paris had surpassed all her expectations. First the Louvre with hall after hall of famous paintings and sculpture, and now, the opera! The adolescent's love of music and drama caused her to savour every note and every stick of scenery for this remarkable production of *La Traviata*. Adele had never read the story nor seen the famed play *La Dame aux camélias*, but a woman sitting in a nearby box had told her the tale whilst Charles endured a long harangue by a Frenchman about the Portmanteau Murders.

"And it's a love story?" she asked the neighbour.

"A very tragic one," the older woman whispered. "All about a courtesan—do you know what that means?"

Della nodded. "I think so. Does it mean a woman who attends on peers at court?"

"In a way. In France, it refers to women who trade favours for money. That sort of thing."

"What favours?" the girl asked innocently.

"Ah, well, you should ask your father, I suppose," the woman replied. "But this woman is dying of consumption and falls in love with a card-playing *bourgeois* named Armand in the play, but called Alfredo in Verdi's opera."

"Do they get married?"

"No, I'm afraid it ends badly. I shan't spoil it. Do you speak Italian?"

"Enough to converse, I suppose."

"Ah, well, then you'll be able to follow. Does your father speak it?"

She turned to look at Sinclair, still fending off the French businessman's barrage of questions. "I'm not sure. Probably. Thank you for the help. What part of England are you from?"

"Kent," the woman replied.

"Really? Then, you must know Branham Hall."

"Everyone knows Branham, my dear. Wait, are you also from Kent?"

"Yes. My father is the Duke of Haimsbury," she said.

"Is he? Oh, that's the duke! But he's far more handsome than the photographs. I'd thought the duchess's children weren't yet born."

"He's my adoptive father. It's very complicated."

"Oh, I see," the woman answered. "Might I meet him?"

"I suppose so," the girl told her. Della turned and tapped him on the shoulder. "Excuse me for interrupting, Father, but this woman hoped to meet you."

Sinclair appeared grateful for any excuse to quit the unwanted conversation. "Forgive me, Sir Alan, but I'm needed by my daughter. Yes?"

"This woman hoped to meet you. She's been kind enough to explain the opera's story to me."

Charles stood politely and took the woman's gloved hand. "A pleasure, madam. I'm Duke Charles Sinclair. And you are?"

"Oh, it's Arabella Adamson, Your Grace! Miss Adamson. My father is the editor of the Kent County Register. A modest little paper, but he's here to meet up with fellow publishers. I've just been talking with your delightful adopted daughter. I'd no idea you and the duchess had done so, but she certainly speaks highly of you."

"She is indeed my daughter," he said proudly. "And this is our first night in Paris together. My wife has always loved *La Traviata*, and I understand our Violetta tonight is famous for the role."

"She is, sir. Oh, I hear the applause beginning. That must be the conductor now. I hope to talk more later, Your Grace!" she giggled as she returned to her box.

Charles sat once again with Adele to his left. She reached for his hand. "Thank you."

"For what?" he asked.

"For bringing me here. For adopting me."

"I should thank you, Della. Calling you daughter makes me happier than you can ever know."

She inched closer, nearly in his pocket. "Father," she whispered, as he stroked her hair. "I do love calling you that, and I love you."

Following the overture, the velvet proscenium drapes parted, revealing a dinner scene. In the wings, the first notes of the chorus rose up to the fly space, and the make-believe doors flew open to the raucous strains of revellers, entering a grand party scene, celebrating Violetta's recovery from illness. Violetta is told that a young man named Alfredo Germont has prayed for her recovery and called each day during her illness. After several tense encounters amongst the *demimondaine's* many lovers, the current one, Baron Douphol refuses to offer the first toast, but the moment is saved, when Alfredo agrees to sing a *brindisi* or drinking song.

The orchestra then commenced the first big duet with chorus, *Libiamo ne' lieti calici*, Italian for 'Let's drink from the joyful cups'.

The opera progressed into Act II, and young Della wept as it became clear Violetta had grown ill again. When Alfredo's father entered to insist the courtesan leave his son, she gripped her new father's hand tightly. Once the act finished, the curtains closed, and the *entr'acte* began.

The lights came up, and the duke turned to his adopted child to find her weeping. "Tears?" he asked.

"It's just so sad! Poor Violetta!" Della sighed. "All she wants is to be happy! Must she leave him, Father? Will she?"

"I'm not sure, but shall we find refreshments whilst we wait?"

"Yes, let's do. I want everyone to meet my new father!"

As they climbed down the staircase to the main areas and salons, she babbled on and on about the opera. "Are such women always unhappy? Must they be?" she asked innocently, unaware that her own mother had lived such a life.

"I cannot say," he replied, wishing he'd chosen a different theatre. *La Traviata*'s plot was far too close to Adele's parents' real lives. Cozette du Barroux had given her life to keep her child happy, all because of her great love for Paul Stuart, who'd become her lover as the disguised artist, David Saunders.

They're reached a wide hallway with many doors, and she tugged on his hand. "Do you mind? I should like the powder room. I need to... I mean. I promise not to be long."

Charles understood her implied message and guided the adolescent safely through the bustling intermission crowd to find the nearest water closet, or *chambres de repos*, as the French signs declared. The beautifully decorated chamber was placed near an equally beautiful salon, where several dozen ladies in the latest fashions gossiped about the terrifying Portmanteau Murders, but also about a certain handsome Englishman.

"I cannot go into the chamber with you, darling. Will you be all right?"

"There's always a maid inside to help, and I shan't be long. You could sit with those women over there. It might be fun to see how they'd react."

"You are a mischievous young lady," he said as she disappeared through the oak door.

Charles waited for Adele near the salon, saying good evening as people bid the same to him, unaware of the ladies' stares.

"Do you wait for the Lady Adele?" a woman asked in accented English.

Charles moved away to allow several women wearing voluminously bustled dresses to pass. "Princess Eluna, forgive me. I hadn't expected to see you here."

"It is a pleasant surprise, I hope," replied the princess.

"Oh, yes, of course." He took a moment to look at her carefully, that same odd sense of familiarity tugging at his memory. "Are you certain we've not met before?"

"If only we had," she said, taking his bare hand. "Then I might have won your heart before your duchess claimed it. Such a pity! But I'm sure women often tell you that."

"No, not really," he answered, not wishing to admit that women often did just that, lately.

Eluna kept hold of his hand, massaging the thumb. "You have very nice eyes. You know, it strikes me that Adele's eyes are much like yours. She might pass for your natural daughter! Indeed, the resemblance is quite profound. I'm surprised I hadn't noticed it last night."

"If her eyes resemble mine, it's because of family traits, I suppose. Adele was orphaned three years ago, but is also my cousin."

"How generous of you to bring her beneath your protection. And do you treat her to a night of music and theatre as celebration? Had my brother and I known you wished to come, we'd have shared our box with you."

"My aunt also has a box here, Highness, and we made use of hers. Though that's kind of you. I'll admit surprise that you and the prince have already obtained an opera box at so prestigious a theatre. In London, these boxes are inherited almost like titles."

She leaned close, placing her hand at his back. "Titles never truly reveal the man inside the box, now do they?"

"I'm not sure what you mean."

"Only a little joke!" she laughed, and the momentary rise and fall of pitch struck the duke as eerily familiar. He felt sure they'd met before, long ago.

"You are sensitive. I like that. No doubt, you are a wonderful father, too. Little Adele, I mean. But also these twins! Our new friend tells us that your duchess will bring you two new babies in June. Have you named them yet?"

"No, not yet," he lied, deciding she'd learnt enough about him "Von Siebenbürgen?" he asked, changing the topic. "Is that German?"

"It is, though my heritage is not. My family home is far away, near the Apuseni Mountains. Apuseni means 'mountains of the sunset'. It is a fierce but beautiful region with many dark caves and steep sides. Few humans could manage such climbs. The goats and rock badgers rule those lands—along with the ghosts, of course."

"I'm hardly a climber," he said, deliberately ignoring her mention of ghosts, "but I've a friend who enjoys it. Those are in the Carpathians, are they not?"

Her green eyes glinted like emeralds, and the ruby mouth lifted into a curved smile. "They are. Have you been to Romania?"

"No, I've not yet had the pleasure."

"Perhaps, one day," she whispered. "Oh, here is my brother. Ara! Come! See who I have found. Let us all share wine!"

The muscular prince passed through the knot of silk-bustled women, bowing politely to each, who all responded with giggles. His dark hair was braided down his back and tied with a red velvet ribbon. Flouting his sister's demands for English attire, the prince had chosen a bold costume of gold and red brocade, trimmed in black silk, with a wide belt of satin that accented his physique. He approached the duke, standing a head taller than Sinclair.

The prince bowed gracefully. "I am honoured to see you again, Duke Charles. But where is the lovely Lady Adele?"

A giggling ingenue dressed in a low-cut, sky-blue satin gown whispered in Sinclair's ear. "He's a wealthy prince, Your Grace. From Romania, I think."

Charles turned briefly to the interloper. "Yes, the prince and I've met, Miss?"

"Carson. My father is Sir Thomas Carson. He's over there ordering buckets of champagne. Will you join us?"

Araqiel answered for them. "Dear lady, would you steal this gentleman from us so soon? He is a new friend. I had hoped to meet him again, and sweet providence has smiled upon me! If you allow us a few moments, then we shall direct our conversation towards you and your good father."

He snapped his long fingers to call a uniformed waiter.

"Boy! Here, please! Champagne for my new English friends, the Carsons. Your finest vintage and spare no expense. Arrange all in the *Salle des Miroirs*, and see to it a large table is prepared with refreshments and fine wines. Do this, and you shall be rewarded."

He handed the slender youth twenty francs.

"*Oui, monsieur! Merci beaucoup!*"

"Do you enjoy the opera, Duke Charles?" asked von Siebenbürgen after the servant departed. "Verdi is rich with tonal mastery, but I find French composers more daring. Bizet, for instance. His *Carmen* is raw and wonderfully carnal."

"Is it? I'm hardly an expert, but my wife is," Sinclair replied, the mention of *Carmen* triggering memories of Antoinette Gévaudan. "Elizabeth has a voice to rival any other."

"Does she? This is the Duchess Elizabeth, no? Of Branham in Kent. The Lady Victoria is her aunt?"

"Yes. Beth's late father and I were cousins."

"Ah, so I see. Lady Adele tells me that you and your duchess host a great festival soon. She called it a fête. I find it an interesting word."

"It's an annual event, and this will mark four hundred years."

"Oh, we've been to the Branham fête!" the Carson girl interrupted with a brash giggle. "And we're going again this year. It's ever so much fun, and we'll attend the ball on Saturday. Is it true you and Lord Aubrey will wear armour that afternoon for a duel, Your Grace? Just like the old knights?"

"Well, not a duel," Charles began, thoroughly surprised by the question. He'd rather hoped to talk Beth out of the strange request, but someone had let the armour-plated cat out of the bag.

Feeling all at sea, Charles suddenly noticed small fingers take his, and a sweet voice whispered, "Holmes, do you need rescuing?"

"I think I do, Watson," he answered. "We've been invited to sit with the von Siebenbürgens and a group of English tourists in one of the salons. Shall we say yes?"

Prince Araqiel and his sister had turned briefly to speak with the city's mayor, and now rejoined the conversation. "Ah, it is my new friend Lady Adele! Fortune smiles upon me once again this night."

Adele curtsied politely. "A pleasure to see you again, Your Highness."

"You're the duke's cousin?" asked the ingenue. "Are you also a Sinclair?"

"She is my adopted daughter, actually," Charles answered proudly, "which makes her a Stuart-Sinclair."

Della beamed. "I like that name. But my brother is Lord Aubrey."

"Oh, I see!" the young woman replied, clearly familiar with the name. "Your brother's so very dashing."

"And he's so very married," Adele told the girl without a blink. "Should we find the salon, Father?"

"Yes, I think we should," he agreed, taking her hand.

The group wound their way through the dense thicket of silk hats, walking sticks, and rustling taffeta to a private area guarded by a pair of uniformed ushers. The prince whispered to one, and the man opened the door to their party.

"Your table is ready, sir," he told them, accepting a pair of gold coins from von Siebenbürgen.

The salon known as the *Salle des Miroirs*, or Hall of Mirrors, greeted them with gleams of multi-hued light. A trio of crystal chandeliers bounced rainbow prisms against the mirrored walls in imitation of the famed corridor in the Palace of Versailles. Adele marvelled at the ornate walls bearing the miraculous mirrors, the glittering gold leaf and the silks, and the muralled ceiling. Soaring over their heads, the gods Mercury, Zeus, and Hercules discoursed with Wotan, Fricka, and Erda, whilst Artemis and Apollo kept watch. Then, Adele noticed a curious inclusion, which didn't immediately make sense: a red ribbon that wound its way along the ceiling, weaving in and out amongst the gods, touching some, avoiding others, and ending finally in a circular formation near the centre.

She tugged at Haimsbury's sleeve. "Do you see that?" she asked.

"What, little daughter?"

She laughed, happy to be called 'little daughter'. "The red ribbon. I wonder what it means?"

"No idea," he answered. "We should find seats."

Their banquet table sat in a quiet corner, laden with rich pastries, cheeses, and fruit. A magnum of 1859 Moët champagne chilled in an ice bucket, and a selection of fine French reds and whites stood like tempting soldiers upon a buffet nearby. Della sat next to her new father, opposite the prince and his sister, with the Carson family taking the remaining chairs. The Carsons featured four giggling daughters, Sir Thomas, and his wife Rosalind. A string trio with piano accompaniment provided constant music to accompany the conversation, which quickly turned to Jack the Ripper.

"Has he been caught?" asked von Siebenbürgen.

"I'm afraid not," replied Sinclair. "Though, we have several, very promising leads. Thankfully, no new crimes have emerged; not Ripper murders, I mean. As with any city, criminals stalk the weak and unwary. And Paris is hardly immune. These recent victims found in portmanteaus, for instance."

"I've seen one of them!" exclaimed Lady Carstairs in a somewhat enebriated voice. "The Paris police actually display the bodies of murder victims in their morgue window. Can you imagine it? London would be shocked if our police did that. The poor man's head and hands lie upon a table with that hideous bloodstained bag beside them. The police say the purpose is to allow everyone who walks past to examine the poor fellow in hopes of identifying him, but it seems ghastly to me."

"Yet you walked past, did you not, Lady Carson?" asked Eluna. "Female curiosity is overwhelming. Pandora always opens the box."

"I admit to curiosity, Highness, but I stood back whilst many others pushed in front, crowding the sidewalk like so many ravenous birds.

"Birds," whispered the prince. "It seems the streets of Paris are alive with them. Pigeons, doves, owls, even hawks."

"Hawks?" asked one of the Carson girls. "Why hawks?"

"I imagine they come here to feast, much as we do," Ara replied. "I've seen hawks and falcons swooping down to catch the weaker birds."

Sir Thomas finished his champagne and poured another from the half-empty magnum. "Most European cities use them to thin out nuisance birds, Your Highness. London considered doing it, but thus far, the plan has been repeatedly vetoed. Duke Charles, you have considerable influence with government. Perhaps you might persuade the new council to approve it. Pigeons are forever damaging our buildings and befouling our streets. It's quite unnatural!"

Adele laughed. "How can it be unnatural, Sir Thomas, when God created birds just as he created man? Surely, their behaviour is determined by their nature."

"Such life and death struggle is not natural at all. It's a product of sin," the baronet's tipsy wife declared. "There are far too many husbands sneaking about with backstreet women. Not mine, of course," she added, realising she may have spoken out of turn. "Tommy would never do that."

Prince Ara waved his arm high to draw everyone's attention upwards. "My new friends, look to the skies. The designers of this most beautiful room have included a ceiling of puzzles. They show us gods and goddesses, and at first look, it seems they only talk, but observe. See them as they watch and intermingle! It is a lesson in paint."

Della looked up, as did everyone else, including the servants and most of the salon's patrons. Skyward, their eyes beheld the same entities Adele had previously noticed, but now others joined the oil and plaster revelries. Poseidon, Ares, Aphrodite, Vulcan, Hera, Dionysus, and a hundred others. It seemed to everyone that the painted figures slowly began to move and interact, their mouths opening, hands and fingers clasping, and the musicians changed to a strange selection, a minor key arrangement evocative of primordial seas and magnificent heights.

Adele inched closer to Sinclair, taking his hand beneath the table as they watched. "That music's from *Parsifal*," she whispered to him. "Wagner's opera about the Holy Grail."

"What?" he asked.

"The music. But up there, you can see some of the characters. Surrounding the central chandelier, see? There's a ring of knights. I don't like this, Father. May we leave?"

"Of course. I'm sure the next act is about to begin."

Her grip tightened. "Actually, I'd like to go back to the hotel, if it isn't too much trouble. May we? I've a very strong feeling about it."

"Is that so? Then, we'll leave, little daughter," he whispered, kissing the top of her head. "Give me just a moment longer."

The Carsons lowered their heads, and Lady Carson actually hiccupped. "Oh, I am sorry! It's this champagne, I'm sure. Too many bubbles!"

The prince laughed. "Wine is the water of life, my dear Lady Carson." He looked to Sinclair. "Tell me, Duke, what think you of the murals? Do they seem familiar?"

"Gods and goddesses," Charles replied. "I've seen similar paintings in nearly every theatre and even some peerage homes. It's a common theme."

"Ah, yes, it is, but why? If you believe these are but myths, bits of starlight and imagination, then why do artists repeatedly paint them? In fact, since we sit in a magnificent salon within an opera house, consider the great musical themes. Most tell the stories of the ancient rulers of the heavens and the earth. Very few musicians write of Biblical heroes. I wonder why that is?"

"Perhaps, the writers cater to the whims of their patrons," Haimsbury suggested. "Money is the arbiter of many a man's soul."

"Ah! You are a philosopher, but are you sighted, I wonder? Look again at the ceiling. What do you find there?"

Charles glanced overhead once again, but this time the Roman and Greek pantheons had vanished, leaving only the circle of knights round the central chandelier. The white plaster background had altered into a midnight blue canvas of stars, and he could see motion within it. The constellations Draco, Bootes, Ursa Major and Minor, and Virgo. Then, the great hunter Orion appeared, his bow at the ready. Amongst these, arose seven stars, brighter than all the others, and these streaked across the nightscape pursued by an eighth. The knights turned round, their backs to the great lamp at their centre. Charles shut his eyes, for he couldn't watch any longer. Opening them again, he stood in a forest, and a woman approached.

Where have I gone? he thought. *Another waking vision. Where's Adele?*

"You are lost," the woman's voice spoke inside his mind.

"Leave me," he ordered her, refusing to look, for she wore no clothing at all.

Her hand touched his face. "Join us, my King. Join the dance and lead our revels. You are the blood, the red ribbon, which binds and unbinds. The scarlet thread of hope!"

She kissed him, her mouth warm and inviting, but the kiss was sharp; her teeth moving to his throat. Charles could feel her stealing his blood, his strength. He tried to summon up Beth's face to counter the attack, but his mind refused to obey. He could feel her hands upon his body, and he stood frozen; unable to move or protest. He felt dizzy, as though disappearing into a great chasm, or falling upwards into the heavens.

Small fingers of light touched his hand. A whisper from the past.

"Father?" a voice spoke from another world. "Father, please!"

His eyes snapped open. Adele held his hand, and he looked down. She was crying.

"Sorry, darling. I must have lost myself for a moment," he told her.

Von Siebenbürgen's sister had moved to his side, and her fingers were clamped round his left arm. "It is easy to lose one's self in music, no? But you look tired."

"Yes, I am. I fear the day is catching up to me. It's been very pleasant, but if you'll excuse us, my daughter longs to retire, as do I."

"But the opera's final acts must play out, friend Duke," the prince insisted. "And would you take Adele away from us so soon?"

"I'm afraid I must," Charles insisted. "Again, it's been a pleasure, Prince Ara. Thank you for the hospitality. Sir Thomas, I promise to bring up the hawk plan to Lord Rosebery of the LCC the next time I see him."

Carson shook the duke's hand. "I'm in the War Office building. Third floor. Come see me, when the opportunity arises, and I'll introduce you to my son, Herbert. He's the architect of that plan."

"I look forward to it," Charles answered politely. "Good evening, ladies. Sir Thomas. Your Highnesses. I pray you all enjoy the remainder of the performance."

He took Della's hand, and the two of them departed, heading for the lobby; a difficult journey which took them upstream through a collection of human waves, all heading towards the upper level boxes and main floor stalls. The interval, it seemed, was at an end.

A hand tapped his shoulder, and Haimsbury turned, finding to his very great shock a most familiar and welcome face. It was Prince Anatole Romanov, dressed in a simple suit with his long hair tucked beneath a large hat. Despite the sedate attire, the prince's face was unmistakable, and Charles gasped in surprise.

"I hope I do not appear at an inopportune moment, my friend," the Russian whispered. "My coach is outside. You and Adele are in danger. Please, come this way."

He turned about and headed towards a side exit, and Sinclair followed with Adele. A part of him wondered if this were really the mysterious messenger who'd so often protected his family, and he kept Adele close, just in case.

In a few minutes, they reached the sidewalk to find a gentle rain had begun. Large drops of silver splashed into puddles and pinged off metal awnings. An unmarked landau awaited at the corner, hitched to a pair of dappled greys. A nondescript driver hopped down and opened the door. Sinclair entered, placing Della to his left. The prince sat opposite.

"What's this all about?" Sinclair asked.

"We've met before, haven't we?" Della interrupted.

"Indeed we have, Lady Adele. At the duke's wedding. You were most graceful as you walked the aisle that morning."

She broke into a happy smile. "That's right! You're that other prince. The one who knows the tsar's family. I remember talking to you at the reception. You were very nice."

"It was a most pleasant conversation," he answered as the coach pulled away from the curb. "Charles, I beg forgiveness for interfering in your plans, but I have much to tell you."

"Where've you been?" asked the duke.

"Here, in France, watching those who watch. Your hotel isn't far, but I wonder if I might steal some time with you once the Lady Adele is safely in her room?"

"Della, do you mind?" asked Sinclair.

"I don't mind at all, Father. I imagine you need to speak about grown-up things. I understand."

Romanov smiled, causing his light blue eyes to sparkle. "You are a most intuitive young lady. Yes, it is adult matters we must discuss. One day, I shall share them with you. I promise. But not today."

"I'll remind you," she laughed. "Are you related to Prince Ara, sir? I'd wondered when we first met why he looked so familiar. I realise now it's because of you."

"We are distantly related, but our branches diverged long ago. Where and when did you meet him?"

"In the woods close to Auntie Tory's house. My dog chased after a hare, I think. I only saw a flash of colour, so I'm not sure. Anyway, she ran off, and I became lost. Prince Ara found my dog and later drove me home in his carriage. Is he—is he *safe?*" she asked, her voice hinting at tension. "Trustworthy, I mean. Not everyone is, and my brother insists I learn to distinguish friend from foe. I'm to assume strangers are an unknown factor, erring on the side of caution, or so he told me."

"Your brother offers sound advice. Prince Ara is complicated," Anatole replied, "and I suggest great caution with him. If he ever approaches you again, you must go to trusted friends, if they're nearby; but pray for guidance if alone. God will send aid. Will you do that?"

She nodded. "I will. It is very sound advice."

Charles pulled her close. "I shall do my best to keep close to you, Della. But God is always with you, and he protects you."

In less than five minutes, they arrived at the *Hotel Terminus*, a newly built, exceedingly elegant four-storey luxury accommodation near the entrance to the Exposition Centre. The majestic building epitomised the *belle epoch* atmosphere of late nineteenth-century Paris. Extravagant luxury and excess ruled the style, and every wall, every niche, every tile of the ceiling, every chandelier, every nook and cranny shouted wealth and privilege. Despite the late hour, three smartly attired bellmen met the duke inside the doors, one to open his suite, a second to inspect the interior to make sure the maid had cleaned it properly and turned down the beds, and the third man was the nighttime concierge and wore a gold braid upon his uniform, indicating superior rank.

"Good evening, Your Grace, Lady Adele," greeted the concierge. "We're pleased to have you back again. Your rooms are prepared, and the heating has been set as you requested. Two messages and a letter await you, sir. We've left them on your desk. If you require anything at all, our staff stands by to offer assistance," he explained as they climbed the stairs and then followed a wide hallway to the three-bedroom suite. "Tea awaits along with lemonade for Lady Adele. Is there anything else you need, Your Grace?"

Anatole had said nothing, not bothering to reveal his title to the concierge. He merely followed Sinclair and his daughter into the magnificent suite as if he were a servant, waiting near the entry as the first and second bellmen fussed with the drapes, fluffed pillows, and straightened glassware on the dining area's table.

Realising the reason for their delay, Charles handed the concierge thirty francs. "Thank you. We shan't be needing anything else."

The concierge bowed. "Very good, sir. You are most generous."

The men left, and Adele glanced at the messages. "Two telegrams," she said. "They so often mean trouble. I do hope nothing's happened to call you back to London already, Father."

"Father?" echoed Romanov. "Then, you've told her."

"You knew?" asked Charles.

"I know a great deal. A lemonade would be most refreshing. Shall I pour one for you Lady Adele?"

"Thank you, sir, but I think I'll retire, if Father doesn't mind. I'm sure he wishes to talk to you. I'll take the lemonade to my bedroom and listen to the music cylinders you bought me this afternoon, so I shan't overhear a thing. But if you need a female opinion on anything, I'm sure I'll be awake for a little while yet. Goodnight, Father mine," she said, rising on tiptoe to offer a kiss.

"Goodnight, Daughter mine," Charles said, kissing her cheek. "Sweet dreams."

"Goodnight, Your Highness," she added, happily. "It was very nice to see you again."

"Rest well, bright angel," the prince said with a bow. "May your dreams be of starlight."

The girl left the parlour and disappeared into the second bedchamber.

"She is very fond of you, and this adoption has made her happier than you can know," Anatole said, removing his hat. The long dark hair tumbled out, falling like a rich sheath of sable across his broad shoulders. He took a seat near the window. "You should read the telegrams," Romanov began.

"As you know so much, I take it you're already familiar with the contents?" asked the duke as he reached for the envelopes.

"Yes, I am."

Sinclair opened the first, from Aubrey. It was in code. It took the duke a few moments to mentally decipher it.

"The earl mentions a problem at Sir Simon Pembroke's home. I suppose you know all about that as well?"

"It's one reason for my visit, but not the primary reason."

The duke opened the second telegram from Inspector Elbert Stanley. His dark brows pinched into a line of worry. "Stanley says Meg Hansen is in trouble. He links this to Lorena MacKey. What's this all about, Anatole?"

"MacKey isn't your problem, my friend. Not yet. The One has despatched another of my kind to take them to a new hiding place. He will keep them safe."

"Them? Plural? Do you refer to MacKey and Hansen?"

"Not exactly. MacKey and another woman have been living with a trusted friend of mine. A priest. He has taught Lorena much about the One and Christ the Redeemer. The other is Violet Stuart."

"Violet Stuart?" he repeated. "Wait, do you mean Henry MacAlpin's former patient? You know where she is? Why haven't you told Henry? The poor man's been frantic!"

"There is no cause for alarm," Anatole said in that calm voice he so often used. "Henry will see her again, when it is safe. That day is nearing."

Charles sat, the messages in his hand. "Why do you dispense information with such parsimonious delight, Anatole?"

"I do not delight in secrets, Charles Robert. But information must be offered at the appropriate moment. Free will matters."

"That makes no sense!"

"Ah, but it does, only you presently choose anger over intuition. I promise you, my friend. All will become clear very soon. That letter is from the woman you met on the channel crossing. She is one reason I've come to you now. Adele is the other."

CHAPTER TWENTY
Branham Hall – The Anjou Suite

"I'm so very glad you're here," Paul told his wife as Ada MacKenzie unpacked the countess's cases. "Looks as though you brought plenty of clothing. Good. Beth's asked us to remain here for a few weeks. Is that all right?"

"Yes, of course," Delia answered in an odd voice. "It's actually helpful. Mama's decided to redecorate half the house in my absence. She might come down for the fête, but she's enjoying herself and your bank account, so don't be disappointed if she remains in London the entire time we're away."

"It's money well spent, then," he laughed.

"Yes, isn't it?" she agreed, her eyes alight. "Paul, it's very good of you to put her name on your accounts, but she's likely to spend a great deal of money."

The earl laughed, his arms round his wife's waist. "If it keeps Connie occupied, then it's all for the good. Besides, she'll likely hire the leading decorators, just so she can brag. The house can only benefit from her talents."

"You're very understanding. I didn't see Charles when I arrived. Is he still in London?"

"Gone to Paris, remember? He's bringing Della back. I've missed my sister. And I look forward to telling her our news. How are you feeling? Any more nausea?"

"A little. Mornings are difficult now, but bearable."

MacKenzie entered and curtsied. "All unpacked, my lady. My lord, shall I unpack the cases Lady Aubrey brought for you, or have you a valet?"

"Thank you, Ada, but as you know, I seldom use a valet, and I'm accustomed to unpacking myself. Go on downstairs and have something to eat. I think the servants take their supper about now. You'll find Mrs. Stephens very pleasant company. We'll ring if we need anything else."

"Very good, my lord," the young maid answered, leaving the apartment by way of the servants' corridor.

"Where did she go?" asked Delia, crossing to the hidden panel.

"The hall's secret passages," the earl whispered. "See this small emblem in the wallpaper?"

"The lion?" she asked.

"Yes, push against it."

Cordelia did as instructed, and the panel opened again, revealing a cool corridor lit by gas sconces. "Oh, my! I'd no idea there was a hallway back here. Where does it lead?"

"Everywhere. These are honeycombed throughout the house," he told her. "Many older homes have these, but are unused. Our home has them as well. They're like a secret highway linking all the state rooms and suites. The head butler before Baxter always insisted his team perform their duties in 'whispered efficiency', which meant so quietly that the family aren't aware of their activities. Not everyone uses them now, but you'd be surprised how useful they can be."

"How?"

"There are tales about some of the old dukes and these passages. How they used them to meet their mistresses or maids for a tryst. Actually, it sounds rather fun. Shall I meet you for a tryst this evening, Lady Aubrey?"

Cordelia laughed. "Can't we meet in here?"

"I suppose we could," he answered.

"I'm not sure I like the idea of secret passages, Paul. I read a novel once where the butler spied on everyone through passages like these. And he used the eyes of paintings to do it!"

He kissed her cheek. "There are no eye holes in the paintings here, and no one spies on us. Although, Beth used to spy on Sir William Trent using these tunnels. As a girl, she'd wind her way throughout the house and even into the old rock tunnels beneath the ground."

"How could she do that?"

"Some of the suites have concealed entries that link to the underground system. There are entire warrens of tunnels beneath Branham. Remember, darling? That's where I found Seth Holloway last year."

"Oh, yes. I remember," she answered wearily. "Paul, would you be angry if I suggested waiting until later for our, uh, tryst? I've a little headache coming on, and I'd love to lie down for an hour before supper. Would you mind?"

He felt her forehead, checking for fever. "Yes, perhaps you should. You're a bit warm. Delia, are you upset about something?"

"No, not really," she whispered, avoiding his eyes. "Only..."

"Only what, *mo bhean*?" he asked sweetly, kissing her cheek.

"Only... Oh, you'll be angry with me!"

He drew her to the sofa, sitting beside her. "Why would you think that?"

"Because I've been stupid. I shouldn't have looked, but Mama insisted. I'm very sorry for snooping. I didn't mean to do it!"

"Snooping?" he asked.

"Bailey packed your cases whilst Ada packed mine. Mama helped me choose what to bring, so she was in our apartment at the time, you see. That's how she saw it."

"Saw what?"

"Well, your pistols for a start. Bailey was packing them along with a metal box of ammunition. Mama had been in your bedchamber, measuring the wardrobe closet for new built-ins, or so she said, when she came upon a broken box. It looked as though someone had forced it open, and she worried it had been tampered with it."

Paul's smile vanished. His closet had been rifled the previous December by some phantom, and he wondered if the same intrusion had happened again.

"Was anything else in the closet disturbed? Did Bailey seem alarmed?"

"He mentioned a previous incident, when your clothing had been thrown about, and you'd thought someone had searched the closet. Who would do that, Paul? And why? It makes me feel so very vulnerable when you're not there!"

"I'll always protect you, *mo bhean*. Always. And I promise not to leave you alone again. From now on, if I travel, you come with me. Would you like that?" He held her close, his mind sorting through the idea that someone had targeted him again. "Was anything missing?"

"Bailey didn't think so, and he sent a note for you. It's inside your suitcase. But Paul, there's something else. Please, I didn't intend to snoop. But Mama brought it in and showed it to me. And I... Well, I kept it."

She rose from the couch and removed a beaded drawstring handbag from its place inside the closet. Opening the strings, she withdrew a leather packet. Paul instantly recognised it, and his mood turned sour.

"Your mother brought you this?" he asked as she handed him the packet.

Delia nodded. "I'm very sorry, as I said. Paul, why do you keep Elizabeth's letters? And there's a poem you wrote for her, called 'For My Princess'."

"That was before I met you, darling. Long ago."

"But then whose picture is it? There's one of Beth. That one's obvious, but the other isn't, and it's dedicated on the back to someone named David. I don't understand. Scold me, if you wish, but please, would you explain?"

The earl opened the packet and removed several dozen letters, an unfinished sonnet, and two photographs. One was of Elizabeth at eighteen. On the back, he'd written ''My dark-eyed Princess, April 1886'. The other was a hand-coloured image of a woman with fair hair and azure eyes.

A mixture of anger and fear warred inside the earl's mind as he struggled to keep his temper. He had no wish to injure his wife's fragile heart, but he also had no idea how to explain why he'd kept Cozette du Barroux's photograph or Beth's heartfelt letters—worst of all the poem! Paul had a terrible feeling that this moment would determine the course of his marriage.

And he was right.

CHAPTER TWENTY-ONE

Hôtel Terminus, Paris

Charles stared at Romanov, that same familiar tingle running along his hands and the back of his neck. "Why are you here, really?"

Anatole smiled. "I have anticipated this moment for many years, Charles Robert."

"What moment is that?"

"When I tell you of your life," Anatole answered. "It was the very last thing I said to you on the journey to the registry office in Liverpool. Do you remember?" he asked, lifting his hands and waving them across Charles's face.

The gesture caused a series of images to tumble like photographs through Sinclair's mind, memories of long ago. He could see himself as a boy, sitting across from Romanov in a sumptuous carriage that smelled of leather and oranges. The boy Charles wore the costume of English youth: short trousers, knee socks, a shirt and tie. He looked as though he were ready for a day at Eton or Harrow. Prince Anatole was dressed in a fur-trimmed coat and matching hat, a long carved cane by his side. He looked typically Russian and extremely wealthy.

"Do you remember?" asked Romanov.

"I remember the carriage ride, but other things, too. You took me to the office and paid the registrar to falsify my birth certificate. Why do that? Why would you steal my childhood?"

"I did it to protect you, Charles. When I found you on the docks of Liverpool, you were in a terrible state. Your mother had lost her mind already, for she'd suffered from a fragile nervous condition since January of that year."

"My sister's death," he replied. "She was only one day old."

"Yes, your sister's tragic disappearance."

Charles shook his head. "No, no. She died. My father—everyone insisted she died!"

Romanov touched the duke's hand, and Charles began to calm. "Remember that later," he told him. "Not yet. For now, think only of our time together. It was raining that day on the Liverpool wharf. The One had told me to meet you and keep you for two years in my home. Saraqael had slain your father. Can you remember that?"

"Some of it," the duke admitted, part of his mind wandering in the past. "The other Russian. Mother trusted him, but he—he did something to her."

"Do not become lost, my friend," Romanov warned the duke. "Watch the past, but do not follow after it. Learn from its truth, but remember you are now a man. You need not fear these memories, Charles."

"Koshmar," the human murmured. Just speaking the name sent a shiver down his spine. "I think his name was Koshmar. My mother befriended him, years earlier. As a girl."

"Yes, and he paid many visits to Rose House."

"He did."

"Koshmar presented himself as a mystic, and Angela Sinclair trusted him, sometimes even more than she trusted your good father."

"He tried to befriend me, but I never liked him."

"Yes, that is true. You've always had great instinct and discernment, but they needed refinement. Koshmar gave you many gifts, including two mechanical clocks and a tall mirror. Do you remember the mirror?"

Charles's eyes blinked, as if returning from a trance. "Yes. It all came back at Tory's home. I was climbing the tower stairs to reach Adele's apartment, and I felt something pull me into the past."

"Another waking vision," Anatole explained. "They will come more often now, Charles. This is why I am here, because you have recalled both the clocks and the mirror. What other memories call to you?"

He rose and crossed to the windows. Outside, he could see the street lights of Paris, flickering along the *Rue Saint Lazare*, and beyond to the *Qaui de Tuilleries* and the mighty Seine. The sidewalks were alive with theatre-goers and late-night sight-seers. The entire city hummed with life. The layout of the buildings and boulevards looked like a great maze, and the people within them moved within the labyrinth, oblivious to the dangers surrounding them.

Why did he think of a maze?

He'd longed to recall his childhood, but now as all the old thoughts and events clicked into place, the reality of it hung upon his heart like unbearable chains.

"The memories hurt, do they not?" Romanov asked. "I do not understand all of human emotions, but I've noticed pain is a constant. Never before had I seen such anguish as when I found you standing upon that dock, Charles Robert. Your mother had lost herself in grief, and the shock of watching your father die had left you void of all memory. And so I took you, whilst another of my brethren saw to it a woman rescued your mother. Angela is with the Savior now, my friend, and she awaits the day when you join her and your father."

"Why?" he asked, tears staining his face. "Why would God allow such horrors to visit my family? I don't understand it."

Romanov joined him at the window, placing a comforting hand upon Sinclair's shoulder. "These trials come from the enemy, Charles Robert, but the One allows them, to form within you the strength of marrow that rivals any steel! You have been designed for a great purpose, Charles Sinclair. In the coming century, your hand will guide England through very troubled waters. You and your sons will change the world."

Charles turned, wiping the tears away as if trying to remove the pain. "Tell me about my sons. You keep using that plural."

"Ah, yes," the angel answered smiling. "I've been given permission to reveal some of that to you, but only that which does not endanger your free will choices."

"Yes, and?"

"Your duchess will give you seven children," Romanov told him plainly. "Six sons who will stand upon the world like great trees, rooted firmly within God's word, and a daughter with the courage of a lion. Adele will be an elder sister to these seven, teaching them and helping to sharpen their minds and hearts. Eight children in all; eight warriors who will change the world. You and your children will rise to great heights, spreading branches across the earth and reaching even unto the heavens. It is this responsibility that requires their father pass through fire, for only flames can separate gold from dross."

"The files Goron gave me," he said pointing to the metal box. "Are they part of this fire?"

"You'd already sensed it, but some of the language is beyond you presently. Here, allow me to help."

Anatole reached out and touched the duke's forehead. "Your French is now fully restored. It's always been there, within your mind, but other worries crowded it out, and formed a block. You say you have no talent for language, but you spoke fluent French as a boy. Your Uncle Robert taught you."

"Paul's father? Wait," he said wistfully, returning to the sofa. "I can remember it now. I remember him. Uncle Robert did teach me French, but also German. And Kepelheim—Uncle Marty," he continued, breaking into a smile. "He helped. They'd speak to me in French and German for hours sometimes. They said it was to prepare me for the future."

"Yes, they did. You were a brilliant child, and you had a great capacity for learning."

"And the mirror? Why is that important, and why do I sometimes have such terrible visions about them?"

"You see your enemy's face?" asked the prince.

"Red eyes," he whispered tightly. "But surely that is my imagination."

"It is not," the angel stated. "More will come as you continue to remember, sometimes in waking visions that will come when you least expect them. Let them wash over you, Charles, for they are meant to prepare you."

"Prepare me for what?"

"For the coming war."

"What war?" he asked, dreading the answer.

"Black, red, and white. You have met the black and the red, but the white remains hidden."

"You mean God's dove? The Holy Spirit? Is that the white division of this war?"

The angel shook his head, his pale eyes serious. "No, but it will present itself as an agent for good. My loyal brethren and I also fight the spirit rulers of these three colours, and we shall do our best to protect you. Remember, Charles, anything that reaches you is allowed by the One to strengthen and refine you. And now, you can read everything Chief Goron's friend wrote, for some is in German.

Three colours, human, hybrid, and spirit. Unseen and seen, their poison seeping slowly into world of men, and you stand at the very heart of this war."

"I don't want to be at the heart of any war!" the duke exclaimed, jumping to his feet. "I've never wanted to be anything more than a man who loves and is loved. Why must I be more than that? Why may I not live my life in peace?"

"Because this is your calling. All created beings are given free will, but some are destined for greatness. Yes, you may choose to avoid it all by retreating from the world, but the rebels who plan to use your blood will not stop, Charles. If not you, then it will be your children who endure these trials. They will face those red eyes. They will feel the rake of the Dragon's claw!"

A shudder ran down Sinclair's back and arms, and he pictured Georgianna or Adele at the mercy of that hideous, scaly face from the attic mirror. Hearing that voice, feeling its fetid breath upon their sweet faces.

No, he could not allow it. *Would not allow it.*

"How do I take this stand you speak of? You see the battle from a different perspective, Anatole. Your vision is clear, but I'm half blind; sometimes totally blind." He leaned closer to whisper. "And you implied this affects Adele. Why? What has she to do with this war?"

"The answer to that lies within the pages of those files," he said, indicating the locked box. "Chief Goron only guesses at the truth, but once you've read these reports, all will become clear. Do you think the rebel angels occupy only the unseen realm?"

"Of course not. You live here, and we've dealt with Raziel and his vampire brother Saraqael. If they're here, then there must be others."

"More than you could count. The Earth is home to many kinds of creatures, most invisible to your eyes, unless they choose to reveal themselves. Think of this world as a multi-layered maze, Charles. A living equation with endless solutions, based upon free will choices. Just as in the Stone Realms, this multiple-possibility maze has doors that lead to secondary doors, that then lead to endless other doors. Pagan priests use roots and herbs to open these portals, but the One would keep them shut, permitting entrance at His will only. I may pass through them, moving into one of these other hallways, you might say; but to you, I'd simply vanish. I see the doors clearly. You do not. It is how I arrived at the theatre this evening."

"Why is this important? I'm very tired, Anatole. My brain cannot decipher these equations."

"Yes, I know, but hear me out. A very long and twisted path has led to your birth, Charles Robert. I have told you that you are central to the future, but I am not permitted to reveal your future choices. The rebels believe it is they who created you with this unique ability, but it is the One—*and only He*—who has done it. He allows the rebels to pursue a futile plan, because it is a trap which will snap shut upon them!"

"Are you saying I'm the bait? Or that my children will be?" asked the duke, his blue eyes wide.

Romanov reached out to touch the duke's forearm. "Forgive me. It is a poor metaphor, but in a way, you are. In a similar way, you could say Adam and Eve were bait, but the trap for the rebel Nachash was also a test. A test to see if the Nachash might actually choose to obey the One, and a test of Adam's character."

"Am I being tested?"

"Yes. Your decisions matter, Charles. It is why you now stand a breath away from England's throne. Think of that throne of England as a tempting fruit. What will you do, if this fruit is presented as both delectable and deadly, all at once? You eat and are pleased, but if you do not eat, the world and even your children will suffer?"

"I don't understand. Please, Anatole, if you're trying to teach me, my brain cannot accept it."

"I wish I could be more clear, my friend, but it is not yet permitted."

Charles ran a hand through his curling black hair, slumping into the sofa. "Are you saying I was wrong to accept this shadow version of kingship? Is becoming a secret ruler foolish? I can still tell her no. I can write to the queen now, send a telegram, Anatole. I prefer not to take it anyway. I want only to live in peace!"

"Which is why you are the best man for the job, my friend," the angel told him, his eyes filled with empathy and kindness. "Other men would accept with the intention of slowly assuming greater and greater responsibility; reshaping the throne into a personal podium for dictatorship. But you will not. You are one of the strongest men to ever live, Charles Robert Arthur. Your character is upright and seeks only good for others. It is that quality which the duchess saw in your eyes the first time she met you. Very few men with so bright a heart have ever lived."

"And Della? Why do you say she's important?"

"Her blood derives from the same wellspring as your own. It is why she is drawn to you. Somehow, deep within her, Adele knows you and she belong together."

"Why? Paul's her father, not I."

It took so long for the angel to reply that Charles began to doubt his senses. He wasn't in Paris in '76, when Della was conceived; he was in London, working as a policeman, newly married to Amelia Winstone. Yet Adele's eyes looked more and more like his own, and he felt connected to her in the same indecipherable way he'd always felt connected to Elizabeth.

Why?

Finally, after what seemed like an eternity, Romanov waved his hand, causing the locked metal box to unlatch on its own. He reached for the file and opened it. "I have communed with the One. I am permitted to explain."

"You've been speaking to God?" he asked, wondering yet again if all this were all a dream.

"I have. Do you see this name inside the first file? Reverend Georgio Georgiadis Lambelet of St. Sophia in London. He holds many secrets. He has just received a telegram from his archbishop, commanding his presence at a special ecumenical meeting in Canterbury. He will arrive there on Saturday at 9:27 am, staying with the dean, Robert Smith."

"Isn't it rather odd for a Greek priest to be invited to stay with an Anglican dean and confer with him on matters of faith?"

"Perhaps, but a patron to both churches has suggested the conference and provided funding to cover all expenses."

"And I suppose this patron is you?"

Anatole smiled. "Lambelet and I have known one another since he trained in Paris. He was but a student, and I offered him advice. He serves on the same side as you and I, Charles. He speaks seven languages, but more to the point, he understands much about the birds that roost here and in England."

The angel stood. "I shall leave you to rest. A telegram will arrive for you in five minutes. I must deal with a problem in Kent."

"At Branham?" the duke whispered anxiously. "Is my wife in danger?"

"Not yet, but one of my kind seeks to plant himself there. And a new danger is about to arise. You have other guardians here, but take care around Prince Araqiel and his sister. They are of my kind, and they seek to ensnare you in their perverted plans."

"I'd thought both seemed too interested in us for coincidence. How do I protect Adele?"

"By keeping her close. The One looks after you, but your free will must never be compromised. Rest in His promises, Charles Robert. Do the best you can with each day, understanding that a single failure is not the end of all things. A journey of many steps sometimes includes a moment of doubt. Press onward, my friend. And *believe*."

The angel vanished, and Sinclair collapsed against the cushions, the box once again in his lap—shut, locked, and silent.

It was as though the prince had never been there.

CHAPTER TWENTY-TWO
Midnight, 2nd May - 33 Wormwood, City of London

"Why are we here?" asked Honoria Chandler. "I do have things to do, Urquhart, and it's very late."

Sir Clive paced back and forth. He'd called the Round Table remnant to an emergency meeting, but now he'd begun to doubt his own plans. "A moment, madam! One moment. My brain is busy!"

"You have no brain, Clive," Dr. Alvin Meyerbridge complained. "If this is about Alex Collins, we already know. Some man named Alphonse Theseus had been visiting him at the London and insists on his release. Just who is this Theseus fellow anyway? I've no records on him."

"Quiet!" the builder shouted, his head aching. At long last, he sat, looking at the faces before him. "Where is Serena?"

"Gone to Russia with Saraqael, I imagine," Sir Robert Cartwright muttered, pouring himself a glass of wine. "And I say good riddance to them both! Clive, those of us who remain alive have met privately, and we think that..."

"You think? You think!" the portly builder shouted, his cheeks red as apples. "What brain cells do you use for such impossible pursuits, Sir Robert? I suppose these newcomers think they have the right to redirect our mission, eh? Is that so, Baron Wychwright? Do you and your two miserable little friends think yourselves now worthy to claim leadership? Bah! You are a trio of infant sheep in the short pants, that's what you are! Squealing pigs with your noses deep in the trough, unaware that the butcher's knife awaits you! I am sick to death of all of you, and I think I create a new Round Table, eh? One with men who have brains!"

Honoria smiled. "Men? Whatever's gotten into you, Clive? I've never seen you actually take charge. Not since Trent died, anyway. And what of women?"

"Men, women? All the same," Clive muttered as he wiped his brow, his breathing somewhat laboured. "Nothing has gotten into me, madam. Nothing save the realisation that we are all doomed if we do not change our strategy. Here, if you want to see it! Look at this telegram!"

He threw a piece of yellow paper onto the oval table where the group had gathered in the great chamber beneath 33 Wormwood's impressive edifice. Chandler placed a pair of golden spectacles upon her nose, preparing to read the printed message, but Sir Richard Treversham grabbed it away.

"Here, let someone with young eyes read it." He smiled as he silently read the text. "I see. No wonder you're in such a tizzy, Clive. Here's what it says, my friends: 'On my way back. Three deaths required for next phase. Draw straws to choose.' And it is signed Koshmar. Our wolf prince dictates his will."

"He thinks we will simply lie down and die for him?" asked Chandler. "Why does anyone else have to die? This is ridiculous! When I became part of the Round Table twenty years ago, I was promised power, and thus far I've seen very little of it. And where the hell is Prince Alexei or Raziel or whatever it is we're to call the creature?" She lit a cigarette, blowing smoke into the air. "I begin to see your point, Clive. Perhaps, we'd be much better off on our own."

William Wychwright stood. "There are nine of us left, right? Urquhart, Chandler, Cartwright, Meyerbridge, Malford-Jones, Wisling, myself, Treversham, and Cecil Brandon here. If we give this fellow Koshmar three more lives, then he's whittled us down to nothing. No, he's trying to divide us. I say we stand and fight!"

Clive sat, his head in his hands. "Fight? Fight? With what do we fight? We have no power against such beings!" Chandler blew smoke into Clive's eyes, and the builder choked, grabbing the cylinder from her and stomping on it. "Please! I must think, and your ceaseless efforts at assuming control..." He paused, his beady eyes brightening. "Oh, but wait. Wait! Maybe. There could be a way out, but it may prove dangerous."

"And that is?" asked Brandon.

"We are nothing without the powers of the other realms, no?" All nodded. "Then, I say we ally ourselves with another. One more powerful than Koshmar, perhaps more powerful than Grigor. It's clear that the great powers and thrones we were promised is but a lure to madness."

"And death," Chandler reminded them, lighting another cigarette. "I've an idea. I was contacted by a representative from Germany. They seek an alliance. Red wings and black wings joining together."

"What does that mean?" asked Wychwright. "Who the devil are the black wings?"

"These blackbirds, madam," Clive moaned. "They will peck out your eyes and devour them along with your tasteless cigarettes! No, I will not allow it!"

"I've spoken with Alphonse Theseus, and he thinks it's a wise move," Lord Wisling told the group. The earl stood, his tall, straight-backed form commanding. "I rarely speak in this assembly, but it's become clear to me that we lack direction. Ever since Trent died, we've lost track of our original aim. All this focus on controlling Sinclair is madness and comes from some old, spiritual plan that very likely excludes us. Why can't we all go back to the original plan to produce an army of our own? If we create enough successful hybrids, as Malford-Jones believes we can, then mightn't we have the power to overthrow the kingdom without the need for these unreliable spirit creatures? Really, it seems that the infighting amongst these Watchers will be our downfall, if not our deaths!"

Clive looked up, a glimmer of hope glinting in his eyes. "Dr. Malford-Jones, are we able to continue this program without the Lords Raziel and Saraqael? Have we the scientific means?"

Laurence Malford-Jones was sixty-one but looked much younger, thanks to an elixir he'd created. He stood before the group, his lean hands upon the table's edge. "I am pleased to answer yes, Sir Clive. As with the good earl, I seldom speak in these gatherings, but I have never ceased to pursue an improved version of our hybrids or of ourselves. And I am also pleased to tell you that the Pollux Project is a rousing success! As a consequence, we're shutting down Castor, for it's drawn far too much attention from Sinclair and his ICI organisation. Also, I can now reveal that it is Dr. Theseus who has harvested the dead for our project."

Wychwright's blonde brows arched with dismay. "Harvested the dead? What the devil do you mean by that?"

Malford-Jones smiled, his light grey eyes fixed upon the baron. "You are William Wychwright, correct? Your father was David Wychwright."

"Yes. Why?"

"Because we have him. We have all the so-called 'missing' of London."

"You have him? See here, sir, my late father was interred at Marylebone last December!"

"Is that what you think? Truly, I'd thought you had greater insight than that, Baron."

A knock sounded on the door to the vault; the metallic material of the portal reverberated like a death knell throughout the candlelit chamber. Sir Richard Treversham rose to answer, admitting a tall individual with silver hair and an impressive face.

Clive Urquhart grew livid at seeing the newcomer.

"No! No! We will not do this! When Trent was our leader, he refused to admit you, sir. We pledged ourselves to Collins, not to your mad plans. Your science is far too risky. No, sir. You may turn about and leave now!"

Alphonse Theseus seemed to grow even taller, and he smiled, revealing perfect, white teeth that looked as strong as iron. The effect dropped the ambient temperature of the room by twenty degrees. Chandler drew a shawl round her bony shoulders, and most of the men seemed to shrink in their chairs.

"Your opinion no longer matters, Clive. If you wish to remain alive, I suggest you sit and listen. I am now in control of this assembly, and it is I who will protect you against Saraqael and the others."

"Others? What others? How many others?" muttered poor Brandon.

Treversham placed a protective hand on his less than brilliant friend. "And you are?" he asked, standing. "My friends and I know nothing about you, sir. Why should we follow anything you say? We joined this organisation because the Round Table promised access to the seats of power in London. It now seems this assembly is nothing more than a bunch of limp reeds in a sea of doubt. For my part, I'm finished with the lot of you. Will, I'm leaving. If you and Brandon wish to stay, that's your business. If I wanted to playact, I'd have joined the Masons!"

Theseus held up his hand, and Treversham froze in place. "How dare you speak to me with such insolence, boy? I could still your heart with a mere thought," the straight-backed stranger told the smug baronet. "When you joined this table, you pledged your life, Sir Richard. Shall I call in that pledge?"

Treversham's eyes bulged, as he struggled for even a single breath.

Theseus smiled once again, pleased with the effect.

"Let him go!" Honoria shouted. "You needn't demonstrate your abilities, Theseus! Please, let's have no more bloodshed. Not amongst us. Please, enough of us have died. Let's have an end to it!"

Theseus waved his hand, and Treversham's lungs began to fill with air. The baronet clutched at his throat, gasping in the rich oxygen mixture.

"I do hope I won't have to make my point again," Theseus told them.

"Are you one of them?" asked Lord Wisling. "One of those Watchers?"

"Oh, I'm much better than that," Theseus answered. "Their blood flows in my veins, but along with that is the purest human blood that ever filled a heart, making me stronger and wiser than either. Think of me as what you all may yet become. But to achieve it, you must follow all my commands from now on."

"And the others? These princes who think they rule us? How do we explain our shift in loyalty to them? They'll kill us all!" Urquhart shouted.

"Leave Saraqael and Raziel to me, Sir Clive. My alliance is with an elohim who is much more powerful than any you've yet met. He is removing the pretenders to his throne, and already, this great Power has taken Prince Raziel prisoner. Saraqael is next on his list."

"Raziel is a p-p-prisoner?" Clive stuttered, his cheeks paling. "But how? No, it is impossible! You must be mistaken, or else you lie!"

Theseus walked round the table to the builder's large chair. He peered down at the shorter man, his cold grey eyes sparking flame. "Think yourself powerful, little man? Think again. The old plans

revive, and the new turn to stone. Shall I turn *you* into a stone statue as I've done to so many others? Prisoners who lie beneath the
waves or crumble within the earth? I am he who gathers the dead,
the founder of nations, and ruler of kingdoms. My walk upon this
earth has taken me into every nation and every continent. My arm is
long, as is my shadow. I am he whom Ariadne loved, the spinner of
magical threads, conqueror of the underworld. I defeated the great
Horned One, and he now follows my commands. I mix the blood of
the great and the greater, and I unmask the pretenders of this world."

"Are you another Watcher?" Sir Clive asked, his heart pounding. "If so, then leave now. We have had enough of your kind's
games. We want no more of them!"

"Did I say so?" Theseus asked them. "My alliances are few, but
what few I make are unbreakable. Now, shall we talk?"

He waved his hands, and Urquhart's chair toppled to the side,
forcing the builder onto the floor. Theseus waved the hand again,
uprighting the chair, which he then took as his own. He glanced
down at Clive. "Will you remain on the floor like a dead pig or take
a lesser place with the living?"

Urquhart pushed himself up, and then limped to the next empty
chair, offering no reply, but if looks had the power to kill, then surely, Theseus would be dead.

All the other humans looked to their new leader with eyes of
cowed deference.

Except for one.

Baron William Wychwright crossed his arms, stubbornly. "I insist you explain yourself, sir! What the hell is this gathering of the
dead? And why did you mention my father? What has he to do with
any of this? Albert Wendaway killed him, we all know that. Where
is the vengeance I was promised? That big-toothed freak that calls
himself Striga vowed to give me retribution and power. I see none
of that here."

Alphonse Theseus laughed at the bombastic baron. "My, my
what a curious fellow you are, Captain. You actually see yourself as
in charge of the entire world, don't you? Others may find that tiresome, but I can work with it. You remind me of myself in my younger days. Very well. You shall have your retribution, but the limping
cockerel you call Wendaway had nothing to do with slaying your
father. He merely had the misfortune to be there when it happened,

for the real murderer had lured him there to act as bait. I will give that information to the ICI soon. Sinclair and his tribe of investigators will make short work of giving you vengeance. Rest assured, you shall get *all* that is coming to you, Baron. You shall drain every last dreg of that trembling cup."

CHAPTER TWENTY-THREE

3rd May, 2:14 am – Branham Hall

Paul Stuart's eyes popped open, seeing the coffered ceiling of the main bedchamber of the Anjou Suite. For a moment, he'd forgotten where he was, who he was. He rolled left, finding Cordelia sound asleep. Her young body was curled up, her knees drawn close to her chest. She often slept like this, as if protecting herself. He stroked her fair curls, kissing her cheek. Paul quietly slipped out of bed and donned a dressing gown over his pyjamas. He had the oddest sensation that he was needed.

Creeping quietly down the servants' staircase, the earl wound his way through a labyrinth of state rooms and galleries to the main floor drawing room, know simply as 'the red room'. A fire burnt inside its hearth, and he entered to find Elizabeth reading near its warm flames.

"Why are you awake?" he asked as he joined her on the sofa.

Beth set the book aside. "Because two active children conspire to keep me awake. Why are you?"

"I'm not sure. Are you all right?"

"Yes, of course," she answered. "Darling, you look upset. I hope you're not still concerned about our talk this afternoon. Really, Paul, I'm very happy for you both."

"No, it isn't that," he told her. "I'm not sure what's bothering me, actually. Some days it seems to me that our lives have taken a turn into some fanciful dreamscape. We certainly aren't living the lives we pictured."

"I suppose not," Elizabeth answered. "Is Cordelia feeling unwell? I noticed she hardly ate this evening."

"Her stomach rebels now and then, just as yours did, but overall, she seems healthy. Is Gehlen still coming down next week?"

"He thought Monday, yes. Why? Are you worried?"

He managed a weary smile. "No, not really worried. I suppose I still take my job as your champion to heart. With Charles away, it falls to me to look after you. You need to sleep, Beth."

"If only I could! When the babies begin to move about, it's difficult."

"You can feel them move?" he asked in amazement. "What's it like?"

She laughed. "Charles has never asked me that. What does it feel like?" she mused aloud. "Well, sometimes, it's a swift kick, other times a bit like a tickle. I find it quite miraculous, actually. I feel like I'm carrying the future pages of a great history book. Knowing that makes the odd sleepless night worth it. I'm sure Delia will feel the same way, when your baby begins to move."

"I'm not sure she's speaking to me these days," he admitted.

She moved closer, touching his face the way she'd done a thousand times before. It felt familiar, comforting. He hadn't expected tears to fall, but fall they did, and she drew him close, as a mother might do for a wounded son.

"What is it?" she whispered, stroking his long hair. "Surely, it's not that bad."

"Cordelia found the portrait of Cozette. And your old letters, along with a few I'd written to you but never posted."

"Oh," the duchess whispered.

"Beth, she's so delicate, and now she isn't sure she can trust me. I've worked so hard to gain that trust, and in one day, it's gone to ruin!"

"Darling, I'm sure she'll come round. I keep all your letters. Where's the harm? Charles found them once in an old photo box, and he read them all. At first, he was a bit hurt, but then he realised you'd written those to me long before he and I became engaged, that it was nothing more than history. The letters are part of a past that makes me who I am today. I'm sure Cordelia will realise that as well. Besides, we never shared anything truly intimate in those letters. You were always more protector than lover. Well, until last summer."

He sighed. "I think my unposted letters hurt the most. I wrote them the night of your birthday ball and contain language somewhat more intimate. But I didn't know how to tell you what was in my heart, Beth. Not then. Rasha and Seth buzzed all round you, and I knew Charles was never far from your thoughts. You'd forgotten your old childhood friend."

She kissed his hand. "Never. Not for one minute did I ever forget you! But even those letters can be explained, Paul. Give her time. Remember, that carrying a baby plays with a woman's emotions. As you're well aware, I find myself crying at the slightest thing."

"I pray you're right," he answered. "Beth, I love Delia more than I ever thought possible! Now, she worries that I've kept more secrets from her."

"Does she know about Della? Were you forced to tell her?"

"Not yet, but we talked about Cozette. The photo of her bore a personal inscription to David."

"The name you used whilst spying for England?"

"Yes. Delia said she accepts my explanation, but I think she carries doubts."

"Shall I talk to her?"

He shook his head. "I fear that would only add fuel to the fire. It's my fault, really. I gave her mother too much rope, and she's managed to hang me with it."

"Nonsense," Elizabeth whispered, kissing his cheek. "Darling, these dark clouds will pass, and you'll see sunshine again. I promise. Now, go back upstairs and keep your wife warm. That apartment never heats properly, and I'm sure she's cold without you."

He tried to smile, and she laughed softly.

"Do you find me amusing?" he asked.

"No, but I was thinking of all the times you comforted me when I was little. You've always been my hero, Sir Paul."

He did smile now, taking her hand. "And you've always been my little princess."

"I think Cordelia is your princess now, dear."

"Yes," he whispered. "She is, Beth. I really do love her."

"I'm glad."

All the hall's dozens of clocks began to strike three, one after another, and as the final chimes sounded, a high piercing scream rose above the musical chorus.

"That came from the east wing!" Beth shouted as Aubrey rushed out of the drawing room. "Paul, it's Delia!"

The earl was already climbing the stairs, and Elizabeth dashed after as quickly as her condition allowed, but remained at the bottom of the long case. She could see Paul race to the right once he reached the broad landing, heading towards the northeastern Anjou suite. The screams continued unabated, a series of terrifying calls that roused every member of the household, be it guest or staff. Even the night watchmen on the grounds responded, and by three minutes past three, the entire house was alight.

Whitechapel

Two hours away, in East London, another woman screamed. Molly Porter, proprietress of the Porter Inn, a lodging house within walking distance of the London Hospital, had heard a noise at her back door. Fearing one of her two boys had been taken again by that 'awful Russian', she threw on a robe and raced through the inn to the source of the noise.

What she found precipitated the screams, and in a moment, a policeman's whistle joined her frantic shouts, answered by half a dozen patrolmen.

What Porter had found at the base of her back steps was neither of her boys, nor was it the hated Russian who sometimes stayed there. No, it was the bloodless body of a portly man with a waxed moustache and not one stitch of clothing.

A light rain began to fall, spattering the dismembered corpse's open eyes and slowly cooling the lifeless body of Sir Clive Urquhart. A long curved dagger protruded from his heart, and a series of peculiar symbols were carved upon his soft belly.

CHAPTER TWENTY-FOUR

3rd May – Hôtel Terminus, Paris

To Sinclair's surprise, both he and Adele slept soundly that night, not waking until well after eight. He could hear her singing as she dressed, and Charles knocked to see if she required a lady's maid, offering to ring the front desk and ask that one be sent up. After hearing a quick, 'No, not this morning, Father!', he removed the mysterious locked metal box from its secure location and began to sift through the files.

Most were Montmartre cases: thefts, swindles, reports of un-savoury foreigners, hanging about the tangled web of streets. The Montmartre district took its name from a small hill on the *rive droit* side of the Seine; that is the bank which sits on one's right hand, assuming you faced west, or downstream, of the Seine. Montmartre had once sat outside the city limits, but in 1860 the area became part of the 18th *arrondissement*, or administration area. Though steeped in religious history, the hill also had military advantage. In 1814, Russian soldiers claimed the hill during the Battle of Paris, and later Montmartre served as an anarchist birthing ground to the rebels of the infamous Paris Commune, a fleeting, coup government which died in just over two months.

Artists and anarchy formed the colourful parents to the trou-bled children of Montmartre, making Paul Stuart's clandestine ac-tivities easy to pursue. Whilst fulfilling England's orders, the wily young Viscount Marlbury haunted these streets in the guises of sea-man, tinker, concierge, baker, pickpocket, even *gendarme*, and in the summer of 1876, he used the false identity of a struggling artist named David Saunders.

Goron had spoken truly. According to the files in Sinclair's hands, a secretive clique within government, calling itself '*le cercle intérieur*' had kept records on all the young viscount's activities. Entire files mentioned his remarkable exploits, and a few were coded reports, received directly from Paul, and given to the French inner circle's leaders.

One file bore the name 'Cozette du Barroux' typed upon the outer cover, and within its pages, Charles found dozens of photographs of the young woman at different ages. Some of these were somewhat blurry, for one of the French circle spies had used a prototype of Kodak's new film camera to secretly snap photos of the girl as she walked along the street. He also found watercolours and sketches, signed 'D. Saunders'; no doubt composed by Paul in his artist guise. His cousin certainly had talent.

Turning forward in the file, he discovered a certificate of adoption, listing a female infant, referred to as a '*princess du sang*', aged three days. Her birthplace was listed 'overlooking the ruins of Mt. Avalon, England'. She was described as well-formed with flaxen hair and blue eyes of unusual colour. A woman named Madame de la Ronchelle had served as intermediary during the exchange, stating she'd received the infant from a traveller whilst in London. When asked to look after the child, she'd agreed, and brought her to Lyon, where she kept a country house. He'd just turned to the page describing the house, when a voice broke his concentration.

"Good morning," Della called as she joined him in the main room. "You look gloomy, Holmes. Why?"

"Do I?" he asked, shutting the file and returning the stack to the box and locking it. "Then, I'm conveying the wrong message, for my heart is full, Watson. Did you sleep well?"

"Very well. I dreamt of stars and planets and music! It was ever so nice. Did you? Sleep well, I mean?"

He drew her to his side and kissed her cheek. "I did. I dreamt of Robby and Georgianna, and you were helping to teach them how to ride on horseback."

Adele smiled, but then a little cloud fell across her eyes. "Did Tory tell you about how I met Prince Ara?"

"Some of it, yes."

"I'm not sure he's to be trusted, Father. And his sister stood far too close to you last night. She watched you all the time. I didn't like it."

He laughed. "Are you my guardian now?"

"If I must be, yes. She likes you, but not as a friend should like you. She wants to be your *maîtresse-en-titre*, I think."

"Whatever is that?" he asked, smiling.

"I read it in one of my history books. The French kings often kept a *maîtresse-en-titre*. In English, it would probably be an entitled or official mistress. The king slept with this woman as though she were his wife, if you can believe it, and she had a great deal of power at the court. I told M'sieur Roubolet that no honest husband would do such a thing, but he said it was quite common with French royalty. That kings need extra wives to have more children."

"And you think this Princess Eluna wants me to take her as my mistress? I doubt that, little one, but just in case, I shall keep you close, as my official guardian."

She kissed his hand. "I shall be ever vigilant, Holmes. You're far too nice to tell her to go away, but I shan't be so nice; not if I think she's trying to seduce you."

"Seduce me?" he smiled. "Is that another new vocabulary word?"

"Not exactly. It's in one my novels. I looked it up. The French word is *séduire*. When do we return to England?"

"Tomorrow. I've armour to wear on Saturday, and I may need to practise riding in it first."

"Armour? Like a real knight?"

"So says your mother. I may need help with that, too."

"Of course," she said seriously. "Shall I be *la page du chevalier*? Your knight's page?"

"*Mais oui, mon petit. J'aurai besoin de votre aide pour tout ça.*"

Della laughed. "Your French has certainly improved, Father! Mother will be surprised."

"Not as much as I've been," he smiled. "Hungry?"

"Famished," she answered. "There are seven restaurants downstairs."

"Seven? Can you eat seven meals?"

Della laughed. "I'd need seven heads, but I've only the two, remember?"

Charles kissed her once again, rising to place a telephone call to the front desk, intending to make reservations, when someone knocked.

"Yes?" he asked, opening the door.

The face on the other side of the door was of a stranger. He stood about five feet, four inches tall. He wore an overcoat that was too sizes too large, making him seem all the more childlike. He held the edge of a broad-brimmed hat, and his light blue eyes blinked from behind a pair of wire spectacles. The cheeks sagged slightly, making him look a little like a Basset Hound, but the small mouth was firm and determined.

"Are you Sinclair?" asked the man in English.

"Yes. I'm Sinclair."

"Oh, good. I was afraid I might have the wrong hotel," the Basset Hound replied in a British accent. "My name is Cherubino. Archibald Cherubino. Prince Anatole sent me."

"Have you anything to prove it?" asked Charles.

The man's sagging cheeks lifted as he laughed. "Ah, well, the prince said you'd ask me that. He spoke with you last night, after rescuing you from Araqiel at the theatre, didn't he? And he restored your childhood French. Oh, and the German, too. Shall I go on?"

"I suppose not," Sinclair muttered. "May I ask why the prince sent you?"

"I'm to watch after Lady Adele whilst you go on an errand. It will make sense in a few minutes. Sir Thomas Galton will ring that telephone in six seconds."

Adele had joined them at the door, and she asked, "Six seconds? How can you know that?"

The phone's bell jingled.

"Well?" asked Cherubino. "Aren't you going to answer?"

Adele did it for her father, picking up the receiver. "*Oui? Allô.*"

She paused and listened. "Oh, yes. He's here. Just a moment. Father? It's Sir Thomas Galton. He's downstairs."

Charles kept watch on the peculiar little man at the door whilst he took the receiver. "Tom?" He listened. "Yes, I see. How long?" Another pause. "All right. I'll come down."

He hung up. "Adele, this gentleman is Mr. Archibald Cherubino. Would you feel safe with him whilst I make a call with Sir Thomas?"

Adele walked up to the stranger. "You have nice eyes. He's all right, Father. I can see heaven in his eyes."

Cherubino laughed. "I was told you had insight, Adele Marie. I wonder if you'd like to read a book with me? We could have a lovely breakfast, and when your father returns, you'll be packed and ready."

"Packed?" asked Charles.

"Oh, yes. It's all arranged. Your passage is booked to depart Calais at seven. Lady Victoria has decided to remain in France until June, when the babies will be born. Lady Patterson-Smythe has offered to stay with her. As I said, it's all arranged. One might say, it was decided eons ago."

"I see," Charles managed to answer. "I shan't be long, little one. Will you be all right?"

"Very all right," she assured him as she picked up one of her books. "I'll read this one to my new friend, Father. You go on." She opened the book to the first page. "This one's called *From the Earth to the Moon*. I don't have it in French, I'm afraid, only English, but it's a wonderful adventure. Do you like adventures, Mr. Cherubino?"

"Oh, yes! I love adventures. You read for a little while, and then I'll share some of mine with you. They're quite exciting."

"I should enjoy that. Very well," Della began, "this story commences with the story of the Gun Club..."

Confident that Adele was in safe hands, Charles descended the hotel stairs quickly, wondering just what adventure he was about to experience.

"Tom, I'd no idea you were in Paris," he told Galton as he approached. "It's good to see you as well, Inspector Stanley. Why are you two here? You should both be in London."

"Mr. Kepelheim asked me to come, sir," Galton told him. "He's concerned for your welfare, and Lord Aubrey agrees. Both insist you return to England at once, and that you bring Lady Adele with you."

"I'd already planned to do that. Is that why you're here, Inspector Stanley?"

"Not exactly, sir. I ran into Sir Thomas outside the hotel. It seems our basic mission is the same. To bring you home, but my message comes from my wife. She's spoken with Margaret Hansen.

She believes the Round Table is planning a major strike at the inner circle."

"Which we now know to be true," Galton continued, his hat turning in his hands. "I always stop by the Sûreté whenever I'm in Paris, and Chief Goron had just received news from Edmund Reid. There's been another Round Table death. Sir Clive Urquhart." Galton withdrew a dossier from within his greatcoat. "This is a list of crimes we've been tracking here in Paris. Many are repetitions of what we're seeing in London, these Portmanteau Murders, for instance, echo our own Embankment Killings. We've identified two of the three Portmanteau victims as Redwing members. And now Clive is dead. We'd all feel better, sir, if you were home and under our protection."

Charles ignored the implication that he was at risk. All Romanov's warnings were coming true, and he must step up and prepare to enter the fire. "Red versus black. The war of the birds. Civil war within the ranks, but why take the bodies?"

"We're uncertain, sir, but when questioned, every family involved, every mortician, mentions the appearance of a blackbird moments before the body is found missing. It cannot be coincidence. We've placed guards on Urquhart's body."

"And the events at Branham? What are they?"

Galton moved the duke further to the side, and Stanley followed. "These are twofold, Your Grace. Firstly, do you recall Sir Simon Pembroke mentioning a series of tunnels that lead to Queen Eleanor's old castle?"

"Yes, he said Blackstone once asked to access them, and he refused. Why?"

"Despite that refusal, someone has been digging beneath Eleanor's castle and using the Pembroke tunnels to gain access. We think it was the late Colonel Collinwood, who also ran the covert operation at Anjou Castle for Blackstone."

"And the second of these twofold reasons?"

"Ah, now that was discovered by Mr. Blinkmire in a most peculiar way. A statue emerged from the depths of Queen's Lake a few days ago. It is identical to one beneath St. Arilda's."

"The bird or the man?"

"The man, sir. The plumbers have dug into the area and discovered more tunnels beneath the lake. Powers and his team worked without rest to drain it thoroughly, so that we might explore it. No one knew it existed, but apparently, the water concealed an entrance to a great artificial cavern. The cavern is well-constructed. One can walk without stooping, for it is broad and high, much like its twin 'neath St. Arilda. When I explored its length, I emerged into a glade of Henry's Woods, precisely where the little duchess says she found the faery house."

"That damnable glade! I begin to distrust everything about that property, Galton," Charles declared angrily. "That ground, perhaps, that entire village and all that surrounds are like a viper's nest!"

"So it would seem, sir, but then much of the world is like that. May I wire Lord Aubrey and say you're on your way?"

Charles glanced at Elbert Stanley. "Is Margaret Hansen safe?"

"For now, sir. Ida is in a state about all this, sir. And she spoke of two other women as well. One is Dr. MacKey."

Charles felt that peculiar electric tingle again, and his hands felt as though fire ran through them.

Hello, boy. Are you ready to play?

"Can you make arrangements for me and Adele?"

"We've already seen to it, sir. We can leave here in an hour."

"Good, we can be ready by then."

"Your Grace!" a man's voice called in a heavy French accent.

Charles glanced in the direction of the caller. The daytime concierge was running down the main staircase, carrying a pair of pillows.

"Yes?" asked the duke as the huffing man ran up to him.

"Forgive me, sir," panted the hotel employee as he handed the pillows to a bellman. "It is the note. Gerard!" he called to a thin man behind the desk. "The note for Duke Charles! Bring it to me!"

The thin fellow fetched an envelope from a bay of letter boxes and handed it across the desk to the concierge.

"For you, my lord," the manager said, still catching his breath. "It came overnight, and we dared not wake you. I hope we have not made mistake."

Charles took the envelope. Inside he found a single slip of paper which read:

> I know about du Barroux. See me. No police.
> 12 rue Chabanais. Ask for Marie.

"Who left this? Man or woman?"

The concierge conversed with the thin man in French for a moment, his words somewhat heated. He swiped at his sweating brow. "Pardon, *m'sieur le Duc*. Pierre, he think he make mistake, sir. It was a woman who brought the note. She wrote it on our note paper, as you see."

"She asked for me by name? Very few know I'm here."

"*Oui, m'sieur*. She did."

"Can you describe this woman?" he asked the frustrated concierge.

Another heated conversation took place, and the poor man turned at last, offering an apologetic answer. "I do hope we have not made mistake, Your Grace. The woman, she is dark-haired and quite petite. Fine figure but with a sadness about her, Pierre claim. He is—how you say?—imaginate. In the head."

"How old?"

"Pierre say she is not so young. Thirty perhaps. Educated from how she talk. She seem tidy, well-ordered. Small hands, but they shake as if she afraid."

"Pierre is quite observant."

The thin desk attendant smiled, daring to speak to the duke directly. "It is my job to see things, Your Grace," he said in English. "I hope is not woman you hope to see last night. If so, I apologise."

It took a second for the man's implication to seat itself in Sinclair's mind. "Oh, no!" he exclaimed, glancing at Galton self-consciously. "No, not at all. I'm not interested in pursuing that side of Parisian life. I am married to the most beautiful woman in all the world and love her dearly. If you met her, you'd understand. The duchess is my heart and soul."

"Then you are lucky man, Your Grace," the young man said, bowing.

The concierge waved at the desk boy as if to dismiss him and then turned his attention to the duke once more. "Forgive Pierre's insolence, Your Grace. We see many things here, and though our hotel is only now opening; already, these halls have witnessed arguments, breakups, flirtations, and assignations to fill the river ten times over! No, my lord Duke, you are blessed to have such a wife."

"Thank you. I thank the Lord for her every day."

Charles showed the note to Galton. "Do we go?"

Thomas handed the slip to Stanley. "Elbert, I'll go with the duke. You stay and protect Lady Adele."

"I believe Adele is in good hands, but I don't wish to be away long. If you'd remain, Elbert, I'd appreciate it. She's with Mr. Cherubino, in the royal suite. Top floor."

With Adele protected and given an activity to keep her occupied, he and Galton left for the very place where Adele had been conceived. 12 rue Chabanais. As their coach turned in that direction, Charles prayed for guidance. Perhaps, this is why Victoria turned her ankle, for it was that which brought Charles to France—that and the possibility of arresting Wendaway and Wentworth. More and more, his life had become a fantastic maze of never-ending journeys through unfamiliar corridors.

He thought of Adele, and of the paperwork making him the girl's adoptive father.

I came to Paris because of her, he realised at last. *I'm not here on ICI business, but to uncover the truth of Adele's birth. And just who her mother really was.*

CHAPTER TWENTY-FIVE

Just before dawn, 3ʳᵈ May, 1889 - Branham Hall

Paul Stuart had slept very little since his wife's terrifying screaming episode, having kept watch on her during the remaining hours. He stood and stretched, his clear blue eyes on the south lawn and long gravel drive, visible from their bedchamber window. The original east-wing apartments all opened to the south, and this large suite had once been used by the 3ʳᵈ Duke of Branham as his own. Because that peer's marriage had never been the most satisfying, his duchess, a Palatinate princess named Katerina von Ezzonen, resided in a separate apartment in the west wing. Paul always felt comfortable in this magnificent chamber, for it appealed to men rather than ladies. The heavy beams of the Tudor-style, coffered ceiling along with walls covered in rich mahogany reflected the tastes of men's club more than a country manor. In fact, the only hint of femininity anywhere in the overtly masculine space lay one foot away, curled into an innocent c-shape, the thick quilts pulled up to her chin.

The earl's compassionate heart ached as he watched Cordelia sleep. She'd screamed because of a shadow at their window, which Paul had convinced her must have been an owl. Delia had insisted over and over that she'd seen a man, not an owl. Knowing the home's history and the many times Elizabeth had seen strange faces in her childhood, the earl promised to remain awake and keep watch whilst his wife slept. Only then, did Cordelia Stuart finally relax enough to rest.

Paul walked to the deceptive window, his eyes on the moon's round white face. The lunar orb peered back at him, floating upon thin clouds twixt the willow and elm trees that bordered the circular drive. To the east, a pale pink hue began to creep across the trees' limbs: the sun, rising once more to banish the cruel moon. Morning had come at last.

The earl crossed the room to tend the gas fire, turning up the jet. In just minutes, the higher flames began to warm the cold room. He entered the second chamber, once used by the third duke's many mistresses, a sumptuous room with a canopied bed, draped in overly heavy brocades. He'd put his own cases in here when Cordelia arrived from London, but he'd not yet unpacked. Opening the largest trunk, he found a matched set of pistols, the box of ammunition Delia had mentioned seeing, and a selection of personal linen, socks, braces, silk shirts, waistcoats, and trousers. The second trunk held a formal coat, two white waistcoats, a black frock coat, a silver-grey cutaway, and a morning coat. He also found a velvet box filled with shirt studs, cufflinks, his father's watch, and other Aubrey jewellery. He removed all the items to the bed and began to hang the coats, trousers, and shirts in the cedar wardrobe.

"What are you are doing?" asked his wife as she entered the room. "Tell me you didn't sleep in here."

He kissed her cheek. "Of course, I didn't. I promised to keep watch over you, and I did just that. You'll find my chair still next to the bed, if you doubt it. Were you able to rest?"

She pulled him close, her bare arms round his waist. "A little. I kept dreaming about you, and I was apologising to you again and again, but you never seemed to hear me. Paul, I am sorry. So, so sorry! I never should have looked in your personal things. Whatever you and the duchess wrote to one another before we met is private, for you alone. And that other woman, Cozette; that affair was long ago. All that matters now, is that we love one another. Isn't that right?"

"Very right, *mo bhean*. My darling, you are all I want in the world. You and our child."

She grew quiet, and he could see the idea of another woman still dragged at her heart.

"If you want to talk about it, I'm listening."

"No, I mustn't be a nag. I don't want to be like my mother, Paul. She nagged poor Father all the time. I want you to act according to your own thoughts, not mine."

"But your thoughts matters to me, Delia. Don't you see that? Darling, Cozette was a lost waif. When I first met her, my only reason was to use her. I'm being honest now." He sat on the bed, pulling her close. "I'm about to tell you something about myself that's quite awful."

"You could never be awful."

"Oh, but I could. I can. When I'm working, I must take on another man's life and behaviours. Another mind. I dress differently, I think differently, and I speak with a different voice. I become another man, for that is how I can fool others into believing me. Do you understand?"

"Yes, but it only makes sense, Paul. If you're ordered to spy on someone, then you must make that man trust you."

"That's right," he said, running his hand through her long tresses. "That year, my orders were to uncover the acts of a man named Fermin. He was evil, Delia. And dangerous. I had to be very careful, and so I found people around him who might have information. One was Cozette du Barroux, his mistress."

"You said she worked at a brothel."

He nodded, taking her hand. "Yes, she did, and she was quite young. She was a French *demimondaine*."

"What is that?" she asked innocently.

"A young woman who's been raised and trained to become a rich man's mistress. She spoke many languages, knew literature and some science, and she understood enough politics to impress the average man. This made her an amusing companion to powerful government men. I was pretending to be this artist, David Saunders. I can paint well enough to pose convincingly, and she and I became friends. I found her very likeable."

"Did you fall in love with her?" she asked in a small voice.

He paused, wondering how honest he dared be with her. Cordelia's mind was still healing from the horrors of December's attack, and he sensed it was at risk of cracking further. How could any woman heal completely from such a thing? Henry had warned Paul again and again to be very careful with Delia, lest she revert to a dangerous mental state.

"No, darling, I didn't."

She leaned in close, and he felt her shivering.

"Cold?"

"A little. Are you sure that was an owl last night?"

He drew her into his arms, offering warmth and protection. "Yes, I'm sure it was. Della used to see them out of her window all the time."

"But this was a human face, Paul. Not an owl. You won't leave me again tonight, will you? Please, I can't be in here alone!"

"No, dear, I'll never leave you again," he whispered, kissing her lips. "Now, shall we dress and perhaps take a walk? I'm afraid the area near the lake has been roped off, but the reflecting pool's lovely this time of the morning, and I understand the rest of the exhibitors begin arriving later today, making this our last opportunity for a quiet walk."

"Yes, I'd like that. May we spend the entire day together?"

"Yes, of course. Oh, but Beth said something about a fitting for my suit of armour. Would you like to help?"

She giggled. "A suit of armour? Like a real knight? Whatever is it for?"

"Apparently, my cousin and I are to put on a display of some sort tomorrow afternoon. It's all a bit mad, if you ask me, but Charles has agreed to it, so I'll play along."

"But you won't actually swing a sword or anything, will you? That sounds dangerous."

"Not if I can help it. Beth may call me Sir Paul, but I do not consider myself a true knight."

"Will you be my knight?" she asked him, her eyes soft as she drew him back into the larger bedchamber. "Now?"

"Dear lady, how can I refuse?"

The newlyweds returned to the warm bed, and afterward, as they lay together in the quilts, Cordelia whispered sweetly, "I'm so glad there are no more secrets between us, husband. You know all the dark things about me, and now, I know about this woman Cozette. If you'd loved her, it would be different, but—well, I'm just so glad you didn't. I want to be the only maiden you ever rescue, Sir Paul. Forever and ever. Yours and only yours."

She closed her eyes, and Aubrey stared at the ceiling. How could he tell her he had loved Cozette? And what of Adele? Would Cordelia understand if she knew Cozette had given him a child? She felt so very fragile in his arms. So innocent and trusting.

And he'd lied.

Paul drifted into a fitful sleep, his last thoughts of Cozette and her dying words: 'Remember me, my beautiful Paul. Remember me and take care of our child."

12 rue Chabanais, Paris
Charles had left Adele in the capable company of the mysterious being named Archibald Cherubino and Elbert Stanley, whilst he and Sir Thomas Galton paid a call on the proprietress of the infamous brothel, Le Chabanais.

The main floor of the hotel reminded Charles of the Empress back in Whitechapel. Every square inch of vertical and horizontal space was arrayed with extravagant decor in the finest materials, splashed in deep reds and rich golds. The heavy smell of incense filled the air, riding upon notes of sweet perfume and sharp tobacco. However, unlike the Empress, the flesh pedaled here wore costumes from a variety of regions to tantalise customers with exotic delights and storybook suites. Some of the women dressed as African slave girls, others wore tight Chinese dresses or flowing geisha robes, still others were arrayed as eighteenth-century courtesans, their faces a stark white, hair piled into elaborate poufs of powdered perfection. Some were fully clothed, but most left bits of clothing elsewhere, their breasts exposed, limbs bare.

The duke had brought Galton as a witness to his behaviour as much as fellow investigator. With so many tourists in Paris, Charles had no wish for his actions to be misconstrued or misreported. As he stood in the crowded lobby, enduring the overt seductions, he kept his mind fixed on business and his wife. Most of these young women looked less than twenty-five, a few less than twenty, but several as young as twelve. Sinclair thought of Adele, and the idea that any normal man might desire so tender and vulnerable a child ignited rage within his father's heart. Twelve was the legal age of 'consent' in many countries; therefore, Charles forced himself to keep calm and not make a scene.

"*Puis-je vous aider, Monsieur? Que désirez-vous?*" asked an older woman in eighteenth-century garb. She looked as if she'd just left a party at the palace of Versailles, where King Louis XIV considered all women as potential conquests.

"Do you speak English?" he asked, deciding to avoid the native language for the moment.

The woman smiled. "Oh, yes, I speak it, sir. How may we please you?"

"I'm not here for pleasure, madam," he told the matron in a measured voice. "But for conversation only. Is Marie available to speak?"

"Marie sees men by advance appointment only, *m'sieur*, and it is the same price. Talk, no talk. It is the same. One hundred francs. You want the best, you pay a premium."

Charles considered the ridiculously high price. His attire was bespoke and immaculately pressed. It might also be that the woman recognised him, for his photograph still graced many of Parisian newspapers. He'd noticed reporters hanging about the hotel since his arrival. Was he being followed? Would Beth hear he'd visited a famous *maison close?* Was the note sent as a trap?

Rather than make a scene, he paid the money. The woman grinned, revealing a gold incisor.

"Follow me, *m'sieur.*" Galton started to accompany them, but the woman put her hand on Thomas's chest. "No, sir. If you both go, then the price is five hundred francs. I do not ask Marie to take on two without asking more."

Charles nodded to Galton. "It's all right. I'll go alone."

"Sir, I'm not sure it's wise."

"Stay here, Thomas." He turned to the proprietress. "Might you serve my friend a cup of coffee, madam?"

"We have many libations," she grinned, showing the gold front tooth. "Come, *m'sieur.* We shall entertain you whilst your friend enjoys Marie."

Thomas looked thoroughly ill-at-ease, but followed a young girl, who was dressed as a boy. The matron led Charles up the main staircase to a second storey, high-ceilinged floor containing a labyrinth of painted doors. He could hear ribald laughter and a variety of music coming from several of the rooms, along with the unmistakable sounds of men and women in intimate congress.

How can a man who loves his wife engage in such activities? he wondered. As a policeman, he'd spent fourteen years in such depressing places, sometimes arresting the patrons, other times the women. He hated the whole idea of prostitution, for it spread disease and shattered marriages, but more to the point, it was the ruin and death of the women involved.

His guide stopped at a red door. "Half an hour, *m'sieur*. No longer. We keep track."

She knocked, and the door opened to a velvety darkness. Heavy perfume mixed with musky sweat met his nostrils, and he could hear the strains of music coming from within. A player of some kind, offering accompaniment by Ravel.

"Marie?" he asked as he entered the dark chamber. *Please, Lord, don't let this be a trap!* he prayed silently.

A small voice replied from the far corner, and a lamp switched on. "I am she. What may I do for you, *m'sieur?* Have you a special fantasy, or shall I act out one of my own? I can pretend to be anything you like. Anyone you like."

She spoke in French, and Charles answered in English.

"You asked to meet with me, Marie. You left a note at my hotel."

"You are the Duke Charles of Haimsbury, no?" she asked in English.

"I am. What is it you want, mademoiselle? Why did you wish to see me?"

She pulled her robe closed, no longer displaying her supple body. "Forgive me. I didn't know it would be you. Please, my lord, sit. We have but twenty-eight minutes now. I must speak quickly."

"I'm listening," he said, taking a chair several feet away.

"I am Marie LaGrande. I knew Cozette du Barroux from childhood. We grew up in same house, you see. A place that—a place that train girls to work in houses such as this. They make us whores but teach us to speak like ladies. Such places take children from the street or orphanage, but only if they are pretty or from special background, and they raise them in luxury, *m'sieur,* making sure all graces be taught. When young, we are treated like princess. The matrons, they make sure our health, our skin, both are perfect. We learn to read and speak well, in many languages. I was only three, when my mother sold me to the *Maison de Beauté.*"

"House of Beauty?" he asked.

"*Oui,* but it is a very ugly place at heart. It is in a great mansion near Lyon. When I arrive, Cozette was already there. She come there as baby, you see. The madame, she tell me so. But a rich man, her *patron*, he sometimes come to visit her. He pay much money for

Cozette's education, her fine clothes, her everything, sir. When she is twelve, she leave with him, and this man, he offer to take me, too, for she and I are friends, no? Like sisters."

She paused, taking a drink of red wine, despite the early hour. "I not say what happen when we come, for it was shameful. Men and women, they teach us what we must do to please the customers. How we act, you know? I am given many gentlemen to please, but Cozette was left alone, for only the man who pay for her at *Maison de Beauté*. Only he and his friends could be with her. Then, one day, she tell me of a sweet boy who make her friend. His name is David Saunders. I meet him. He had beautiful eyes and long hair like the poet, no? He draw our pictures, and buy us sweets. He never ask to do bad things to us. David spend more time with Cozette. She fall in love with him, *m'sieur*, but he never sleep with her. Not once. Not until, one night, after this rich patron, he beat her."

She sipped the wine again, wiping tears from her eyes.

"That night," she continued, "the beautiful David, he stay, and Cozette say he treat her like princess. For three week, he come here to visit, staying each night. Then, he not come. Cozette cry most terrible tears, *m'sieur*. She weep and weep, and the rich man beat her again. One day, she is gone. Her room empty. I ask everywhere, but only a year later, do I find her. She is living in Montmartre, in a small house. She have baby. Such pretty eyes! Like M'sieur Saunders! But Cozette is coughing. She claim it little thing, but she ask me to find David for her. Only later, she admit she is dying and want him to take their child and keep her safe from the evil patron. Cozette worry that little Adele would be taken to *Maison de Beauté* and end up like her mother. I look and look for David. No one know where he go. I even talk to the police, and they tell me they have no time for whores. Then, one day, a man come. He is dressed well, and he look like David, only he is Scottish with great title. He ask about Cozette. I tell him where she go, and he give me money. Oh, *m'sieur*, tell me I did not do wrong! Tell me, please!"

Charles crossed the room and knelt before her, offering a handkerchief to dry her eyes. "Marie, you did very well. That man was Adele's father, and he took her to safety. She's with me now. My adopted daughter. All grown up and healthy. But tell me, why did you send for me? Who told you where to find me?"

"I know because of what the tall man tell me, *m'sieur*. Last night, he come to see me, ask for me by name. He say Cozette's daughter is here. In Paris. And he give me package. That I must ask for the Duke Charles of Haimsbury at *Hôtel Terminus*. He say this package, it belong to you and only you."

"What package?" he asked gently.

Marie unlocked a drawer within a nearby bureau. She pushed aside numerous frilly intimates, her powdered face growing flush as he saw them. It occurred to Sinclair that the young woman felt embarrassed by her profession in the presence of a man who had no wish to use her body.

"Marie, have you enough money?"

She turned, a silver box in her hands. "Money? Do you wish to pay for me again, sir?" she asked, a tremor in her voice.

"No. I wonder, though, if I might help you to leave this place. To find a more noble profession?"

Hope entered her eyes, but it quickly died. "No, *m'sieur*. I am not fit for anything but this. I shall die here."

"That isn't true. Not if you wish to choose a new path. Let me help you." He wrote a name on the same slip of paper she'd left for him at the hotel. "This man is a very good friend, and he will find you a lovely house. Tell him the Captain sent you. He'll help you to begin anew."

She took the paper, clutching at it as she would a lifeline. "*Merci!* Oh, *merci, m'sieur!* I did not think to send for you because of such a thing! I only hope to obey the tall man."

He took the small box and placed it inside his overcoat pocket. "Marie, can you describe this man?"

"*Oui.* He is much taller than you. Long black hair like the poet. Pale eyes."

"Did the man carry a carved walking stick?"

"*Oui!* Do you know him, *m'sieur?*"

"Yes, I imagine I do," answered Charles, assuming the man was Romanov. "Speak to my friend and be ready to leave this house tonight. I'll arrange everything."

Charles kissed her hand and left, wishing he could do more. He'd send for André Deniau immediately, the circle agent who worked with the French government. If anyone could find a place to hide a fragile witness, it was Deniau, Paul's right-hand man in France.

Thomas Galton looked relieved when the duke returned to the lobby. "Let's go," Haimsbury said. "We're finished."

Once inside the coach, Charles opened the box, showing it to Galton.

"What is it?" asked Thomas.

"I'm not sure, but I suspect Romanov has some plan in mind."

"Romanov?"

"Yes, it looks as though our Russian prince once again makes an appearance. Let's see what he thought so important, and why it connects to Cozette du Barroux, though I'm surprised he didn't simply bring it to me last night."

Charles opened the box and found a letter, folded many times over and stained with blood.

"What does it say? Who wrote it?" asked Galton.

"It's in English, dated the 1st of May, 1860. Here's what it says.

'My Dearest Ramone,
    This is your life insurance against unforeseeable circumstances. If anything happens to me, you're to give this letter to the marquess. If by chance, Robert Sinclair has died, you're to give it to his son and heir, Charles. This is my confession, and I pray the Lord forgives me!
    In late 1859, a man approached me with a proposal. As you know, Ramone, my winery had failed to produce again, and I faced bankruptcy. My grandfather planted those vines! How could I not do all within my power to save it? That August, as if brought by providential messenger, a man entered my life and offered to pay all my debts and even give me ten thousand francs beside. All I need do to earn it was transfer a child. I asked what child? How can this be legal? He laughed and asked me if it mattered. To my shame, I said it did not.
    I assumed this child was an orphan or one of a hundred left upon the streets of Sancerre. I asked if I had to take it from its home. No, he said. He would

do that. All I need do was carry it on the train from Kirby-Stephen, England to London. A woman would meet me there, and the child would pass to her. She would give me two thousand more francs if the child was in good condition. A total of twelve thousand in all! A fortune!

When? I asked him.

He said he would contact me.

In December, I received a letter telling me to leave France for this Kirby-Stephen village. I had to look at a railroad map, and even then the place was difficult to find. When I arrive there, it was Christmas. Everyone treat me well, as if I am honoured guest. I feel like monster. The people at the inn, they sing carols and give gifts. A snow fall everywhere. That night, the man he come to see me. The same one from before. He say the baby will soon be born, and will be brought to me. I'm to meet him at the castle ruins of Uther Pendragon. Inside the old gates. He will give me the baby then."

When? I ask.

In a few days. I will know.

Days pass, and the people at the inn toast the new year. Then, a message comes. It say only one word.

NOW.

I pack, and outside, I find a coach waiting. A scowling man drives. He speak not one word to me, but take me to an old ruin beside a river. I climb a little hill, pass by sheep. A wolf is howling. Inside the old castle, is a man so tall I must look up to speak. His face is dark, his hair long and blowing in the wind. Snow falls all around, and the wolf, it howls! A raven lights upon the rocks, watching me.

The tall man hand me a tiny bundle. It is warm. The face is sweet.

"Her name is Charlotte Sinclair," he tell me. "But as of today, she is no one. Do you understand? She is dead to her mother, and must remain so. Speak to anyone of this, and I will slice your throat and then do the same to your children."

"What will she eat?" I ask him. "I have no milk."

The tall shadow say I will find a woman on the road. She will suckle the infant. He say to trust him. I leave with the baby, walking back to the coach in deep snow.

He did not lie! We pass by a pale woman upon the road to London, and she enter the coach. She is unsure why she is walking, but she take the baby and nurse her. The woman does not know her own name, so I call her Michelle, my late wife's name. By the sixth of January, we are in London. The woman she come and take the child. She give me two thousand francs.

Two days later, Michelle dies.

I am cursed! I do not know how this happen to me, but I pray is not too late! Since that day, my business prosper, but last week, my daughter die in childbirth. It is a sign. Then my son die in shooting. Another sign.

Now, I plan to take my life. I pray God forgive me. I pray Lord Haimsbury and his poor wife forgive. I am cursed!

Goodbye, Ramone.'"

Charles grew quiet as he considered the letter, for it implied a harsh and painful truth. Cozette du Barroux was stolen as an infant from the Kirkby-Stephen area, the village near Rose House. Charles remembered everything now, the final pieces of his childhood. The reason he'd fallen into illness that winter, why he'd needed to see so many doctors.

His baby sister, Roberta Abigail Charlotte Sinclair. He'd heard her cry out as a strange man took her from the cot. Everyone said he was wrong, that he'd imagine it; but he'd been right. She lived. She breathed. He'd even touched her.

Then, the next morning, his father broke the news of her death. No, Charles insisted. The long-haired man had taken his sister.

And the thief escaped using the mirror!

Yes! Just as Trent took Elizabeth through a mirror, the tall man had taken his sister *through a mirror!* That was why his father had ordered it stored in the attic. Charles had told him the truth, but his father refused to believe it.

Wait, the adult Charles thought. *They had buried a baby.*

Whose was it?

He thought of the woman on the road—the one who'd just given birth but had no memory. The one this confessor thief called Michelle.

It must have been *her baby* they'd buried.

And the tall stranger? The shadowy man in the mirror.

It was *the very same man who'd killed his father*.

Prince Aleksandr Koshmar.

Charles remembered the day of his birthday. The morning search in the attics. He'd gone to confront the mirror.

And he'd *passed through it*, finding himself in an entirely different house. A strange room filled with symbols.

Then, the world went black.

Both to the boy—and to the man.

Charles Sinclair had fainted in the coach.

CHAPTER TWENTY-SIX

Pollux Institute – Paradise St., Lambeth

Trevor Killian had once worked on the railroads, but ill health and the loss of his wife had cost him a job and his sanity. Finally, after the third arrest for public drunkenness, a commiserating judge had sentenced the thirty-two-year-old to confinement at Pollux Sanitorium until doctors there deemed him cured and fit to return to society. The rooms at Pollux were light and airy, and the staff considerate and friendly. After only ten days, Killian's thirst for drink had significantly diminished, and the electric shock treatments had successfully removed all memories of his late wife from the patient's thoughts. Only now and again, did her ghost appear to him, but then only in dreams. A morphine injection banished even that.

Killian had resided at the institute for six weeks when Dr. Theseus approached him with an offer to remain and take part in a special experiment. Trevor's strong physique and height had impressed the eminent physician, who insisted that the former railroad worker would be perfect for the radical new trial. The treatment, he warned Killian, could alter him profoundly, but make him stronger and forever cured of his desire for self-destruction.

He would, in fact, become almost godlike.

Trevor had never imagined himself as 'godlike', but the allure of such a promise certainly proved tempting. After just one night's consideration, the reformed drunk signed consent papers and entered a new phase of his life. An altered phase, becoming a forever-changed man.

That third of May was Killian's thirteenth day of treatment, and he awoke as usual, his eyes somewhat dismayed by the strong lights in his room. He pressed the buzzer next to his bed to summon a nurse. A fresh-faced girl who couldn't be more than twenty answered.

"Yes, Mr. Killian?"

"The lights," he told her. "They're very bright."

She switched off the overhead fixture. "Is that better?"

"A little, but the lights in the hallway are also quite disturbing. I'm sorry to be a bother."

"Not at all, sir. Dr. Theseus warned us you might find them troubling. I'll see if there's a way to block them. We need to see you understand, sir. Our eyes don't function well in darkness."

"Yes, of course."

She left momentarily, and whilst she searched the store rooms for canvas sheeting to block his windows, a strange compulsion overwhelmed the experimental subject. He found his sense of smell had heightened, and he could discern a hundred different scents: sweating men, perfumed women, an unborn child within the womb of a nurse named Wilson. Rum on the breath of a porter who'd come directly to work from an overnight at a brothel. Men's cologne, a familiar scent, which reminded Trevor of Alphonse Theseus. Toast, eggs, dogs, cats, and something else. Something rich and sweet and *oh so tasty*.

Blood.

Hot, wet blood.

Pumping blood.

Human blood.

When the fresh-faced girl returned to Room 1C, she found the room empty. Or so she thought.

She was just about to call the matron, when the darkened room gave birth to a monster. Trevor Killian had somehow elevated to the ceiling, and now hung suspended above the befuddled young nurse.

He slammed the door shut with his mind, and fell upon the victim. The half-drunk porter raced to the room when the screams began, and he managed to rescue the nurse before Killian drained her of blood, but the bite had infected poor Nurse Trowbridge.

Within thirteen days, she, too, would be sensitive to light and shivering inside a subterranean room, not far from the man who'd bitten her. Theseus declared the event 'an unfortunate side effect', but it seemed to everyone working in the special unit that the insti- tute's director was pleased with the results. By August, the lower wards would teem with blood-thirsty hybrids; their minds sharp as their teeth, and with strength to rival Hercules.

But on that third day of May, Alphonse Theseus did nothing to reveal his ultimate plans for these trusting patients. Nor did he reveal the existence of a second experiment, taking place in Fulham, next door to Henry MacAlpin's Montmore House. That neighbouring estate had once belonged to Round Table member Lord Hemsworth. But as the earl had died suddenly, without an heir, the land, house, and all associated properties were purchased at auction by a wealthy Romanian prince. Each locked room of that regal home was currently filled with dead men and dead women; thirty-three in all at present with plans to add many more. These bodies were devoid of natural life, stored in chemically infused coffins that kept the tissues from decaying.

And one of these unhappy dead had been known in life as Baron David Wychwright, his metal coffin marked in paint as 'Subject 12'.

By October, the blood of patients like Killian and Trowbridge would be used in a devilish plan to resurrect these human dead as living portals for demon habitation.

Alphonse Theseus was building a private army.

A battalion of inhuman monsters.

CHAPTER TWENTY-SEVEN

As Charles Sinclair regained consciousness, he could hear hushed voices in the darkened room. He had trouble remembering where he was—Paris? London? Rose House? A tangle of images swirled in his brain, struggling to form a cohesive pattern, and he felt a hand upon his. Small and warm.

He opened his eyes.

"Father?"

The duke slowly smiled. "Charlotte," he whispered, not knowing why. "I mean, Adele, of course. Sorry to worry you."

"Sir Thomas brought you back to the hotel, and you wouldn't wake up for the longest time. Mr. Cherubino talked to you, but still you slept. I was afraid you were in a coma again, Father. Did you hit your head?"

"Where am I?" he asked, not finding the room familiar.

"We're in a different hotel now. Sir Thomas had you moved. He said it was for our safety. He's very nice."

"Tom's still here?"

"He's gone now, but Auntie Tory and Dolly are here. We're all taking the train to Calais. Won't that be nice? We're going home to England. Sir Thomas is making the arrangements."

His eyes hurt, and the room's light seemed bright. *Tory? Dolly? No, that isn't right.*

Another hand touched his, this time from the opposite side of the bed. He felt the mattress depress as someone sat beside him.

"Captain?"

Charles thought he might faint again, so much did his heart leap at the sound!

"Beth? Can that be you?"

"Yes, darling, it's your Beth. Galton wired me, and when I read it, I insisted on coming immediately. I've been here three days, but you've slept and slept. It must be the same fever you had in Scotland last year, but your head's much cooler now. How I've missed you!"

"And I you," he whispered. "Am I dreaming? What day is it?"

"Sunday. Rest now."

He held her hand to keep her from leaving.

"Don't go. I need to talk to you. There's so much I've learnt. About Paul. No, I mustn't think about it."

"What do you mean?" she asked.

"The box with the letter in it. I had it with me. Where's my coat?"

"Don't think about it," she cooed, kissing his forehead.

Then he noticed it. Her body. It was different.

She isn't pregnant.

"Who are you?" he asked angrily.

"I'm your little one," the figure told him in a voice achingly close to Beth's.

"You're lying!"

"Doctor, he's delirious again," the lying Beth told a man in a tall hat. The man's scarecrow face hovered before Sinclair's eyes, the skin as pale as waxwork, and a pair of bony fingers shoved a pill down his throat.

"Sleep, my king," he whispered. "Sleep! We need you strong and healthy for the Machine. Your blood must be strong. Sleep. Sleep..."

Charles awoke with a start, still inside the carriage. The jostling movement of the wooden wheels upon the street's uneven cobbles jarred his senses, but the waking dream caused him far worse distress. His nerves felt raw, and that same electric sensation still ran along his hands.

Charlotte. Du Barroux's true name had been Charlotte Sinclair. Adele was his dead sister's child. And what was this machine the spidery man had mentioned?

"You all right, sir?" Galton asked.

"What?"

"I asked if you wanted me to wire Lord Aubrey about the new plans. You started to reply, but then your face went—well, somewhat strange. As though you'd fallen asleep for a moment."

"No, I'm all right. A waking dream, you might say."

"What, sir?"

"Yes, wire my cousin with our new departure time. Seven?"

"Yes, sir. Shall we find a doctor, sir?"

"No, Thomas. I'm all right. I do have one call to make first, though. There's a woman I promised to help. She's also staying at the Terminus."

"Is it an errand I can run for you? Or Deniau?"

Charles couldn't shake that persistent tingle, and the vision couldn't let go. *What is this machine?*

"No, I should do it. I promised."

Galton made several notes in a leather book; orders for his lieutenants. "Do you have luggage at Lady Victoria's house? I can go to there myself and collect it."

"Thank you, Tom, but let another agent go. Also, ask Deniau to go at once to Marie at La Chabanais. I'll withdraw funds from my bank here before we leave. I want the woman secured in one of our safe houses tonight."

"Do you worry about her safety?" asked Galton.

"She's told us information that Redwing's tried to hide for nearly thirty years, and I suspect there's a reason why this Pandora's box opens now. If I'm not making sense to you, Thomas, please just trust me. Right now, my only thought is to get Della out of France."

The coach stopped, and Charles checked to make sure the box was still in his pocket. An old truth was emerging, he realised. His hidden past had come to call with a vengeance. He'd never imagined the truth, hidden for years within his brain, would have anything to do with Adele, but it explained why he felt so very connected to her. She was Charlotte's very own. His blood niece—and now, his daughter.

And when he next saw his Cousin Paul, he prayed he could maintain his temper.

10:33 pm – RMS Padstow, middle of the channel
Charles and Della boarded the steamer on time, meeting Deniau, who'd collected all their luggage from Château Rothesay along with a note from Victoria, wishing them a pleasant crossing and a lovely

time at the fête. She promised to be at Branham for the babies' arrival in June, and added how pleased she was Charles had adopted Adele.

Keeping his promise, Sinclair had called on Miss Calabrese's suite, only to discover she'd checked out, and he wondered if he'd missed an opportunity to learn more about her father, Antonio Calabrese. He could form his own opinion on Tuesday, however, so he put it out his mind, happy for another evening with his beautiful new daughter.

They'd enjoyed dinner with the captain and an hour watching men play cards, before retiring to their two-room cabin. Charles took the larger bedroom, whilst Adele the single, and she kissed him goodnight, thanking him for making her so very happy. He'd been asleep for an hour, dreaming about Georgianna's help in the Stone Realm's confusing maze, but as he dreamt, Georgianna's face became Adele's. The dream child had been explaining the next phase of their journey, when she suddenly began to weep. And as dreams often do, this one began to blend with reality, and Charles slowly opened his eyes, realising he heard actual crying, coming from Adele's room. He jumped from the bed and pulled on a robe.

"Della? Darling, are you awake?" he asked, knocking on her door.

There was no reply, but the weeping and little cries grew louder.

Charles entered without a summons, finding the small room dark and cold. He lit a gas lamp. Adele lay beneath a silk coverlet, her chestnut hair braided, her slender hands clenched, eyes shut tightly. She appeared to be dreaming, and he touched her forehead.

"Della?" he whispered. He took her hand, and her eyes popped open.

"Father?" she asked. "Is that you?"

He sat beside her. "Yes, darling, it's your father."

She sat up, pulling into his embrace, sobbing into his chest. "I dreamt of Briarcliff. I was following Paul, and he ignored me. I kept asking him to turn round, but when he did, he wasn't Paul at all— but my old father. My dead father. He told me I was adopted! And then, I remembered someone else telling me that. Why would he say that? Wasn't Lord Aubrey my father?"

An ache ran through Sinclair's heart, for he'd dreaded this moment, prayed she'd never have to hear this truth about her life. By adopting her himself, he'd hoped to remove that Damoclean sword from over her head.

"Tell you what, there's a beautiful moon tonight, and the stars at sea are breathtaking. Let's dress, and we'll walk the decks. All right?"

"Yes, all right," she snuffled. "I'm sorry I woke you."

"I am always available to you, Daughter mine. No matter the hour. Now, dress quickly but warmly. The sea winds are often cold."

Within ten minutes, both had donned appropriate clothing and shoes, and left their cabin for the main deck. As they reached the port side, Charles drew her close. "See what I mean? Breathtaking, aren't they?"

"Yes," she answered. "May I talk first?"

"Of course. Say whatever you wish."

"And you'll be honest with me?" she asked.

He kissed the top of her head. "I promise to be honest with you every day of my life."

She took a moment to compose her thoughts, and he noticed her gloved hands seemed tense. "I suppose I started thinking about it a few months ago. It was Winnie who mentioned it. He said I was adopted, but I told he was a liar. I thought he was terribly cruel, actually. But even then, I had a dreadful feeling it was all true."

Bracing himself for a long and difficult conversation, Charles prayed silently for inspiration. Where to begin? And how does one include information about prostitution when explaining an out-of-wedlock pregnancy?

The moon stood high against the inky vault, and the constellations had come out to play. "Look up there. Do you see the Plough?" he asked.

"Yes. I see it. M'sieur Roubolet calls it Odin's Wain."

"Is that so?" he asked, watching her eyes. "My father called it Odin's Wain, as well. He used to quote Homer's *Iliad*, whenever we'd see it in the skies over Rose House. Let me see if I can remember how it goes." He shut his eyes, and Charles could hear his father's voice speaking, and he repeated the words:

"'Thereon were figured earth, and sky, and sea; the ever-circling sun and full-orb'd moon; and all the signs that crown the vault of Heav'n: Pleiades, and Hyades, and Orion's might; and Arctos, called the Wain, who wheels on high, his circling course, and on Orion waits; sole star that never bathes in Ocean wave.'"

"That's beautiful, Father. What does it mean? Is Arctos waiting on Orion?" she asked.

Charles shook his head. "Perhaps. Wain's an old English word for a wagon, but I'm not sure why my father thought the passage important. Perhaps, Homer wrote in code. My father loved riddles. He often pointed it out. Arthur's Wain is your destiny, he'd say."

"Did he? That's very strange," she said, reaching for his hand. "Auntie Dolly called the constellation something else. She said she'd read it in a book. 'Charles's Wain'. I asked her what she meant, for I thought it most peculiar that it would have your name, but she said the book linked it to Charlemagne. Charles the Great. I think you might be called Charles the Great, Father, for you're the most important man in England."

"Not really," he answered, his mind whirling through the idea of the constellation's alternate name. *Might it be connected to the constellations in the secret passageway of my home?* "So, ask me."

Her hands gripped the railing, just as Angiolina Calabrese's had on the crossing to Calais. It seemed all Della's words were caught up in her throat, and so he pulled over a pair of deck chairs and placed her into one, whilst he took the other.

"Shall I address it for you, little one? I assure you the news might not be what you want to hear, but it's the truth. Truth is always best, I find. I've learnt many new truths about my life in the past seven months. I prefer knowing to blind ignorance."

She took a deep breath. "All right, Holmes. Give me the truth. Am I adopted?"

"Yes."

She thought about this for a moment. "Do you mean by you?"

"No, little one, by the late earl. Here now, allow me to explain it, because I've learnt much more about your life than I knew two days ago, and I think you're going to be surprised. First of all, the man you grew up calling Father, the late Robert Stuart, loved you as his own from the moment he first met you, but someone else is your natural father."

"Who?" she whispered.

"Paul."

It took several minutes for the concept to take root, and the young duke marvelled at Adele's ability to manoeuvre through the mine field he'd just thrown her into. He could have broken it gently, but as a policeman, he'd learnt to start with blunt truth and then soothe the wound with explanatory bandages made of smaller truths; those that led to the monstrous blow.

Your husband is dead, Mrs. Adams.

Your sister has been drowned, Miss MacNeill.

I'm afraid your father has been arrested for murder, Mrs. Armstrong.

The jury's decision was guilty, Mary. I'm very sorry, but your brother will hang.

He'd wounded many a heart since donning Met Blue fourteen years earlier. But he'd also made a difference in thousands of lives. He prayed he might be able to help just one more now, by aiding Adele through her recovery.

"How is my brother also my father?" she asked at last, pain in her eyes and voice. "How is that possible?"

Charles pulled his chair closer and placed an arm round the girl he now called 'daughter'. "Do you know how Paul spends most of his professional life?"

"He's a spy," she said proudly. "And he's one of the best, perhaps *the best*."

"He is the best," Charles concurred, "and he's been serving England and Scotland as a spy since he was your age. As a youth, Paul used to travel with his father and Uncle James, and he'd pretend to be all manner of boys: grooms, pages, shopkeeper's assistants, even a policeman's runner. This was his education in spy craft: learning how to become someone else. He learnt to look and live like another person, speak like him, and perform a job that made everyone believe he really was a page or a shop assistant. Whilst his friends at Eton spent summers playing cricket, Paul was working, and he developed a marvellous ability to blend into any crowd."

"It's why he keeps his hair so long," Adele added. "I think he looks quite dashing with long hair. Cordelia likes it, too."

"As do many women, I'm told," Charles laughed. "Shall I grow mine longer yet?"

She reached over and tugged at the three-inch curls creeping over his shirt collar. "It suits you, I think. I'm not sure about the beard, though."

"Neither is my wife, which is why I plan to shave right after the ball. I'll need it for my fifteenth century costume. But Paul uses facial hair as part of his toolkit for spying. As he grew older, he was given much more important assignments. Then, when he was twenty-one, the foreign secretary asked him to unmask a spy who lived in Paris. This meant finding a way to learn all about the man without being observed. He couldn't go to him directly as the Viscount Marlbury, nor could he start asking the man's friends."

"His friends would tell him," Adele agreed. "I imagine my brother—no, wait, you said he's my father—well, is this when it happened?"

"Don't rush me," he smiled, grateful for her calm reaction thus far. "In 1876, Paul sailed to Paris and began living in Montmartre."

"That's where the police think the Portmanteau Killer lives! It's very dangerous!"

"Yes, but that part of Paris allows men to disappear into a crowd. Paul posed as an artist named David Saunders. This disguise allowed him to move freely within many different social circles, for no one notices artists, but society ladies have a fondness for them."

"Was my mother one of those society ladies?"

"Not really," Charles answered patiently. He wondered how best to approach the idea of his sister's profession. *My beautiful sister. She must have looked like Adele at this age.* Taking a long breath, he plunged into the deep end of this metaphorical pool.

"Della, how much has Ida Ross told you about her life?"

"A little. She said she once lived across from your old house in Whitechapel. On Columbia Road. Why?"

He prayed for the right words. This moment would affect the rest of her life. He couldn't make a mistake.

Above their heads, the moon looked down upon them, and *Athene Noctua*, a 'little owl', flew in from the sea and settled close to their position, perching just above the door that led to the cabins. The small bird's grey-brown feathers mixed with white to mark the prominent facial mask, and the eyes set within that somewhat dumpy face, should have been amber, but instead were icy blue. The owl's head tilted as he listened.

Charles decided to offer as clear a picture of prostitution as possible without being overly graphic. He had no desire to alarm the girl. "Darling, not every young woman has the advantages you do. Some have no education and no family. Others are thrown onto the streets when they're only nine or ten. Some women are forced to find bread after their husbands die or go to prison. Life in Whitechapel for many young women is very hard, and I suppose that's also true of Paris. Your mother..." he paused, wondering how much to reveal. Should he mention the abduction of Charlotte as a baby? No. Not yet, for that truth was still unfolding. He wanted to find proof, perhaps locate this Ramone person, named in the confession letter.

First, tell Paul that his liaison in '76 was with my sister.

"I'm still investigating the precise details of your mother's past, but it seems she was born in a very pretty house, into a very nice family, but she was taken from it as an infant by a rich man who brought her to Paris. She grew up there, not knowing her true name."

"How awful for her!" Della gasped. "Do you know her true name? You say you're investigating. What do you know?"

"I am doing all I may to learn the facts, but I've much more to uncover yet. Shall I continue?"

"Oh, yes, please," she said, pulling closer.

"As I said, this man saw to her every need, and one day he moved her from the only home she'd known to a place called a *maison close*. Do you know what that is?"

She shook her head.

"It's rather like the hotel across from my old house. Women who work at these places are paid to please men. They have to sleep with them, I mean."

"They're paid to sleep?" she asked, dumbfounded.

"Not sleep, *per se*. It's a roundabout way of saying they act as a sort of substitute wife." He sighed, realising he was digging a very large hole for himself and wondered if this topic wouldn't be better handled by Elizabeth, for she was Adele's new mother now.

Della gazed at her father, eyes narrowing as she concentrated. Suddenly, her entire face opened with recognition. "Are you talking about sex, Father?" she asked him bluntly.

He stared at her, mouth open. Was he really having this conversation? *Will it be like this with Georgianna? And how will I teach my son the proper way to treat a woman, physically?*

"Yes, I'm talking about sex," he heard himself say.

"I know all about that," she declared without a blink. "My old tutor, Mrs. Chandler, told me, but Mrs. Mac told me first. She's the housekeeper at Briarcliff. Are you saying Ida did that with men? But they weren't married. Isn't that illegal? Did she ever have babies? Mrs. Mac says a girl has to be careful not to get in a 'family way'. She says, 'A man's seed can take root whether you're married or no, girl,'" Della quoted in a thick Scottish accent.

Charles laughed at her imitation of the Highland woman. "I see you're well informed."

"I'm not a child, Father," she told him plainly. "Are you saying my mother had sex with men? With my brother. With Paul?"

"Your brother is an honest, considerate gentleman, Adele. He never planned to take advantage of your mother. Not that way. He introduced himself to her, because he hoped she might answer his questions about this man he was chasing. Fermin was his name. Michel Fermin. Over the course of many weeks, he became fond of your mother, and then one evening, that fondness grew stronger. All men make mistakes, Della, but I've heard Paul say again and again that the greatest mistake he ever made was leaving your mother alone. He'd no idea she'd conceived a child until he saw her again, three years later. Your mother'd become ill by then, and Paul brought in numerous doctors, but it was too late. He lived with you and your mother for three months, until she died in his arms. Once he'd buried her, he brought you back to Scotland with him. His intention was to name you his own child legally, but the late earl feared it would forever ruin Paul's chances for a good marriage and government job. Robert Stuart meant well, Della, and that's why he insisted on adopting you as his own. Because you looked a little like Paul, everyone assumed your adoptive father was your birth father."

He paused, measuring her expression and praying he'd not made a thorough mess of it all. *This is a fine way to start a father-daughter relationship.* "Della, your mother was a beautiful woman who lost her true family as a baby, and her abductor used her mercilessly. But she loved Paul, and he loved her, too. Had he known about you from the beginning, he'd have married your mother. He tried to marry her even then, in '79, but she refused to allow it. I've seen him with her photograph, and just seeing it nearly brought him to his knees with regret. Della, Paul loves you more than you can possibly know, but he's not very good at showing his feelings. I wish he were here to tell you himself, and he should have done long ago, but he didn't. I've done a poor job of it, I'm afraid."

Without warning, she threw her arms round his neck, her blue eyes wide, filled with tears. "No! Oh, no, you've done it beautifully, Father. Really, you have. I know I'm supposed to think of Paul as my true father now, but it's too much, you know? I don't blame him or anything like that. He's very tender-hearted and a little bit timid when it comes to serious talks. He's better at rescuing damsels than actually talking to them, but I love him very much. I do wish he were more like you. I'm so very glad, though, that it's turned out like this. My true father is the brother whom I love, and my adoptive father is you! Thank you for being honest with me. May I ask one thing more?"

"Anything, little one," he whispered, his voice choking with emotion.

"My mother's name. What was it?"

"Cozette," he told her. "Cozette du Barroux."

She thought about this for a moment, then glanced up. "You've begun to investigate her?"

"I have."

"If you know she was born in a nice house, is that because you know which house? Do you know her real name?"

Do I tell her? I've always said, if she asked about her mother, I'd tell her the truth. Do I reveal what little I know? About the letter? I'd want to know.

"Very well, Watson, I shall tell you what I've learnt thus far, but remember that I need to confirm all of this."

"Yes, of course, Holmes, of course! After all, we do investigate together."

"Quite so." He paused, wondering where to start. As he gazed at her azure eyes, it all fell into place in his mind. "Della, have you ever noticed how similar your eyes are to mine?"

"Oh, yes! The older I get the more they look like yours." Then, her face lengthened in confusion as the question seated itself in her thoughts. "Father, what are you saying?"

"This is good news, darling. Earlier today, I had to leave, remember?"

"Yes, and Mr. Archie stayed with me. Mr. Cherubino, I mean. He told me to call him Mr. Archie."

The small owl's head bobbed excitedly, just as a large white owl fluttered to the area and joined the brown bird. The two owls listened intently.

"Whilst away, I was given a letter—a confession of sorts—from the man who brought your mother to France. She was only one day old. I believe I know her real name and where she was born."

"What? Where? Please, tell me! I can help you with the investigation. We'll work together. Please, tell me!"

He kissed her hands. "Yes, yes, of course we will. Here's what little I know. The village where the transporter stayed was Kirby-Stephen, and he received the baby at an old ruined castle by a river. The only ruined castle near that village is Pendragon. As it happens, the mistress of a great noble house overlooking Pendragon Castle had given birth the previous day, and she was told her baby died. It's my belief that her baby was stolen—and that another dead infant was put in her place."

"How can you know that?" she asked. "Did the man put it into his confession?"

"No, but I've surmised it, for the poor woman's son had seen a man steal his infant sister. He told his father and anyone who'd listen that he'd seen it happen, but no one believed him."

"Why? You'd believe me, wouldn't you?"

He kissed her forehead. "I'd believe anything you told me, little one. But they had a dead infant in the cot, you see. They assumed the boy had dreamt it all."

"Can you interview this boy? How old would he be now? Perhaps, we can find him. Isn't that worth trying?"

"Very clever thinking, but I already know what he'd say. He'd be thirty-three years old now. Nearly thirty-four. And I see him every time I look in the mirror."

"You?"

"Yes. Della, your mother was my younger sister Charlotte. You're not only my adoptive daughter. You're also my niece."

The air grew still, and the moon seemed to move closer. The owls' ice blue eyes stared, and their bodies leaned forwards.

Adele took a deep breath, wiping a tear from her cheek. "I'm your niece? My real mother was your sister? But that's wonderful!

Father, that's quite amazing, don't you think? Oh, and it explains why our eyes are the same, doesn't it?"

"It does," he said, grateful to God for granting her the strength to take it all in. "I'm your Uncle Charles, and now, according to all laws of man, you are my daughter."

"Oh, yes, and Mother would be so very happy, Father!" she cried, rising up and kissing his cheek. "It's been like a dream coming true for me, you know? We'll uncover all the truths about my mother's life, won't we? Because we're a father and daughter team, aren't we, Holmes?"

"We are, indeed, Watson."

A thought struck her as she gazed at the owls with the strange blue eyes. "I wonder, Father, am I still Adele Stuart? Or is it Sinclair?"

"That is up to you. We can change it legally, if you wish. What name would you like to use?"

"May I be Adele Stuart Sinclair? I should like to keep the Stuart, in honour of my brother and my late father, for he did adopt me, after all. But I'm both Stuart and Sinclair, aren't I?"

"You carry both blood lines, darling. And the duchess is now your legal mother; also a Stuart and a Sinclair."

"And we'll continue the investigation, won't we? Into my mother's life?"

"Of course, and I intend to bring the man to justice who dared to abduct her. You may rely upon it."

She grew thoughtful, her eyes upon the moon. "Do I look like my mother?"

"Yes," he whispered, pulling her close. "I have a copy of her photograph, if you want it for your bedroom. She had long hair of reddish gold and eyes that spoke of the French Riviera—just like yours and mine."

"Was she tall?"

"I'm told she was quite tall. Taller than Tory, according to Paul."

"And was she musical?"

"I'm not sure, but I can try to find out for you."

"And may I still call Paul my brother? It's how I see him, you know."

"Of course, you may."

Then a thought struck her, and her face grew serious. "Father mine, do you think Paul and Cordelia will have children?"

"It's possible," Charles answered. *I'll let Paul reveal the news of Delia's pregnancy.*

"Then, I shall become an aunt. I prefer to think of it that way. Babies shouldn't have to worry about complications, should they?" They both stood now, and she gazed up and crooked her finger. "Bend down, please."

He obeyed, and she kissed his bearded cheek. "I love you very much, Father mine. Thank you for being open and honest with me. Not all fathers are, you know. And I'll try to be a good example to Robby and Georgie. I'm so very happy!" She kissed him again, her arms round his neck. "I do think shaving is a good idea. You're rather scratchy. I doubt the new babies will like that."

"I'll shave as soon as the fête is over. Now, shall we go inside?"

"Yes, please."

They left the railing, and the owls appeared to smile. The tiny brown one looked up at the majestic white owl, and it seemed as though the two birds conversed. Then, the brown one flew away, heading towards Kent, whilst the white one remained on the ship. He glanced up at the moon, its feathers ruffling as if to send a warning.

The pale face of the sky Watcher darkened with anger, and she drew clouds about herself as if to hide.

Anatole Romanov left his perch and flew towards the clouds, where he passed out of the human realm and into the connecting world called *sen-sen*.

CHAPTER TWENTY-EIGHT

Saturday morning, 4ᵗʰ May – Branham Hall

At the great hall, party preparations had begun for the opening night of the four-hundredth fête. A masked ball was planned, with each attendee dressed in medieval costumes of the late fifteenth century, when the Borgias ruled Rome, Christopher Columbus sailed the ocean in search of a route to India, and Henry VII, descendant of a king's squire from Henry V's court, controlled England as the first Tudor King.

The grounds were alive with exhibitors from all over England and Scotland, providing booths with food, clothing, games, and crafts; as well as jugglers, dancers, acrobats, a huge circus in one of the many tents, and a steam-driven carousel complete with a calliope to provide music. Sinclair and his new daughter had arrived at Dover just shy of 2:00 am, and their train pulled into Branham Hall depot just after 4:00. Too excited to sleep longer, Adele had jumped out of her bed at eight, wolfed down breakfast, and rushed into the flood of pavilions and people. She strolled through the colourful displays, singing as she went, talking with the vendors and circus performers; each and every one hand-picked and approved by her father's inner circle.

As an extra precaution, several dozen of the circle's best agents constantly watched the family and kept a close eye on Adele, per Duke Charles's orders. Adele chatted with a ballerina near one of the many caravans, where the performers lived during the week-long fête, whilst her newly adoptive father grumbled as he tried on the armour his wife had ordered.

"It's certainly not designed for comfort," Charles muttered as Martin Kepelheim examined the hauberk's chainmail. "Am I supposed to ride horseback in this tin can or preserve tomatoes?"

"You may not appreciate it, being on the inside, Charles, but I think the workmanship is remarkable!" Kepelheim answered from his corner chair. "And you hardly look like a tin can. And there's a padded surcoat to go over the entire affair. I believe the duchess ordered one emblazoned with the Haimsbury-Branham coat of arms and colours."

"There's more to add?" the duke asked.

A muscular Frenchman named Henri Brodeur stood nearby, a gold-trimmed armet in his hand. "*M'sieur le duc* is displease? Is fit? Is no fit? You no like?"

"I'm sorry, M'sieur Brodeur. Ignore me. Everything is quite beautifully made, it's just I'm not accustomed to the weight, or the lack of mobility."

The craftsman laughed. "*Oh, oui, je vois!* Englishman tell me when first they wear the armour, is no fit, but this *magnifique!* You are *chevalier extraordinaire!* You ride?"

"I must ride, yes," the duke replied. "Assuming I can even mount the horse."

"Well, well!" a Scottish voice called from the entry to the large dressing area. "I leave England for a few days, and I return to find my nephew has taken up arms. Are we at war?"

Charles broke into a smile at last. "James! It's good to see you. When did you return, sir?"

"Just now, and not a moment too soon, it seems. Has my granddaughter put you up to this? I do hope this is new and not that old stuff from her armoury."

Haimsbury stepped off the dressing block to examine himself in a long mirror. "Tis very strange to see oneself in armour," he said, flexing his elbows and knees. "I cannot imagine how real knights managed to ride horseback in this, much less wield a sword. I remember looking at the suits of armour back at Rose House and marvelling at the knights and thinking how much I wanted to be one of them. I realise now, I'm designed for soft wool and silk, not polished steel."

"You remember the Rose House armoury?" asked Drummond. "Have I missed something important in my absence?"

"I'll tell you all about it later, over a glass of Reserve, sir. Martin, if you'd help, I'd like to return to my nineteenth century self, please."

Betwixt the tailor and the armourer, the young duke resumed his former costume. Drummond examined the beautiful surcoat. "The embroiderer's done a splendid job on this, Charles. When you're done showing off later, we should add all this to the Branham armoury."

"A good idea," Martin concurred. "Duke James, I wonder if you've half an hour? Seth Holloway was hoping to speak with you about circle membership. Henry's sponsoring him."

"Charles, how do you feel about that?" asked Drummond.

"Seth would be an asset. We could use his linguistic and archaeological skills. I've no objection," Sinclair replied as Brodeur's assistant helped Charles with the gambeson, a quilted undershirt worn beneath the armour.

"He's also quite a talented artist," Martin added. "Have you seen the portrait he's made of our duchess? Charles, perhaps you can ask Seth to paint you in this armour. In fact, we should take photographs of you and Paul."

"Photographs are fine, but I don't think I could stand wearing all this for a portrait. If Seth wants to paint me, he'll have to use a photo."

"Come, Kepelheim!" Drummond called to the tailor. "Let's leave the armour to the experts. We can discuss Holloway whilst looking for Della. I've brought her a gift from Scotland."

Paul Stuart had finished his own fitting in the room next door, and he crossed through just as Drummond and Kepelheim left.

"Was that James?" he asked his cousin.

"Yes," Charles replied.

Aubrey smiled, his dimples deep, and he extended his hand to Sinclair. "Welcome back. How was Paris?"

It was the first time Charles had seen the earl since returning to Branham, and a strange darkness fell over his heart as he looked at the man who'd abandoned Charlotte to her fate. No, he shouldn't feel this way, but try as he might, the young duke couldn't help wanting retribution for his sister's sake.

"I take it you spoke with Goron. Any news of Wentworth or Wendaway?" the oblivious earl continued.

"A few leads, but he offered other information which I found interesting," he answered with mild restraint. "Though enlightening might be a better word."

"Goron's Sûreté chief now as I recall," Aubrey answered as the French armourer left to store Haimsbury's suit and gather up the various parts of Aubrey's, granting the two cousins a short span of privacy.

"Yes, he is," Haimsbury replied, buttoning his shirt.

"I worked with François several times," Paul noted casually. "He's a good man."

"So I've learnt. In fact, he had much to say about your Parisian exploits."

The earl laughed, unwittingly causing his cousin to tense ever more. "He called them exploits? That's not the word he used when he and I last spoke. In fact, he usually calls me some rather select names. I think the good detective prefers the British government keep out of French lives. I suppose I can appreciate the sentiment."

Charles gazed down at his shoulder holster and the gleaming gun within. A pair of greenbottle flies buzzed about the room, and outside, on a stand of ash trees, dozens of black birds began to gather. "I doubt Salisbury would concede to President Carnot's wishes, seeing that he so often sends spies against us."

"True, but then all nations have their espionage units. Charles, is everything all right? You appear, oh, I don't know, a bit preoccupied. Is there anything I can do to help?"

Sinclair stared at his hands, silently ordering them to relax, but the fingers felt like ropes of retribution, alive with anger. He'd prayed often during the crossing back to England. Prayed he'd keep his temper when he saw his cousin again. Prayed for God's wisdom to ease the pain. But suddenly, all he could think of was his sister. The crying infant he'd seen stolen that hellish night in 1860. The tall man with the laughing eyes; the one who'd called him 'boy' and dared Charles to come after him, just before vanishing into the mirror.

Charlotte had been pure and innocent, and she was carried away to her death.

Was Paul to blame? Logically, Charles knew the earl had made the best possible choice at the time, but all the logic of Sinclair's mathematical brain was overwhelmed by massive waves of guilt and self-loathing. Truthfully, *it was he* who'd failed Charlotte, but for some reason Charles wanted to make someone else take the blame; another to bear this heart-wrenching burden.

If only Paul had stayed long enough to learn about the pregnancy, what then? What might have happened? How would Charlotte's life have been different? Might the truth have come out? Would she be with him now, as Paul's wife and his beloved sister. Back in the Stuart-Sinclair family, just as he was?

Would Paul really have married the harlot he knew as Cozette du Barroux, or would he have soothed the wound he'd inflicted with money? Charles wanted to believe the best of his cousin, but an uncontrollable outrage boiled inside his breast, crowding out all sense. He had to blame someone. Himself or Paul? Who? Surely, the abductor was at fault. The monster who'd sold her to a procurement place, this *Maison du Beauté*.

"Charles?" asked Stuart again. "What's wrong? Did something happen in Paris?"

The duke cast a cold glance at his cousin, trying to overcome the inner turmoil that threatened to boil over into rage. "There's a new prince living on the opposite side of the woods from Tory, who may prove a threat."

"Another prince? Is he human?" asked Paul.

"That's debatable," the duke muttered, still staring at the deadly weapon.

The earl could sense tension in the air, and he wanted to give his cousin room to relax, to let go of whatever might be churning through his thoughts, but he also wanted to help. Perhaps, changing the topic might do it.

"I'm very glad you brought Della back with you. I've missed my girl."

"Your girl?" Charles heard himself bite back angrily. "Yours? I'd hardly call her that, seeing as you let her go. I've signed those papers you gave me. I registered the change to Adele's legal status with the Paris authorities. If she's anyone's girl, she's mine."

Aubrey's face paled, his mouth open. The Charles Sinclair before him was entirely different; as if another had taken his place. "You're angry with me, but I can't fathom why. What have I done?" Paul asked.

279

The ravens had multiplied into a massive cloud of black upon the ash trees' branches.

"What have you done?" Charles exclaimed, no longer able to control himself. "What have you done! Allow me to explain it to you, as you're so very lost. The something interesting that happened to me whilst in Paris delivered a rather indigestible meal of truth, if you must know. I've recovered many of my childhood memories, and one is directly connected to you!"

"I've no idea what you mean," Paul tried to say, but Charles refused to listen.

"Quiet!" he screamed, his head on fire. "When I was a boy, I saw my one-day-old baby sister stolen from her cot by a tall man with long hair. He took her through a mirror. My family thought me imaginative at best, but some said I'd gone mad, just like my mother."

"Charles, I..."

"I suppose this is one of those distressing childhood memories Martin worried I'd one day recall. Well, I do recall it! All of it! With horrible clarity and hellish reality, I remember it all!"

"Charles, please, I..."

"*And you.* How could I ever imagine that the younger cousin whom I'd called my little brother would betray me? Betray my baby sister?"

"What?"

"Quiet!" the duke shouted, his deep voice echoing throughout the entire floor. "You have no right to speak to me. None at all. My beautiful baby sister never had the chance to grow up in our home. I may have been ripped from my family when I was five, but at least I have memories. I remember my parents' faces. Their love. The moments spent in their arms. Charlotte had one day, Paul. Just one day before she was stolen away and dragged to another country, where she was sold to a devilish place called a *Maison de Beauté!*"

Paul's eyes widened. "Sold to a...? Charles, please, I don't understand." He tried to touch his cousin, but Charles shoved him away angrily, sending the earl stumbling to the floor. Aubrey stared, completely dumbfounded.

"Allow me to enlighten you just as I was, Cousin," Charles continued, yanking the earl to his feet and slamming him into a chair. "My sister Charlotte was taken to this hell-house and groomed for one job and one alone: to please rich men. My precious baby sister was taught to dress provocatively, to temper her voice in soothing tones, and to become a high society mistress. Then, when just twelve years old, Adele's age, she was installed at a notorious *maison close* called La Chabanais. Does that name sound familiar? Shall I tell you the name her abductors gave her? Cozette du Barroux! That is the name, Paul. My sister is the one you used for your own ends. The one you bedded, impregnated, and then abandoned like an old shoe!"

Aubrey's face whitened to ash. "What? No, it can't be. Charles, please, tell me this isn't true. Please!"

"It is true. All of it. You left my sister on her own to raise your child!"

"How could I know that? And I didn't abandon her. I didn't!"

"You have admitted to leaving Paris without giving her the chance to tell you about the child she carried."

"Charles, please! I did speak with her. Several times. She never told me!"

Hearing the loud argument, the duchess rushed into the antechamber to find her husband holding her cousin by the collar and shaking him like a ragdoll.

"You as much as killed her!" Sinclair screamed. Every ounce of rage and guilt over his own failure to protect his baby sister poured into his fists, and suddenly he threw a punch, knocking the shocked earl to the floor.

"Get up! Get up and explain yourself!"

Paul slowly regained his feet, but Charles threw a second punch, this time to the earl's midsection.

Beth screamed. "Stop it! Stop it now!"

The raven's wings fluttered, and they laughed in caws of delight, as if they kept a secret.

Unbeknownst to all, an evil spirit hovered nearby. It had been concealed within the silver box Charles had brought from *La Chabanais*. It hadn't been Romanov who'd spoken to Marie, but Araqiel. And that subtle Dragon had given Marie the malicious box, ordering her to hide the letter inside. Now, the deadly genie within it was twisting his venomous poison into the duke's brain, enflaming him beyond any capacity to resist.

Beth pleaded with her husband, her hand upon his arm. "Charles, I beg you. Stop this now!"

Far away, near the stables, Henry MacAlpin stood inside a green shed with Seth Holloway, examining the strange statue pieces, recovered from the lake. A tiny owl watched from the corner of the shed, its small beak open.

Henry stopped to listen, for a soft voice whispered inside his thoughts. He could hear it clearly: *Charles and Elizabeth need you,* the voice told him. *You must hurry!*

On the great mansion's first floor, Charles Sinclair heard no soft voices, no pleasant admonitions, for the enemy had at last found the duke's weakness: guilt. An irrational guilt born in the mind of a small boy. An elder brother, who believed that somehow *HE* was to blame for his sister's abduction. And that he must likewise take the blame for her death.

The cruel serpent hissed into Charles's spirit: *Hit him, boy! Hit him! He's to blame! He's the one who stands in your way! Kill him! Kill the earl!*

A strange sensation ran through Beth's soul, causing the pregnant duchess to shiver. She couldn't actually see the serpent standing near her husband's left shoulder, but she sensed it, for the room felt cold and evil. Beth pulled at his elbow again, trying desperately to stop his madness.

"Charles, why are you doing this? Paul's your cousin. He's your closest friend!"

But the duke was not himself. Another controlled his actions, and Charles pushed his wife away, causing Beth to stumble.

Cordelia Stuart had heard the commotion, and now joined the duchess in the antechamber. Seeing Elizabeth on the floor, Delia quickly helped her to stand, and pulled her away from the fight. Beth was badly dazed, and Delia left her in the dressing room, where the Frenchmen began to care for her. Cordelia helped her to a fireside chair.

"You'll watch her?" she asked the armourer.

"Oui! Yes!" he answered as his assistant ran for help.

Delia dashed back into the antechamber. The argument had escalated into a full-blown fist-fight, for when Charles struck Paul again, the earl fought back, connecting squarely with Sinclair's jaw.

"Paul, no!" Delia screamed.

"Get out of here!" Aubrey ordered his wife as he ducked his cousin's powerful left hook.

Cordelia refused to obey. "No! Stop this now! Both of you, stop!"

Paul turned aside for the briefest second. His intent was to speak to her again, to order her out, but Charles caught him hard with a hammer blow to the diaphragm, sending the earl to the floor once again, all breath forced from his lungs.

Aubrey gasped for air, clutching at his midsection.

Cordelia ran to the duke and pulled at his elbow. "Please, Charles! Stop! Please! This is madness!"

The noise had drawn the attention of nearly everyone within the upper floors by now, including Duke James who stormed into the room, shouting to both nephews.

"Stop this now! That is an order!"

The ravens stared in unison at the apartment, most with black eyes, but the largest with eerie orbs of bright amber. The avian form of Uriens, also known to humans as the funereal lawyer Albus Flint. He shouted in caws to the cousins, ordering them to fight, assisted by the writhing spectral serpent, who'd been hiding inside the box.

Close behind Drummond, came Henry MacAlpin, who'd run at top speed all the way from the shed to the hall; arriving in a miraculously and most improbable two minutes. That soft voice urged him onward the entire time, and he had the sensation of wings upon his feet as he raced to help his friends.

The scene of supernatural evil inside the study nearly caused the sensitive viscount to fall to his knees, but he kept his balance and cried out with great authority, quoting from 2 Samuel 22.

"The Lord is my rock, my fortress, and my deliverer. The God of my rock; in Him will I trust! He is my shield. The horn of my salvation! My high tower! My refuge and my strength!"

The slithering serpent's fiery eyes turned towards Salperton in rage, briefly releasing its hold on the besieged duke.

"YOU!" the dragon screamed, and it seemed to everyone else in the room that a piercing wail coursed through the air. Only Charles and Henry could discern the voices clearly. "I'm not done here yet, Son of Scotland! Begone before I eat you up!"

Henry stood his ground and would not relent. He raised his hand aloft, still quoting the chapter. *"I will call upon the Lord, who alone is worthy to be praised! So shall I be saved from my enemies!"*

The hideous wraith's image faltered, as if its permission to test the duke had waned. By willingly bringing the enchanted box with him, Charles had offered the serpent entry to all his houses, but Henry's words formed a prayer, and God answered.

"In my distress I called upon the Lord and cried to my God. And He did hear my voice out of His temple, and my cry did enter His ears," the viscount quoted, praising God for his mercies.

A second shimmer formed in the study, near the duke's right hand, and it raised a gleaming brass arm against the cruel serpent. No one else discerned the battle, however Henry and Charles both saw the otherworldly beings and heard the bright rescuer's voice cry out with great authority.

"THEN THE EARTH SHOOK AND TREMBLED," the being of light proclaimed, continuing with the Biblical passage.

As he spoke, the entire room was filled with a radiance so great it hurt their eyes, as though each elementary particle of matter emitted packets of rainbow-hued light. A long, curved sword appeared in the rescuer's hand.

"The foundations of the heaven moved, because HE WAS WROTH!" the magnificent being declared, and a flash of fire arced from the sword's tip, directly into the serpent's red eyes.

The whispering dragon wailed as it vanished through a swirling portal. "THIS IS NOT OVER, SAMAEL! I WILL HAVE VENGEANCE!"

The duke collapsed against the wall, and Henry grasped at his friend's shoulder. The victorious angel transformed, becoming the entity known to human governments as Prince Anatole Romanov, though his countenance still gleamed with a serene light. He placed a comforting hand on Charles Sinclair's heart and another upon his head.

"Now, my dear friend, may all darkness leave you. May you remember only your love for this beloved cousin. And remember God's promises. You are not the blame. Charlotte is with her Saviour, and she is eternally happy. Be free of this guilt, my friend. Be free at last."

Henry stared as Samael rose up through the coffered ceiling and in less than a second, he was gone.

Elizabeth had heard Henry's voice, and she rushed to her husband's side. "Henry, help him sit, please. And someone, help Paul!"

Salperton led Haimsbury to a soft chair in the next room, away from the temptation scene. Charles seemed to have fallen into a trance, unable to return to reality. He was lost in the past, remembering the touch of his baby sister's fingers; how they'd curled round his own. Her bright eyes and pink mouth. The trusting gaze.

Henry tried to reach him, as did Paul. But then a tiny voice cut through the thick darkness; the pleading voice of a small girl.

A bright-eyed child he'd met in 1879.

"Captain, please, come back to me."

He blinked, looking towards her. He could feel Beth's soft hands on his face, and the young duke's eyes welled with tears.

"Beth?"

"Yes, Captain. Yes!" she cried out in relief.

Charles drew her close, intending to stand and embrace her, but the duke's knees collapsed, and he fell at her feet instead. He threw his arms round her midsection, his head against her rounded abdomen as he sobbed uncontrollably.

Charles wept bitterly, and Elizabeth stroked his curling black hair. "It's all right, Captain," she whispered sweetly. "Grandfather, would you pour two glasses of brandy, please? If you go to our apartment, Charles keeps some decanted in his study."

"I know just where it is," Drummond told her.

Cordelia had remained in the doorway all this time, not knowing just what she should do. "Paul?" she asked in a tiny voice.

Henry was performing a medical check on the earl. Hearing Cordelia, Aubrey looked up, his right arm reaching out for his wife. "I'm all right. Come here."

She crossed the room, kneeling beside his chair. "Your lip is bleeding. Are you hurt?"

"No, *mo bhean*. I'm quite tough."

"But your lip's cut. And there's a bruise starting on your jaw."

He wiped at the split lower lip. "It's all right."

"I wonder, Countess, might you fetch my medical bag?" Salperton asked the young woman. "It's in my room. The next apartment over. Inside the closet."

She left the room just as Drummond returned with the brandy. "Charles, drink it all down now. No sipping.

Charles took the drink and tipped it back. He set down the empty glass and rose, crossing to his cousin and kneeling before him.

"Forgive me, Paul. Please, forgive me."

The earl smiled. "Forgive you for what? Your poor aim? I must admit, though, you pack a mighty punch, Cousin. No wonder you won so many Met bouts."

Charles broke down completely, falling into his cousin's arms, weeping uncontrollably. "I don't know what got into me. I could have killed you! But it isn't your fault. None of it. I don't know why I said it was. I'm the one to blame. I should have shouted that night. I should have stopped him from taking Charlotte away."

"What are you talking about?" asked Drummond.

"It's about Charlotte, James, " Charles whispered. "My sister. But it isn't your fault, Paul. How could you know Cozette was my sister? If only I'd called out, all this would have been different."

Cordelia had found Henry's medical kit, and she'd just returned, when her husband answered Charles. She paused just beyond his line of sight to listen, her heart quickening as she overheard her husband's confession.

The earl had no idea his wife stood nearby, and he answered his cousin honestly. "Charles, you were but a child. I was twenty-one. I should have listened when Cozette begged me to take her with me. I should have done more than just give her money. God help me, I hadn't realised she was pregnant! If I had, I'd have married her, Charles. I would! That's the honest truth. I loved Cozette. I cherished her, but my mind was fixed on completing my assignment; to find the proof of Fermin's crimes and return to the War Office with the documents in hand. I've regretted my actions a thousand times since. If only I'd stayed another week, I might I have discovered her secret. That's why I'm not fit to be Adele's father. It's why you'll always be better for her than I. Sometimes, I wish I'd died instead, Charles. Because every time I look at Adele, I see her mother's eyes looking back at me." He paused, gazing at Sinclair's face. "It's funny, you see. They're your eyes, too. I suppose the truth's been there all along. The older Della gets, the more her eyes take on your colour. She even has your nose. Or rather, she has your sister's nose."

Charles helped Paul to stand, and the two cousins embraced. "Charles, I am so sorry!"

The young duke's arms tightened round the earl. "Forgive me," he whispered.

Paul pushed back slightly so he could look into his friend's face again, a fierce determination overwhelming his lean features. "Never again, Charles. Never. Never again will we do this. Promise me."

Sinclair wiped his eyes. "Paul, I allowed the enemy to control my thoughts. May God forgive me. I listened to the enemy's lies. If Henry hadn't come in here; if he hadn't called upon the Lord for aid, I might have killed you."

Paul smiled, his brows arched into a familiar line. "I very much doubt it, Cousin. Your right hook needs a lot of work."

Charles sighed in relief. "Perhaps, you can help me with that. And for the record, you're going to make a splendid father."

Paul tucked a tendril of chestnut hair behind his right ear. "Will I? I'm not sure. I pray I rise to the mark. Charles, no matter what the future brings, you will always be my brother. My dearest friend. I would die for you."

"And I for you," Sinclair told Stuart. "Never again."

The two men embraced once more, and Drummond handed each a filled glass. "Now, if this nonsense is over, we've a meeting planned downstairs that requires your attendance. I trust I won't have to intervene further?"

"No, sir," both men replied in unison.

"Good, now, look to your wives, gentlemen, and then join me in the library. Henry, give them the once over to make sure no damage is done."

"I'm fine," Aubrey insisted, rubbing his bruised diaphragm. "I'll admit my cousin is a talented boxer, but he cheats."

"I do not cheat," Charles volleyed back playfully. "You're just lucky I didn't use any of that *savate* nonsense."

"It would have been your downfall, Cousin. I've not taught you all the moves."

Charles reached for Elizabeth's hand. "Forgive me, little one. I cannot explain my actions, but..."

"You needn't say more, Captain," she replied gently. "I can see the agony and regret in your eyes. I shan't add to it with any reproof. Tell me everything later, if you wish. Just know that I love you."

The gratitude in his face told her his thoughts. Charles kissed her cheek. "You are the fairest of women and the greatest of wives. Thank you, little one." He turned to his cousin. "Paul, I pray you can forgive me as well."

The earl laughed. "If I took offence every time someone clipped me on the chin, I'd be angry half the time, Charles. It's nothing." He turned to his wife. "Forgive us, Delia. Men will be boys, I suppose. Oh, I see you've brought the medical bag. Henry? Do you really think I need tending?"

Salperton took the bag from the countess's hand and began sorting through it for a bottle of alcohol. He pointed to Aubrey's split lip. "I can use this or the remainder of your brandy. Which do you prefer?"

"Is that a serious question?" the earl laughed.

As the combatants slowly returned to normal, the French armourer and his assistant shrugged at one another; thoroughly perplexed.

"Perhaps, the two of you are knights, indeed," teased the elder man.

"Perhaps, we are," sighed Haimsbury. "When do we meet at the pavilion, M'sieur Brodeur?"

"No later than three o'clock, my lord."

"Very good. See you both there."

The armourer and his assistant bowed and left the room to pack the pieces into trunks and convey them down the lift.

Paul drew his wife into his arms. "I'm sorry you had to see any of that. It was nothing. A misunderstanding."

"So I see," she whispered.

Charles sat with his wife near the fire, thoroughly exhausted. "Henry, what just happened in there? I'd felt strange ever since that last day in Paris, and during the crossing, it grew worse. But when Paul and I started talking, those dark thoughts converged into overwhelming anger and all I could think of was that Paul was to blame. But deep down I knew it to be a lie. I dearly love my cousin. He isn't to blame for what happened to Charlotte. Why would I do that? And why did you even come here? I'm very glad you did, but did you have a premonition?"

"Of a sort, yes. You mentioned Charlotte." Henry replied. "I don't understand."

"I'll explain it all downstairs, but yes, she was my sister."

Elizabeth touched her husband's hand. "It's clear something unnatural caused it."

"What do you mean, darling?" her husband asked. "Did you see a shadow?"

"Not actually a shadow, and I couldn't actually *see* anything, but some dark creature was in there, Charles. I'm sure of it! I could sense a strange heaviness round you from the moment you came home this morning. I think it's why I kept asking if you were all right."

Henry's thoughts turned back to what he'd seen, trying to interpret them. "Charles, I did see something, a dark presence. Like a great serpent, or more like a dragon, I think. It had scales and red eyes, and it was whispering to you. It reminded me of that slithering creature I saw inside your ballroom last year. Surely, you haven't been back there, I hope?"

"No, not since it's been locked. And Mac says he's cleansed the entire house again, beginning with that room."

"Did you bring any items with you from France? You were telling me earlier that you met another of those strange princes. Might he have given you something?"

"No," the duke replied. "Wait. Wait! That girl. Woman, I mean."

"What woman?" asked Beth.

He kissed her hand. "She's no one for you to worry about, little one. A woman I tried to help, for she helped me. Her name is Marie, and she gave me a box. It struck me as odd that she required a box to hold a simple letter, but that's where she kept it. Wait a moment. I have it in my study."

He left the room for the master apartment, and in a few moments returned with the curious painted box given to him by Charlotte's friend.

Henry took the object. It felt warm. Dark. Unwholesome. "The box is charmed by very powerful magic. You must burn it, Charles, but not in the house. Take it deep into the woods. Burn it thoroughly and then cast the ashes into the sea. Do it, or else the remains can act as a portal again."

"That demon entered our home through this?"

"I believe so, yes. Charmed objects are often used by witches and other pagan worshippers as doorways into a victim's home. Because you willingly brought the box into your home, it is a way to bypass free will law."

"I understand." Charles placed the box in his pocket. He rang for a servant. "We're needed for a meeting, but I'll have Kay send men into the woods to burn this and cast the ashes into the sea right away." He turned to his wife. "Elizabeth, forgive me for allowing the enemy to enter our home. I've tried so hard to fight against them. If it weren't for Henry and you, I shudder to think what I may have done."

Beth gripped his hands. "It's why the Lord brought us Henry, darling. You, Paul, Henry, and I are part of a small battalion, I suppose. And I think Mr. Blinkmire and Riga also serve within that unit. But also Seth. Charles, I know you still harbour distrust towards him, but I really think he's going to be important to us."

He smiled, offering her a kiss. "Forgive me for my foolishness, Duchess. I shall not contend with you."

"No man would," Henry said, smiling.

"Henry, Paul, do you mind allowing us a moment?" asked Sinclair. "I'll join you both downstairs for the meeting."

"Of course," the physician answered. "Lady Aubrey, will you come with us?"

"Yes," she answered, her face pale. "What meeting does Charles mean?" she was asking as Paul led her from the room. Henry began to explain and shut the door to allow the Sinclairs a moment alone.

Charles sat beside his wife. "I'm a great fool."

"No, darling, you're a warrior."

"A warrior? I hardly think so, not even wearing armour."

"Oh, but you are, Charles. And God's placed you at the head of our little battle formation. That's why the enemy keeps trying to take you down. But you never stand alone, my love. God sends his angels to help, and he's placed all of us who love you, here as your support. Adele's now part of that unit, and soon, we shall add two new members. Robby and Georgianna."

He kissed her soft lips. "How did you become so very wise, Mrs. Sinclair?"

Beth laughed. "I'm hardly wise, but all I've been through in my life has taught me to trust. Not only in God and his promises, but in you, Charles. You are a man whom the enemy fears. Today, was but a momentary fall, a metaphorical hit on the chin. God will tend to it. Trust in him, darling."

"I will. I promise. Thank you for understanding, and thank you for your prayers."

Outside, the ravens had been banished from the ash trees, and upon the abandoned branches, sat two owls; one a glorious white with ice blue eyes, the other small and dull brown with the same eyes. They turned to one another, speaking without words, and in a moment, both flew up towards the azure sky; one towards the woods to oversee the destruction of the box, and the other to the highest point on the hall.

For now, the danger had passed, but another was about to arise.

CHAPTER TWENTY-NINE

In the Aubrey apartment, Cordelia had taken to her bed. Paul assumed the pregnancy had begun to wear on her, and he left her to sleep whilst he wrote notes for the coming circle meeting. He was sitting near their parlour fireplace, scribbling in a leather notebook, when Adele knocked.

"May I come in?" she asked through the open door.

"Of course, darling," he told her. "I'd hoped you'd come visit me. Delia's napping."

"I'll whisper so as not to wake her, then."

Della took the chair closest to Paul, and he set his notes aside. "To what do I owe this honour?" he asked. "I see seriousness on your face. I pray nothing's wrong."

"Not wrong, actually," she told him. "Only, I wonder if you know all about the adoption."

He moved from his chair, drawing her up so he could give her a great hug. "I know all about it. As your guardian, I had to sign the papers."

"And as my father," she whispered. "You're my father, which means you had to approve it. Isn't that so?"

"Who told you?" he asked, struck hard by her question.

"My new father told me, but I asked him to tell me the truth, and he did. It's all right, Paul. Really, it is! I think you're the best of men, and I pray I find such a husband one day."

"You're not upset with me?" he asked, a thousand emotions running through him at once. "Honest and true?"

"Honest and true," she answered with a wide smile. "I hope it's all right. Charles being my new father, I mean."

"Della, I've seen how much you love and admire him. Charles is a natural father, and I know he'll watch after you. I'm a bit of a wanderer, and I've always worried about you because of it. Government sends me off at the worst of times, and..."

"You needn't explain, but did my new father did tell you about what we discovered? My mother's real name?"

"In a way," he said, rubbing his chin. Paul had begun to grow his beard back in the previous month in preparation for the fête's medieval theme, which helped to disguise the bruises. "Her name was Charlotte."

"Yes," Della answered happily. "May we sit?"

"Of course." He and Adele took seats next to one another on an overstuffed sofa, which faced the fireplace. The bright, gas-fed flames danced upon their faces as they spoke.

"Did you know my birth mother was also Father's sister? It's all very complicated, isn't it? My mother was actually my cousin, several times over, and now my new father is also my cousin as well as my uncle. I shall have to write a novel about it all one day; using different names, of course."

"Oh, yes, of course," Aubrey told her, trying to keep up.

"It should make for a bestselling book, I should think. My poor mother was stolen as a baby, but my new father saw the man take her. A shadowy man, who gave her to another. This fellow transported her to France in return for money. Poor Mother was then raised in a place called *Maison de Beauté*, where she was taught—well, you know what she learnt to do—and at a very young age, she was sent to Le Chabanais. She wasn't much older than I am now. Poor Mother."

Paul felt as though he'd been slapped. No wonder Charles wanted to hurt him! Cozette's real name was Charlotte Sinclair? He knew the story of Baby Charlotte's death and how it drove his Aunt Angela mad. His mother had told him about it many times. She'd also told Paul that the death had caused his Cousin Charles to withdraw into himself, and that Uncle Robby had hired dozens of doctors, but to no avail. Now, it all crashed into a new, devilish truth. Charles has told the doctors again and again that his sister never died, but they thought him delusional.

But he'd told the truth. Charlotte Sinclair had indeed been stolen! And Paul had taken her to his bed.

Suddenly, the earl felt sick. *No wonder Charles wanted to take my head off!*

"Paul, are you all right?" Della asked him, taking his hand. "Brother mine? Oh, I hope it's all right if I still call you that. I think it's simpler, but do you want me to call you Father?"

He managed to pull himself out of the troubling reverie. "No, dear. You must call Charles your father, but so long as you know that I love you with all my heart, I'm content."

She threw her arms round his shoulders, kissing his cheek. "I shall love you all the more now. I know you'd have married my mother had you known about me. I hope I look like her. I want to live the life she never had, in her honour."

This caused him to smile. "You are the brightest light in any heaven, Della. When I first saw you, honestly, my heart skipped beats. You had large blue eyes and golden curls."

"My hair was lighter as a child?"

"Oh, yes. And it fell in ringlets, much as it does now. I always assumed you bore a resemblance to my mother, but as Aunt Angela was her twin, it's clear you take after your grandmother. Darling, are you happy with this new arrangement? I wasn't trying to rid myself of you. Please, don't think that."

"I don't," she told him. "I know you want the best for me. Paul, I love you dearly, and I shall always think of you as my wonderful, handsome brother, but secretly, I know you're my father. I've had three amazing fathers. My grandfather, the late earl, who raised me as his own; and now I have Charles as my new father, but also you as my secret father. What girl has so much love?"

He smiled, happy tears in his eyes. "How I love you, Della. If you ever need me, I'm here. I hope you know that."

"Of course, I do. And when I marry, both you and my new father can walk me down the aisle."

"Marry? Not Winston, I hope."

She laughed. "No, not Winston. He's too busy to marry. I think someone older. But I shan't marry for another four years at least."

"Good," he declared.

"Paul?" called Cordelia from the connecting room.

"You'd best see to her," his sister told him. "It's all right. I'm going outside to walk the pavilions and perhaps ride the carousel. I know Uncle James has a meeting planned, so I shan't keep you. I just wanted to make sure everything was settled between us. I love you, Brother mine, Secret Father."

"And I love you, Sister mine, Secret Daughter."

She giggled, and Paul knew everything was all right. Della left and closed the door, and the earl smiled.

What a miracle! How did Charles manage to break the news in a way that seemed to heal her?

Because, he's designed for fatherhood, the earl realised.

As he entered his wife's bedchamber, he prayed the Lord might also help him to be a good father. But for the present, he must be a good husband.

"Paul, would you talk to me, please?" she asked as he shut the bedchamber door.

"Of course," he answered, taking a chair nearby. "Are you feeling any better?"

"Not really," the young wife whispered. "Is it true Adele's your daughter?"

The earl suddenly wanted a strong drink. A tall one. No, not one. Many. "Yes," he told her in a whisper.

Delia's face went white, but the cheeks burned with anger. "You said you didn't love that woman, but you told Charles you did! And she was his sister! Paul, why did you lie to me?"

"To spare you," he answered honestly. "Delia, I love you, and I feared hearing me speak of loving someone else might cause you pain."

"This causes me pain," she told him. "The lie. How can I believe anything you say now?"

He sat on the bed, but she withdrew to the other side to avoid him. "Go away."

"Delia, please, let me explain."

A knock sounded in the parlour.

"*Mo bhean*, please, let me explain."

"Don't call me that! I never want to hear that again! You're a liar!"

The knock sounded again; more loudly.

"Delia, please!"

"Go away, or I shall scream!"

"I love you, Cordelia. No matter what you believe now, I only wanted to protect you."

Knock, knock, knock, knock.

"Go answer that and leave me in peace."

"Very well, but I'll return after the meeting. I pray we can talk then. I love you."

She turned on her side, offering no reply.

The earl left the bed, his heart heavy. Crossing back into the parlour, he opened the door to the footman.

"Duke James insists all circle members to join him in the red room, sir."

"Yes, thank you. I'm coming."

Aubrey glanced back into the bedchamber; the panelled door symbolising his marriage at the moment. Closed and silent. Never in his thirty-three years, had Paul Stuart felt so alone.

CHAPTER THIRTY

2:00 pm – Circle Meeting, Red Drawing Room

"Do come in, Mr. Blinkmire," Haimsbury said to the gentle giant. "Count Riga, you're most welcome, sir. Sit, gentlemen. I've just been sharing a little of this past week's events with my uncle. Henry, pour our friends a glass of wine, will you?"

"Is everything all right, sir? Your left cheek is bruised," said Blinkmire as he passed beneath the tall entryway. The eight-foot man's head cleared the opening by just four inches.

"A misunderstanding, but yes, I'm fine. We're delighted you've joined us."

Lord Salperton filled everyone's glass and returned to the great fireplace, where seventeen men had gathered round a pair of tables. "Seems like only yesterday, we all celebrated Christmas in this room. Now, we're but a month away from welcoming Robby and Georgianna into the family. Life goes on."

"Indeed it does," answered Drummond. He took to his feet, his face alight with pride. "May I have your attention? Before we commence the meeting, I propose we all toast to the next generation of circle members. May we all be upstanding?"

Everyone stood, each raising his glass. Drummond spoke, his eyes bright. "Before I propose my toast, I'd like to say a few words."

Several in the company laughed, in particular all who'd known the duke for many years. "Yes, I see my penchant for long speeches is well known," Drummond told them. "But I'll keep it short. It's just that, seeing all of you in this beautiful home, means more to me than words have the power to convey. This hall is steeped in English history, but also circle history. It represents the very reason for creating the inner circle in the first place. And if Charles's wanderings in those strange realms are true, then in just one month, his twin children Robby and Georgianna will be born in this house. Is that right, son? You're not heading back to London for the birth?"

Sinclair answered, "No, sir. Beth's insistent that our children be born at Branham, and I'd never contend with our little duchess."

"Nor would any sane man," Drummond chuckled. "And now I return to hear that Paul is also to become a father. It seems I've missed a lot whilst in Scotland."

The earl glanced at his cousin somewhat sheepishly. Their violent argument had shaken Aubrey more than he dared admit, but the truth it revealed had torn his marriage into shreds. Cordelia thought him a liar, and Paul's own heart accused him as well. Adele was not only his daughter, but also Charles's niece. It felt like the plot of some Greek tragedy, and his precious wife's fragile mind was caught in that tragedian vice. But he was grateful for the one miracle that no argument could alter; the innocent child now growing within his wife's womb.

"It's true, sir," he told Drummond, trying to disguise his doubts beneath a smile. "And we couldn't be happier, but I owe my cousin a debt. Charles, I want everyone in this fellowship to know that..." Paul stopped, the words catching in his throat. His smile slipped as fear and doubt overwhelmed him, and he broke into tears.

The men looked one to another, trying to unravel this strange mystery, for Paul Stuart never wept openly. Charles went to his cousin, his arm round Aubrey's shoulders. Paul turned to Sinclair and loosed a torrent of regret upon his comforting arms.

"It's all my fault," the earl muttered. "I'm sorry, Charles! I'm so sorry! If I could take it all back, I would. If I could relive those years, I'd do it. If it meant losing my life, I'd happily give it, just to bring your sister back!"

Charles felt completely undone. As with other memories, recently whirling through his brain, a new torrent of memories eddied into his consciousness of childhood moments with his younger cousin, and Charles realised how close he'd come to losing that childhood brother.

The young duke kissed his cousin's cheek and placed his hands upon Aubrey's shoulders. "No, Paul, I must apologise to you. When we were children, I promised to look after you. I remember all of it now. The Lord has given the memories back to me. Do you remember how we'd chase one another through the old hedge maze at Rose House? We'd spend hours in the old armoury pretending to be knights and proclaiming ourselves champions of the king! Or we'd lie upon the grassy hill that overlooked the Eden, our eyes upon the night's glittering stars, and we'd call out the names of all the constellations overhead, wondering at the tales my father had told us about each."

Paul wiped his eyes, nodding and breaking into a happy smile.

"Yes, I do remember. You used to teach me about the stars. You had such a fine mind, Charles. You could speak fluent French, or at least it sounded fluent to my ears. And you kept watch over me. Protecting me against anyone or anything that might harm me. But I remember strange things happening, too."

"Strange things? Such as?"

"Well, once, in the hedge maze, you were helping me to learn the turns, and I followed you faithfully. But when I reached the centre, only a few steps behind, you'd vanished. I never did discover where you'd gone."

Martin Kepelheim stepped close and touched the earl's shoulder. "I believe I can explain that. Duke James, may I interrupt your toast to offer clarification?"

"If it provides insight, of course. Please, do sit, everyone."

Before taking his seat, Sinclair touched his forehead to that of his younger cousin. "We used to do this, remember? We found it amusing that we looked a bit alike, and we'd always touch foreheads in union."

"And I'd say 'this makes us one'."

Charles nodded, tears forming on his lashes. "Yes, that's what you'd say. That our minds and hearts were one. My mother used to call us the Stuart-Sinclair Twins. Paul, I take back every angry word, and I beg you to forgive me."

"Let's both put aside all hasty words, Cousin. No, my Brother."

Charles began to laugh. "Perhaps, this is why Georgie calls you Uncle Paul, eh? You truly are my brother, but also my dearest friend in all the world." He wiped the tears from his eyes and then turned to Kepelheim. "Martin, what clarity do we lack in our memories of the Rose House maze?"

"I suggest you both take seats, my friends. And perhaps a glass of brandy for our twin cousins?"

Paul poured the last of the Danflou from the decanter. Baxter started to rise. "Shall I decant some more, my lord?"

"No, Cornelius. You're an inspector now, remember?" Charles answered. "If we need more, I'm sure Kay or one of his footmen can bring it. Go on, Martin. We are all attention."

The former butler returned to his chair with a glass of Bordeaux, which he enbibed happily whilst listening. Duke James had whisky, but was so riveted to the ensuing story that he forgot all about it finishing it.

"Now, that we're all settled, allow me to begin this strange tale. Charles, your father asked me to keep this secret, but as our young earl has already mentioned it—and, perhaps you also remember?"

Sinclair sipped at the cognac, thoughtfully. "I remember most of it, I believe. Martin, you once told the inner circle gathering at Drummond Castle that the return of my memories might leave me a little lost for a time. I now know why you made that statement."

"Yes, I think what I said was that we might lose you. I knew what dark secrets were locked inside your mind—or some of them at least—and I feared a relapse of your childhood amnesia. After your sister was taken, you drifted in and out of brain fevers. Then, when your father was killed, your memory lapsed entirely."

"Oddly, enough I recall that strange period now, but go on. Tell us of the maze."

Kepelheim took a sip of his drink. "I wonder, how many here realise that the Rose House hedge maze is identical to the one at Branham?"

Most of the men showed surprise in their faces, but Charles did not. Instead, the young duke smiled. "I realised that the first time I ran it. Boxing Day last year, when I had a very distressing encounter with a dragon. What I don't know is why they're identical. Are all mazes built upon the same design?"

"No, but these two are the same, because they are linked," the tailor replied. "I didn't notice the patterns were the same until that time I became lost in the maze here. Our good Inspector Baxter served as butler then, and found me quite exhausted when I finally emerged from those passages. It was then he taught me to run the new lift."

"I remember it, sir," Cornelius noted, his dark eyes thoughtful. "Your colour had gone quite pale, if I may say so, Mr. Kepelheim."

"You may, for it was true!" the tailor exclaimed. "But it wasn't only the maze's difficulty that caused me to grow faint. No, it was the unsettling sensation of being in two places at once. I could hear an odd mixture of sounds whilst nearing the centre, as though they arose from two locales simultaneously. And certain floral scents came and went, as if from two different gardens. But also it was a *feeling* as much as anything else, and it brought to mind something Charles had told me as a boy. You said the maze took you to other places, just like the mirror did."

Sinclair gasped, for another set of memories raced forward to demand attention. Then, without warning or preamble, everyone in the room froze into statues, and the fire's flames became nothing more than still-life, waiting for an artist's brush. A voice spoke, and Charles turned to find Anatole Romanov standing beside him.

"I'm getting more accustomed to your dramatic entrances, Romanov."

The mysterious messenger laughed, stepping closer. "I come when I'm summoned."

"I didn't summon you."

"No, but the One did, and it is He who sent me to you. Come with me, Charles."

The duke followed the entity out of the drawing room, through the foyer, and out into the afternoon. The panorama upon the gardens, pavilions, and lakeside of the grounds seemed eerily similar to a living diorama from a museum. Horses, people, the carousel, even the circus animals; all had frozen into a single second of motion. Charles could see dogs in mid-stride as they chased a cat through the waggons; children running and laughing; campfires, meat sizzling upon spits, water from the many fountains, all frozen in a single moment; even three sets of combatants in full armour, practising their swordplay in preparation for that afternoon's tilt yard performances. And far to the north, he could see the sawdust covered yard and the wooden list which formed the dividing line for mounted combatants. He could see a pair of majestic horses in battle dress, their tails extended, manes flying, hooves poised in mid-air as their riders raced towards one another, lances pressed against their sides, ready to strike.

"It's all impossible," Sinclair told the angelic companion. "The world stands still. None of them will be harmed, I hope? When they return to normal, this won't cause them to lose concentration?"

"To all but yourself, the world continues without interruption. They notice no pause or break in time, for I speak to you in the long breath betwixt seconds. We have stepped out of human time, you might say."

"I think I understand. Can your kind do this at will?" he asked as they walked towards the hedge maze.

"Yes, and I do so only with permission. The fallen also have this ability, but do not seek permission. My rebellious brethren often watch and interfere with humans. To those with the gift of 'sight', their presence might be felt as a tingle across one's nerves or seen as an unwelcome shadow."

"I often get that sensation," Charles told his friend. "And I'm beginning to remember other times when this happened, when I was a boy."

"Yes, I know. It is why I'm here. Next, you will remember the truth of the Arthur clocks, and the greatest test will come. But for now, I've been given permission to aid you in the maze. Come. Let us discover what comes into your mind."

CHAPTER THIRTY-ONE

2:13 pm - 33 Wormwood, City of London

As so often happens in human events, just as Charles Sinclair was reliving his childhood inside the Branham maze, a meeting was taking place in London that would undo all such pleasantries and send the duke and his inner circle running in a dozen different directions. Coincidence might be blamed for this confluential catastrophe, but humans who use such a word have no idea of the invisible spiders that design these sticky webs of correlation. Moonlit sprites in congress with devilish demons would soon lead to sleepless nights for the duke's new family, and the spidery filaments now being spun at 33 Wormwood would catch the unwary ducal fly in a trap that would send the entire Stuart-Sinclair family reeling.

With Sir Clive Urquhart dead and his body left for the police, an argument had erupted amongst the surviving members of the former Round Table of Redwing; that argument led by Baron William Wychwright and his toady friends, Sir Richard Treversham and Cecil Brandon. The self-absorbed threesome waged vociferous war with the staid and somewhat somnolent core members over what to do about Lord Aubrey. Wychwright's anger over his sister's marriage to the wealthy and intractable earl had boiled over into seething hatred, and he sought permission to—quote, 'put an end to the Scotsman's damnable interference once and for all!'—unquote. Three of the Round Table council favoured this radical solution (with decided relish), but the remaining five did not. Without oversight from Saraqael, now in Russia grooming a mystic named Gregory Rasputin, it seemed the squabbling humans stood at an impasse.

Now, Honoria Chandler, who'd voted against killing Aubrey, raised her hand to speak. "My friends and colleagues," the rail-thin woman began in an intentionally honeyed voice, "let us not quibble over so small a matter."

"Small?" shouted Wychwright. "You're not the one living in humiliation! I'm the one must face my friends at the regimental club. Their smug looks and snide remarks may as well be polished swords for the wounding I'm taking. Aubrey's lies about my activities have marked me as an outcast amongst my own friends. Ask Brandon, if you don't believe me!"

"It's true," the somewhat less intelligent, younger man agreed, his hand upon the baron's arm. "Poor Will's become a laughingstock at our club. How is he expected to mount a successful campaign for Parliament in such a tempest?"

"A tempest, you say?" Lord Wisling noted with a wry grin. "And which of you is Prospero and which Antonio, eh? Are you the designer or the victim of this supernatural tempest, Lord Wychwright? Do you work with spirits, or do you use the hand of man only?"

"What?" asked the baron, blinking his eyes. "You really are a puffed up little fraud, Wisling. What the devil does any of that nonsense have to do with Stuart?"

"Everything. You speak of a tempest, yet you know nothing of wind. You talk of vengeance, but what is there to your plans other than complaint and moaning? You and your Silver Spoon pals are no better than a woman who groans to give birth but releases only air. If you really want to hurt Aubrey, there are much better ways to wound him than violence."

"Such as?" Sir Richard asked, his face intense. Of the three young men, Treversham was the brightest and probably the most devious. Despite Wychwright's belief that his baronet friend hung upon his every word and command, Sir Richard de la Pole Treversham, descendent of the famed pretender to the English crown, considered his childhood companion little more than a friendly rung on a very tall ladder, and he felt ready and eager to climb up further, which required stepping upon his ignorant friend.

However, Sir Richard's question would lead to a very unexpected answer, for the hastily called meeting now received two most unwelcome attendees: the mysterious Dr. Theseus and Prince Araqiel, who popped into existence without one bit of warning.

The prince spoke first to the startled Round Table assembly. "Is this supposed to be the core of evil in England? You are nothing but a bunch of children!" Ara laughed. "Theseus, my old friend, why do we even bother with these paltry humans?"

Alphonse Theseus tapped the baron on the shoulder. "You're in my seat," he grumbled in that superior, almost liquified Greek accent. "Do sit, Ara. I had doubted your idea, but I now believe this might prove to be fun."

Araqiel's ebony hair draped across his broad shoulders like a sable collar. He wore a dazzling fifteenth-century coat of silk velvet in claret red and trimmed in sable. His long legs were clad in black velvet breeches, tucked securely into supple black boots that cuffed over his knees. The tunic was gold brocade and closed with jewels. A great chain of power hung from his shoulders, crossing over his chest, each link made of golden dragon heads set with ruby eyes. He could have passed for a wealthy Carpathian prince visiting the English court.

"And just what are you made up for? And while we're about it, who the hell are you?" asked Sir Richard boldly.

"Who the hell am I?" repeated Araqiel. "Such a curious expression, don't you think, Theseus? Who the hell!" The two laughed, and Ara snapped his fingers, transforming the room's decorated walls into screens of flame. The room instantly grew intolerably hot, and the members gasped for air, and all began screaming.

Ara snapped his fingers once more, and the walls returned to normal. "*That* is who the hell I am, Sir Richard. I bring demon fire and a great tail, long enough and strong enough to sweep away all of you. After all, if you'll remember, it was you who resurrected me in the first place. You who formed an alliance with my brothers, and you who sought to use *my* power for yourselves. But we do not share power, do we Theseus?"

The Greek physician grinned, his salt and pepper beard widening with the handsome smile. "No, we do not."

"You call those other demon creatures brother? Then, I assume you're one of them," Wychwright declared, rising to his feet. Despite the overwhelming odds, the army captain still saw himself as superior to all others.

"You're a bold little monkey," Araqiel answered, stealing the wine glass from Treversham. "Do you humans drink blood?" he laughed. "Who taught you this ritual? Saraqael? How typical of my brother. He's always been a glutton."

The baronet reached for the glass, but Ara threw the contents against the wall. "How revolting. I taste pork in this blood," he said wiping his finger along the bottom of the empty glass. "I've never cared much for pigs, though they do have their uses."

Honoria Chandler stared at Wisling, who'd provided the so-called 'vintage' for their meeting. "Pig? You give us pig blood to drink?"

The middle-aged earl's double chin sagged. "It's all I could find at the last minute."

Theseus began to laugh, and the deep, roaring sound echoed throughout the room. "We've much to teach you about appeasing the princes and powers of this miserable realm. Captain, your Round Table must make a decision. Is that not so, Ara?"

"It is," the tall prince replied, rising and walking round the oval table. He touched everyone, either on the hand, or the forehead. "As you have freely given your hearts to evil, I may now freely leave my mark upon you, claiming you as mine. By joining this amateur group, you have pledged yourselves to darkness, which means free will laws are satisfied. Now, my dear friend Theseus and I intend to build a new organisation in London. The amateur club is officially disbanded. We are building a mighty army of the dead, and we will place a deified human as this army's king. It will take some time, and we mustn't show our hand until we're ready to mount the first assault. And so, I've purchased this building along with several others in London, and I shall be your general. If any of you steps out of line, I'll leave your body parts for Scotland Yard's bumbling detectives to puzzle out. Is that clear?"

"You can't speak to us that way," Sir Richard insisted, his hand burning where Araqiel had touched it. "We're hardly amateurs! I'm a member of the Spoons, dash it all! We worship the old ones in our meetings, and their power is greater than any of yours. Surely, if you have any sort of supernatural abilities, you'd know that."

"Ah, yes the Spoons," Theseus whispered greedily. "You do worship the old gods. Herne the Hunter? The moon goddess? She is the real reason you call yourselves Spoons, no? That silly nursery rhyme. How does it go again?"

Prince Araqiel waved his hand, and a shadow play danced upon the far wall, colouring the painted plaster with a Magic Lantern show.

"Hey Diddle Diddle, the cat played the fiddle, and the cow jumped over the moon," the prince sang out as the animated image of a cat began to fiddle upon the wall.

A spotted cow leapt high into the air of the miraculous display, soaring over a silvery full moon. "The little dog laughed to see such sport, and the dish ran away with the spoon."

As the prince finished the recitation, a huge dog began to laugh, but unlike in the rhyme, the dog's snout lengthened, his spotted tail grew longer and longer. It sprouted spikes and scales. The dog's soft paws grew talons, and the laughing mouth breathed blazing fire, consuming the terrified cow and cat in one monstrous exhale. The quivering spoon hid behind the dish, but the moon spied the terrified china plate and crashed into it, the collision bending the spoon into a shape familiar to everyone at the table.

The symbol of the Stuart-Sinclair inner circle.

The assembly of humans gasped, and Lord Wisling slapped the table angrily. "How dare you, sir! If this childish display is meant to signify the predominance of that hated inner circle, then I must insist you leave. Redwing will not tolerate such blatant treachery!"

"But Redwing no longer exists, Lord Risling," Araqiel said, moving to the earl's position. "Much like you no longer exist."

"What?" muttered the peer.

Ara turned to Theseus. "Alphonse, would you like the honour?"

The alienist hybrid's head tilted as he surveyed the earl. "Hmm. He isn't much to look at, but I might make use of some of his skin as a lamp shade or perhaps a book."

"What the devil does that mean?" Wisling bit back, taking to his feet and backing away from the table. "Stay right there, sir! I'm a member of the House of Lords! I head the committee on the new French treaty! You cannot injure me!"

"Oh, but all that is past. You *did* head that committee, Lord Weasley."

"It's Wisling!" the earl shouted. "Why aren't any of you do-ing anything? Cartwright! Honoria! Wychwright! Do you intend to allow this latecomer to ride roughshod on our group? We are Red-wing, sir! We run England!"

"Hush now," whispered Theseus, his right forefinger to his lips. "No more talking, my dearly departed friend. Cease your protest and allow slumber to take you."

Wisling's mouth grew taut, his hands to his throat as though choking, but as Theseus stepped nearer, the earl's cheeks paled to powder, and his hands fell limp. Gerald St. Ives, 5th Earl of Wisling collapsed into a heap of dead flesh, his heart stilled.

Honoria gasped, clutching at her scrawny throat. "Is he—dead?"

"Of course he's dead. At least, for the present," Theseus declared. "Shall we leave his body for this new Intelligence Branch to ponder, Ara? I do so like to watch them scramble about, trying to make sense of our puzzles."

"A perfect solution," Araqiel answered. "Now, to those of you left alive, I suggest you leave my building and scamper to your homes to await my summons. You work for us now. Theseus and myself. I warn you, though: Saraqael will soon return, and he'll try to lure you back to his side, but pay him no mind. I have better plans for Sara. He is not long for this world."

With that final warning, the mysterious prince vanished into a puff of smoke. Theseus laughed, twirling his black cane as he stared into the humans' eyes. "He's off to enjoy a joust! And later, we'll attend a delightful masquerade ball and dance in the fabled ballroom at Branham. Take care, all of you, lest you imagine yourselves capable of overcoming the prince and myself. One death, two, a dozen. A hundred. We care not. Human lives are cheap, and they can always be revivified as demon suits. Remember that."

With another twirl of the carved cane, both Theseus and Lord Wisling's body vanished into the aether with a loud *pop!*, and every surviving member of William Trent's demised Round Table scrambled for the exits. Before another minute passed, the room stood empty, save for a shimmering presence, shining in the southeast corner. The glimmering cloud transformed into a familiar shape with arms, legs, and a distinctive set of dark eyes.

It was Saraqael the Trickster, wearing the guise of Striga of old, his favourite Carpathian 'suit'. He emerged fully into the empty space and then leapt upon the table. The cigars and cigarettes, lit and left to burn by the humans, smouldered within their ash trays. One second later, a pair of ugly imps popped into the material world, their flat noses upturned towards their master.

"I smell pig's blood," Sara told his gargoyles.

"Ooh! It smells so sweet," the shorter imp snarled. "Might I have a sip, my lord? I could lap it up from the floor and wall, if you'd allow it."

"Help yourself, Shishak. Lap all to your fill, if such is possible. But there are pigs aplenty in Kent. Globnick, do you hear any echoes?"

"He was here, my lord. I can still smell him."

"Yes, he was here," Saraqael concurred. "Now, I wonder why my brother is keeping company with our old nemesis Theseus? Methinks I smell an enormous metaphorical rat."

"A rat, my lord? Where?" Shishak asked greedily, his scaly lips covered in porcine blood.

"Not a real rat, idiot!" his master shouted as he clapped the gargoyle on his scaly head. "Cleverness is clearly wasted on the likes of you. Why did Raziel create the two of you, I wonder?"

"To serve, my lord," Shishak smacked hungrily. "To fly and spy, my lord. To bite and smite. To hunt prey all day, and..."

"Yes! That is quite enough of your idea of poetry. Really, I must alter your DNA soon, else I'll have to create my own imps. Still, you both joined me against him, didn't you? Perhaps, you're not as dull-witted as you appear. Now, let's leave this room of soiled trousers and grovelling gums and fly to Kent, where I shall loose a hundred pigs for you to devour!"

Saraqael vanished, and the two gargoyles happily flapped their leathery wings to perform a similar trick. Shishak took one last lick at the blood before following his brother into *sen-sen*, and from that mirror realm, all three crossed quickly through another door to the human realm of Kent.

CHAPTER THIRTY-TWO
Branham grounds

Time had stopped for Charles Sinclair, and only he could see the otherworldly being who led him through the field of frozen statues. Anatole Romanov's face grew still, and he appeared to be listening. He turned towards the human, speaking patiently. "I am limited on time, Charles. Red, black, white. Three ancient enemies converge, and a new battle will soon begin."

"Will this battle affect my family?"

"An insightful question. You begin to learn. The answer is yes, but your armour has strengthened since you called yourself St. Clair. Do you recall our conversations? Those when you were young?"

The human smiled. "Is this another test? Is that why you've come here now? You know that I remember all those talks. I remember how you found me, wandering alone along the docks of Liverpool. My mother had wandered off without me, and I had no idea of my name or my family. I'd been in shock since that moment I touched the attic mirror."

"But do you remember what happened after?"

He grew silent. "I don't want to remember that."

"Ah, but you must. Everything depends on what happened then, Charles. You must face the truth!"

"I can't! Don't ask me to go there again. I haven't the courage yet."

"Your courage has always come from another's heart, Charles. Even when you were a child, the two of you were connected. Though born years apart, even time could not prevent you from meeting."

"What do you mean?"

"I must go," the messenger declared.

"No, please! Don't leave me!"

Anatole Romanov had vanished, but the world remained frozen. *I must face the mirror. No, I can't. Not again.*

"Father, please, show me how to do this," he prayed as he stood at the maze's centre. The miniature version in boxwood stood before him, but the water of its central fountain still flowed. "Lord, how is this possible? I see birds overhead whose flight is stilled, yet this water moves? How?"

He stepped closer to the water, putting his hands into it. Only an hour earlier, he'd tried to kill his cousin—the man he loved like a brother—with these hands. "Forgive me, Lord. Create in me a clean heart, my King. Help me to see why I'm here."

Charles felt small, warm fingers upon his thumb, and then a sweet voice called to him, "Do I know you?"

He looked down, finding a small child. She looked no older than five or six, but her eyes, mouth, and hair told him this had to be Georgianna again, come to rescue him.

"Georgie?" he asked. "Are you Georgianna?"

"That's one of my names," the child said, her dark eyes fixed on his. "Are you another angel?"

"No," he told her, bending down to her level. "I'm just a man. Can you tell me your other names?"

"Yes. My full name is Lady Elizabeth Georgianna Victoria Regina Stuart, but I'm sometimes called Lady Anjou. Who are you?"

Charles's voice caught in his throat. This wasn't Georgie at all. He was looking into his wife's eyes, when she was a child. Much younger than when he'd met her.

"How old are you?"

"Eight. Well, almost eight. Are you my cousin? You look a little like Paul."

"Yes, I am your cousin. Why are you here?"

"Do you mean the maze?"

He nodded.

"I'm hiding," she whispered. "William doesn't know how to find the centre. Not this one. This is the secret place. How did you find it?"

Charles realised why everything felt different now. It wasn't just that time had stopped, but it was the smell, the very air, the sky. Everything here had changed from Branham.

"Where are we?" he asked the young Elizabeth.

"Don't you know? It's the other house. The one from my dreams. Are you dreaming, or are you hiding?"

"A little of both, I think," he replied, marvelling at the very idea that he could be conversing with the mother of his children when she was only eight. "Do you remember meeting Hal? The one who helped you when you were lost in the woods?"

Her face brightened, and her eyes sparkled with joy. "Oh, yes! Hal is very nice, and he taught me a psalm to recite whenever I'm afraid. He carried me through the snow and let me wear his coat. Do you know him?"

"Yes, Hal's my cousin. His real name is Henry, but he's sometimes called Hal, but only by very dear friends."

"My friends call me Beth. Do you live in this place or at Branham? Can you cross through the secret door? Because I don't remember seeing you before, though something about you is familiar. I sometimes see children in this place, but they don't always see me. You can see me, though. And there's a boy with black hair and sea-blue eyes who sees me, too. Do you know him? Is he also your cousin?"

Charles pondered her words, wondering if they meant what he'd begun to realise. "Do you know the boy's name?"

She nodded eagerly. "Oh, yes! He's told me his name many times, but he's often sad. He's an only child just as I am. He sometimes meets me at Branham's maze. He comes through the secret door."

"I see. And his name?"

"Oh, it's Charles."

Sinclair's face paled, but only a little, for he'd begun to understand. His memories of the Rose House maze had remained stuck inside his mind until that very moment. But how could such a thing happen? Had he met Elizabeth the girl, inside his childhood maze? Was it even possible to travel across time as well as distance in an instant?

Then, it hit him. His blood. Her blood. Their children's blood.

It was why Redwing's minions and spirit masters wanted them so very badly. For some strange reason, both he and Elizabeth had the ability to cross through hidden doorways. He'd not seen the portal, but he'd crossed it. And so had she.

Anatole had led him here for this reason.

"May I ask a rather odd question?" he said.

This caused her to laugh, and the sound was so unabashedly joyful, he wanted to hear that healing music forever; to place it inside his watch so he might hear it again each time he opened it!

"Am I funny?" he asked her, hoping to elicit the laughter again. His efforts found reward, and the eight-year-old's giggles fell upon his heart like summer rain.

"I'm sorry for laughing," she said, taking his hand. "It's just that adults don't usually ask permission of me—unless they're servants, of course. But all our servants are very nice. Especially Mr. Baxter. He carries me on his shoulders. Paul put a snake in his pantry once, but he still likes Paul. Everyone likes Paul. He's going to marry me one day, but..."

"But what?" he asked, wanting this moment to last longer, praying it would last hours and hours.

"Paul's always leaving. You wouldn't leave me, would you? I think you're very nice, and I like your eyes. They're so very honest and true. And they look like the sea, I think. Sea-blue eyes, just like the boy's."

Charles's joy turned into happy tears, and she wiped them dry with her hand. "I've never seen anyone cry except my father. He died last year," she added, her voice growing soft. "Mother's going to marry William. That's why I'm hiding. Oh, I'm sorry! You wanted to ask me something, and I kept talking. What would you like to know?"

The tears threatened to fall again, and he lifted her into his arms rather than remain kneeling. "Is this all right?"

"Oh, yes. You're very tall. I like that! I hope some day to have children as tall as you, and I hope to grow tall myself, but Mother says I'll always be little and useless."

"Is your mother nearby?" he asked, wondering if this strange visitation would allow him to actually meet his wife's mother.

"Yes, but she's talking to another of her friends. She'll be cross if I interrupt."

"I'll stay with you. I promise." He'd intended to ask her the year, but everything she said made it clear that he'd crossed distance to Rose House and entered the year 1877. But would it still be '77 when they crossed back to Branham? Or would he return to 1889 and Beth to 1877?

"You wouldn't leave me?" she asked him.

"Never. Not for a moment, little one."

She smiled. "I like that name. May I call you Captain Nemo?"

His breath stopped. "What?"

"Captain Nemo. I read the book last year with my father, and I found his character sad. Like you. You look sad and a little lost."

He began to weep again, thinking of how—in her future, his past—this beautiful child would meet him again and say the very same thing. "Yes, you're right. I am sad and a bit lost. May I call you Beth?"

"Yes, but I like little one, too."

"Come now, let's see if we can find our way home, all right? Do you know how we do that?"

"Oh, yes. All you have to do is walk into that," she said, pointing to the miniature hedge maze that formed the centre of the great yew labyrinth. "Just step towards it, and you'll be there. I've never met anyone else who can do it, but I've always been able to. I wonder if there's a reason for that?"

"I think there is, little one. Now, hold on tightly. I'm going to step into the small maze."

CHAPTER THIRTY-THREE

3:33 pm - Chicksand Street, Whitechapel

Edmund Reid had been eating a late luncheon at the Brown Bear, when a constable reported the discovery. One fifteen-minute hansom ride later, and he entered a quiet sort of Hell. The doss house at No. 45 Chicksand stood amongst one of the poorer sections of Whitechapel. The area played host to an assembly of fleabag hotels that rented rooms by the hour, most shared with a dozen other tenants, not counting the roaches.

"Some days, I truly hate my job," he told Arthur France. "Is Stanley back yet?"

With the duchess residing at Branham under the careful eye of Stephen Blinkmire, Arthur now worked with the ICI as an investigator, but he knew Elbert Stanley acted as liaison twixt the police and the Intelligence Branch. The question of talking with Stanley, implied a need to call in Commissioner Sinclair.

"He is, sir. Got back about eight this morning. Shall I wire the duke?"

Reid sighed. "Yes, I'm afraid so. Despite the condition of the body, it's clear from the man's face—or what remains of it—that we've probably got the Earl of Wisling here. He's Redwing, but he's also a prominent member of the Lords. This will make Michael O'Brien's day. Oh, talk of the devil, and he comes to call, in fancy dress, no less."

"Good morning to you, too, Inspector Reid," greeted the reporter. "Is this the work of the Dybbuk? And will you be sending for this local rabbi you've been consulting?"

"No answers, O'Brien. Leave before we place you in irons. They'd look quite fetching with your new coat." The inspector turned to a thin gentleman sporting a bristle-brush moustache. "Sergeant Upton, pull those men back. No one's to breech this crime scene without my approval."

"But we were invited, Inspector," O'Brien countered. "Our paper received a letter from the Dybbuk, telling us of his latest artistic display. His words, not mine."

"Hand it over," Edmund told the reporter. "If this killer sent you a message, then it's evidence. Give it to me, Michael."

O'Brien fished in the inner pocket of his elegantly tailored coat and withdrew a brown paper packet. He handed it to Reid. "The note's in there. Along with his thumb mark. Rather interesting, I think."

The note was written in black ink, but the signature was indeed a bloody thumb mark, though not anything Reid had seen before. It lacked whorls or ridges and the contour was elongated, as though the thumb itself were three times the length of a normal man's. And it ended in a peculiar point, like a long and tapering nail.

Edmund had a very bad feeling about this. "Arthur, send for Galton. And ask him to bring Sir Percy as well. Ask them to hurry."

"Right away!" Arthur replied, hastening to call a hansom cab. In ten minutes, he was back at the station house, where he started the telegraph wires humming—bouncing the message from Leman Street to Whitehall, care of Thomas Galton.

The baronet read the disturbing news and sent a commissionaire to inform Sir Percy Smythe-Daniels, praying he'd not already left for the joust at Branham. Another Redwing death; and this one a high-ranking peer and MP.

It looked like Thomas wouldn't be attending the ball tonight.

Branham Hall Maze, 1877
"Do you think we made it?" Charles asked Beth.

The eight-year-old looked up into the sky, nodding her head. "Yes, this is Branham. Can't you tell? The clouds are different."

He set her down, and they walked together through the maze's many turns, arriving after several minutes at the statuary garden's entrance. Beth led Charles along the gravel path, through the statues of dukes and duchesses, coming at last to the very spot where

Charles had once noticed a light in Beth's childhood rooms. He pointed to the statue of the first Duke Henry.

"Beth, is this the statue where you once saw the Shadow Man?" Her eyes grew wide, and she paled. "You know about him?"

"I've seen him, too," he told her. "But you mustn't be afraid. You're never alone, little one. Not ever."

"Beth?" called a woman's voice from beyond the corner of the house. "Elizabeth Georgianna Stuart, where are you? If you've gone into that maze again, the spider men will eat you! Come out now, or I shall be very cross!"

Beth took Sinclair's hand and moved closer.

"That's Mother," she told him. "She's angry that I ran away."

A tall figure rounded the house. Charles stared in amazement, for he now saw the oil paintings of Patricia Stuart come to life. No portrait artist had every managed to capture the vitality and intense beauty of this vision of womanhood. Flaxen hair so gleaming it shone like pure gold. A swanlike neck, ample bosom, small waist set within a tall frame. Trish Stuart stood five foot nine at least, but the three-inch heels made her even taller.

But her perfect figure paled against the radiant face. Eyes of purest blue, a straight nose, and full lips that Charles imagined once kissed Connor Stuart—and all the while the treasonous wife had been thinking of her equally treacherous lover, Sir William Trent.

Suddenly, Charles wanted to slap the woman, but no sooner had the thought come to him, than the entire world winked out, and he fainted.

The same time - Baron Wychwright's London home

"Did you see what that creature did to Wisling?" asked Brandon. "The poor old fellow just fell down dead! Right then and there, as if done with magic! I'm not sure this Redwing business is for me, Will. Let's stick to the Spoons, old man, what there is left of them. They're a good deal safer. And a damn sight saner!"

The former army captain struck his companion in the face, leaving an angry red welt on the effeminate young man's cheek.

"Be a man for once, Brandon! It's a jolly good thing you weren't in the Sudan. We'd have been knee-deep in Musselmen with our heads chopped off. You're a disgrace to real men."

"Yes, but I'm alive, and I'm not sorry, either," the cowardly man answered. "Not everyone is built of iron, Wychwright. Am I right, Treversham?"

The handsome baronet sat in the corner of the parlour, his long legs crossed, smoking a meerschaum pipe carved in the image of a wolf. He exhaled deeply, and then tapped the spent ash into a nearby candy dish, not caring that he'd just spoiled the peppermints.

"Face it, old boy, you are a bit of a coward," he told Brandon. "Always were, but I've never really been bothered by it. Why are you so hell-bent to impress these Redwing maniacs, Will? I mean, what do we actually gain from it? Thus far, the only powers any of us has achieved are a few additional gaming invitations, but even those left us flat broke. With Urquhart and Wisling both dead, it seems to me that retreat is the better part of valour."

"You wouldn't understand valour if it met you at the theatre with its own definition branded on its head."

"What the devil does that mean?" Brandon asked. "Will, why are you so enamoured with these peculiar fellows?"

"I'm looking to our futures, gentlemen. One of us must. We'll get no satisfaction from my mother, that much is obvious. I called on her at Aubrey House this morning, and the scheming witch made it clear she's jumped camps. And she's got her cap set on Lord Brackamore of all things!"

"Witch? That's a helluva a way to talk about one's mother," Brandon moaned.

"It's accurate, though," Sir Richard laughed. "Connie's always been a scheming witch, and if Brackamore's looking her way, then he'll soon fall beneath her money-grubbing spell. Brackamore's a toad, but he sits on a great pile. I say, Will, might she be vulnerable to blackmail? After all, if Aubrey ever learnt she conspired with us to deflower your sweet little sister..."

Wychwright threw an apple at his friend, narrowly missing the baronet's head.

"Jolly bad aim, Will!" Treversham laughed, picking up the apple and taking a juicy bite.

The baron started to reply angrily, but suddenly a thought entered his head, and he smiled. "Aim," he muttered. "Now, why hadn't I thought of that?"

"Thought of what?" Brandon asked, praying his friend had no more apples to throw.

"I'm the finest sharpshooter in the British army. Isn't that so, Rich?"

"I've always heard it said, why?"

"Do you know what I did in Africa?" the baron asked as he turned to stare into a silver mirror overhanging the fireplace.

"Fought Musselmen, I suppose. Some uprising or other."

"Yes, the Mahdi uprising, but I had a specialty during those assaults. I led the aerial corps."

"Aerial?" asked Brandon, whose mental capacity ran somewhat lean. "What's that?"

"Balloon corps," Wychwright answered as he admired himself. "The enemy's rifles hadn't the distance or accuracy of ours. Inferior design. My men and I flew beyond their range, but with field glasses trained on their positions. And we often flew at night, which allowed us to report enemy positions to HQ using Morse's code and a lantern. I always flew with just an aeronaut. He manned the lines, whilst I took out specific targets."

"Took them out?" asked Brandon.

"Shot them dead in the head, didn't you, Will?" Sir Richard clarified. "Top marks for marksmanship. Always did have a steady hand."

"And I still do. This Branham fête. It will be quite crowded, I imagine."

"The papers say it's to have as many as fifty thousand visitors over the course of the next week," answered Brandon, still not getting it. "Why? I doubt they'd allow us to go. None of us received an invitation to this fancy ball the duke's hosting tonight. We're off everyone's list, Will. Even my old dad ejects me these days."

"But it is a *costume* ball."

Richard leaned forward, finishing his apple and tossing the core onto the rug. "No. You'd tip your hand and put those circle men on alert, old man. Best to give the ball a miss."

"Yes, perhaps," Will murmured.

"If you're thinking what I believe you are, then you'll not want to give Aubrey any advance warning. The man's practically a mentalist as it is," Richard argued.

"Where's that newspaper?" asked the baron, crossing to a stack of recent broadsheets. "It had the events listing for the week. I saw it a day or two ago."

"This one?" asked Brandon, who'd been sitting on Thursday's copy of the *Pall Mall Gazette*.

"Give it here!" William seethed, snatching the paper away from his friend. "Let's see. I remember something about a—yes! Today, there's to be a tilt yard demonstration."

"They're tilting the yard?" Brandon asked. "Why?"

"It's a medieval joust, idiot," Richard explained. "But the actual passes will be done by experts not Aubrey, Will. All he and Haimsbury are doing is riding the list to put on a show. There's to be no weapons."

"So I see, but the right shot at just the right time could do wonders. And you'll notice, there's to be tethered balloon rides the entire time. No one will think it odd if a second appeared in the sky, now would they? With everyone's attention on the joust, who'd notice a second balloon?"

Sir Richard began to smile. "Better still, what if the operator of the first balloon took a sudden nap, eh? We'd not need to find our own, which at this late date could prove challenging. And we'll need to go right away, if we're to make it. The trains to Branham can take over an hour, and then there's the drive to the hall. Another half hour."

Wychwright rubbed his hands together greedily and then clapped his friend round the neck. "Yes, but we can do it. I've managed more with less. And with Aubrey dead, who'll be there to comfort his poor, grieving widow, eh?"

"Why, her brother, of course," Treversham answered.

"Yes, and that faithful brother would then advise her on how to spend the money she'd inherit."

"Would she inherit?" asked Brandon.

"She would if she were carrying a child," William said, his eyes aglow. "I learnt something very interesting whilst at Aubrey House this morning, lads. The entire place is buzzing with pricey decorators, and though my mother had little to say to me, the furniture maker did. I asked how the plans were going, and he said all would be ready in time for the happy event."

"Happy event?" Brandon repeated. "Oh! I see! Then, she's...?"

"Oh, she is indeed! Congratulate me, chaps. I'm about to become an uncle, and I shall happily act as his guardian as little Lord Aubrey grows up—all alone, without a father."

CHAPTER THIRTY-FOUR
Branham Hall Statuary Park

Cornelius Baxter had just left the circle meeting to search for Sinclair, when he ran directly into him—or more accurately, nearly tripped over the prostrate duke.

Once Charles had reverted back to his own time, he'd landed unconscious in the very spot where he'd stood, twelve years before. "My goodness!" cried Baxter as he bent to help the fallen peer to his feet. "My lord, however did you get out here and in such a condition? It's a mystery to be sure, for one minute you were standing with Lord Aubrey, then, quick as a blink, you vanished! We thought we'd all fallen into a trance, for it was most strange. Are you all right, sir? Shall I send for Dr. MacAlpin?"

"No, that won't be necessary, Mr. Baxter. If you'll just give me a moment. I'm a bit dizzy."

"Then lean on me, sir, and we'll find our way together."

Charles followed his friend's orders, and the two men returned via the north entrance, which was closest. They passed by the armourer on their journey, who nodded and called out, "One hour, sir, and we must begin to dress you!"

"Dress you, sir?" asked Baxter.

"For the tilt. I'm to dress in armour, if you can imagine it."

"Well, sir, I believe I can. If ever a man had regal and knightly bearing, it's you, Your Grace. Now, I don't wish to interfere with any plans already made, but I have served as knight's page several times over the years. Our fête themes have often included tilt yards and medieval themes. I wonder if I might offer my services."

Sinclair laughed. "As always, Cornelius, you meet my need before I even know I need it! Yes, of course. It's in an hour, which means we'll need to conclude our meeting quickly. I'll explain everything once we get inside."

"And I think brandy, sir?"

"Drummond Reserve is more appropriate," the duke told his friend.

"Reserve it is, then."

It took five minutes before the men reached the red drawing room, and everyone applauded when Baxter returned with the young duke. Aubrey rushed over, for he'd worried when Charles had vanished.

"Sit down, now!" he ordered his cousin. "That vanishing act brought back my childhood!"

Taking the chair nearest the fire, Charles asked, "Your childhood? Why?"

"Because I saw you disappear more than once when we were children. Don't you remember? Your father and mine used to search everywhere for you, sometimes for hours, because you'd simply vanish without warning. Sometimes, it happened inside the maze, sometimes in the attic, and others whilst we played at Pendragon Castle. Don't ever do that again!"

"I cannot promise, for I had no control over it, but I'll do my best. If the members don't mind, I'd like to explain many things."

"But tell us, what happened?" Kepelheim asked, clearly worried, for his face had flushed. "Where did you go?"

The young duke glanced up just as Baxter returned from the drinks cabinet, bearing a large glass of Reserve. "Thank you, Cornelius. Where've I been? Now, there's a loaded question. Sit, everyone. This could take some time, but sadly, we must move quickly. Paul and I have an appointment at the tilt yard."

76 Leman Street

Edmund Reid longed for a drink, but such was not to be. The clock behind the booking desk read quarter past five. He'd been awake and working since six that morning, and it was beginning to look as though he'd miss tea, and most certainly would miss the Branham Joust. His belly cried out for food, and he could almost smell bacon.

"Inspector?" a sergeant asked from the other side of the desk. "Sandwich, sir?"

Reid felt as if a magical genie had appeared with the answer to his inner longing. Alfred Williams held out a bacon sarnie, dripping with creamery butter. "That explains the smell in my head. Tell me, Alf, are you reading minds these days?"

"Let's just say I've come to know you, sir. I've a pint of ale back here as well, and a fresh pot o' coffee boilin' on the fire."

"I'll take the coffee when it's done. Best to have a clear head when Galton arrives."

"I'll keep the ale, just in case, Inspector. Oh, there's a woman waiting to see you. Over in the constables' lounge."

Reid wiped his eyes and returned the delicious looking sandwich to the sergeant, sighing. "So close. Just keep this until I'm finished speaking to our guest."

"Lordy, what now?" Williams asked as he took the sandwich. The main doors to the station had opened to two unwelcome men. Michael O'Brien and Harry Dam. Dam noticed the pretty female sitting in the lounge and quickly snapped several photos, just in case she proved to be interesting.

"Are you turning yourself in, O'Brien?" Reid asked the reporter.

"Merely serving the public, Inspector," Michael replied. "We understand a telegram's been sent to summon ICI agents to the scene. We'd be remiss if we failed to add that element to our murder report. We shan't get in your way. Harry and I shall stay in this humble corner. Carry on, Inspector. Act as though we aren't even here."

"I shall act, O'Brien, but not in the way you'd like. If you and Dam aren't out of this station house in one minute, I shall find a dungeon where you may spend the remainder of your days whilst I live in peace."

"Really, Inspector, such threats! If I were any other man, I should consider myself in danger. However, I know your intentions are made under duress."

"Duress?"

"Lack of sustenance. I'd be happy to offer a meal at a fine restaurant in return for an interview."

The reporter's words left his mouth, unheard by human ears, for at that moment, the doors opened again, admitting a pair of well-dressed peers.

"Evening, Inspector," said Galton. "Sergeant Williams. I hadn't expected to find your station infested with rats, Edmund. Shall we offer our help? Percy, you're good with your fists."

"Now, now, gentlemen," the American, Harry Dam, replied, glancing at O'Brien. "We're just here for interviews, that's all."

Galton laughed. "We'd be pleased to interview you, if you wish, Mr. Dam. Percy, I believe we have our own American at the ICI, don't we? A former Texas Ranger. Shall we give him your name, gents?"

O'Brien slowly began backing towards the door. "Harry, let's see if we can talk with the people living near the crime scene. But then after, we'll look into that rumour about Aubrey's wife."

Galton's eyes turned into slits, and he poked the smaller man in the chest. "If you so much as whisper that dear lady's name, you will discover why I was called Two-Ton Thomas at Oxford. I may not stand as tall as Aubrey, but I have a punch that knocks through brick. Care to test that?"

The two men spoke briefly, and then O'Brien added one last parting remark before they escaped through the door. "Look to the skies, Two-Ton. We hear it may rain brass today."

Edmund Reid could barely contain himself, he laughed so hard. "You've made my day, Tom! Two-Ton Thomas. Really! You never boxed at Oxford."

"No, but O'Brien doesn't know that. The man's a coward with a yellow streak for a spine. Now, tell me about your summons. Word at Whitehall is the body you found was Wisling. Is that true?"

"I'm afraid so. Did you send word to the duke?"

"Not yet. I started to do so, but then decided to look for myself first. Is the body here?"

"In the dead room downstairs. Sunders is giving it the once over, but there's another inhabitant of that room already. Clive Urquhart."

"Oh, Inspector," Williams interrupted, "that woman I mentioned? That's her," he told Reid, pointing to a dark-haired visitor, sitting on the constables' bench.

Edmund heaved a sigh. "Fetch her out here, Alf. We'll get this over, and then I'll take Galton down to see Sunders."

The sergeant obeyed and returned with a beautiful woman with Mediterranean features and wearing high-class clothing. Before Williams could make introductions, Tom Galton spoke up.

"It's Angiolina Calabrese, isn't it?" he asked without preamble.

"Yes, but I'm at a loss, sir," she answered in a polished British accent.

"You'd not know me from Adam," he laughed, "but I know you quite well. My mother knew yours. I was sad to hear of her passing. I'm Sir Thomas Galton."

"Galton?" she asked, her dark eyes searching his face. "No, I'm afraid the name's not familiar."

The disguised Princess Eluna von Siebenbürgen hesitated, wishing she'd copied the real Angiolina Calabrese's memories before leaving her body to rot in the Thames three months earlier.

Who is this Galton person? she wondered.

That person was about to reply, when a man entered the station house and began insisting on seeing Reid. He had silver hair and a trimmed beard, and he honed in on poor Edmund like a rhino with a grudge.

"Inspector Reid, I grow weary of your attempts to delay legal due process. You will release Alexander Collins to me or suffer the consequences, sir! If my friend is not in a coach within an hour, I shall bring the wroth of the gods down upon this station!"

"Ed, what's going on here?" Thomas asked his friend.

"Sir Thomas Galton, allow me to introduce Dr. Alphonse Theseus. The good doctor has a paper from Home Secretary Matthews demanding we release Dr. Collins. Understandably, I've refused, but the good doctor doesn't seem to hear the word no."

The baronet barely reached six feet, and the commanding and powerfully built Theseus passed him by five inches, but Galton refused to be intimidated. "Dr. Collins, has been charged with numerous violations of the law, Dr. Theseus. I'm afraid Home Secretary Matthews is out of line to order anyone to release him, because Collins is under Intelligence Branch jurisdiction."

"And your position with the Intelligence Branch, sir?"

"I am Deputy Commander," replied Galton, showing his warrant card.

"I see," harrumphed the irate physician. "But it's my understanding that this Intelligence Branch is part of Scotland Yard, which makes you beholden to the Home Secretary, meaning you must release him to me."

"No."

"You dare to defy a legal writ?"

Thomas smiled. "I do not defy it. Mr. Matthews is not my superior. My position with government is rather complicated, but I assure you that if you try to exert influence on the IB or our sister organisation, the ICI, then you'll need to climb a lot higher to do it. Collins will remain under arrest until we release him."

"And if he dies in custody?" Theseus asked angrily.

"Why would he? He's under twenty-four hour guard."

Theseus paused, a slight smile creeping along his handsome face. He softened his tone. "Sir Thomas, please, I am Alexander's lifelong friend, and I fear for his life. My friend became involved with a group of foolhardy men and women who've been targeted by a person or persons unknown. Surely, you understand my meaning? If someone from your family were in danger, would you not move heaven and earth to help? Many of the others within this organisation have died in recent months, and only last night, another. Lord Wisling. And two days ago, Sir Clive Urquhart. Must my friend be dead before he receives justice?"

"Who says Wisling is dead?" asked Galton.

Eluna von Siebenbürgen watched the interesting exchange from within her Calabrese disguise. This Galton works with the same group as Sinclair. Perhaps, he might prove useful.

"The reporters outside say it," Theseus answered.

Tom had no intention of caving to the man's continued pressure, but he'd begun to wonder if there were more than just 'friendship' behind the demand.

"Dr. Theseus, where may I ask do you intend to take Dr. Collins, if we release him? And that is a monumental 'if', you understand."

"I'd bring him to my own facility. Pollux Institute. It's the sister hospital to Castor. I'm afraid Castor has failed in the original mandate imposed by our benefactors. As such, Collins cannot return there, but I believe he can be cured. It's my conviction that Mr. Treves misdiagnosed Alex. I have methods to return my friend's sanity and his dignity. Won't you allow me to try?" he asked in a silken voice. "If you want to post your officers by his door at Pollux, then you have my permission. My only concern is for Alexander's safety and his health."

Thomas took the paper signed by Matthews and read it over. In truth, the Home Secretary did have a small amount of oversight to the IB, but none regarding ICI activities, but Galton had a gut feeling about Theseus, and he wanted to try an alternative approach: Let the minnow serve as bait to lure in the big fish.

"These papers are worthless, Dr. Theseus, but I shall allow you to transfer Collins from the London to Pollux. Not today. On Tuesday afternoon, and I'll assign my own men to oversee the transfer. You may provide two men, and the London will provide two. We'll provide six men and the transportation. Inspector Reid, have you someone who can type up the arrangement?"

"Yes, of course, Sir Thomas."

"Good. Have him type it in triplicate, but let me see it before anyone signs."

Dr. Sunders chose that moment to appear in the corridor that led to the below stairs dead room and cold storage areas. He waved to Ed and Thomas.

"Forgive me a moment, Dr. Theseus," Edmund told the irritated alienist.

"Have you found something?" he asked Sunders.

"Carving, sir. On the dead man's back. If you have a moment?"

Ed motioned to Galton, who apologised to Theseus. "If you don't mind waiting in the lounge whilst the typist prepares the release orders? The inspector and I will return shortly."

Theseus turned towards the lounge, pausing to look at Calabrese. She saw his eyes blink red, and Eluna took him by the arm. "Tell me, Doctor, just what it is you do, for I found your conversation very interesting. Are you acquainted with the tale of the Minotaur?" she asked him in a honeyed voice.

The hybrid human laughed. "Intimately, my dear. I know that tale as though I'd lived it."

Galton and Reid followed the H-Division surgeon down two flights of steps to a cold surgery filled with enamel sinks, gurneys, cots, test tubes, microscopes, and beakers. A Bunsen burner's flame flickered yellow and blue on a lab bench in a far corner, whilst a pale green liquid simmered above it. The smell of carbolic acid mixed with blood and urine was overwhelming.

Sunders pushed through a swinging door to a second area within the large surgery. They'd entered the primary examination parlour. The walls were finished in white tiles to the ceiling, stopping at chair rail height line of black, then finished to the floor with cobalt blue tiles. Two porcelain sinks on opposing walls allowed for handwashing, whilst a broad but shallow third, looking almost like a chest-high tub, provided a place to examine excised organs.

The room contained two bodies, one chopped into three sections.

"That's Sir Clive over there," Sunders told Galton. "Strangely, he died of a heart attack. The wounding was all post-mortem. This poor fellow, however, wasn't so lucky," he continued, standing before the main table. "His heart looks as though it's been crushed—squeezed in a vice. I've never seen anything like it. Help me turn him over, Constable Brixton," Sunders told the assistant.

The fresh-faced lad pulled the naked body towards himself, then efficiently flipped him onto his face. Sunders moved close, pointing to a series of deep cuts on the late earl's upper back.

It was a good thing Galton had a strong stomach. "I may have seen these before, Edmund."

"Then you know what this means, Sir Thomas?" asked Sunders. "The writing makes sense to you?"

He nodded. "Perhaps. Is this the only message you've found on these Redwing corpses, Dr. Sunders?"

"There was one other, sir. Carved into Sir Clive's stomach. I'll show you."

Sunders led the detective to the second gurney, and the surgeon lifted the white cotton sheeting, revealing the victim's bloated trunk.

"We've similar wording here," Sunders explained, "though the hand that carved them seems different. These are slanted to the left, rather than the right."

"Have you noticed any other markings on any of the recent bodies? The Embankment corpses, for instance. Or the victims of this so-called Dybbuk?"

"No, sir. Just these two."

Galton headed for the door. "Dr. Sunders, could you send me a copy of your reports as soon as you finish the autopsies? I'll be back next Tuesday."

"Very good, sir. Do you understand the message?"

"I'm not sure. I'll need to consult with Duke Charles and Martin Kepelheim. Thank you, Dr. Sunders. Please, keep this information secret for the moment. Show the markings to no one else."

Returning to the main floor, Reid and Galton found their friend Inspector Elbert Stanley in a heated argument with Theseus.

Galton interrupted. "Inspector, is there a problem?"

"Is it true Collins will be released, Sir Thomas?"

"We've worked out a compromise, but not because of Home Secretary Matthews. Come this way, Mr. Stanley." Galton led the inspector into a small room, behind the desk sergeant's office, then shut the door to ensure privacy.

"I take it Alfred sent for you?"

"Yes, sir. I thought it might be because of this Theseus blowhard as I see he's here again."

"No, I can handle men like Theseus," Galton smiled. "When did you move Meg Hansen? I stopped by her safe house to find her gone."

Elbert's face went slack with shock, "What? When?"

"The moment I got back to London. Have you moved her?"

"Of course, not, sir. How could I? I was in Paris with you."

"And no one else knew of her whereabouts?"

"Not a soul," the inspector assured him. "Ida knew, of course, but no one else."

"I doubt your wife would dare interfere," Galton said, scratching his nose. "I fear Haimsbury will not be happy. What about these other women? Did your wife give you names for them?" Galton asked.

"Just the one, sir. Cause it's someone claims to know Duke Charles and Lord Aubrey."

Sir Thomas stared. Rescuing Meg Hansen was one thing. She'd worked with Ida and lived across from Sinclair for years. What other harlot might the duke know?

"Who, Elbert?"

"Someone named MacKey, sir. Lorena MacKey."

CHAPTER THIRTY-FIVE

4:10 pm - Branham Hall, North Gardens

In just one hour and twenty minutes, the jousting would begin. Adele Stuart Sinclair's Aunt Victoria had sent her back to England with a beautiful, medieval-era gown for the festivities, made of pure silk velvet in a muted lavender shade, trimmed in gold lacing, which cross-crossed at the bodice. The sleeves fell past her wrists in delicate bell shapes, and the collar stood high behind her neck; denoting peerage. Ada MacKenzie arranged Della's chestnut hair in two braids and then twisted them round to form a heart. As any fifteenth-century princess might have done, Adele added a modest velvet hat, the same colour as the gown, with an attached veil that fell behind the graceful girl's head and draped almost to the ground.

Whilst waiting to join the others in the Royal Court seating area, Adele had chosen to stroll through the area with her dear friend and protector, Stephen Blinkmire. The spring sun smiled down upon them, and not one cloud marred the sky.

"Look, Mr. Blinkmire!" she said excitedly. "It's the hot air balloon!"

The gentle giant had refused to wear fifteenth-century hosiery, but instead chose soft trousers, a simple cotton shirt, and a reddish brown doublet. Despite his sedate choices, Stephen felt rather foolish, but he'd decided to put that out of his mind and enjoy the day.

"Oh, yes, I see it!" he cried, a hand against his brow to shield his eyes from the bright sun. "Oh, but it's magnificent!"

"That's the Queen of the Meadow," the girl told him proudly. "My father bought it for Inspector Reid last Christmas. It's a shame Mr. Reid isn't here to pilot it, though," she sighed.

"Then, who is flying it?" asked Blinkmire.

"A very capable pilot named Adamson, I believe. He's a friend to my Uncle James, though I suppose I may now call him Great-Grandfather, as my new mother's his granddaughter. Which do you think is better?"

Blinkmire took a deep breath as he pondered the question. "I suppose that's for you and Duke James to decide."

"Is this where you found it?" asked Adele as their walk took them close to the edge of the lake. After surveying its secrets, Powers had refilled it for the fête, but the waters still had a dark appearance, and Blinkmire had no wish to step any closer.

At that very moment, all five puppies chose to appear, as if to replay their earlier adventure. First Aramis, then his four siblings emerged from a nearby pavilion, each carrying a sizzling sausage. A portly pie man chased after, shouting in German.

Aramis ran up to his friend, as if to plead for help. Blinkmire picked him up, hoping to steal back the sausage, but the pup had already gobbled it down. He waved to the irate vendor.

"Es tut mir leid!" he told him in perfect German. "Ich werde dafür bezahlen!"

The man stopped, apparently cowed by Blinkmire's size. "Is nothing," he replied in English. "No need for pay, but thanking you."

Blinkmire handed the man the two shillings anyway. "Vielen dank."

The pie man bowed and hurried back to the tent, richer by half for the loss, but convinced the puppies had a powerful friend. Adele laughed at the scene, for she understood enough German to follow the conversation.

"You look intimidating, Mr. Blinkmire, but not when one gets to know you. I think you're quite nice and very helpful. I'd not realised you spoke German."

"Oh, yes," the giant answered, still holding the puppy whilst the others trailed behind them. "I speak several languages. I so love to read, and Prince Anatole used to help me with conversations. Let's not get too close to the edge," he added, referring to the dark lake.

"Is this where it happened?" she asked.

"Very close to it, yes. I'm told thirteen pieces were discovered to this new statue. Or rather old statue. New to us, but certainly an antique of very old origin. Oh, do keep away from the edge, my lady! It's still somewhat muddy, and you might slip."

Della laughed as she turned about, climbing back up the sloping lawn towards her protector. "You're right, Mr. Blinkmire. I shouldn't want to cause trouble on such a lovely day."

They walked up the hill to a refreshment tent, containing a dozen cloth-covered tables, surrounded by chairs. A drinks selection stood nearby with a large spigoted crock filled with cold lemonade. Already the day had warmed to nearly seventy degrees, but the interior of the tent felt somewhat chilly.

"Will you be joining us at the ball tonight?" she asked him as Stephen held out the chair for Adele to sit.

"I doubt it, my lady. I'm not very graceful. No one ever bothered to teach me dancing."

"Oh, but you must learn to dance, Mr. Blinkmire. Everyone must. Society's filled with dances. It's a requirement."

The giant took a seat in a nearby sturdy chair and then released the wriggling puppy onto the grass. "Aramis dances his own way it seems. Will tonight's ball be different?"

"In what way?" the adolescent asked.

"The theme is medieval, isn't it? The fifteenth century. King Henry VII's court, I believe. I rather think their dance styles would differ from now."

Adele reached down to scratch Aramis behind his pale ears. "I'd not thought of that. You're right, I suppose. Oh, but the costumes are very beautiful, aren't they? I love my new gown, but you should see the dress my mother gave me for tonight! It's like a princess would wear! And Mr. Kepelheim showed me the costumes he'd chosen for my brother and father."

"I take it you mean the earl and duke?" asked Blinkmire. "I'm still working it all out."

Adele beamed with delight. "Yes. It's to be announced tonight at the ball. Charles Sinclair is my legal and most wonderful father. When I talked with Paul about it, he cried. I'd never seen my brother cry before. Well, he's actually my father, but not legally. Not now."

Blinkmire's small eyes stared in puzzlement. "Am I to make sense of this?"

Adele smiled. "No, I suppose not. I recently learnt that my brother is actually my father. Apparently, it's all very secret."

"How can that be true?" asked her protector.

"Paul was assigned to follow a man in Paris. Years ago. That's where he met my mother, who happened to be his cousin, but also my father's sister."

"I'm not sure that makes it clearer."

"Sorry. It is rather a bit of a knot."

"Indeed, it is."

"Charles, my new father, had a baby sister, who was stolen when she was only one day old. A rotten-hearted man did it, and he took her to Paris and forced her into a very horrid life." Della leaned forward to whisper, her hands cupped. "She worked in a brothel. Do you know what that is?"

Stephen's eyes rounded. "Oh, yes! I've heard of them, but never seen one. The duke's sister suffered so?"

"Yes, she did. Her name was Charlotte. Well, this awful man changed her name to Cozette, and when Paul was in Paris to follow this evil man, he discovered the man often visited Cozette—who was really Charlotte, of course."

"Yes, I think I'm following you."

"Well, Paul fell in love with her, but shortly after that, he was ordered back to England. Three years or so later, he returned to Paris, and whilst there, he discovered I'd been born, and my poor mother was very ill. Paul made sure she had doctors, but Mother died anyway. Her grave is in Paris presently, a very lovely spot amongst a stand of myrtle trees, but Charles, who's now my remarkable father, well, he's bringing her back to England to be buried at Haimsbury House."

"I see. Or I believe I do. And the earl brought you back to England?"

"Yes. Paul was a viscount then, and he actually brought me to Scotland. As Paul had no wife, the late earl, Robert Stuart, adopted me, and I grew up thinking he was my father, but now I know the whole truth. I shall continue to call Paul my brother, though. It makes the most sense, I think. Don't you?"

Blinkmire did just what his name implied: he blinked rapidly. "Yes, I suppose it does. But why can't the earl call you his daughter now? He is married, after all."

Adele's serene face took on a very grown-up expression as she answered, her hand on Blinkmire's. "It's because my brother has trouble showing affection, and he worries that I lack stability in my life. My new father, Duke Charles, has a father's loving and very open heart, don't you think? And now that my brother's wife is expecting a baby..."

"A baby?" Blinkmire echoed excitedly. "Oh, that is wonderful news!"

Della laughed. "Yes, I think so, too. Now, that he's to be a father again, Paul worried that I might feel jealous, but I'm actually very happy. I shall be that baby's Aunt Adele, but first, I'll become a big sister to the twins. I shall be quite busy soon, don't you think, Mr. Blinkmire?"

"I think that you have a remarkably mature attitude about it all, Lady Adele," he said in admiration.

"It comes from feeling secure, I suppose," she told him. "I wonder, though. Should I change my name to Sinclair or make it Stuart Sinclair? My father's said it's up to me."

"I've no idea. What does the law state?"

"I'm not sure, so I shall ask my new father. Oh, I do like calling him my father, Mr. Blinkmire!"

The sound of music arose on the air, and Adele rushed to the tent's opening to find its source. "The calliope's starting up, Mr. Blinkmire. Come, let's watch the carousel horses go round."

The giant followed his charge past the sunny gardens, and they made their way through the crowded field of golden cloth and exhibitors, towards a large, steam-powered carousel. The carved wooden animals varied, and each was unique. A tiger with open jaws and jewelled eyes, a white unicorn whose long horn gleamed with golden paint, an exotic ostrich with flecks of silver in its black feathers, an African lion, a grizzly bear, an Indian elephant, South American panther, a hippopotamus, a grey wolf with ruby-coloured eyes, and lastly a fire-breathing dragon.

Adele walked all round the remarkable ride, touching each animal and remarking to her protector regarding design and decoration. She stopped at the wolf, and Stephen thought her voice trembled slightly. "I don't like this one," she told him.

He touched her shoulder gently. "You've nothing to fear whilst I'm here, Lady Della."

She looked up at the eight-foot-tall man. "I wish you'd been in Scotland with us last year. It was so very frightening, Mr. Blinkmire. I've told everyone that I don't remember much, but the truth is I remember all of it. A great wolf stood only a few feet from me. It meant to eat me, I know it!"

He lifted her onto the wolf's back. "Then, sit here. Take command of it. Do not allow it to frighten you."

She touched the painted fur. It felt strangely warm. "I don't like it."

"Tell me what happened," he encouraged. "Speaking fear helps to release it."

She took a deep breath. "I'd started walking in my sleep when I was very small. That night, in Scotland, I must have done it again. The first thing I remember, is seeing a woman coming towards me, and all I could think of was that she was my mother. I called her that. And it's very strange, Mr. Blinkmire, but it was Elizabeth. And she is my mother now. She said I could call her that. Isn't that strange that I'd call her Mother then?"

"The world is filled with very strange things," he told her. "Shall I help you down?"

"No, you're right. Speaking fear does help. And perhaps sitting here on this make-believe wolf will help me dispel the horrors of the real one. I need to be brave, just as my new mother was brave that night. The wolf we saw was enormous! Much larger than this one."

"How terrifying!"

She nodded, putting out her hand to take his. "If only you'd been there, Mr. Blinkmire. We'd not have been so afraid, but you should have seen my new mother. Cousin Beth, I mean. Oh, she was so very brave! She faced the wolf, Mr. Blinkmire. She dared him to come after her. And she did it all to protect me!"

Stephen's face lengthened in awe. "Did she? But she's so tiny!"

"Yes, she is, but my mother is the bravest woman ever born! Paul shot it, though. It was such a dreadful night, Mr. Blinkmire!" She grew quiet for a moment, touching the carved and painted wood, her small hands shaking. "Do you think there are unseen creatures who follow us?"

Blinkmire thought of the enigmatic Prince Anatole Romanov, and he nodded. "Yes, I do. I've met one who is able to come and go in a heartbeat. And he's so very good! I think he might be one of God's angels. Is that what you mean?"

"Yes, I suppose God sends angels to watch over us. But there are other creatures, too. Have you ever seen anything like that? Something that seems beautiful but feels quite dangerous?"

Stephen lifted her off the wolf, worried now about unseen dangers. "Perhaps, we should return to the house. There are hundreds of strangers hereabouts now, Lady Della. We could visit Mrs. Stephens and see if she's baked any cakes for tonight's ball."

Adele glanced back at the wolf, but she noticed a glimmering light nearby. Not coming from the wolf. From the Dragon.

"Yes, I think we should go," she said, taking his massive hand. "I don't like this carousel at all. The calliope music is off-tune."

They left the area, passing through the dense crowds of shouting exhibitors, brightly-dressed clowns practising their acts, jugglers tossing rings and clubs, acrobats in Chinese garb, several harlequins acting out mimed plays, a sawdust ring with tethered ponies, large cages filled with wild animals; the last of which held a large grey wolf, whose owner claimed the beast was caught in the wilds of the Hebrides—the last of its kind.

Adele cast a glance at the massive grey carnivore, noting its red eyes. Suddenly, she wanted her father's comforting arms.

"May we go to the tilt yard now, Mr. Blinkmire? I want to see my father."

"Yes, Lady Adele, we'll go there right away, and I think it a very good idea."

CHAPTER THIRTY-SIX

Haimsbury Pavilion, near the tilt yard

Charles Sinclair shook his head. "Go over it again, M'sieur Brodeur. Do the earl and I charge at one another, or do we simply ride past one another?"

Six men stood nearby, each in charge of a different aspect of the complex armour. Henri Brodeur, a man of small stature but a quick mind and an expert in medieval chivalry, oversaw every aspect of the joust and armoury. Cornelius Baxter stood at the duke's right hand, making sure the overseer did his job correctly.

"Is simple, my lord," Brodeur answered in his accented English. "You and the earl nod to one another, bending forward slightly, like so," he said, demonstrating the action by bowing his head and upper back. "Then, you lower your lance."

"We're carrying no weapons, M'sieur Brodeur."

"Oh, *oui*. I mean, yes, I see, but surely a frangible lance?"

"No weapons. My wife is adamant, and so am I."

"I see," he answered, turning to one of the other men and speaking rapidly in French. The second man handed Brodeur a short lance, emblazoned with Haimsbury's colours and bearing his name. "But, sir, this made for you. The Lord Aubrey, he have one, too. Made for him. These break with slightest touch. Little hit. Here, I use another to show."

Brodeur picked out a black lance, placed it against his hip and then thrust it into the duke's shield, which still hung on one of the tent poles. The lance's tip and ferrule broke away, falling to the gravel and sawdust floor of the tent. The overseer showed the shattered lance to the duke. "You see? Is simple. Not much effort to break the ferrule."

"Is the ferrule that metal tip?" asked Baxter.

"*Oui*. You use, my lord Duke?"

Charles had no wish to argue, but he'd felt certain Beth asked that no weapons at all be used in the display. "I'm not sure."

"I show again," the man said patiently. He repeated the demonstration, and once again, the lance tip broke. "No one can be harmed, sir. No one."

Baxter stepped closer, whispering, "Allow me to walk over to Lord Aubrey's pavilion, my lord, and enquire as to his dresser's suggestions. If he is also told the lance is required, then..."

"Good idea, Baxter. Ask Mr. Kepelheim to step over this way whilst you're there. And see if the stands are filling yet."

"Very good, sir."

Whilst Cornelius was away, Charles took a few moments to assess his appearance. *Beth wants this,* he told himself as he gazed into the tall, cheval mirror. The medieval body harness consisted of a chain-mail gorget round his neck, bright metal pauldrons on each shoulder, rembrace on upper arms, vambraces at the elbows, a gleaming breastplate, a plackart to protect his abdomen, fould over his hips, tasset below that, a cuisse on each thigh, poleyn and fan plate at the knees, and greave on the chin, finished by sabaton over each boot. He'd add the visored helm just before mounting his horse. The entire assembly weighed more than forty pounds, but it wasn't the weight so much as the restricted movement that he found daunting. He was just about to ask Brodeur a question when he noticed the tent's flap open, admitting the most beautiful woman in all creation.

And he proudly called her wife.

"You're not supposed to see me before the joust," he told her turning round.

Beth laughed. "I believe that only applies to brides before a wedding, Captain. My, you look quite splendid! Honestly, Charles, you are every inch a knight. And the beard and longer hair are perfect for the era. Darling, you truly are my knight in shining armour!"

The duke laughed, bending to give her a kiss. "If you're pleased, then so am I. But you are a vision, Beth. Turn round and let me see you."

The duchess showed off her medieval costume, a copy of the one worn by the very first Duchess of Branham at the 1489 fête:

A rouched-sleeved dress of apricot silk, topped by an overdress of royal blue velvet, trimmed in gold embroidery. The high lace collar framed her slender neck and brought the eye to Beth's lovely face. The inner and overdresses fell across her round abdomen in a way that minimised her pregnancy a little. Her hair was arranged in braids that wrapped in a circle round her head, upon which sat the first Branham ducal coronet; a glimmering circlet of gold and filigreed strawberry leaves, scattered with large pearls and sapphires. She looked every inch a queen.

"You're positively breathtaking, little one. Where will you be sitting? I'm told we're to carry these breakable lances, and I thought you might consider offering me your favour to wrap round mine."

Her brow furrowed. "Lances? I thought you weren't to carry anything, Charles. This is merely a show of royalty, representing the first joust by my ancestor and yours."

"Mine? The Duke of Drummond was here as well?"

"Oh, yes. Didn't I tell you? But he wasn't the first duke. Henry Charles had died by then, about two months before. It was his eldest son, Charles Edward, who rode the list. Paul represents him today. Are you sure those lances will break?"

"Brodeur has demonstrated it, and they break quite readily. I'm sure it will be fun. He's shown me how to brace the lance against the arrêt. It's just here," he explained, "beneath my right arm. I'll be fine, darling. In fact, I might just signal for a mercy pass, meaning we'll keep our lances raised. Don't worry."

"If you say so," she said. "Please, though, pray before you come out. I've asked the same of Paul."

"You've seen him as well?"

"Yes, but you're much handsomer," she smiled. "Are you going to put on the brigandine?"

"The surcoat?"

"Yes. It has the Haimsbury-Branham coat of arms embroidered on it. Esther Alcorn did the needlework. She did a splendid job."

"She did indeed. Shall I wear all this for you later?" he teased. "Or perhaps after the babies are born, and we leave for our wedding trip?"

Elizabeth laughed, her eyes brightening. "I think I prefer you in far less clothing, Captain."

"As I do you," he replied with a wink. "Now, my lady, go find your seat and await your knights. We shall do our best to entertain."

He bowed, his lengthening curls falling forward, and she pushed them back behind his ears. "You look more and more like Paul."

Charles paused, a thought distilling in his mind. "Say that again."

"What? That you begin to look like Paul?"

"That's it!" he declared. "Beth, when the demonstration is over, and you and I return to change for the ball, remind me to tell you about my experience this afternoon in the maze. Suddenly, I understand a great deal about our first meeting in '79."

She shook her head. "Such as?"

"Just remind me," he said, kissing her cheek. "See you soon."

Elizabeth left, just as Baxter returned. The former butler bowed to her. "May I say that you look grander than any queen, my lady?"

Beth laughed. "You're gallant as always, Mr. Baxter. Oh, I keep forgetting! It's Inspector Baxter. Thank you."

"My pleasure, Your Grace."

The duchess left the tent, and Baxter decided to examine the decorated lance his master would use. "This looks rather sturdy," he told the duke.

"Yes, but when the ferrule strikes anything solid, it causes the tip to break. I'm sure M'sieur Brodeur has examined it. I'd hate to break it now. Whatever artist decorated the lance would be very disappointed."

Just then, an artist entered the tent, only not the armoury artist, but one familiar to Sinclair. "It's all very King Arthur hereabouts," Seth Holloway said, shaking the duke's hand. "I hope you'll be wearing better gloves, Charles."

"Gauntlets, actually. These leather ones are intended to protect my hands from the gauntlet's interior, apparently. I can tell you this much. This is the very last time you'll ever see me in battle dress."

Baxter's large head tilted, and he inhaled deeply, preparing to speak. "Ah, but, if I may be so bold, sir, you wear battle dress every day. Metaphorically, perhaps, but it's my belief that the armour is quite real. In the spirit realm, sir."

Holloway seemed perplexed. "How so, Mr. B.?"

"Ephesians six, sir. Have you had time to read it yet? I believe Mr. Kepelheim and Dr. MacPherson often quote it."

"Honestly, Baxter, I've an entire notebook filled with verses those two gentlemen have recommended to me. Having been raised an atheist, my Christian education lags far behind any of yours. What's the passage about?"

"Let me see if I can recall it for you, sir," the servant replied. "It is the eleventh verse which begins it. *Put on the whole armour of God, that you may be able to stand against the wiles of the devil. For we do not wrestle against flesh and blood, but against principalities, against powers, against the rulers of the darkness of this world, against spiritual wickedness in high places.*"

Charles smiled. "Well said, Cornelius. But the passage then lists the armour we're to wear. The breastplate of righteousness, the footwear of peace, shield of faith, belt of truth, helmet of salvation, and the sword of the Spirit, which is the word of God. And Paul adds that the armour requires that we pray always—in the Spirit—and that we keep watch. This armour is defensive, but wearing it is a call to action."

"What call is that?" asked a familiar voice. Aubrey entered, garbed in full armour, carrying his helmet, shield, and lance. He set the lance beside his cousin's. David Saunders, Henry MacAlpin and Duke James followed him into the tent.

"We're discussing Ephesians, chapter six," Haimsbury told his cousin. "And so you've entered just in time, because I was about to suggest we all pray. Baxter, I wonder if you'd be willing to offer up a prayer on our behalf?"

"I should be honoured," the former butler said in a deep voice. "Gentlemen, let us bow our heads and hearts unto the Almighty."

Charles and Paul knelt in unison, as though some external force ordained it. Seeing his nephews on their knees, James did likewise, and so did Anderson, MacAlpin, and Holloway. The armourer and his six assistants glanced one to another, and they, too, fell to their knees. And then, with all men kneeling and heads bowed, Cornelius Baxter raised up his voice unto God.

"Lord Almighty, maker of the universe, the stars, planets, and all we see round us. Maker of human minds and hearts. Creator of animals and seas, of pastures and glens, of trees, rocks, and even the unseen air—to you we lift up our voices. We men here are but dust. We may put on fancy clothing, take noble titles, even call ourselves king, but when we compare ourselves to you, all such vanity must vanish. How can we match what is matchless? Climb higher than the highest? Your throne sits beyond our eyes, and yet lives within our hearts. This is marvellous to me!

"Today, sir, we men of clay participate in a festival marking human achievements. In a very real way, my Lord, it is a vain thing, but we seek your blessing as we begin it. If I may, sir, I should ask your protection over these two precious cousins. It is my belief that you've raised them up for your reasons, and for such a time as this. Whatever spirits might seek to harm them, I ask that you enrobe them both with armour of another kind. Spiritual armaments that no sword, no lance, no spear, no arrow, no missile of any human or spiritual design might penetrate. Place your hand upon their hearts so that they might honour only you, and may they always lift up Christ as their true banner!

"My precious Saviour, we rely solely upon your blood as our clothing. Upon your salvation as our helmet. Your righteousness as our breastplate. Your Spirit and Word as our sword. Your truth as our belt. And with your peace upon our feet, we march forward to the battlefield each day, where only our faith in you might shield us, for we know that you and you alone stand twixt us and death. And when that moment comes that you call us home, we pray that it will only come, when our battle is done. And may we then hear those precious words, 'Well done, thou good and faithful servant.'

"Lead us now into this day, hand in hand, heart to heart, and shoulder to shoulder, with our shields of faith locked together: an impenetrable force so firm it makes the enemy quake! We ask all this in the name of your most wonderful Son, even our Lord Jesus Christ, who taught us to pray, 'Our Father," he continued, and every man joined together as they recited the Lord's prayer.

As Charles prayed, he reached for his cousin's arm, and Aubrey removed his gauntlet and held the hand of his dearest friend firmly. The two men wept together as they prayed, and they sensed a presence within the tent. Charles lifted up his eyes, finding the tent filled with beings of light, and outside, he perceived many more; thousands upon thousands, filling the entire grounds and reaching up to heaven.

For the first time in his life, Paul Stuart also saw them, and the vision he now shared with his cousin left him weeping and almost breathless. Anatole Romanov then appeared, standing beside another, the being whom Charles called 'the gardener', the angel Shelumiel. Romanov, known as Samael in the spirit realm, approached and spoke to the duke.

"We stand now out of time, and we have opened the earl's eyes so that he, too, might be encouraged. You are about to face great danger, but fear not! The Lord is with you always."

Shelumiel placed his hand on Aubrey's head. "Your eyes are opened, so that your heart might heal, Paul Stuart, beloved of God. Your wife carries a son, and that son will one day join with those of your cousin in a battle that will raise up a great cup of trembling, the promised nation; and the world will marvel at its beauty. Let not the past destroy that which is to come. Trust only in the nail-scarred hands."

Then, Shelumiel turned to Charles and placed his hand upon the duke's head. "Charles Sinclair, beloved of the Most High, your walk upon this earth is a difficult one, but Paul Stuart will walk beside you. You and he have been united as closer than brothers for a reason, for your two families will pave the road to a bright future, and that road will prove difficult to walk. You must encourage and protect one another. Charles, your wife will bear you six strong sons and a brave daughter. Adele makes the eighth child, for she has always been meant to be yours, and you and Paul Stuart will help her to become a mighty force in England. You, Charles, will rise higher and higher, but beware of temptation, for the enemy seeks permission to sift and test you. If you fall, your children will fall. Wear the armour daily—both of you. Today, your battle begins."

Shelumiel vanished to their eyes, along with the great battalion of angels, but Samael remained.

"One last thing, Charles. Remember to look up. You'll know when. God loves you and is stands ever beside you, keeping watch."

The mysterious angel left them, and the two cousins opened their eyes, realising only then, that they'd shared the vision whilst their heads remained physically bowed. As they glanced round, their friends were only just finishing the prayer.

"For thine is the kingdom and the power and the glory forever," the two cousins recited along with the company. "Amen."

Charles helped Paul to his feet, and the two men embraced. Paul's eyes were filled with tears as he spoke. "If it means my life,

Charles, I will stand beside you so long as God permits it. I have never been so moved in all my days."

Sinclair touched foreheads with his cousin, as they'd done as children. "And my life is yours, should God ever require it, Paul. You are closer than any brother, and I love you."

Aubrey sniffed, wiping tears. "I feel the same. Now, strange as it may seem, you and I have to make a pretense of fighting."

"But we're surrounded by a great cloud of God's witnesses."

"So we are," Paul answered.

James placed a hand on each man's shoulder. "I've no idea just what you mean by that, but I've a feeling the two of you experienced more than we other men did during the prayer."

"Let's just say that our inner circle has gotten much larger," Charles told his uncle. "Baxter, shall we make a show of it?"

Cornelius grinned from ear to ear, for his heart felt full to bursting. He picked up the lance and handed it to Haimsbury, and then the decorated shield. "These are but symbols of the real armour you wear, sir."

"No truer words were ever spoken," the duke told Baxter. "And now, everyone. Let's see if I can manage to mount my horse without making a great fool of myself."

CHAPTER THIRTY-SEVEN

Langham Hotel, London

Just as Cornelius Baxter led the prayer eighty miles away, an entirely different type of gathering, accompanied by an entirely opposite type of spiritual witnesses, occurred in the West End of London.

"I hope your rooms are to your liking, Mr. Calabrese," simpered the day manager of one of the city's finest luxury hotels.

The Chicago entrepreneur had just returned from a long meeting with Theseus and the Austrian Group, and he smiled at the employee, his thick black moustache upturning with the full lips. "Marvellous," he said in Italian-accented English. "Few of our American hotels have such charm, though they are newer, of course. Is my daughter returned?"

"Actually, sir, she left in a hired carriage about two hours ago. Shall I send someone to her rooms?"

"No, I look myself. Several of my business friends, they come to see me today. You send them up, no?"

"Yes, of course, sir. I shall be pleased to escort them up personally."

"No need for escort, no. Just send, please," the Sicilian insisted.

"Ah, well, then, will you be needing our salon?" asked the obsequious man.

"No, my room is okay. I ring for wine and refreshments, no? You have plenty?"

"Of course, of course! We can supply all your dining requirements, sir. I'll come up myself with our wine and aperitif listings. Will you be wanting a full-course meal or finger foods?"

Calabrese laughed. "Fingers for food? Is English dish?"

"No, sir, I mean small sandwiches and desserts, *petit fours* and the like. Appetizers, all that."

"Yes, yes, I know you mean this. I make the fun, no? Bring antipasto, sweet cakes, pastries, bruschetta, fig salad, prosciutto, anchovies, all these, you see? Italiano. I live in America, but my stomach still Sicilian."

"We shall deliver you a bountiful selection, sir! It happens, one of our chefs is Sicilian. He'll be pleased to provide a taste of your home country."

"*Si. Bene.* Is good. Now, I go make ready for my friends. You come up with menu in half-hour, no?"

"Yes, sir. Half an hour, and I'll let your daughter know you asked after her as soon as she arrives."

Once the manager left, the scheming Sicilian shut the door. He crossed the large parlour and opened the windows to allow the afternoon breeze to freshen the suite. The noise of London always reminded him of Hell, but he found its music sweet. Breathing in the smells of food, chimney smoke, horses, sweat, and humans, the peculiar being allowed himself to change back into his usual 'human suit', that of a Carpathian prince known to many as Striga.

And by six that evening, Saraqael would form his own new 'inner circle' within Redwing, and with any luck, the scheming trickster would soon own England, Scotland, France, and America, with his hungry eyes cast upon Germany and Russia. He'd met the real Calabrese in Paris, but a snap of the neck and a splash in the Seine soon gave Saraqael a new suit to wear. He'd been playacting as Calabrese for weeks now, and he'd noticed the man's so-called daughter had a familiar scent about her. Sulfur and champagne.

"I'll soon find you, Eluna. Or shall I call you Antoinette? Better still, I may just call out your ancient name and cause the lower realms to shudder. I'm sure your old husband, Dumuzi, would enjoy seeing you humbled."

But Eluna must wait. First, Saraqael would turn his eyes towards his scheming brother. Already, Raziel lay inside a prison box, and Sara suspected Araqiel intended to do the same to him.

"What are you planning, Ara?" he asked the winds. "Might it be the Machine? The great Crucible of Time? Do as thou wilt, Brother, for that machine will be your undoing. I shall see to that!" Saraqael laughed aloud, the roaring of his voice growing louder and louder, until every citizen in the West End felt sure he'd just heard the Devil call his name.

That same hour - Canterbury Cathedral Chapter House,
Father Georgio paced back and forth, his papery hands clenched in
worry. "Where is he?" he asked his host. "You're certain that the
telegram said the duke would pay call here, today?"

"I cannot swear that it meant today, but I can read it to you
again," answered his host, seventy-one-year-old Robert Payne
Smith. He took the slip of paper from his desk and read aloud:

> FATHER GEORGIO:
> WAIT IN CANTERBURY TIL I COME.
> – HAIMSBURY.

"Surely, the duke plans to come today?" asked the Orthodox
priest of his Anglican friend.

"One cannot derive that from so brief a message, Georgio. Ex-
egesis not isogesis, remember? I believe it means little more than
soon. Look, there's no rush to leave here. The ladies seem content,
and we've plenty room. Be patient!"

"How can I be patient, when someone has already tried to kill
them? I'm their guardian, Rob. If the prince hadn't promised we'd
be safe, I'd not have one hair left upon my head!"

Payne smiled at this, for his own head had practically no hair,
whilst Georgiades's bore a bounty of silvering strands. "As to hair,
it is a concept no longer relevant to me, but I appreciate your sentiment. Will you allow me to lead the women in prayer? I know that
you've been teaching them according to your liturgy, but I should be
pleased to offer you a respite. It's nearing the hour for vespers, and
prayer will begin in the chapel. Do you think they'd enjoy it?"

"I cannot say," the priest admitted. "But I think prayer is important at this moment, though I cannot explain why. Robert, I've
this dreadful feeling something monumental is about to happen—
that a darkness is falling round us that only God's light can banish.
Yes, let's find the women and pray!"

CHAPTER THIRTY-EIGHT

6 pm – Branham Hall Tilt Yard

Adele took her seat beside Cordelia and Elizabeth in the Lady's Court, a subsection of a much larger area, reserved for family and special guests. Traditionally, this 'court' formed the decision-making panel of a joust, or lists, as they were called during Henry VII's day. If a winner didn't become obvious, or if the Knight Marshal declared no victor, then the combatants could appeal to the court for a ruling. As Charles would open the games, Beth's grandfather, Duke James, sat to her right until his nephew returned from the dressing tent later. James wore a costume similar to that worn by his own ancestor, the 2nd Duke of Drummond, four hundred years earlier, and he glanced down the rows at the various lords and ladies of the kingdom, arrayed in medieval finery.

"Salisbury's not here," he told his granddaughter. "I imagine there's Whitehall business keeping him in London. Ah, but Matthews seems to think his presence important. I wonder if he's planning to corner Charles later regarding a certain matter at H-Division."

"No business today," Elizabeth warned her grandfather. "Once all this is done, we'll enjoy the banquet inside the grand pavilion, and then rest for two hours or so before the ball."

"You're certain everyone will have a bed?" laughed Drummond. "You only have three hundred of them."

"And there are only two hundred guests, but I get your point. It may prove to be a very crowded house, but no one except close friends and family are overnighting here. The ball ends at two, and we've provided special trains to convey everyone back to London. I've no intention of becoming a hotel."

"The place could pass for one," Holloway inserted as he took a seat nearby. "Della, you look quite splendid, if you don't mind my saying," he told the adolescent. Adele's figure was taking on the silhouette of a young woman, and it seemed men had begun to notice.

The young girl smiled, her dimples deepening. "Thank you, Lord Paynton. That's very kind of you."

Elizabeth reached for Della's hand, already assuming the protective role of her mother. "He's right, you know," she whispered, "you do look splendid. Very grown up."

Adele's face brightened even further. "Thank you, Mother."

Beth smiled. "I like being called that," she told Adele. "And I know my husband is delighted whenever you call him Father. Oh, there's Henry. Henry!" she called, waving to Salperton. "We've saved you a chair!"

The viscount wriggled through the dense crowd of two hundred peers in fancy dress, climbing up the steps to the higher platform of the Lady's Court.

"Oh," he muttered as he reached them, "I'd been told this is for ladies, but as I see James here, then I suppose I was misinformed."

James moved down a chair to allow the newcomer to take the place beside Beth. "You'll need to move to that other chair once our victorious duke returns, Henry," Drummond told him with a grin.

"Ah, yes, I see. Strange to call it a ladies' anything then," he muttered. "Lady Adele, it's lovely to see you here. My, you look rather grownup! Quite beautiful, if I'm not too bold."

Adele practically lit up, and she bashfully replied in a soft voice, "That's very kind of you, Lord Salperton. Thank you."

Henry had no idea of his effect on the budding adolescent, but he did notice a certain 'something' about her that day that stuck in his head, and he made a mental note to speak to Charles about it later.

"So, what is it exactly that we're supposed to do here?" he asked Beth. "Are we judges or audience?"

"A little of both," she explained. "During the original joust four hundred years ago, the final tilt involved our two ancestors, Dukes Drummond and Branham, but it was called a draw by the marshal. Both men were unhorsed, you see. The two dukes then looked to the court for a decision. As it happened, the court that day included Henry VII, who is supposed to have looked to Duchess Eleanor and asked for her thoughts on the matter. The duchess, knowing that Henry wanted to forge a treaty with France and needed her husband's help, voted for Branham. It could have gone terribly awry, but Duke Charles Edward was only twenty-nine and quite fond of his uncle, and he offered to withdraw. The king then took to his feet, applauding Drummond's wisdom, and declared both men winners."

"Is that a true story?" asked Della.

"So our archivist tells me. I suppose it's possible the Drummond records indicate something different," she said, winking at her grandfather.

"No," Drummond answered. "That's what ours say as well, but they do mention the 2nd Duke of Drummond was also hoping to receive his uncle's approval for a marriage with the 2nd Lord Aubrey's Cousin Amarissa. From where I sit, everyone won."

The next few minutes passed in pleasant conversation, and Elizabeth noticed that Seth spoke often with Adele, and each time her new daughter paid close attention, but of the two men, Henry's comments drew the most blushes. Knowing how her own heart had longed for her 'Captain' for years before he knew it, she decided to allow life to play out according to God's plans.

Just then, the trumpets blared, announcing the beginning of the games. The Official Crier, a big man named Elgin Stout, stepped onto a tall box and addressed the gathering. "My lords and ladies! It is my great pleasure to announce the commencement of the four-hundredth-year celebration of the Branham Games! Shortly, we shall begin the lists with demonstrations of genuine and most breathtaking valour, but first, we have a very special replay of the final joust from 1489, twixt Duke Henry Edward of Branham and his nephew, Duke Charles of Drummond! On your left, turn your eyes to see our first rider. He wears the colours green and gold, and the chosen symbol of House Aubrey, the rampant lion. I give you Lord Robert James Paul Ian Stuart, 12th Earl of Aubrey as Duke Charles of Drummond!"

The crowd broke into wild applause, for everyone knew and loved the handsome earl. Paul had chosen to ride Beth's second best hunter, a stallion named Bucephalus, named for Alexander the Great's famous horse. The stallion had been dressed in armour and colours to match Aubrey's, and the earl bowed from the saddle, waving to the crowd and throwing a kiss to his beautiful wife. The earl rode to the rail and lowered the tip of his lance, his eyes on Cordelia.

"Lady Aubrey, I wonder if I might have the honour of your favour?"

As she'd practised, Delia withdrew a green and gold scarf from her belt and tied in at the end of Paul's lance. "May God grant you courage and victory," she told him. Then she leaned forward to whisper, "I love you, Paul, and I'm very sorry."

He smiled. "And I love you, *mo bhean*. With your love, I can move mountains, my lady."

Paul bowed once again and threw her another kiss. Afterward, he directed his horse to the far end of the tilt.

Crier Stout's voice rose up once more as the trumpets blared, announcing another rider. "Our next combatant has joined the list!" he called. "My lords and ladies, allow me to introduce our second contestant! Wearing the red and gold of his own house and the chosen symbols, the unicorn and the dragon, and representing his wife's ancestor, Lord Henry Edward, 1st Duke of Branham, I give you, Lord Charles Robert Arthur Sinclair III, 1st Duke of Haimsbury!"

The crowd went wild now, every person on his or her feet, and the thunderous applause made the skies ring. Charles rode the magnificent white stallion, Paladin, who'd been dressed in equine armour and adorned in the Haimsbury colours and crest. Even Paladin's saffron, the shield that covers a horse's face, was painted in red and gold. The sun glittered off Sinclair's shield and lance as he positioned himself opposite his cousin. Each man prayed to God Almighty that the lances would break as promised and that he would protect his friend from any harm.

The audience watched in hushed anticipation, their eyes fixed on the list. Above them, the skies shone blue without a cloud, and the sun's late afternoon rays painted the tops of the wood line with orangey pink. Torches had been placed all over the grounds for night lighting, and many of the pavilions had similar lighting inside. Beth had even ordered the grounds men to run electric lines from the power station to the main pavilion and the family tents, where strings of faery lights would soon be switched on. The fifteenth century was about to meet the nineteenth.

Also in the sky, the Queen of the Meadow aerial balloon floated just above the packed grandstands, a sight which had become somewhat commonplace during the past two days as vendors and exhibitors took turns, paying to ride up and down above the grounds.

However, this flight was different. Deadly different.

For an intruder had disabled the usual pilot and replaced him with his own, and now both devious men looked down upon the lists, one with a hand on the lines—the other with his hands on a rifle.

CHAPTER THIRTY-NINE

Chapter House Chapel - Canterbury

Lorena MacKey and her friend Violet Stuart began to pray at precisely six o'clock, remaining there for what felt like forever. Though they'd spent many hours in prayer since coming to live with Lambelet in December, both felt a heavy burden for Margaret Hansen and for their friends, Paul Stuart and Charles Sinclair. Violet prayed that God would help her to forget the love she still bore for Stuart, whilst Lorena prayed for the removal of her own love for Sinclair. Though never married, Lambelet had once loved before taking orders, and he recognised the symptoms in his charges, and had often counselled them to ask God's leading in finding future husbands, or else choose to take holy orders themselves.

It was nearing half past, when the doors to the chapel thrust inward with a great *bang!*, and both women turned from their place near the altar, shocked to see a flock of crows invading the chapel's serene interior. MacKey screamed, and Stuart threw up her hands to protect her friend, deciding that she'd 'died' once already, and the world would never miss a woman without a real name.

Seeing the women in danger, Father Georgio Lambelet rushed from the connecting vestibule, armed with naught but his courage and a broom, and began to battle the swirling cloud of madness, his face taking many slashes in the process. Georgio's longtime friend, Robert Smith, had been speaking with one of the cathedral's new musicians, when the doors slammed inward, and he and the young man quickly joined the fray, each one using arms and hymnals to beat back the deadly birds.

Despite the danger, Lorena continued to pray, for a very strange sensation had overcome the young woman, and she believed the birds had come to stop their petitions to God.

"Please, protect Charles," she asked again and again, not sure just why she was saying it, for the physician had no idea what danger the duke might be facing, but the deep conviction would not release her heart, and so pray she did, even though she might die doing it. To MacKey, losing her life to protect Sinclair would be the finest way to die.

In the midst of the black cloud, a ball of brilliant light emerged; appearing first at the top of the chapel, and then descending and broadening its spherical circumference as it did so. The birds parted, terrified by the light, and they formed a ring outside it. The great and glowing orb pushed the avian ring outward, outward, and evermore outward, until the ring of birds seemed to cause the chapel's walls to warp. The priests, musician, and Stuart gaped in wonder, watching the impossible ballet, certain that the bending bricks meant the roof would soon collapse upon them, but the display proved so charismatic that they felt drawn to it, as a moth to a flame.

However, this holy flame burnt only evil, not the good.

By ten past the first bird's cawing, the entire event had ended, except for the light, which slowly diminished its circumference until it grew small enough for a man to hold in one hand. This final ball of light floated down the aisle, towards the altar, stopping over Lorena's head. The doctor had continued to pray, and only now, did she stop. As she opened her eyes, the sphere of light transformed into the semblance of a man.

Anatole Romanov.

The heavenly messenger smiled at MacKey and placed his hand upon her head. "Your prayer has been answered, Daughter of Eve, beloved of God. Because you were willing to give up your life for another, your own has forever been changed. From this moment forward, the love which you've felt for Charles Sinclair will become only friendship. You will be a much-cherished counsellor to his children and a lifelong friend to him. Rise, Lorena Melissa. You have passed the test."

Lorena started to ask what Romanov meant by that, but before she could, the messenger turned his attention to the others. "Violet Stuart, once called Susanna, named at birth Cassandra, I call you

Violet, for it is the name which you, yourself, have chosen. Your willingness to protect your friend at the cost of your own shows how much your heart has changed. Beginning in the coming weeks, a new path will emerge for you, and your feet will walk towards a far different future. I would remove the love which you bear for Paul Stuart from your heart, but God knows that you wish to retain it, for the present. He has charged me to tell you that your future is bright. Within a few days, Margaret Hansen will meet you here, and together, the three of you will form a great friendship."

"May I ask what this new future is?" Stuart dared speak.

"You may, but that must remain shrouded for the present. All will be revealed very soon."

"And what of the duke?" asked Lorena.

"I go now to see to his welfare, but your prayers availeth much, Lorena Melissa. Fear not. You will see him again."

Branham Tilt Yard
Charles took a deep breath, his left hand on Paladin's decorated rein, his right on the lance. "Father, protect Paul, please. If this lance fails to break or anything else goes amiss, I ask only that you protect him. Be his shield, please."

At the end of the list, Paul Stuart prayed a similar prayer, his eye on his cousin's horse. The marshal stood in the centre of the ground, within sight of both riders, a large white scarf in his hand. Once he released it, either rider could commence to speed. The cousins had practised riding the tilt many times, but neither had done so carrying a lance. The frangible lances the armourers had offered both men were half the weight of an ordinary weapon, but for some reason, Sinclair's felt heavier than it should. He glanced down at it again, noticing the tip was different.

Pointed, not blunted.

He'd been given the wrong lance. A second later, the marshal would drop the scarf, but before Charles could raise the alarm, a tiny brown owl flew over his head. As he noticed the bird, time seemed to slow down.

The owl circled round his head, whispering into the duke's thoughts.

Look up! Look up! Danger! Danger!

The duke's eyes turned skyward, and he saw the Queen of the Meadow, but the setting sun's rosy fingers glanced off something uncharacteristically shiny near the basket's rim. Charles looked closer, praying for an eagle's vision. At that very moment, an eagle crossed the heavens, and the duke could 'see' the object reflecting the sun. He saw it in his mind as clearly as if he might see it on the ground.

It was the barrel of a rifle, and it was trained on the tilt yard.

Sinclair looked at his cousin, a wild thought entering his mind.

"Lord, make this missile fly higher than possible! And make my aim true, please!"

The marshal's hand opened, and the white scarf began its fluttering descent to the earth. Paul spurred his horse, but Charles did no such thing. Instead, he raised his right arm as far back as he could, praying again as he extended it, straining every muscle. He released the lance, sending it upwards into the evening sky like a winged warrior. Paul saw the movement and pulled up his horse; gravel and sawdust billowing behind the animal's hooves. The crowd stared in disbelief, their brains perceiving truth mere seconds behind the actions.

The lance sped higher and higher, but the shooter failed to notice it, for the sun suddenly winked into his eyes. William Wychwright pulled the trigger regardless, hoping to hit either one of the Stuart clan members, not caring if the bullet struck a bystander. The bullet slammed into the ground, mere inches from Paul Stuart's position.

The lance, however, continued aloft like a majestic eagle, defying gravity, defying physics; until it sliced through the primary rope that tethered the great balloon to the ground. Cut free and without a skilled pilot aboard, the Queen of the Meadow was at the mercy of the wind. Though the day had been calm, a sudden, powerful breeze arose from the west and blew the balloon and its passengers towards Kent's coast and the sea.

Charles spurred his horse to Paul's position and leapt off, turning his ankle in the process. The light swelling would prevent the duke from dancing more than a few dances with his wife at that night's ball, but would heal in less than a week.

The earl managed a little better and helped his cousin from the list to the nearest tent, where both peers began stripping off their armour. "What happened?" Aubrey asked his friend once both doffed their helmets.

"I think God answered our prayers, that's what," Charles answered. "Didn't you see the rifle?"

"What rifle? Above? Is that why you threw your lance?"

"Yes," Charles told him, his breathing quick from the rush of adrenalin. Baxter's long legs reached their tent first, and he helped with the armour. "Did you see the gun?" he asked the former butler.

"Gun?"

"You must have the best eyes in England," Paul said as several others arrived to help the two peers undress. "And the finest arm. Never have I seen so straight a flight as that lance, Charles! Honestly, it must be the greatest javelin throw in history!"

"If it flew straight and true, then an angel bore it, Paul. Baxter, will you go tell our wives that all of this was but a practised performance? That we're both fine. Nothing's amiss."

"Yes, sir!"

Cornelius raced from the tent, his large feet denting the earth as he ran towards the Ladies' Court.

Brodeur entered the tent, his face pale. "M'sieur le Duc, my lord. Forgive! I am now only learn that my assistant give you the wrong lance! It is the one that our expert, M'sieur LaGrande will use. His ferrule is sharp, not blunted. You might have killed your friend!"

Rather than shout at the man, Charles began to laugh, and everyone stared, wondering if the duke had embibed a drink before the contest. "Prayer, Paul. It was the prayer. The Lord switched that lance. I'd noticed the sharp ferrule before the marshal dropped his cloth, but at the same time, a sweet word came, telling me to look up. And God allowed me to see the rifle."

Paul began to smile, finally breaking into laughter. "Hence the javelin! You're right, Cousin. It was prayer."

"And a little owl," Haimsbury added.

High above their heads, that same little owl joined with a majestic white one, and the two flew out towards the sea to make sure the Queen of the Meadow never returned to Branham.

CHAPTER FORTY

3 am – Master Apartment, Branham

"Did you have a good day?" the duke asked his duchess.

"I did, darling. Thank you for making it so very nice. Everyone talked about your amazing performance at the tilt yard. I still wonder what really happened."

"We put on a show. Isn't that what you wanted?" he asked as he sat beside her.

"Yes, but I hadn't expected anything like that! You know, I've just remembered. You asked me to remind you of something earlier. What was it?"

He and his wife occupied the centre of a velvet settee, and they'd been watching the fire for several minutes, dressed for bed. "Oh, that," he said, glad she'd brought it up. "I've already told some of this to the circle, but I wanted you to know it. In fact, once the babies are born, I'd like for you to be more involved in our work. Would you enjoy that?"

"I don't know," she whispered, her head against his shoulder. "It isn't that I'm afraid, it's just that you are so good at protecting me. Is that selfish of me?"

"Not at all," he said, kissing her hand. "For now, we'll keep it as it is. I look after you, and you look after our children."

"Including Adele?"

"Especially Adele. I saw all the young gentlemen looking at her at the ball. There was one who paid far too much attention."

"Prince Araqiel?"

"How did you know his name? I never introduced you."

"No, he introduced himself. You'd gone off to talk with Henry, and the prince came over to see if I needed a glass of punch. I don't trust him, Charles. He asked if he might overnight here, but I said we hadn't the room. Do you think me terrible for the lie?"

He laughed. "Not that lie, darling. I don't like the prince at all, and Adele finds him unsettling. Della is growing up so quickly. How will we ever keep watch on her?"

Beth tweaked his nose. "Are you already worrying about young men? You truly do have a father's heart, Charles. But you needn't worry about any prince. I think Della has her eyes set on a viscount."

"Holloway? Please, tell me, she's not pining for him as well!"

Beth sat up. "As well? Do you know about Henry, then?"

"I know she's infatuated with him, but I very much doubt Henry returns her feelings. For one thing, Della's not yet twelve..."

"Woman can marry at twelve in Scotland, Charles. Gretna Green isn't that far away."

"Twelve years old? That's ridiculous! But look here, Henry's not going to whisk her off to the border anytime soon, and besides, she'll set her sights on someone else before she's eighteen."

Beth laughed. "You'd let her marry at eighteen?"

"I might."

"And seventeen?"

"It depends on the man, I suppose."

She ran her hand along his bare arm. "And what about sixteen?"

"Far too young."

"I was only sixteen, when you saw me at Aubrey House," she reminded him. "If you'd not been married, would you have kissed me?"

He responded with a deep, passionate kiss. "Yes," he whispered. "Message received."

"And the message you meant to tell me?" she asked.

"Message?"

"The reminder I was to give you."

"Oh? Whatever it was, I seem to have forgotten."

He decided against telling her. How does a man explain the impossible? For some reason, Beth had met him as an eight-year-old and apparently forgotten it. Yet, in 1879, something in her unconscious mind recognised him as her childhood Captain Nemo, the man she'd met in the maze.

"Never mind, Captain. If you think of it later, you can tell me." Her eyes looked tired, and he had a mind to stretch his legs and work out the swelling in his ankle.

"Cocoa?"

"No one's in the kitchen, darling. They're all abed, except for whatever footman's on duty."

"I know how to boil water, you know. Peppermint?"

She laughed. "Yes, if you're determined. Cocoa with peppermint—oh, and a plate of those lovely almond biscuits. Your children are hungry again."

Charles went downstairs to the vast kitchens and found the tea kettle just where Mrs. Stephens always stored it. He wrote her a note, letting her know that it was he who invaded her kitchen overnight. He was passing through the south gallery, carrying a tray with two cups of cocoa and half a dozen biscuits, when he noticed moving shadows in the foyer area. Wishing he'd brought his pistol, the duke set down the cocoa and hastened down the staircase. He could hear whispers to his right, and so followed them to the great drawing area known as the Anjou State Room.

As with all the formal gathering areas in the hall, the Anjou had a four-foot-deep anteroom, where servants could stand at the ready or prepare trays for presentation; but the primary reason for anterooms was because of the service passages. Branham Hall was honeycombed with them, and in previous centuries, these secret corridors hummed with activity.

Approaching the anteroom, Charles found the disguised entrance sprung inward, and he could see lights flickering within. "Hello?" he called into the dark interior.

Electric wires ran through the entire main floor, and the duke planned to continue the service up into the rest of the house once he and his new family returned to London in July, meaning the passages were lit by gas, but the sconces were presently cold. He searched several tables until he located a candle and matches. Placing the lit candle into a brass stick, he used it to light his way through the unfamiliar realm.

He could still hear the whispered conversation, and it sounded like several people to his ears. Charles followed their voices for five minutes at least, and was just about to turn back and find help, when light flooded an area just ahead, caused by the opening of a chamber door. He could see the shadow of a man step into the passageway, and Charles doused the candle.

"Who's there?" the newcomer asked, striking a match to his own candle.

Charles sighed in great relief. "It's your cousin, Paul," he replied, lighting his candle once again.

"Charles, what on earth are you doing in here?"

"I might ask you the same thing."

"I heard voices," the earl told him. "Coming from that direction. Towards the old tunnels."

"I heard them, too," Sinclair said. "The old tunnels? Do you know these hallways?"

"I should. Beth used to take me through them when we'd play hide-and-seek. I usually found her, but once in a while, she'd avoid me entirely."

"You know..." Charles began, but the earl placed a hand on his mouth.

"Ssh," Stuart whispered. "They're talking again."

The two cousins listened, and within seconds, both heard the mystery intruders' voices. Paul pointed towards the far end, and together, he and Charles crept along the dark hallway.

Five minutes passed, and then ten.

The two men followed in silence, not wishing to give away their presence. Twice, they climbed staircases, and each time, they could hear arguments ahead; as though the intruders differed on direction. They'd reached the northeast portion of the secret highway, when a door opened ahead of them, and they saw three individuals leave the corridor and pass through the opening. Then, the door shut, leaving the passage dark and silent.

Paul rushed ahead, using his candle for light as he searched for the door. "These are usually mounted on springs, which allows them to sit flush against the wall," he whispered.

"Are they in all the rooms?"

"Oh, yes. Before Beth assumed the title, most dukes and duchesses insisted staff remain hidden from view, so they all used this system to reach the apartments. Why isn't this opening? I can feel the edges."

"Can the doors be locked?"

"Not that I'm aware," Paul replied. He pushed harder, and the latch finally released, emitting a soft clicking noise. The door sprang inward. "After you," he told Sinclair.

The duke peered into the chamber beyond, stepping into the unknown. He emerged into a vast library, but Charles recognised none of the decor. Branham Hall had five libraries, six if you included the private library in his study. One had soundproofing and was used only for circle or private meetings. Two were used by guests, placed near the galleries on the first and second floors. Then, there was the main library on the ground floor, which drew scholars from all across the country to study the rare collections. And there was one final library, built by Duke Henry, Beth's great-grandfather. Beth's grandfather, Duke George Linnhe, had shuttered that library the very moment he took the title, for he claimed his late father had participated in hellish rituals using Satanic books and grimoires he'd collected and stored within the library's crowded stacks.

The cousins stood still, listening to the hushed whispers ahead of them. Two men and a woman. They were discussing a book, or perhaps looking for one.

Charles thought he heard a familiar name that caused an angry shudder to run through his bones.

Raziel.

Without any warning, Sinclair left the corner where he and Aubrey had hidden themselves. "This is a fine way to treat your hosts," he boldly greeted the intruding trio.

The woman turned round, and Charles nearly gasped. "May I ask why you and your companions are raiding my library, Miss Calabrese?"

Angiolina's face was lit only by the candle in her hand. "Your Grace," she whispered. Her companions also turned towards the two cousins. Charles thought he recognised one, but it was the earl who spoke next.

"Patrick MacAllen. Now here's a surprise. What is the new head of Special Branch doing skulking around Branham Hall at three in the morning?"

MacAllen cleared his throat, the features in his lean face performing a series of acrobatic manouevres. "Ah, well, we're following a lead, actually. That mess at this afternoon's tilt is all down to the IB. Surely, you're aware of that."

Charles used his matches to light the gas on a nearby wall sconce, helping to illuminate the intruders more clearly. "What has the Irish Brotherhood to do with it? And why, for that matter, have you brought Miss Calabrese along? Perhaps, I should simply arrest all of you for trespassing."

"That would hardly stick," the second man insisted as he moved closer. It began to make a twisted sense to Charles, for he knew this one well. So well, that rather than reply verbally, the duke punched the man in the nose.

MacAllen and Calabrese (or rather the Watcher using her skin) jumped aside, both surprised by the duke's response, but instead of striking back, the man began to wail.

"You broke my nose, you bully!"

Sinclair grasped the screaming man by the jacket and threw him against the nearest stack of books.

"You're the bully, Lowry, and I'll break more than your nose unless you explain what you and these friends are doing in my home, and why you're talking about Raziel. And I'd better hear the truth, else all three of you will be wearing irons before the sun rises!"

Harold Lowry slumped against the wall, cupping his bleeding nose with both hands. The pretending 'Angiolina' knelt beside him, using her handkerchief to daub the bright blood.

MacAllen glared at the man that he considered his enemy. "If anyone wears irons, Haimsbury, it'll be you. Assault is against the law."

"Defense of one's own home is not, MacAllen," Aubrey intervened. "I don't believe any of you was on my cousin's guest list, which means you entered this house illegally." He calmly walked through the library to a red velvet cord, hanging near the largest of the room's two fireplaces. He pulled on the rope. "There's always a footman on duty in the bell parlour, which means you have no more than five minutes before half the staff come running to this room."

'Angiolina' smiled up at the two cousins. "That may be true, but the only way to access this library is through the servants' passage, meaning your men will have to come through them or else break down the library door."

"Is that so?" asked Charles. He handed his candle to Aubrey and then crossed the room, stopping once to light a gas sconce closer to the main door. Once there, Sinclair used the savate move Aubrey had taught him and kicked down the door with one strike of his foot, causing a cloud of ancient dust to billow into the air.

"There," he said, wiping dust from his hands. "That should do it. Who wants to explain why you're here? There's a reduced charge for the first person to offer me the truth."

CHAPTER FORTY-ONE

7 am - H-Division Station House, 76 Leman Street

The very last person Edmund Reid expected on that Sunday morning was Charles Sinclair, but as the detective inspector walked through the bright blue entry door to the station house lobby, the first sight to meet him was his old friend, apparently booking three individuals into lock-up. Alfred Williams nodded towards Reid as the puzzled inspector approached the booking desk.

"And what have we here?" asked Edmund. "Commissioner, did I miss an overnight call-out?"

Charles shook his friend's hand in fellowship. "No call-out, not here at least. I've brought these three in from Kent, actually. Sergeant Williams has all the details, but if you have a few minutes, I'd appreciate a meeting."

"Yes, of course," Reid muttered, noticing one of the booked individuals was Patrick MacAllen, the man rumoured to be the next head of Special Branch. And that man looked very angry indeed.

Once upstairs, the inspector sent a constable for coffee and welcomed the duke into his cramped office. "Forgive the clutter. It's been rather busy lately. Bodies almost nightly. Just move those files to one side, Charles, and take a seat."

Sinclair noticed familiar names on many of the files: Barnett, Gantry, Hillwell, Haxton; known pickpockets or housebreakers who often called Leman Street their temporary homes. But also Urquhart, Wisling, and Wychwright.

"Crime never stops," he said soberly, taking a seat on a new-looking, striped sofa. "Where's the old floral couch? Ed, you promised I could have it, if you ever replaced it."

"Never fear. I've saved it. I know how much sentimentality's attached to that battered old bit of history. It's downstairs, waiting for you. Now, tell me about our newest guests, because MacAllen's likely to have lawyers here before I can get a cup of coffee."

"I doubt that," Sinclair answered. "I've already spoken to Salisbury, and our new Scottish earl is hardly the prime minister's favourite person at the moment. MacAllen may be an old pal to Matthews, but even that friendship will likely crack, if I have any say in it."

"And your reason?"

"Patrick and his two cellmates broke into Branham Hall overnight and were searching Duke Henry's library."

Reid's face grew pale, and he rose to shut his office door. "The occult library?" he asked in a whisper.

"So Paul informs me, yes. I'd no idea the room had such a reputation."

"That library contains some powerful spells, Charles. Beth's grandfather planned to tear it down, but suddenly had a change of heart after Patricia nearly died from typhus."

"It'll be gone soon, if I have any say in it. I've no wish to keep evil books in our home. If a small box can bring a demon, I dare not imagine what such books conceal!"

Edmund's brows furrowed together. "What box?"

"I'll tell you at the next meeting. I want to interview Lowry right away. When given the chance to sing, he began an entire repertoire regarding the break-in and much more. And his songs include a litany of information about Redwing, Ed. I want all three kept here until we can arrange a more permanent lodging at one of our ICI buildings. That's why I've been talking to Salisbury. He and the privy council have to approve the arrangement."

"Because of MacAllen's peerage?" asked Reid.

"That's part of it, but apparently, Miss Calabrese's late mother had deep connexions to the royal family. Long story, but trust me, when I say this will not go down well. Especially, since Calabrese's father runs Chicago."

Reid slumped into his chair. "Thank you for bringing this to my door."

"It's only temporary, Ed. A day at most. Perhaps, a few hours. I had no wish to keep them at Branham, and the village jail's security is half-hearted at best. My wife could break out of those cells."

"And is this Lowry the same man you told me about?"

Charles's facial muscles tightened. "Yes. He's the man who took Amelia to Ireland and then abandoned her when she became ill. Truthfully, Edmund, it was all I could not to strangle the man!"

"Yes, I noticed the broken nose."

"I wanted to break his entire face," Sinclair whispered tightly. "Oh, and be sure to put a matron on Calabrese. There's something about the woman that screams deceit. She struck up a conversation with me on my crossing over to France, and I'm ashamed to say I fell for her claims. If I knew where Susanna Morgan was, I'd bring her in and have her talk to the woman."

"Charles, her father is staying in London. Tom Galton says he's checked into the Carlton."

"The hotel Paul owns?"

"The very same."

Charles sat back, growing quiet. Reid had seen that same look on his friend's face many times; as though the duke were performing a thousand calculations. A constable knocked, breaking the peer's concentration, and Reid called for the youthful police officer to come in.

"Hot and fresh, sirs. And I've brought a telegram for you, Commissioner."

"Thank you, Constable," replied the duke as he took a cup and the slip of paper.

"Are our new prisoners settling in?" asked Reid.

"The sergeant's booked them into the lower cells, sir. That tall skinny one insists on seeing you. And the woman does, too. The shorter fella's talkin' like a preacher on Sundays. He's been put into an interview room, sir. Hope that's all right."

"Perfect. Thank you again," the duke said.

"That's all, son," Reid told the boy.

The door closed, and Sinclair read through his telegram. "It's from Paul. He's keeping watch on Branham. He and Baxter have combed through the old duke's library and all the passages our housebreakers used. They've found no book by Raziel, but plan to keep looking."

"Raziel? Isn't that the name of a Watcher?"

"Yes. Long story. I'll stay in London tonight. I plan to visit Aubrey House as well as a certain house in Hanover Square. I'm not sure if you heard, but there was an assassination attempt at Branham yesterday afternoon. We've kept it quiet. I doubt it will make the papers. Paul and I explained it away as part of a rehearsed performance."

"What happened?" asked Reid, sitting forward in his chair.

"We think it was Captain Wychwright. This goes no further, Ed, and I'm telling you only because you sit on the circle. Which reminds me, I should call a meeting. Would you send a wire to Galton and ask him to round up as many members as possible. We'll meet at my home. Say, eight o'clock?"

"Yes, I can do that. Shall I help with Lowry's interview? You'll want a witness, just in case, his face is rearranged again."

Harold Winston Lowry III was a ne'r-do-well sort who enjoyed gambling, theatre, turf clubs, and women. Despite having spent nearly half his thirty-one years in idle pursuits and illegal activities, he'd never been arrested. Not until today. As Charles entered the small room with Reid, Lowry did his best to appear nonchalant. The swollen nose did little to assist that effort.

Charles took the lead. "I have your booking information here, Mr. Lowry. It states your next of kin is Prince Albert Victor. Now, why on earth would you include a blatant lie on a police form?"

Lowry tried to laugh, but his wounded nasal passages betrayed him by inserting a high-pitched whistle. "Eddy's a mate and a distant cousin. Why shouldn't I put his name down? And once he learns what you've done, he'll..."

"What I've done?" Sinclair interrupted, nearly losing his temper again. He waited a beat to continue, realising what Lowry was trying to achieve. Deciding the best approach was clinical and clear, the duke continued. "I'll send for the prince myself," he told the prisoner. "My wife and he are close, and I've come to know him rather well myself in recent months. I'm sure he could be here in half an hour. Shall I send a coach for him?"

"Uh, no. That isn't necessary, but I should like to see a doctor. You did break my nose, after all."

Charles rose and called into the corridor. "Fetch Dr. Sunders, will you, Greeves?"

Shutting the door again, he returned to the chair. "Happy? Now, Mr. Lowry, please, explain to Inspector Reid and myself just why you, Patrick MacAllen, and Angiolina Calabrese were snooping through the papers in my library?"

"Is it yours?" he asked, trying to assume control of the conversation. "I thought it belonged to the Branham line."

Charles smiled. "Perhaps, you've not read recent headlines, Mr. Lowry. I know you've been touring the lesser known cities of the continent since departing Ireland two years ago, but since marrying the duchess, I've been given control over the entire Branham estate, per my wife's wishes. Now, you have one minute to start talking before I have a constable take you to a cell. Your window for improving your future is closing."

Harold blinked. "All right, then. First of all, that woman isn't Angiolina Calabrese. At least, that's not the name she used when I met the first time. In Venice a year ago, and she was with MacAllen. I've no idea who this man Calabrese is, but I heard them both talk about him like he's a king."

"Hardly that, but go on. Where in Venice?" asked Sinclair.

"A castle. I'd gone there with Albert."

"Wendaway?" asked Reid.

"That's right."

"Do you know his current whereabouts?" asked Charles.

"If I tell you, they'll kill me for sure! It's already likely they'll put me through hell, but if I grass on Albert, I'm as good as dead. You've seen the bodies stacking up, Charles. Please, I know we've got history, but..."

"Do not presume to call me Charles!" Sinclair shouted. "Just because you ate at my table once, does not make us friends. Had I even an inkling that you were seeing my wife behind my back, you'd have suffered much more than a broken nose. I brought your dead children back to England. Did you know that? And Amelia's body as well. What kind of man leaves a woman to die from typhus, all alone in a flea-infested flat?"

"There's more to it," Lowry muttered. "If I told you everything I know..." He stopped, staring at the ceiling as though wishing he had wings. "Look here, Commissioner, I understand why you hate me, but if information can buy anything at all, then you need to keep me alive. There's so much more to what happened back then than you can ever imagine. Amelia and I—well, I was ordered to take her to Ireland."

"What do you mean?" asked Sinclair. "Ordered? By whom, and why?"

He shook his head. "Put me somewhere safe, and I'll tell you everything I know. Don't you understand? It's the reason Wendaway's in hiding! Not to avoid you lot, but because of *them!*"

"And who are they?" asked Sinclair.

Lowry's eyes looked this way and that, as though searching for shadows. "Not here. I can't tell you here, but trust me when I say they are more powerful than any—than any human."

Suddenly, Charles was all ears. "Give me one name, and I'll see about granting you asylum."

The man's hands shook as he placed them on the table. He took a deep breath, leaning forward to whisper, "Saraqael."

It was enough for the moment. "Very well. Remain here, and I'll see about finding you a secure location. Edmund, I'll need your telegraph room. If you'd stay with our prisoner?"

"Yes, of course. Ask Constable Davis to join me."

Charles left the interview room, and climbed the next flight up to the detectives' offices, turning right at the last desk to reach the telegraph room. The area had once been used as the police commander's office, and it had three large windows that overlooked Leman Street. Charles used the telegraph to rapidly send messages to Aubrey and to Galton, but a final message went to Goron in Paris. Once done, he rose to leave, but the open windows brought more than fresh breezes. At that moment, they also brought commotion and chaos.

He rushed over and leaned out, looking towards Commercial. Several flies buzzed past his left ear, but he saw nothing to cause the noise. Then, Charles looked towards the Thames. From his vantage point, he could just make out the tall masts of ships along St. Katherine's dock, and twixt here and there, he could see the cause of the commotion. A warehouse had caught fire, already sending spirals of smoke and flame high over East London. Running down the steps, he dashed past the interview rooms and sped down to the main floor.

"Call the fire brigade!" he ordered Williams before slamming through the main doors. People had begun to gather on the sidewalks, and it looked to Charles as though night were coming, for already the black smoke of the chemical warehouse had begun to obscure the sun. Bells clanged all round, and in another moment, the fire brigade waggons raced past, their horses' hooves ringing on the limestone cobbles. Running back into the station, Charles took command, ordering men to form up ranks to offer help to the brigade.

"I want ten men to remain here, guarding the cells. Everyone else with me!"

By now, Reid had returned Lowry to a cell in the basement, and he joined his friend at the booking desk. "Charles, the timing of this fire couldn't be worse."

"Yes, I'd noticed that," Sinclair whispered. "Williams, you stay here. Let no one into the cells. No one, not even the crown prince. Come on, Ed. Let's find our batons and help keep order."

"Charles, you should stay here. Let me lead the division."

"And let you have all the fun?" he joked. "No, Ed. We'll do this together. Come on now!"

The two brave men ran out of the station house door, leading over thirty men in uniform along with half a dozen detectives in civilian attire. Sunders followed, too, bringing his medical kit, and over the next three hours, the men of H-Division worked alongside three from the ICI, Sinclair, Stanley, and France, to keep order and fight a blaze that would soon engulf two warehouses, a church, and seven homes along Leman and Cable Streets.

By the time the fire was extinguished, Sinclair and company were exhausted and hungry. Charles ordered meals for everyone from the Brown Bear along with pints of ale for all who served. He'd no intention of asking these men to continue their shifts, and once they'd eaten, all were told to go home.

As he entered the station house lobby, exhausted, sweaty, and covered in soot, Charles was met by an apologetic Williams.

"I dunno how he managed it, sir, but that fella MacAllen's lawyer came by an hour ago with orders for his release, signed by Home Secretary Matthews. The release order promised to return the earl to your care tomorrow for questioning. Someone here wired the home office that Leman Street had a fire, and that everyone in the cells was in danger of injury. I've tried to find out who sent it, sir, but no one's willing to confess. The woman went with him, but Lowry's still here. Leastways, I've not seen any paperwork for his release."

"Good," Charles said. "Have Sunders take a look at every man who worked the fire before he goes home. I'll be downstairs."

Sinclair quickstepped down to the lower cell area, finding the electric lights switched off, and no one manning the guard's desk. "Sergeant?" he called into the darkness.

A fly landed on his nose, and Charles swatted at it. He'd seen dozens of flies near the fire, he realised, and that same familiar tingle ran along his neck and hands, as though someone breathed upon him. He turned round, expecting a phantom, but found no one there.

"Lowry?" he called into the long chamber of cells.

All were empty, save for one.

The last cell in the eastern block held a shadow sitting at the back corner.

"Lowry? Let's get you out of here. I'll take you myself."

As he reached the cell, Charles noticed a slick wetness to the floor. The tingle along his hands began to scream at his brain cells, sending out a warning of yet another of the enemy's twisted tricks.

The door to the cell was unlocked, yet Lowry remained inside.

"Harold?" he asked as he opened the door.

The thing on the chair didn't answer, yet it seemed alive.

Moving closer, Charles could just make it out: the reason for the movement and for the sickening slickness on the stone floor.

Lowry was dead, his throat torn open. Blood had rushed from the wound until the man's heart stopped beating, and now provided a feast for flies.

The dead man was covered in them.

A voice whispered into the duke's left ear:

We're just getting started, boy. Playtime is over now. Let the real games begin.

CHAPTER FORTY-TWO
Saturday, 8th June – Branham Hall

Newspapers ran stories about the second great Whitechapel fire for weeks, and Charles Sinclair's photo once again graced their front pages, often beside his comments regarding police matters, but also because of what reporters had begun to call the 'Branham Baby Watch'. All across London, betting parlours took odds on whether or not the duchess would have the twins early, late, and if they'd be girls, boys, or a mix. Some bookies took bets regarding the very distant possibility of triplets, for a rumour circulated that one physician had observed certain behaviours and physical signs in the duchess that indicated she might have as many as four babies!

The feud twixt Charles and Patrick MacAllen slowly cooled, and the new Lord Granddach even sent an olive branch in the form of a gift: a stuffed bear wearing a police hat, meant for the twins' nursery. Charles found the gift less than amusing and ordered it given to an orphanage. The enquiry into Lowry's death concluded that the station had no liability, for the fire had allowed the prisoner the opportunity to use a knife which he'd hidden upon his person, slicing his own throat. Charles had no idea what secret information his late wife's lover might have offered.

A month passed in relative peace, and Charles remained at Branham on a rotating schedule: two days in London, the rest of the week in Kent. He and Paul visited with Sir Simon Pembroke several times, discussing the Collinwood murder and the coded book the baronet had given to Kepelheim and Aubrey. Seth Holloway assembled the statue found in Queen's Lake, and its resemblance to the one Blackstone had uncovered in the tunnel system was uncanny.

In late May, Paul took Cordelia into London to visit with her mother, and the couple even joined the dowager baroness and her new gentleman friend, Lord Brackamore, at the Lyceum one evening to watch *Lucia di Lammermoor*. The earl left the Aubrey box momentarily during the 'mad scene' of Act III, in response to a note supposedly sent by Salisbury, but was told the prime minister wasn't in attendance that night. Puzzled, he returned to the lobby, but as he passed the main doors, Delia suddenly came tumbling down the steps, screaming the entire way.

His wife lay unconscious, and a rush of men and women crowded round as Paul checked her neck, back, and limbs for injury. The audience that night included several prominent physicians, including Michael and Andrea Emerson, who left with the Aubreys in a coach.

Cordelia spent three days in St. Mary's hospital. Paul allowed no one other else to visit, for when she regained consciousness, Cordelia told him her brother had pushed her down the stairs.

The earl realised Wychwright had lured him away with evil intent, and Paul considered taking vengeance at once, but he feared leaving his wife alone. And so he remained with her, day and night, until Emerson allowed her to return to Branham. To his very great relief, Michael and Andrea packed their bags and joined the Aubreys in the Scottish Knight.

"I can help with the twins as well," Michael told the earl. "Besides, Andrea wants to see the duchess."

June arrived with mild temperatures and almost daily rain, which nourished the flower beds but made it difficult for Beth to take even short walks.

As her delivery date approached, she grew anxious, and Henry MacAlpin moved into the hall as an adjunct physician to Emerson and Gehlen, but also as companion to Elizabeth.

That Saturday morning saw the first sunshine in days, and the bright morning enlivened everyone living at the hall. As he finished an outdoor breakfast, Stephen Blinkmire turned to Adele. "Shall we take a walk through the rose gardens? Or perhaps, we could watercolour! I'd love to practise mixing those new paints the duke brought us last week. What do you think, Lady Della?"

The newest member of the Sinclair household had been daydreaming, thinking about what her father had said about taking her wherever she liked as a belated birthday celebration. With the babies due to be born in two days' time, Charles feared the new arrivals would dominate everyone's thoughts for the near future, and therefore set a date with his daughter for early August, when father and daughter would celebrate their June birthdays together.

"I'm sorry, Mr. Blinkmire," she said, roused from her reverie. "I was far away. What was it you said?"

The gentle giant laughed, his heart filled with joy at belonging to so happy a household. "I was merely commenting on how cheerful the morning is. I do love sitting outdoors as the sun warms the air, don't you?"

Adele nibbled on a strawberry scone. "Yes, I suppose so. Though the sun seldom shone back in Scotland. Most of the time, it rained. Or snowed. Of course, it was very green. A miraculous sort of green. Greener than even the greens of England."

"What's all this about green?" asked Tory Stuart as she joined the others on the flower strewn patio. "Why ever are we eating out here?"

Adele laughed. "You're already cross, Auntie Tory, and it's not yet ten. I suppose that portends a very irregular day. Has Auntie Dolly gotten up yet?"

"Like most sane people, Dolly has slept in this morning. As has your Cousin Beth, it seems. And where is Charles?"

"Do you mean my father?" Della sang back happily, emphasising the parental noun, her smile broad as a church and twice as dependable.

"Ah, yes, do forgive me. I'm half asleep yet. Yes, Della, I mean your father. You know, it occurs to me that day after tomorrow is his birthday. Have we planned anything?"

"Other than the birth of two children?" asked Count Riga from across the table. "I should think that would be gift enough."

Victoria managed a wan smile, for she had a severe migraine that morning and had very nearly remained abed. "Yes, I suppose you're right. Hand me the scones, will you, Della?"

Adele stood and helped to fill her aunt's plate with fruit, two scones, one with strawberry, another with apple, a slim wedge of gouda, and a slice of ham. She then poured Victoria a cup of strong black tea with milk and three sugars before sitting once again.

"Will that do?" the almost twelve-year-old asked.

"For the moment," Tory replied with a wink. "Now, who is here this morning? I seem to remember our viscounts mentioning a trip to the village."

"If you mean Henry," Della offered, lingering on the physician's name with an interesting inflection, "he and Mr. Holloway have gone to visit Sir Simon Pembroke. He's a very nice man."

"Which?" asked Riga as he used his fork to cut a slice of ham. "Salperton, Paynton, or Sir Simon?"

"Oh, all three, of course," replied Adele diplomatically, "but I meant Sir Simon. I met him at the fête, you see. He won several prizes for me at the tombola tent. He laughs a lot. Who was that strange woman, Auntie Tory?"

"Was there a strange woman?" asked the spinster. "Butter, please, if you don't mind, Mr. Blinkmire. Does that look like a rain cloud?"

"The dark-haired one. You know, Mother disliked her."

"Mother? Oh, do forgive me, darling. You mean Beth."

"Yes, she is my mother now, you know."

"And she's soon to become mother to your baby brother and sister," the giant added happily. "Oh, I do love babies! I've seldom been allowed round them, and I've never held one. I suppose it's my hands, you see. They're so much larger than most men's hands that it frightens people."

Riga handed the butter to Stuart, then offered his dear friend a smile. "Stephen, your hands may be large, but they are delicately strung. As with a fine instrument, they make music to soften any heart! I'm sure the duchess will be pleased for you to hold them. Of course, if our hostess is correct, then the babies will arrive in two days."

"That's right," Adele declared to all. "Both Father and Mother say the babies will be born on the tenth, and it shall be the tenth. It's all been agreed."

"Then, our dear newborns will be somewhat early, which may be why Dr. Gehlen has installed so much medical equipment in the nursery, including something he's calling the Holtzapple device."

"Whatever is that?" asked Stephen.

"It's an enclosed bed of some kind with an attached container filled with oxygen. I asked our learned Dr. Gehlen how he intended to use it, and he said the unit would offer an enriched atmosphere for filling a newborn's lungs."

"Nonsense," Tory huffed. "Children breathe on their own, don't they?"

"Apparently, our obstetrician has experience with babies born before their time. Anthony referred to a German set of twins born at only thirty-four weeks, who survived and recovered quite well with such a unit. He says he's aided babies born as early as thirty-one weeks with it."

"How long should babies grow before being born, Uncle Riga?" asked Adele.

"I understand that forty weeks is considered optimum, but twins are often early. I suppose because they run out of growing room."

Adele laughed at this. "Poor Mother is already huge. She lost sight of her feet long ago!"

"I shouldn't use that word with your mother," Tory warned the girl. "No woman wants to be told they are 'huge'. Talking of children, how is Cordelia feeling? Is she any better?"

"She is still suffering, I fear," Stephen answered. "I spoke with her yesterday. Riga and I took turns reading to her. I should love to strangle that brother of hers!"

Riga touched his friend's hand, tapping it as if to calm the giant. "Now, Stephen, we mustn't judge. God says that vengeance is his alone. William Wychwright will pay for his sins. If not on this earth, then afterward. If the earl has managed to keep his temper, then so must we."

"But to intentionally push his own sister down the stairs! Surely, that demands justice here on earth!"

"And our young duke has promised that earthly justice is served. He and the earl look to that very thing today, I understand. Is that not so, Lady Victoria?"

"So I understand, and I pray Charles is able to find some legal yardarm to hang that villain from! Really, I believe in God's right to vengeance, but to do such a horrid thing to one's own sister! Well, I..."

"Good morning, everyone," a woman's voice called from the little hill near the house. Tory turned, wishing she'd said nothing at all about Charles.

"Beth, you shouldn't be down here. Gehlen put you on confinement in your apartment, didn't he?"

"Yes, but the children aren't coming until Monday. I thought I'd spend as much of today enjoying the outdoors as I can. Oh, smell those lilacs! Isn't this a perfect day? Did I hear you talking about William Wychwright?"

"We mentioned him in passing. Really, Beth, you promised Charles you'd remain in bed."

"And I will, after I've had a scone. Mrs. Stephens added fresh strawberries to these, I see. How nice."

"You're certainly chipper," Tory noted, swatting a fly. "I do hate summers in England!"

"You hate summer everywhere, Auntie Tory," Della noted with a giggle.

"That's simply untrue," the spinster argued. "I love summers in Scotland. They're decidedly pleasant, except for the midges, of course."

"And the rain," Elizabeth noted, her face paling slightly. She put down the teacup.

"Are you feeling ill?" asked her aunt.

The duchess shook her head as she wiped her mouth. "No, not really. Just a bit odd." She turned to the count. "And how are summers in Romania, Count Riga?"

Viktor Riga sighed. "Ah, lovely, quite lovely; however, summer here is pleasant. As you know, Duchess, both Stephen and I spent twenty years with Prince Anatole at his castle, where spring never faded. Each day was perfect. Some days, I miss that life."

"Do you?" Beth asked, her voice grown softer.

The count took her hand. "Dear lady, life with you surpasses all days at Istseleniye. All days. Even when it rains, we have your countenance to cheer us, and when the sun is out, we've the lilacs. And we have Della now, too! Our Blinkmire's thinking of trying his hand at painting, and Lady Della offered to teach us how to mix watercolours."

"It's very easy," the girl answered as she poured her mother a cup of tea. "Two sugars?" she asked the duchess.

"Yes, two, dear," Beth replied. "No milk. Not this morning. It sometimes unsettles my stomach."

Adele prepared the tea and then placed it in front of her mother. "There now. And I asked Mrs. Stephens to blend it just the way you like, with bergamot and lemon rind added. Oh, and a tiny bit of cinnamon."

Beth took a sip of the hot beverage, smiling as she set down the cup. "Perfect. My father would have approved. You say Charles has gone? I failed to hear him leave, I guess. Where's he gone?"

"Just to the village," Lady Victoria lied. "He promised to return after speaking to..." she paused, scrambling for the second half of the story. "After speaking to Sir Simon. That's it. Oh, this migraine is beginning to fiddle with my memory!"

"Is it?" Elizabeth asked, her dark eyes narrow, for she knew her aunt very well and detected a familiar sound to her voice. One Victoria used when deflecting truth. "Now, Adele, where has your father really gone?"

Della stared at Victoria, wishing suddenly that she had remained in bed or perhaps decided to read in the library. "I, uh..."

A newcomer broke the silence by spoiling Tory's tale.

"Morning all! Why are we eating out here?" asked Dolly Patterson-Smythe from the little rise that led to the side entrance of the hall. "Oh, scones!"

Elizabeth took another sip of her tea. "I'm waiting," she told the adolescent.

"You see, Father's gone to..."

"Father? Oh, you mean Charles, don't you, dear?" asked Dolly. "He's in London, isn't he? He and Paul left before the sun even came up. A positively mad time of the day. I heard them talking in the corridor, for I couldn't sleep. Their voices really do carry, even when whispering. Something about the timbre of deep voices, I suppose. Resonance and all that. I can't blame them, of course. Dickie is positively livid about it! Honestly, he's talking about closing all Wychwright's bank accounts, but I think Duke James may have already done it. I've known James Stuart all my life, and never have I seen that man so angry. And with good cause, don't you all think?" she asked, pausing at last.

Everyone stared at Elizabeth, waiting for her reaction. It was like an entire herd of elephants, holding their breath, waiting for their leader to sound the call to charge or retreat. One could have heard a feather fall, and even the insects stopped buzzing.

But the duchess surprised everyone. She smiled.

"Good," Beth declared, the single word accompanied by a group exhale. "William Wychwright deserves my husband's wroth, and woe to the man who angers my grandfather! But if he *ever* touches his sister again, he will wish he'd remained in North Africa with the army! War is far less dangerous than being Lord Aubrey's enemy. I'm surprised Paul didn't throw him down the stairs that very night!" She paused, the smile returning to her face as she sipped the tea. "So tell me, how is our Delia this morning?"

Dolly nudged Tory in the ribs, for the maiden aunt had frozen in place, still a bit shocked by her niece's reaction. "Delia? Oh, yes, I stopped in to check on her before coming down. Poor thing's still woozy from her morning medicine."

"And the baby?" asked Elizabeth.

"Gehlen and Emerson both insist everything is fine. And those same physicians will likely be quite angry that you've ignored specific orders to remain in your apartment."

"Was it an order?" asked Beth playfully. "Really, Tory, I feel quite strong this morning. I think the children are building up their strength. I still feel them move now and then, but the motion is different. More downward, rather than sideways. It's hard to explain. Honestly, with the exception of those first two months, I've felt rather well during all this. I think I'll have a child every year until we have eight."

Victoria's eyes widened. "Eight? That's a very decisive number. Didn't you originally tell me you wanted seven?"

Beth laughed and took Della's hand. "I already have a daughter, Tory. A very beautiful one at that. The twins will make three, which means just five more years until our family is complete."

"That is a very ambitious plan," the count noted with a wink. "Have you discussed it with our duke?"

"Not yet," Beth answered, "but I'm sure he'll agree. Now, did that duke say when he planned to return? And where are our handsome viscounts this morning? And the well-educated Dr. Gehlen? Is he still with Cordelia?"

"No, Gehlen's gone into Branham to buy supplies," Riga answered. "And our two viscounts are spending the morning at Sir Simon Pembroke's home. Something about that old statue our Mr. Blinkmire found in the lake last month."

"Oh, I don't like that statue at all," Beth noted.

"I think it looks like Father," Della said, buttering a slice of toast.

"It's a dreadful thing, though the carving does show great talent. Why is Sir Simon interested?" asked Tory.

Riga replied, "Apparently, Sir Simon found one very similar to it beneath his rose garden two weeks ago. He'd mentioned it to Duke Charles, and our duke asked Salperton and Paynton to go have a look. The statues could prove to be from the same era."

Beth slowly nibbled on the strawberry scone as she answered. "The same era. I wonder what era that might be?"

"Lord Paynton thought it pre-Christian," Dolly told the group. "The style is Greek. The resemblance to Charles is striking, though. It's just like the one Seth sketched in those awful tunnels last year!"

Beth set the butter knife to one side and pushed back from the table. "Perhaps, I should go inside."

Riga stood as did Blinkmire. "Forgive us, Duchess. We are thoughtless men. Of course, that statue distressed you last month, and here we are bringing it up again. Do forgive us."

She took Riga's hand. "No, dear Count, that isn't it. I'm just—I don't know. Suddenly, I feel somewhat strange. A bit too warm. Perhaps, it's the sunshine. I wonder if you might lend me your arm? Tory, if you'd ask Kay to send a tray of tea and biscuits to our apartment, I think I'll..."

She never completed the sentence.

The duchess let out a cry and collapsed into Riga's arms.

CHAPTER FORTY-THREE

Loudain House – Whitehall, London

At that very same moment, two hours away, William Wychwright wished he'd never even heard of Paul Stuart. ICI's executive headquarters occupied the main floor of Queen Anne House—a ten-minute drive by coach to the southwest—but the field agent offices, armoury, and rifle range were housed at the four storey house built by Charles Sinclair's great-great-grandfather, the 5th Earl of Loudain. The house came into the Haimsbury portfolio, when James Robert Sinclair married Anna Marie, the only child of Harold Wipscombe, the fifth earl. A year later, James Robert Wipscombe Sinclair opened his newborn eyes to the world of peerage privilege, becoming heir to the earldom and the powerful Haimsbury marquessate.

For months, a team of trusted carpenters and electricians had worked round the clock to ready the magnificent home for its new direction. Drawing rooms that once hosted crowned heads and ministers now hosted offices for Sir Thomas Galton, Lord Malcolm Risling, and Sir Percy Smythe-Daniels; with smaller areas converted for Matthew Laurence, Arthur France, and Captain Thomas Crenshaw, a reliable and gifted Texas Ranger, whom the two cousins had met at the now defunct Royal Estate Agency, once owned by the late Lewis Merriweather.

Aside from offices, the layout included a surgery for tending to the injured and assessing a recruit's fitness level; a 'disguise' chamber, filled with a wide variety of clothing, from leather aprons worn by butchers to uniforms of sailors, army officers, tinkers, longshoremen, and nearly every occupation and social level known to man. The former wine cellars served as makeshift holding cells for anyone the ICI agents needed to 'question'; whilst the butler's spacious pantry was transformed into a secure repository of every imaginable type of weapon: rifles, shotguns, pistols, revolvers, crossbows, explosives, knives, and even swords; all kept in locked compartments.

It was that very pantry that now hosted the devious and very angry baron, William David Wychwright.

Sitting before Wychwright were five men: Inspector Elbert Stanley, Duke James Stuart, Duke Charles Sinclair, and Paul Stuart, Earl of Aubrey. This last gentleman looked as though he could spit rocks, and the trajectory of said stoney orbs would certainly be directed at the man sitting in a wooden chair, the aforementioned Baron Wychwright.

The outraged baron's hands were tied behind his back whilst the other four men barraged him with questions. Thus far, no one had laid a glove on the arrogant baron, but had he done this alone, it's likely Paul Stuart would have long ago wiped the floor with the man's smug little face.

"My wife!" the earl shouted as Matthew Laurence entered the interrogation room. "Weren't you satisfied with the money we gave you? Good heavens, man, we signed the Marylebone property over to you as well as Cordelia's inheritance! Yet, you managed to lose it all in one fell swoop. Gambling will be the death of you, Wychwright. Unless I get to you first!"

"Now, now, Cousin, we mustn't ruffle the baron's pretty feathers," Charles interrupted, leaning into Wychwright's face. "We want to present him to Newgate's prison system intact, for all the hungry inmates to see. Nothing pleases a pickpocket or housebreaker more than having a bit of fun with a banged-up baron."

William twisted in the chair, pulling against the rope. "I take it none of you knows the law?"

Charles grinned. "I've only spent fourteen years prosecuting it."

"Then, tell me, Commissioner, what are the charges against me? I see no legal authority. No warrant. No booking desk. No legitimate reason why I should be held against my will!"

Everyone produced warrant cards, and Charles showed two: one for the ICI, the other for the Intelligence Branch. "I see enough warrants to satisfy any court, Wychwright. If you wish to blame someone, blame yourself. You're the one pushed your sister down the theatre steps."

"It was an accident! I had nothing to do with my sister's fall down those stairs. In fact, I tried to help. Ask Cecil Brandon if you don't believe me. Or my mother, for that matter. She saw it. I insist you allow me to contact my solicitor!"

Drummond took a deep breath, the fingers of his right hand twisting the end of his thick moustache. "Which solicitor might that be, William? Sir David Kilmeade? Peter Donnelly? Both are Spoons men, aren't they? Silver Spoons. It's a very elite club, as I recall. Now, I'm an Oxford man, as is the earl, but Commissioner Sinclair attended Cambridge. Charles, are you a member of the Silver Spoons?"

The young duke sat in the chair opposite the prisoner. "The Spoons are mythical, Uncle. They don't really exist. Well, not any longer."

"You ignorant, jumped-up policeman!" Wychwright seethed. "I'll show you what a Spoons man can do! If you dare to touch me, if you so much as make a move towards sending me to Newgate or any other prison, I guarantee you a rude and most unwholesome education."

"Is that right?" Charles asked easily. "Strange. I wrote to the Master at Trinity, the college that once allowed the Spoons to exist. Henry Butler's a close friend, you see, and I asked after this alleged club. We discussed it at length over luncheon, actually. As of two days ago, all Spoons affiliations have been banned and deemed illegal. If a Cambridge alum even mentions the organisation with hopes of using it for advantage, that alum will lose all privileges at the college. Now, that would disclude you from High Table and use of the library and all associated lounges, clubs, and offices, wouldn't it?"

"You can't do that!" Wychwright shouted. "You wouldn't dare. No one can take down the Spoons. We're everywhere, you numbskull!"

"Is name-calling the best you can do?" Charles responded.

"I'll go there myself and make you out for the liar you are!" Wychwright threatened. "Trinity College leadership doesn't simply jump because you tell it to."

"Oh, but they already have," the earl interjected. "You see, we three have just endowed the Stuart-Sinclair Applied Sciences Chair at Trinity. The endowment is substantial enough to melt all the metal of your precious Silver Spoons, for the one condition to the endowment is the removal of all Spoons privileges. You are now *persona non grata*, old boy. Choke on that spoon."

"And to simply your life, William," Drummond added, "we've locked you out of all your bank accounts."

Wychwright's face paled to ash. "You can't do that. No one can do that!"

Drummond grinned. "I can, and I did. I'm good friends with all of London's bankers, and when I informed them of your mounting debts, my friends grew quite concerned. I'm afraid, all your promissory notes are about to be called. Charles, did you know the baron's London house is mortgaged?"

"Is it? Now, that is a shame," Haimsbury answered.

Paul Stuart untied the ropes on Wychwright's wrists.

"You're free to go now, but if I weren't a Christian, you'd already be floating in the Thames without head nor hands. The only reason you're alive is because I am a Christian, but don't depend on that saving you should you *ever* touch my wife again. Do you understand me?"

The baron stood, rubbing his wrists. "Yes, I understand all of you perfectly. You three are a pack of inner circle vermin, and I guarantee you will pay for this insult." He grabbed his hat and coat from the table near the door. "Watch your shadows, gentlemen. Revenge is a far tastier dish when served up cold."

He stormed out of the pantry and dashed up the servants' staircase to the sidewalk shared with the Oxbridge Club. The baron hailed a hansom and sat into its open-air seat. The driver peered down through the ceiling flap. "Where to, guv?"

"Anywhere! I don't care, just drive," he said. The flap closed, and the driver's whip flicked upon the horse's back. As they sped towards the Strand, Wychwright started to plot, his mind fixed on how to forever remove the inner circle from his life.

As if by magic, the trickster Saraqael, known in government as Prince Aleksandr Koshmar, appeared in the cab. "Why the long face?" asked the impish fallen angel. "That's actually the punch line to a joke, but I imagine you've other things on your mind. Might I help?"

"Go away," the baron ordered the supernatural guest. "I'm sick of you and all your kind! You're filled with empty promises and empty ideas!"

"Oh, I don't think my ideas are empty at all, and that rather hurts my feelings. If I were like most of my brothers, you'd be roasting on a spit for such insolence, but I'll let it pass. I'm feeling magnanimous today. It's a very special day, you see. A day that will go down in history. Or is that infamy? Catchy, no? I shall have to remember that one."

"What do you want?"

"Want?" echoed Sara. "I'm crushed that you'd ask. Besides, I want nothing. Now, ask me what I'm offering."

Wychwright stared at the elohim. "What?"

"Say *please*."

"What? Get out!"

"You're just as rude as that other one. The special boy."

"What boy?" asked Wychwright. "Why are you always jabbering on about a boy? Do you have unnatural desires for some fairhaired youth? Huh?" he dare suggest.

"Unnatural?" laughed Saraqael. "If we're going to throw *those* stones, Baron, then let us begin at home. And home is what it's all about, isn't it? You're about to lose yours, but I can help. I'd hate to see such a fine house lost to the auctioneer's hammer. I wonder, how did you manage to mortgage it in the first place? The house is entailed to the barony, isn't it? And yet three different banks allowed you to borrow against it. Spoons men, no doubt, but still fools to lend money on a lie. I wonder what they'll get for the old place? A thousand? Two?"

"A thousand! I'll have you know, Wychwright House was one of the first homes on Fitzmaurice Place, and it dates back to Tudor times."

"I don't think so," Saraqael said, playing with his hair. "Not unless George III was a Tudor. House of Hanover, wasn't he? I do get my kings and queens mixed up. Except for one king, that is. Everyone knows him, but I won't name names. Keeping peers and princes straight is such a chore. This realm, that realm; past, present, future—they're all the same."

"You're demented. Get out!"

"Really? After I've offered to pay off your house? What will your future heirs think? Assuming there is an heir, that is. And I can help with the Stuarts. I have a very good friend, who also bears a grudge against that pesky clan."

William sighed, feeling utterly trapped. Their coach passed a group of businessmen in morning suits, mounting the steps to the new Courts of Justice, and he longed to leap out and plead for their help.

"What friend is that?" he asked after several minutes.

"I shan't tell you," the irritating creature answered. Saraqael stared at the long nails of his left hand, his head tilted to the side. "Perhaps, I should cut these. I notice you humans keep your nails short. I ask you, why? How can you rake a man's flesh with stubby little nails?"

"Who?" Wychwright shouted.

"Ah," Sara whispered, gazing at the baron with a smile. "I have finally gained your attention. His name is Patrick MacAllen, and he has similar cravings to yours. In fact, he can often be found at a particular address on Cleveland Street. I'm sure you know it."

This caused the baron's left eye to twitch. "What of it?"

"Oh, I'm not condemning your inclinations, William. I find all living things beautiful and alluring, don't you? Why limit yourself, I say. MacAllen's inheritance is endangered simply because of his—*inclinations*. His late grandfather was such a prude about those things. It seems the late earl's will states that poor Patrick must marry and produce a male heir within the next five years or else forfeit the entire inheritance and titles to another."

"Balderdash! I doubt that's even legal!" Wychwright exclaimed.

"Oh, but it is legal. Patrick's challenging it, of course, but I'm afraid he's going to lose. And he will never have an heir. Also, the will stipulates that he cannot touch any of the entailed funds until that heir is born. He may live in the house, but he must pay one pound a year for that privilege. His hands are practically tied—a condition you can surely appreciate. And in five years, everything will go to the secondary heir."

"Just who is that?" asked William.

"Charles Sinclair."

"Sinclair? How? Why?" shouted the outraged baron.

"Because the late earl was Sinclair's great-uncle. The lucky little boy is the nearest next-of-kin."

"Boy? Why do you always call him that?"

"Oh, I have my reasons," Saraqael grinned. "But shouldn't we find a way to help poor Patrick? After all, he's a Spoons man, too."

Wychwright's brain began to sort through a series of possibilities. Tempting whispers arose amongst those thoughts, like evil wind upon a ship's mainsail. Saraqael's twisted desires conjoined with the human's, but William believed it all his own idea. "An aerial assault," he declared as they passed St. Paul's.

"Aerial?" asked Saraqael, knowing full well what the baron intended. "Hasn't that been tried?"

"It should have worked, but Sinclair managed to cut the tether and the winds sent us off towards the east. But I don't need a balloon to take aim, do I?"

"Not at all," the tempter hissed. "A rooftop would suffice. Or even a balcony rail. One with sufficient height and cover. It would take some planning."

"And advance warning of the target's itinerary."

"I imagine a man's secretary would have all that. An innocuous enquiry from an innocent visitor could prove very useful," Saraqael whispered, his arm wrapped round the prey's shoulders.

"Yes, that might work. I've a friend who knows Pennyweather's mother. She might be persuaded, providing she believes the enquiry is in the duke's best interest."

Sara sat back against the leather seat. "My, but you're clever! Your star shines so much brighter than that Round Table rabble. And who needs Silver Spoons, eh? They're school boys compared to you, Will. I've a mind to start a real centre of power in England, with a new leader. Are you game?"

The conceited baron's pride was about to lead to a very great fall. "If by 'game' you mean, am I ready to mount the world? Then yes, I am very game, indeed."

The fallen angel smiled, his dark eyes glinting red for the briefest of seconds. "Oh, I do like the way you put that, William. Mount the world! Such delicious imagery! Yes, my dear friend, let us do just that. We shall mount the world."

CHAPTER FORTY-FOUR

Anthony Gehlen had no sooner arrived in Branham Village than he was summoned back to the hall by way of a terse telegram. It was Constable Tower who delivered the news to the physician. Anthony had just started to enquire regarding the local apothecary's supply of morphine, carbolic acid, and ergot. The young apprentice who was working the counter that morning asked regarding the last item, and Gehlen stared in amazement.

"Son, you are aware that ergot in small doses has been used for centuries to stop post-partum bleeding?"

"No, Dr. Gehlen. I wasn't. Do many doctors use it?"

"Those who know what they're doing use it," he declared. He was preparing to give a lecture on the efficacy of plant-based medicines in obstetrics, when Constable Tower arrived with the telegram.

"Mornin', Ken. Mornin', Dr. Gehlen, sir. I'm to give you this right away."

Gehlen took the sealed message, read it, and jammed it back into the envelope. "Send a runner to Sir Simon Pembroke's house and tell the Viscounts Paynton and Salperton to hoof it back to the hall at once! I'm taking the hall's train back to the depot. Ask everyone to pray, Constable Tower. The duchess has gone into labour."

Westminster - London
Charles Sinclair checked his pocket watch. "It's nearly lunchtime, James. Shall we eat at the Royale? I don't think Mrs. Paget is expecting me, so I'm free."

"Why not?" the elder duke replied. Drummond sat opposite his nephews in a black-and-red brougham coach. They'd just left Loudain House. "Do you think Wychwright will nibble at our bait? He's smug, but he might smell a rat."

"How can a rat smell anything but rat?" asked Paul as he leaned against the leather, his clear eyes serious. "Will's nose is dull. For a military man, he lacks discipline, and he's hot-headed, which guarantees he's already devising ways to bring us down. All we need do now is wait and catch him in the act. The man insists we charge him with a crime, then, let us give him what he wants."

"Even attempted murder?" asked Sinclair. "It's a big risk."

"Yes, but I play to win," the earl said in a chillingly cold voice. "And I never lose. William brought this on himself. He threw Delia down those stairs at the Lyceum. True, no one saw it, but I'm convinced of his guilt. Delia says her brother did it, and I believe her."

"Are she and the baby going to be all right?" asked his cousin. "Paul, if there's anything we can do—anything at all, just name it. I'll send for the best doctors from France and Germany, if we must."

The earl seldom revealed his feelings, but Charles had learnt to read his cousin's mind. He perceived the telltale signs: tension in Aubrey's jaw as well as repeated tapping on the window glass.

"Thank you, Charles, but Gehlen is the best obstetrician alive," Stuart answered, drumming the curtained window. "Ask any specialist on the continent, he'll give you Anthony Gehlen's name as tops in his field. We're blessed to have him, and now that he's a believer and member of the circle, we needn't worry about either of our wives. Are you sure we shouldn't go back right away? I know you say the children aren't due until Monday, but women sometimes go into labour hours before a child is born."

"Not two days' worth of labour. At least, I pray not. But perhaps, you're right. We could order a take-out luncheon from The Red Lion. It's on the next block, and their food's generally quite good."

Drummond made the decision for all of them. "The Red Lion it is. You know me, gentlemen. The Royale may be where other dukes and earls prefer to be seen, but I'm happy with a beef and cheddar next to a roaring home fire."

"I suspect the Duke of Haimsbury agrees with you, Uncle," Aubrey retorted.

Charles tapped on the ceiling of the coach to alert Hamish Granger, their driver. The brougham came to a stop, and the burly Scotsman appeared at the window.

"Yes, sir?"

"We're going to order sandwiches and ale from The Red Lion, Mr. Granger. If you'd be kind enough to stop as close as possible and send Mr. Lowell in with our order?"

"Of course, Your Grace. Have you a list?"

"We will by the time you stop."

The driver returned to his seat and Haimsbury quickly scribbled out orders for all. "Shall we add food for the Baxters?"

"We're meeting them at Victoria?" asked Drummond.

"Yes, but I think we told Cornelius two o'clock. It's not yet noon."

The coach stopped in front of the pub, and the young footman's freckled face appeared at the window. "My lords?"

Charles handed his servant the paper. "Do you know if there's a telegraph agency nearby, Mr. Lowell?"

The lad looked east and west, then stepped away from the coach for a few seconds before reappearing at the window. "Two blocks over, sir. Have you a message?"

Sinclair nodded. "Yes. Give me a minute." He wrote a quick note for Baxter and handed it to the footman along with ten pounds. "That should cover the food and the telegram. Keep anything that's left. Thank you."

The footman grinned, for he knew the most the meals and telegram would cost was five pounds. "Thank you, sir!"

James laughed. "You're very generous, son. I'm glad to see it. An employer should always treat his staff with respect, and reward loyalty. That lad will serve you faithfully for the rest of his days. Is he new?"

"Actually, Miles hired him last year for Queen Anne. He came over as sixth footman at my home when Miles replaced Baxter, just before Christmas. Della thinks he's 'rather dishy'—her words, sir, not mine. I'm not sure where she picks up these modern phrases, but I find it instructive to talk with her each evening."

Paul smiled at last. "Charles, you've made her very happy. She came to our apartment at Branham last night, and all she could talk about was the new babies. She hopes Robby will have Sinclair eyes, like hers." He grew quiet for a moment. "I wonder if Della's Sinclair blood makes her a target?"

James had been watching a pair of men arguing on the next corner, and this last caught his ear. "Ah, there you'll want to speak with our tailor. Kepelheim's keeper of the lines, as you're aware, and he mentioned an entire list of connecting threads he's uncovered. Not only is Della a Sinclair, but Henry is as well—a cousin, I think. But Beth carries Sinclair blood as well. I think hers is through Anjou. Or perhaps d'Orsay."

"D'Orsay?" Charles repeated. "She's mentioned that before."

"I imagine she would," the elder man replied. "Beth's archivist keeps a book with all her titles in it. Some six or seven dozen at least. There may even be a hundred, if one includes all the minor ones. But she talked to me about seeking permission to name Georgianna the Countess d'Orsay, in the event she's born second."

"Yes, she mentioned that to me as well," Charles told his uncle. "Here comes our Mr. Lowell."

The freckled-faced lad scampered across the busy thoroughfare, carrying an envelope in his left hand. He reached the window, breathless from having run at top speed. "I sent the telegram, my lord, but the manager overheard, and he came over to tell me a message has been sent to all offices in the city. It's from Branham, sir."

Charles took the cream envelope and tore it open. His eyes widened as he read the simple line:

DUCHESS IN LABOUR. COME AT ONCE.

"Thank you, Mr. Lowell," Haimsbury answered as calmly as he could manage. "We'll forego the meals. Hop up and tell Mr. Granger to take us to Victoria."

"What is it, son?" asked Drummond.

Charles gave his uncle the slip of paper. "How could she go into labour already? The twins aren't due until Monday!"

"Keep calm now, Charles," the wise senior told him. Drummond rapped on the coach's roof, and Granger's face popped into view a moment later. "Drive past Haimsbury House, Hamish. We'll fetch the Baxters along the way."

"Very good, sir."

Charles's hands shook, and his uncle reached over to take them. "She'll be fine, son. Why, when my Ellie gave birth to Connor, she was in labour for two days."

"Two days?" the younger duke echoed mournfully. "How can a woman endure two days of pain? Amelia had Albert in just two hours, and she screamed the entire time. I can't bear the thought of Beth going through that for two minutes, much less two days."

"It's a process, Charles," the Scotsman assured him. "Ellie's waters didn't break right away, and she had periods of pain followed by intermittent periods of rest. Our doctor had her walk now and then. Good old Victor Adamson. Wish he'd been alive last October. He surpassed Lemuel's abilities, and he'd not have betrayed us. Adamson was a distant cousin to us somewhere along the lines. Through the MacAlpins, I think, which makes him kin to Henry as well. As you can imagine, I wasn't one to let my wife go through agony on her own, and I bullied my way into the room and helped her walk myself. She and I spent those two, long days together, and I got to see my son take his first breath."

Drummond's face glowed with the pleasant memory.

"Charles, there's nothing more beautiful in this entire world. What a miracle! Trust me, laddy," he whispered affectionately, "Beth can do this. She may be a whip of a thing, but my girl's got a lion's heart."

Sinclair nodded, only slightly reassured. "Thank you, sir. Honestly, I'm trying to trust in God for her welfare, but it's my own failing to worry. Do you think Gehlen will allow me to be with her the entire time?"

Drummond laughed. "You're the twins' father, Charles! Do as I did and push your way in! If you need another set o' bull's horns, I'll help. There are few men in this world who won't step aside for me."

Aubrey laughed, his own concerns banished for a moment. "If the Duke of Drummond wants it done, then woe to him who refuses."

The Scotsman grinned, swiping at his thick moustache. "It has been said," he answered proudly. "My father had the same reputation. And old George Linnhe had a similar character."

"Trish's father?" asked Haimsbury.

"Aye, that's the one. Crusty old crab. If he ordered it done in the Lords, then by St. Michael's trousers, it got done! Branham or ban 'em, that's how the privy council put it. Every Parliamentarian cowered at old Linnhe's big voice. He'd get up at meetings and shout 'em all down. Bonnie times, they were, too. Ah, but George had his dark side. Many's the time he and I cracked heads at circle meetings. Especially over Patricia."

"Why's that, sir?" asked Charles as the coach sped quickly past Marlborough House. The brougham bore the familiar crest of Haimsbury-Branham, and many of those along the sidewalks bowed or curtsied politely at seeing the famous coach.

Aubrey waved, smiling. "Even the people of Westminster think of you as a prince, Cousin."

"Really, I wish they wouldn't."

"I suspect most would be happy to call you king."

James intervened, seeing the younger duke's obvious discomfort. "Well, I think your compromise was brilliant, Charles. And Drina's pleased as punch! It was the idea of putting one of our own on England's throne that drove George Linnhe a bit mad, if you ask me. He refused to allow his daughter to marry Ian Stuart, because he wanted a Drummond-Branham heir. A final union of the twins' blood in one body. A son to take command of England. George was besotted with the idea. Truly, it drove him to madness, and it ended his life."

"How?" asked Aubrey. "Father sometimes mentioned the old duke with disdain, but I always assumed it had to do with Ian. What happened?"

"I think George listened to dark whispers, much like his father did," Drummond said, his eyes on the passing scenery. "And so Trish married Connor, and within a year lost a son. Tragic."

Charles's azure eyes focused intensely on his uncle's face. "You knew about the miscarriages?"

"Of course, I did," Drummond replied. "Three sons born before their time. Do you think Connor didn't tell me?"

"Moira Stopes saw to their deaths," Haimsbury declared.

"Aye, she did," his uncle sighed. "How I wish we'd kept a closer eye, but Trish wouldn't allow it. She pushed us all away. As I said, after that first son was lost, old George got peculiar. He died the very day of the baby's funeral."

"No one's told me that," Charles replied as the coach drove past Queen Anne, turning at the southwest corner of the formal park towards Haimsbury House. "I'd thought the old duke died before that child was born."

Paul interrupted. "The circle altered some of the official records to protect George's reputation, but the truth is he may have ended his own life, Charles. Baxter claims it's because George began keeping long hours in his father's occult library. That's where they found him. Slumped over one of the grimoires. Trish refused to allow an autopsy, but signs pointed to poison."

Sinclair grew thoughtful. "Sometimes I wish Beth were having our children at Queen Anne. Of all our homes, it has the fewest ghosts."

"We're here, son. Shall I run in and fetch our Inspector Baxter and his missus?"

"I'll do it," answered the younger duke as the coach stopped before the magnificent north edifice of the Haimsbury London estate. Charles intended to go inside, but to his surprise, the Baxters stood waiting at the top of the limestone steps, surrounded by luggage.

Granger jumped down, his red-bearded face appearing at the window. "Leave it to me, sir." The tall Scotsman helped two footmen secure the trunks in the boot of the coach whilst Cornelius helped his bride into the luxurious interior. Aubrey joined his cousin and uncle on one side, whilst Esther Baxter sank into the padded leather seat opposite.

"Oh, sirs! It's sure a jolly thing ta see you all again. And in such a fine coach, too. These seats feel like kid gloves."

Cornelius entered, his great weight causing the springs and struts of the coach to compress and creak. He sighed as he joined his wife, a large basket betwixt them.

"Good afternoon, my lords. It's good of you to come fetch us. I take it you, also, received the telegram about our little duchess?"

"We did," Sinclair told his friend. "I'm afraid we hadn't the time to order any lunch. Our next meal will likely be taken at Branham."

Baxter grinned. "My dear wife thought of that, sir." He lifted the lid on the basket. "We have a lovely claret and glasses. The sandwiches are egg and bacon, pork shoulder, and of course beef and cheddar for Duke James. We also have apples, raspberry tarts, and a jar of milky tea for anyone who prefers it."

Charles smiled at long last. "If only Mrs. Baxter could organise my life."

Esther handed out sandwiches to the men. "I'd give it a try, Your Grace, but I expect you'd be hard pressed to follow my orders."

"I'm afraid that's true," Sinclair answered. "Egg and bacon for me. If my sweet wife is to spend the next two days working to deliver our children, then I'll require sustenance."

Cornelius poured the claret and passed glasses to all. He raised his glass high, saying, "To our little duchess and the next generation of the House of Haimsbury-Branham. May God bless them all!"

James raised his as well. "To my great-grandchildren! May there be many more to come!"

CHAPTER FORTY-FIVE

1:35 pm - Branham Hall – Master Apartment

"Have you heard from my husband yet?" asked the duchess as she walked back and forth along the upper gallery.

"No, my lady," Mrs. Reston replied. "But he'll be here. And there's plenty of time. Doctor says you're not yet dilated. These pains are just the beginning."

Beth held the tall nurse's hand with her right, with her left sometimes touching the furnishings of the gallery to keep her balance. Her back ached, and the pangs came irregularly, lasting about a minute each time. She prayed during these, asking the Lord to strengthen the hearts of her children that they might thrive despite the early arrival.

"Is it dangerous for twins who come so soon, Mrs. Reston?" she asked, her breathing coming in gasps.

"It's very common for them to come early, my lady," replied the efficient woman as a man approached from the opposite side of the long gallery. "Here's Dr. MacAlpin, Your Grace. Sir, if you might take over whilst I check on Lady Aubrey?"

"Yes, of course!" Henry rushed over, allowing Beth to lean on him. "Lady Aubrey is sleeping at present, Reston. I believe Lady Victoria planned to keep watch this shift." The private nurse left, and Salperton placed his left arm round Elizabeth's waist. "You're doing very well. I've not delivered nearly the number of babies as Gehlen, but I've overseen the birth of two sets of twins. Both times, the pangs began early. As though the body was preparing for the extra job of managing two births."

Elizabeth stopped. "Might I sit for a few minutes?"

"Yes, of course. Do you need water?"

"I had two glasses half an hour ago. Mrs. Reston is regimental about such things. Is it warm?" she asked. Her face shone with a thin film of sweat, and she cooled her cheeks with a small silk fan.

"Let me do that," the viscount offered, taking the fan and waving it back and forth. He took her pulse with his free hand. "I must say, Beth, you're really doing well."

The duchess managed a smile. "Am I? I keep asking myself if I can do this year after year. I told Charles I want to have five more children at least—one every year. Do women do that?"

"Yes, many do. Though not by choice in all cases," he said, drawing a second chair close, so he could sit. He continued using the fan, causing the loose curls of her hair to blow round her flushed face. He felt her forehead. "You're slightly warm. Of course, it's rather warm up here. The chilly morning led to all the main floor fireplaces being lit, and the heated air rises. And the sun's coming in all the interior windows now. I do like these galleries, though. They're rather like cloister walks with glass. Lovely."

She sat with her back to one of the many windows, and the central gardens of the inner courtyard teemed with life and colour. A large white owl perched upon the tallest branch of a nearby elm tree, its cool blue eyes fixed upon the duchess.

"How long will this continue before the pangs grow worse?" she asked.

"Gehlen's the one to ask, but in my narrow experience, it can take a day or two."

She sighed, clutching at her distended abdomen. "Oh, Henry! Two days? I'm not sure my poor feet can take two days of walking. Might I lie down for a little while?"

"Certainly. Lean on me. I'll help you back to your apartment."

She pressed against his arms, slowly standing. Henry held her close, his hand on her rounded waist. The owl moved to a nearer branch, flapping its wings lightly. The physician gazed into the young woman's eyes, his heart suddenly skipping beats. For a fraction of a second, the sensitive Scotsman could see a dark cloud form around the gentle duchess. He saw blood and agony and danger. A vision of Elizabeth upon a death bed filled his mind.

The owl stepped closer still, its icy gaze fixed upon the stunned viscount.

The vision crystallised, becoming grievously real to Henry. He could hear men's voices shouting. A woman screamed, and the duchess's eyes closed. Blood filled the bed, and then all went dark.

"Henry?" he heard her ask, the slender hands upon his own. "Is something wrong?"

The startled visionary forced himself to return to the present, and he pulled her close, wanting to protect her from the horrible future he'd just witnessed.

"Yes, sorry. I suppose I need to eat. Shall we go back to your apartment and ring for a tray?"

"That sounds quite nice, actually. I'm finally hungry again."

"As am I," he answered, slowly helping Elizabeth through the long gallery and towards the west living area.

Was that a warning or a fixed future? Henry wondered as they walked. *God help me! What does it mean?*

33 miles from Branham Hall Depot

The Captain Nemo special stood still as a post, and had done for almost ten minutes. Haimsbury and company assumed the engineer had stopped for water or to allow sheep to cross the track, but ten minutes was too long for either. The young duke for whom the train took its unique name looked out the windows of the first car, trying to discern the reason for the delay.

"It's most likely cows or sheep, Charles," Aubrey assured him as he joined his cousin in the long passenger car. "Shall I walk the tracks to make sure?"

Before the duke could reply, the train's first engineer, Ed Gabberfield, lumbered through the doors that connected to the generator car. "Sorry, Your Grace. We've run into a small problem."

"Yes, we'd thought that might be the case. Sheep?"

"No, sir. We're unable to get pressure on the boiler. I expect it's one of the tubes lining the firebox, or else a valve. I've got Featherberry on it, my lord. He's the best mechanic in the kingdom."

"If it's a valve, is it something that can be repaired quickly? I don't know much about how these engines work, but I'd assume such a part would need to cool before a man can touch it," Charles enquired, doing his best to remain calm.

"We have asbestos gloves, sir. Made just for such a time as this. Not to worry, my lord. We'll be back up and running in no time at all. The electrics are still on, if you require a cup o' tea. That new-fangled electric kettle the duke's scientist asked ta test is in the back. Shall I boil up some water?"

"All I require is to be at Branham, Mr. Gabberfield. Do your best. And thank you for letting us know."

The engineer left the car, and Haimsbury returned to his office, running his hands through the thick curls of his black hair. "What if Robby's born first? He might even come today. Is that even possible?"

"Stop borrowing trouble, son," the duke told his nephew. "Babies come when they come, and nothing a man does can rush or delay it."

Alcorn poured glasses of the milky tea for the men and passed out the tarts. "I can make coffee, if you want, sir. I've never used one o' these new kettles, but it might be an adventure."

"No, this will do nicely. Esther, you mentioned delivering twins. Is long labour usual?" asked Sinclair as he sat into one of the club chairs.

Drummond cleared his throat, his eye on the half-empty bottle of claret. "I've never delivered a baby, but I can tell you Beth's mother was in labour for a very long time. Paul was there. He'll vouch for that. Remember, son? Because of the miscarriages, we all worried she'd lose another. That's why Connor insisted she go into confinement at Drummond, rather than Branham. He no longer trusted that house. Connor didn't tell me then, but I think we can guess his reason."

"William Trent," whispered Charles. "He'd already taken control of the duchess. I wonder if that man is really dead?"

"I suspect he's roasting on a specially built spit," Aubrey answered. "But you're right about Connor, James. I recall something he said to me at the time that never made sense until now."

"What's that?" asked the elder duke.

"I'd arrived earlier that morning, exhausted after spending twenty-four hours travelling from Briarcliff. It was mid-March, and everyone thought Trish was in labour, and Connor was frantic. It was too soon, and he feared she was losing another son. At twelve years old, I didn't appreciate what he was going through, but he just sat in the library, drinking cup after cup of coffee and moaning about some man from France."

"France?" asked Sinclair. "Wasn't Trent English? Had he been living abroad?"

"He didn't say the man was French, but that he lived in Paris. Or rather just outside Paris. Did I tell you I sent Deniau on a quest to follow Trent's trail of breadcrumbs?"

"No," answered his cousin, forgetting for a few minutes that he was about to become a father. "Did he find any?"

"He did. I planned to present his report at our next meeting. When Mac freed Anthony Gehlen of his spirit attachments and led him to Christ, our physician began to share his own history. Mac had asked him whether or not anything in his past might have allowed this spirit entry, and Anthony shared an experience from the early 1870s, possibly '73. Now, let me also tell you that I've been follow-ing the devilish exploits of a chemist named Emile Sandoval. He works with several companies, most recently Sanguis, Ltd."

"Sanguis?" Charles repeated. "The company owned by Anto-nio Calabrese?"

"Yes," Paul replied. "And the so-called father of Angiolina"

"I'd love to find out who she really is. After finding her in the old duke's library, I can't believe anything she told me."

"Sanguis is an evil company," Drummond declared. "Our two circle traitors, Ankerman and Swanson, ran chemicals for Sanguis, remember?"

"Sanguis means blood," Paul muttered. "A disturbing clue, and a bit of bragging. But this Sandoval ran with Redwing, though he tried to hide his affiliation. He operated a clinic for mental illness on the east side of Paris. Sandoval claimed he could use electricity and chemicals to heal broken minds. When Gehlen suffered from brain fever, he was sent to Sandoval's clinic. It's Mac's belief that some-one there opened our friend's mind and soul to infestation."

Charles considered this, dark whispers in his spirit warning him of Gehlen. Was he still a threat? A wolf in sheep's clothing?

"Mac's certain Gehlen is clean?"

"He has no doubts. Charles, we covered all this at Gehlen's induction meeting, remember? Do you think I'd have voted to admit him, if I had any reservations about his loyalty?"

"No, of course, not. Forgive me. I'm not myself."

The earl managed a smile. "No, you're about to become father to twins. Not every man can make that claim. And very few dukes."

"What of Lord Kesson's tale of Trent, Lord Aubrey?" asked Esther as she refilled their glasses.

"Ah, yes," the earl replied. "That is where we connect our story to Sandoval. Connor mentioned that this mysterious man from France had once lived near a sanitorium. He never gave me a name, but offered enough clues for me to weave into Deniau's findings, to deduce the rest."

"Which is?" asked Charles.

"That William Trent is not the man's original name. Indeed, it is but one of a dozen names this demonic creature has used. And I name him demon, for it's likely he is just that. An evil spirit using the form of a human. Or perhaps altering an actual human and unnaturally lengthening his life span."

"You're not implying that Trent is, or rather was this Sandoval, are you, sir?" asked Baxter.

"No, but Trent's demon worked at a hospital near that region in '73. He called himself Favor. Dr. Crispin Favor."

Charles paled. "Tell me you're wrong about that name."

"No, that's what Deniau found. This Favor worked at a women's asylum, where he specialised in ending unwanted pregnancies. But there's more. He had an assistant named Moira Stopes."

Charles threw his glass at the wall of storage lockers. The remaining liquid and shattered glass formed a glittering waterfall as it slid down the metal doors. He stood and began to pace. Everyone held their breath, each eye on the troubled duke.

"Son, what is it?" asked Drummond. "We started this tale to take your mind off Beth, but that may have been a bad idea. She'll be fine, Charles. Believe me."

Sinclair leaned against the locker that held the dial safe, tears filling his eyes. "Favor. That damnable name!" He took a moment, his chest broadening as he gulped in air. He felt as though he'd been stabbed through the heart, and he tried to suck in life-giving oxygen to force the traitorous organ to beat again.

"A couple of months ago, I spoke with Margaret Hansen. Do you remember, Paul?"

"Yes, I'd suggested you were mistaken about her willingness to leave Redwing's nest, but you insisted on meeting her, on your own."

"But I was right about her. I'm sure of it. She just wasn't willing to leave them yet. I met her not from here, at a Greek restaurant, and she told me a great deal about Redwing's organisation and plans. Because they held meetings at her brothel each Saturday and played cards there during the week, she overheard many of their conversations. Even when I was still married to Amelia, those devils met there. It was an easy place to hide, since the same well-dressed men frequented the hotel's rooms, and no one thought to question their comings and goings. Margaret revealed a dark truth to me about my late wife. I'd always suspected she'd married me because she thought a Cambridge graduate might help her climb higher in society. She certainly urged me to apply to the inns and become a solicitor. Amelia dreamt of being the wife of a fashionable and wealthy QC, perhaps even an MP, but I had no ambitions for practising law, only enforcing it as a policeman. Her affection towards me had waned long before our son died. In fact, just two months after he was born, she began paying long visits to a woman named Abernathy. I never questioned my wife about the visits. Why would I? But Margaret told me that my wife had been seen many times with her worthless cousin and his friend at a hotel in Mayfair, where Amelia used the name Mrs. Harold Lowry."

Paul's eyes rounded. "Are you saying she was sleeping with that low dog Lowry, even before Albert died?"

Charles nodded. "Yes, but it's worse. Meg also told me that two days before Albert passed away, Lowry came to our home whilst I went from house to house with my men, looking for victims of the smallpox outbreak. Amelia left with Lowry a few minutes later, and she had my son with her. Meg told me that Lowry often gambled at the Empress, and he later confessed that he'd hired a City doctor to inoculate Albert against the disease for a small fee. Amelia's parents admitted to me that she'd taken Albert to see a doctor, but either they had no knowledge of Lowry's involvement, or they failed to mention it. The doctor's name was Crispin Favor."

"No!" Drummond shouted. "Are you saying William Trent killed your son?"

Charles stared at the fallen shards of glass. Esther had already begun to clean the wall and sweep up the glass, but the young duke stopped her. "Don't. Just don't, Esther. Please. Let it stay there for a few minutes. I need to see it."

"But, sir, you might cut yourself."

"No cut could harm me as much as this. It's all been a long, devilish plan, gentlemen—and lady, of course. Forgive me, Esther," he said, wiping weariness from his eyes. "Trent used Moira Stopes to make certain Duchess Patricia bore only daughters. Once Beth was born, Connor was no longer needed, and Trish began her affair with Trent. At three years old, my precious Elizabeth first saw this Shadow Man. At seven, her father was killed by a monstrous wolf, who was either this Shadow or Trent in another form. With her father dead, Trent was free to marry Patricia, and he brought in his evil friends to live in the hellish second east wing at Branham. In the guise of Crispin Favor, he made sure my son died, leaving me grief-stricken. My wife's affair with another man helped secure this arrangement, and further isolated me. Then, in early February of '79, Bob Morehouse took me to Paris, where he insisted we attend a performance at the Opera Comiqúe. He introduced me to the star, a woman named Antoinette Gévaudan. Bob then insisted we all go to a party, given by an influential politician. I had no choice. Gévaudan tried to seduce me at that party, and may have tampered with my drink, for I awoke with no memory of the night before. She claimed we made love—forgive me, Esther, for such frank language," he said, glancing at Mrs. Baxter. "We did not. I returned to London thoroughly confused. I had no idea that Bob Morehouse's strings were pulled by Redwing at the time."

He paused, taking a deep breath as he worked through the various events that led to now. "Then, I began receiving letters from Antoinette. She claimed to love me. Would I leave my wife, that sort of thing. I never wrote back. On the last day of February, she appeared at Leman Street, asking for me. When I arrived, she claimed to be pregnant—again, Mrs. Baxter, do forgive me. She was not, nor would it have been mine, had she been. On the second of March, Antoinette suddenly left London. My life was, quite frankly, an empty, lifeless cage.

"Then the early morning of the third arrived, and I was called to Commercial Street, where I worked a brutal murder. A mysterious woman had been butchered and left in pieces near Christ Church. After learning all we could at the crime scene, Bob and I returned to Leman Street, where I discovered a beautiful child asleep on Bob's office sofa, and thus my life was reborn. I say all this, because William Trent's evil stench has lingered round both Beth and me for longer than we imagined. If you want to know why I'm so frantic now, let me tell you this: Last month, at the fête, Beth thought she saw a woman from her childhood. She was with Count Riga, and it was he who told me. Beth isn't aware that I know about it, for I've no wish to worry her."

"Whom did she see?" asked Aubrey.

"The name she told Riga was Moira Stopes."

CHAPTER FORTY-SIX

2:45 pm - Branham Hall

"Shall I read to you?" asked Adele from the chair opposite. "Dr. Gehlen says you're to rest for a little while, and I'd be happy to read a little of Mr. Verne's novel. I have a new one, in French."

Elizabeth lay upon a sofa, her feet elevated with cushions, and a thin coverlet across her body. A small table sat to her right with biscuits, water, and ginger tea. Mrs. Reston busied herself near the bed by making sure the waterproof liners, wash pans, and towels were all in place and ready. The duchess's chamber had been transformed during the past week into a birthing room, complete with medicinal supplies, equipment for blood transfusions, two high tables covered in towels ready to receive the newborns for assessment and cleaning. Clamps, lamps, and enough surgical steel instruments to intimidate any newborn father.

"Or would you prefer poetry?" Della asked. "Mother, are you asleep?"

Beth's eyes were shut, but she turned towards the girl. "No, darling, I'm not. Would you mind switching off the chandeliers? They're so very bright. It hurts my eyes."

Reston took care of it, and the room was plunged into semi-darkness, lit only by the bedside lamps. "Is that better, Your Grace?"

"Yes, thank you. Poetry sounds very nice, Della. Or perhaps, you could play the piano."

"But how would you hear it? The music room's down two flights of stairs and all the way to the back of the house."

"There's a piano in your father's study, darling. The door should be unlocked."

Adele set the books aside and crossed through the rooms to her father's bedchamber. She paused, enjoying the reassuring maleness of the space; the powerful security of it. Beyond a large armoire, she found the doors, both open, and she entered the study. As promised, the adolescent found the grand piano and sat upon the stool. She lifted the cover and set her hands upon the keys. Two rooms away, Elizabeth could hear a Johannes Brahms lullaby, and within minutes, she'd fallen asleep.

Adele played for half an hour, providing the duchess accompaniment for a series of odd dreams. In one, Beth saw herself standing on a tall hill with two crosses upon it. In another, she flew over London, and below could see the shapes of two smoking buildings. In the third, she sailed upon a ship, and the captain told her that two people had died tragically, all their blood drained from their bodies.

Beth awoke with a start, her thoughts struggling with the disturbing dreams, and her hands clutching her abdomen. The labour pains had intensified.

4:13 pm – 33 miles from Branham

"And that is how we finished our final day," Baxter told his companions. "Esther and I hadn't caught a single fish, but we'd discovered midges aplenty. My dear wife made poultices, which soothed them quite readily."

"Peppermint helps," Aubrey said, smiling. "But the best solution is to avoid the water in summer."

Enough time had now passed to allow his cousin to calm down and Esther to clean up the broken glass. Charles still paced, but he no longer appeared ready to punch the nearest Redwing member. As he walked back and forth, Sinclair let his mind run through the revelation about Trent. If the evil baronet had assumed other identities, then how many others had there been? He found himself wishing Anatole Romanov would show up with his ambiguous answers.

The door to the next car opened, and the engineer arrived with an update and a note. "The valve is repaired, my lord, and we should be at full steam in five minutes. This came by way of Lord Aubrey's wireless telegraph. For you, my lord."

Haimsbury took the paper, and for the first time in hours he smiled. "It's from Beth. She says I'm not to worry. Here, James. you can read it."

The elder Stuart took the message and read it aloud:

CAPTAIN - ALL IS WELL. LABOUR STALLED. ROBBY AND GEORGIE REFUSE TO APPEAR UNTIL THEIR FATHER IS HERE.
   ALL OUR LOVE. - YOUR WIFE AND CHILDREN.

"It sounds as though our girl's doing fine, son. We'll be there within the hour."

Baxter stood and placed a hand on his employer and friend. "Shall we pray and thank the Lord, sir?"

Sinclair began to weep with relief. "Yes, Cornelius. I think we should. Will you do it?"

"I'd be honoured. Gentlemen, and my dear wife – let us join hands and seek the Lord."

Everyone took hands, each standing. They formed a circle, and Baxter's resonant baritone filled the car with power, softened by humility.

"Lord of all, Lord of always, Lord of now and forever more. You created us and you formed us to bear within us your desire for love. Your image is imprinted upon us. You shaped mankind with your very hands! And you designed him to shape others through an intimacy beyond imagination and description: the love of a husband and a wife. As I learn more about Charles Sinclair, I continue to be humbled and amazed. His is a rare soul, sir. A rare soul indeed! I know not what future you've devised for him, but I know that road will be filled with joys as well as sorrows. We ask today that this be a season of joy! May our little duchess be protected by your mighty angels and covered with your impenetrable shield. I pray for longevity for myself, and for all who stand here now, for it's my hope to share in the lives of yet another generation of inner-circle warriors. Before the foundation of the world, you knew the roads prepared for Robby and Georgianna Sinclair, and I believe that road will encompass the world. Create within them the hearts of lions. May your Holy Spirit shape their lives and fill their mouths with your words. May they stand upon the earth as defenders of truth, lifting up Christ for all the world to see; for you promised if we would do that, then all men would be drawn to you! That is what I foresee for this family. For these children. And I believe this family will shake the world! May you help our young duke to boldly proclaim your Son and His grace. For it is to this, we are called. We ask it all in the name of our Risen Savior. Even the Lord Christ Jesus. Amen."

Charles opened his eyes once more, and he could see Baxter was weeping. He embraced the ageing inspector and kissed him on the cheek. "You're our very dear friend and advisor, Mr. Baxter, and we all love you. Thank you."

Cornelius wept openly for several seconds, his hands on the duke's shoulders. "You, sir, are the greatest man I've ever known. With perhaps the exception of your good uncle, Duke James."

Drummond laughed. "I'd hoped you'd say that, old fellow, but you're right. Our Charles is special. As is our Earl of Aubrey, eh? We're a handsome clan o' Scots, aren't we? And that clan includes you, Mr. B."

The train jerked as the engine took hold, turning the mighty cylinders that drove the pistons that forced the wheels into motion. Soon after, they heard the familiar, rhythmic 'chuffing' sound made when the steam puffed out of the stacks at the end of each stroke.

By five, they arrived at the depot, and by half the hour, Charles Sinclair had taken his wife's hand. Branham was ready for twin miracles.

CHAPTER FORTY-SEVEN

Those precious miracles took their time to make their presence known. All day Sunday, Elizabeth alternately walked and rested, walked and rested. By evening, Gehlen found she'd begun to dilate, and by nine, the duchess entered full labour. At thirteen minutes past nine, her waters broke, and her bed was surrounded by doctors: Anthony Gehlen as lead, Michael Emerson to tend to the first baby to emerge, and Henry MacAlpin eager to greet the second. They'd rehearsed their actions and made plans for any contingency. Transfusion equipment stood at the ready, just in case Elizabeth suffered excessive post-partum bleeding, and both her husband and cousin had been briefed on the procedure, should they need to donate.

Charles had never donated blood to his wife, but Emerson introduced his colleagues to a quick and easy method of cross-matching blood, pioneered in Edinburgh. Whilst caring for his dying brother Laurence, the modest physician had furthered his education by studying with the finest scientists in the kingdom. By mixing the blood of the duchess and any potential donor in a Petri dish, he was able to quickly eliminate or confirm a match. Sinclair's blood had not reacted adversely with the duchess's blood, and to the surprise of many (but not to Sinclair), Henry MacAlpin's blood also matched.

"When Romanov brought you into Beth's life, he knew all of this, I'll wager," Charles told Salperton. "Now, she'll have three of us, should she require transfusion."

Henry laughed it off, in typical fashion. "Yes, but mine would just leave her singing Scottish airs, I'd imagine. Paul's will probably improve her horsemanship, and yours—well, yours, my dear friend, would make our dear lady spout logarithmic equations and quadratic conundrums. Let's just pray none of it affects the babies."

The three men took a vow to drink only water or tea for the fore-seeable future, but Charles added this caveat: "I shall most certainly share in a Drummond Reserve toast once it's all said and done. A man doesn't become a father to twins every day. Not only is it rare, the man's wife would likely not wish to repeat it."

They shared a laugh, but by eleven, every man had stationed himself in position, ready for the final phase.

Charles Sinclair refused to leave the birthing room, and when Gehlen objected, both dukes, Haimsbury and Drummond, made it clear that neither one intended to leave. James remained close to the fireplace, whilst Charles sat by his wife, holding her hand the entire time.

"You're doing beautifully," he told her as he mopped her moist brow. "Anthony says you're nearly there."

Gehlen bent over the foot of the bed. Beth's legs and ankles were covered with sheeting, and Nurse Reston acted as assistant. "Can you push for me once more?" he asked the exhausted duchess. "I'm not sure which one this is, but he or she is just about ready to emerge. One last push."

Charles whispered into her ear, "You can do this, little one. Think of Robby as you saw him. He needs you to help him now, just as he helped you."

Beth took a deep breath, her small features contorted, sweat covering her skin. "Arrgghhhhh!" she cried, pushing with all her might. She gripped her husband's hand with more force than he'd have ever thought possible, but Charles never moved. "Oh! Oh! Arghhhhhhhh!" she screamed, and suddenly the painful contraction ceased, and everyone waited.

One second passed. Two seconds. Three.

"Which is it? Is the baby all right?" asked Charles.

Gehlen turned to Reston, who applied a syringe to the baby's mouth. Anthony massaged the infant's back, and then gently tapped it. Finally, a wail pierced the air, and everyone exhaled in unison.

Gehlen beamed. "Duke Charles, say hello to your son."

Beth began to cry, and Charles left her side to take his first look at the miraculous boy who would one day rescue his mother in the terrifying maze called the Realms of Stone.

"Hello, there," he said. The boy was covered in blood and tis-sue, but he was perfect. Every finger. Every toe. Every limb perfect.

Charles gazed at the little face, realising at once that it bore a resemblance to his own. The boy had mounds of black curly hair, black lashes, and a sharp cupid's bow to his upper lip.

He even had a cleft chin.

"He looks just like you, son," his uncle said proudly.

"Does he?" asked Beth weakly. "May I see him before you take him away?"

"Give me a moment. We need to cut the cord." Gehlen clamped off the umbilical cord, made the cut, and then handed the calm infant to the nurse. Reston quickly cleaned his skin, made a cursory assessment, and then swaddled him in cotton sheeting.

"My lady, meet your son."

Beth reached out and touched the infant's hand. "He's so tiny. It's hard to believe he'll grow to be so very tall."

"We'll need to get him into the tented bed as soon as possible. It's important to keep him warm and provide rich atmosphere," Reston told her.

"Goodbye, Robby. We'll bring you a baby sister very soon," she promised.

Reston handed the boy to Emerson, who left for the nursery, where the specialised cots were arranged. "I'll stay with Robby, Anthony," he said.

"Yes, do that. Duchess, are you sensing any new contractions."

Exhausted, Beth had laid her head against the pillow, her eyes closed. "No. Not yet. Is that normal?"

"It varies," he told her. "Sleep whilst you can."

Gehlen made the delivery area ready for the next baby. Reston prepared the receiving table and arranged the transfusion equipment.

"Gentlemen, prepare yourselves, just in case," she told the three donors.

Charles returned to his wife's side, kissing her moist lips. "Well done, little one. He's beautiful."

"He looks like you."

He kissed her again. "You should rest. Perhaps, Georgianna is sleeping. She did say she was born on my birthday. That isn't for another two hours."

"One hour, fifty-seven minutes," Drummond observed as he came over to kiss his granddaughter. "Robby's to be the next Duke of Haimsbury and Branham. We'll have to find a title for Georgie, I guess. I'll talk with Drina about that next week. Now, sleep an hour, Princess. You've earned it."

Beth closed her eyes, and the men took chairs near the fireplace. James's blood had reacted adversely with Beth's, so he'd been eliminated from donating. Martin Kepelheim knocked on the door, opening it a crack. "Is it clear to enter? I understand congratulations are in order."

Reston made certain the sleeping duchess was covered modestly. "Yes, it's clear, sir."

Martin stepped lightly to the bedside, standing close to the young duke. "I hear we have a new heir."

Charles smiled, his eyes alight. "He's beautiful, Martin. And he can call you Uncle Marty, just as I did."

Kepelheim beamed. "I shall be pleased to serve in that capacity. And perhaps teach him to read code?"

"Of course."

"And our new mother?" he asked.

"She's so brave. And hardly made a sound until the very last push. I can't imagine what it must be like, but Beth took it all without complaint."

"Our little duchess has always been remarkably brave. Oh, where is Lord Aubrey? I'd heard he was to be ready in case blood donors are needed."

"Paul's with Cordelia. George Price is with her as well."

"Ah, and how is our countess faring today?"

"Delia suffered a mild concussion when she fell. That's one reason we can't use her testimony to prosecute her brother. I'd like to punch that smug little baron into next week."

"Yes, as would we all. And the baby?"

"Emerson said Gehlen worked a miracle," Charles answered. "Anthony's expertise is why Delia didn't miscarry. How the fall affected the child is yet to be seen, but thus far, the pregnancy is intact. If we could prove William pushed his sister, then we could charge him with willfully endangering the life of an infant, but there are no witnesses, save Cordelia."

"As William surely planned it," Martin whispered as Adele knocked on the door.

"May I?" she asked timidly.

Drummond rose to admit her, kissing her cheek as she entered. "Your mother has brought us a new Stuart, Della."

"He's a Sinclair," the girl corrected. •

"Ah, but he's got a lot o' Stuart in him! You can see that right off. He looks a bit like me, don't ya think?"

Adele laughed. "Oh, Great-Grandfather! He looks just like my father."

James hugged the adolescent affectionately. "Just call me Grandpa. It's easier. Beth hardly ever calls me that, unless she's trying to butter me up. Shall I teach you how to fish? Just like I will Robby?"

"And Georgie, too," Adele added. "Don't forget her. When will she be born? I thought twins came at the same time."

Gehlen had gone to the bath to wash his hands, and he emerged with a reply. "Not all are born close together, Lady Della. I had one mother whose twins were born almost a month apart. It's very rare, but it can happen."

Adele shook her head. "Georgianna Sinclair will be born on our father's birthday, which begins just after midnight."

Beth opened her eyes, her weary hands clenching. "I don't think she's going to wait too much past midnight. Oh!"

Charles returned to the bed, taking his wife's hand. The entire team reassembled, and Martin convinced Adele to join him in the duke's study.

"Perhaps, piano music might help. Will you play?"

They left, and for the next half-hour, the duchess strained to deliver her daughter. MacAlpin kept a close eye on her pulse and blood pressure, whilst Emerson, who'd left Robby in the oxygen cot supervised by his wet nurse. As the clock's hands struck midnight, Gehlen could feel the head crown.

"One or two more pushes, Beth. But wait until I tell you."

Beth could hardly breathe, and she longed to rest, but she answered as pleasantly as possible. "Yes, all right."

Her husband kissed her cheek. "You can do this, little one."

"Now!" Gehlen cried, and the nurse held out a linen towel. There was a pause, and then Anthony demanded another. "Just once more, Beth. Now!"

Every muscle in Elizabeth Sinclair's body clenched, and she pushed with all her might. As before, she could sense the baby emerge, and she stared at her doctor.

"Is she all right?"

Sinclair moved away from his wife, thinking of the little girl who'd dared to shout at an angry tree. His Georgianna.

"Gehlen, is she...?" he asked.

A loud, sweet cry was his answer. Charles began to weep, and he reached down to touch the infant's hand.

"She's just as I've always pictured," he said.

"Give me a minute," Gehlen was saying as he clamped the umbilical cord. "There. Nurse, if you'd attend to our new girl."

As before, Olivia Reston performed a quick assessment of the infant's appearance and then cleaned and swaddled her. "Your Grace, allow me to present Lady Georgianna Sinclair."

Every muscle in Charles's body released tension, and he feared he might collapse from joy. "She's all right?"

"She's perfect," the nurse answered. "We'll want to get her to the tented cot soon, though. Just as precaution."

"May I?"

"Yes, sir." She handed him the child, and Charles cradled her in his arms. "Do we know how much each weighs?"

"There's a scale in the nursery. Lord Anjou weighed in at five pounds, six ounces, and he's twenty inches long. Remarkable for a premature baby. He'll likely be quite tall, sir."

"Yes, so I hear," Charles answered, his eyes on his daughter. "She's much smaller than Robby. But she's healthy?"

"From what we can see, sir. Dr. Gehlen will perform a more thorough assessment later, after we've seen to the duchess."

Charles took her to Beth and allowed the duchess to touch the girl's hand. "See? She is the image of you. No wonder Paul talks of the moment when he first held you. Beth, there are no words to say how I feel. Thank you, darling. Thank you for making me a father again."

Elizabeth laughed. "You had a bit to do with it, Captain. I should be thanking you for making me a mother." She closed her eyes, and Charles returned the infant to the nurse, who left for the nursery.

"She needs rest," Gehlen told the duke. "There's a little more to do."

"Yes, afterbirth. I recall from when my first son was born," Charles answered. "Shall I wait outside?"

"Go enjoy your new babies, sir," the physician told the duke. "But don't go too far. It's likely the duchess will want to talk when she recovers."

Sinclair left the chamber, his head in the clouds and his heart lingering somewhere twixt the duchess's bed and the nursery.

How wonderful life can be! he thought.

Charles had no idea that within the hour, his entire world would fall apart.

CHAPTER FORTY-EIGHT

76 Leman Street - Whitechapel

Inspector Elbert Stanley had just finished a very late tea, when his fellow inspector Arthur France knocked on the door of Elbert's cramped office. "Sir?"

"How many times do I have to tell you, son? You needn't call me sir."

France shook his head. "But you're... Well, sir, you're a bit older, and also an inspector with the Intelligence Branch, which I'm told makes you my senior."

"Does it? Ah, well, that makes a change. What is it?"

"There's a riot down by the docks. Some fool fisherman's claiming he's seen a woman in white attacking children, and I'm afraid locals just aren't takin' it any more. Men are up in arms with whatever weapons come to hand. Mr. Reid's not here, and that puts you in charge."

Stanley wiped pie crumbs from his mouth, licking at the bits tickling his dark moustache. "The Woman in White again. Next, it'll be more of those Dybbuk rumours."

"I'm afraid that's already happenin', sir. Constable Bright says he's heard Lusk's men intend to tear down the Jewish Men's Rescue."

"Why on earth would they do that?"

"Lusk's been sayin' the Jews brought the Dybbuk with them. He figures eradicating all the Hebrews from Spitalfields will kill the demon."

"Send for Reid and let the Yard and the Intelligence Branch know. I hate disturbing our duke, but he'll want to hear about this. Fetch me a pad and pen. My desk drawer's been cleaned out."

"Yes, sir. Oh, and there's a priest downstairs who claims he needs to speak to you."

"To me? A priest? I'm not Catholic."

"No, sir, but this one's got Duke Charles's card in his pocket."

The ICI inspector sighed. This would be a long night.

Branham Hall

A scream tore though the hall, coming from the far east end of the massive mansion. With three hundred rooms, navigating from one side to the other could take as long as ten minutes, depending on which floor. As Elizabeth had fallen asleep, all the physicians rushed to the sound, finding Lady Aubrey standing on her bed and shouting that she'd seen her brother at her window. Paul did his best to reassure her, but Cordelia would hear none of it, alternatively screaming and weeping like a child, nearly breaking the earl's heart.

"Can't we do something?" he asked the doctors.

Henry stepped from the circle and towards the rumpled bed. "May I?" he asked the earl.

"Yes, of course."

Salperton exchanged places with Delia's husband and gently took the terrified woman's hand. "It's very dark out there," he said easily. "But there are stars out. I wonder if my star is up yet?"

Cordelia had been standing with her hands against the window panes, staring and weeping at something she saw on the south lawn. She turned to look at Henry, her blonde brows pinching together.

"What star? I can't see any stars. My brother's eaten them all."

"Has he?" Henry asked. "May I see?"

Cordelia took a breath, the tension easing slightly in her face.

"I'm not sure. He doesn't want everyone to see him. Only I can see him. But the stars are gone."

"Might I climb up there with you?"

"Very well. Do be careful. There are waves. We're on a ship after all."

"Ah, yes," the viscount replied without a hint of condemnation. "Oh, I see what you mean," he whispered once he'd found a place beside her. The bed's mattress moved beneath their feet, and it occurred to Henry that a troubled mind might perceive the motion as the rocking of a ship. "The waves are certainly high, aren't they? Is that a star?" he asked, pointing to the moon's white face.

The large, round orb peered betwixt the leaves of an elm tree. A large white owl perched several feet away, sitting beside a brown one.

"No, that's the moon. William cannot eat the moon. It's too far away and too large. But the stars are gone. He's a hateful man. Very hateful! He pushed me. As soon as Paul left to speak with Lord Salisbury, my brother came up to see me. I ran after Paul, and when I reached the stairs, William shoved me as hard as he could. He was laughing! I can't remember what happened after that. Paul didn't see, but that other man was there. Surely, he saw."

Everyone looked one to another, for she'd mentioned nothing of a possible witness. Henry remained calm. "Was there? Do you know who the man was?"

She continued to gaze out into the night. "He was out there, too, a little while ago. I saw him fighting with that great white owl. He changed into a large black bird. He wasn't a bird at the theatre, though."

Paul stepped closer. "*Mo bhean*," he said. She froze but did not turn round. "Darling, did this bird man have long dark hair at the theatre?"

She nodded, her hands against the glass. "Yes."

"And was he tall? Much taller than William?"

"Taller even than you."

"Did you see his eyes?" asked Charles, who'd just entered the room.

"Yes. They were like death. Cold and cruel and pale. Like evil ice."

Paul clenched his fists as he turned to look at his cousin. "They're after my wife!" he whispered angrily. "I will find them and..."

Charles reached for Paul's forearm. "No, that's what they want. Paul, this is the ploy we discussed. William's trying to lure us into a misstep, but we must follow his breadcrumbs with our eyes open. If we do so beneath a cloud of rage, we'll fail."

"And if it were Beth that demon pushed down the stairs?"

Charles said nothing, for he had no answer.

"I thought so," the earl replied. "Henry, can you get her back into bed?"

The viscount put his fingers to his lips to call for silence. "Delia, I wonder if you'd help me? The movement of this ship is making me a bit ill. I'm afraid I might fall. Might I lean on you?"

The gentle countess blinked as though waking from a dream. "Of course, I'll help. Be careful now," she told him as both slowly stepped off the tall bed. "Oh, it's so far away," she said, but Henry put his arms round her thick waist and eased her to the floor.

"There now," he said. "Much better. Back on dry land. You look tired, though."

"I am," she said in a childlike whisper. "If only Paul were here."

The earl moved closer, taking her hand. "I'm here, sweet one. I'm here."

Henry left the bed and the room. "Shall we, gentlemen?" Everyone gathered in the small antechamber to the Aubrey's suite. Salperton turned to Gehlen. "I think she's suffered a mental break, but we must make sure her head injury isn't the cause. If you'll rule out a physical pathology, I can help with any remaining nervous condition."

Anthony turned to Reston, who'd run to the suite upon hearing the screams. "Shall I fetch your bag, sir?"

"Yes. How are the twins doing?" Gehlen asked her.

"Very well, sir. I'm happy to say that both are already nursing. They appear to have no trouble eating."

"Another blessing," answered the physician. "Dr. Price, would you go sit with the duchess whilst I perform a quick examination of the countess?"

George Price looked as if he'd aged ten years, but he nodded wearily. "I shall be happy to oblige."

Everyone dispersed to different areas of the house. A calm settled over Branham Hall. That calm would be broken, just as the clock struck three.

CHAPTER FORTY-NINE
2:58 am - Sir Simon Pembroke's Home

The skies over Kent were clear that night, and the moon stood at her fullest. Selene's face was, in fact, abnormally large that June night, for Earth's satellite had reached perigee, that point in the elliptical journey when the ancient goddess came closest to Terra. England's green and pleasant land had looked quite different when the statues found at Branham and Pembroke's home were carved.

What no one knew at the time but would soon discover, was that Branham Hall and the grounds that extended from the village all the way to the sea and even beyond, had once belonged to the gods. By September, Martin Kepelheim would chance upon a map that revealed a long-forgotten truth: That an area known as Doggerland had once connected modern-day Kent to the European continent, sometime before the year 6000 B.C., when giants ruled the land. Long before Noah's birth, enigmatic beings from the heavens, the *Grigori* or Watchers, along with their giant offspring, ruled the tribes and cities of this primeval world, leaving traces here and there. These magnificent gods also bore children, and their exploits inspired sculptors and painters to record their divine images as acts of worship.

Two such gods were called Araqiel and his consort Eluna. The human chieftain of Doggerland's fiercest warrior tribe, a man called Kannu-Ki, or 'horn of the earth', longed to become one with the gods. One night, Kannu-Ki had a dream, and in that vision, Araqiel came to him and promised to fulfill Kannu-Ki's wish to be a god. To achieve this, he must order his magicians to form two statues, anointed in human blood; one of Araqiel, the other of Eluna. Then, he must order these same wizards to design an underground maze to serve as a vast temple to the god and goddess: The Realms of the Dead. This magical maze must extend eastward from the sea, all the way through Doggerland, and also westward for the same distance.

When the floods came to destroy all flesh, Araqiel and Eluna fled, concealing themselves upon the dark side of the moon. The god and goddess thought themselves clever, but Samael allowed the escape, for the One planned to use the Dragon and his consort's mischief against them. Both would be tested at a future time.

As the flood waters rose, the two statues were buried beneath silt and sand and earth, awaiting reactivation by the birth of twin children: Robert and Georgianna Sinclair, who drew their first breaths beneath the rays of a supermoon, the eyes of Eluna.

And thus, the end began.

Blissfully unaware of such eternally complex eschatological events, the very pragmatic Mildred Ketchum awoke with a start. Her hazel eyes searched the room for motion, for her senses shouted of intrusion, and she could hear footsteps outside the house.

"Bill!" she whispered, nudging her sleeping husband. "William Andrew Ketchum, wake up! There's someone about in the gardens!"

Fifty-one-year-old Bill Ketchum turned over, his iron grey hair askew, mouth open. "What the devil's going on, woman?"

"Intruders, that's what's going on. Get out of bed before I fetch the master's shotgun myself!"

Ketchum sat up, scratching his head. "It's prob'ly the wind."

"It's those ruffians the master's been talkin' 'bout. Those that broke into the cellars and killed the poor colonel, God rest his soul. Now, go, else I'll go myself!"

Ketchum wore only a sleep shirt, but he pulled on a pair of brown wool trousers and drew black braces up over his rounded shoulders. Still barefoot, he planned to make a quick search of the house, and then return to much more pleasant dreams. He emerged from their back bedroom and into the hallway towards the kitchen. As he passed the butler's pantry, Ketchum heard a loud scratching. *Likely a tree branch*, he assumed, turning towards the leaded panes that formed the kitchen's north-facing windows.

Not a branch.

A face.

White, cruel, and filled with rage.

Ketchum's ageing heart went into overdrive, and he dashed out of the kitchen and towards the cellars where Sir Simon kept his collection of guns. It took half a minute to reach the door, but the panicked caretaker had forgotten the key, and so he dashed back to his office, fetched the iron key, and ran through the narrow hall back to the cellar door.

It was open.

Bill Ketchum's breath caught in his throat, and he could hear the rapid thumping of his heart in both ears as he entered the cold room. Even in summer, this underground chamber remained cool, but not cold.

Why's it cold? he asked himself. *Must just get cold at night.*

At Seth Holloway's suggestion, Ketchum and a lad named Kevin Jones, who sometimes helped round the house, had loaded the nine-foot-tall statue onto a dog cart and then carefully carried it down the cellar's back stairs to protect it from the weather. Bill could hear a strange sort of humming. Stepping back towards the open doorway, he fumbled in his trouser pocket for matches. Striking one, he intended to light a sconce, but no sooner had he lit the phosphorus tip, than something blew it out!

He struck another.

The flickering yellow flame puffed out again.

A third did the same, but before all went dark, William Ketchum saw her.

The cold marble face.

Eluna.

"Hello, little man," he heard in his left ear. "Tell Sir Simon thank you. Tell Sinclair we will fetch him soon to test his blood. Tell him, Angiolina says *tick tock*."

Ketchum stared into the darkness, but the rods of his eyes flashed signals into his optic nerves, registering the impossible.

The statue had moved, and she was walking up the back stairs and into the night.

William Ketchum fled the cellar, his untucked nightshirt flapping as he ran, and his braces slipping off his shoulders. His face was pale as paper.

And above, the bright light of the supermoon shone upon the capering statue. It ran through the gardens until it reached the entrance to an ancient tunnel system.

Then, the supernaturally animated effigy passed into the Realms of the Dead, bound for Hell itself.

CHAPTER FIFTY

3 am - Branham Hall

Charles Sinclair returned to his wife's bedchamber, happy but exhausted. The room stood in semi-darkness to allow Elizabeth to sleep. A strong smell of alcohol and carbolic soap mixed with ginger root and camphor filled the air. He took his former chair, smiling warily as he gazed at his wife's soft face. She'd worked like a champion to bring his children into the world, not once complaining. Amelia had screamed and shouted a constant stream of obscenities at her nerve-racked husband during delivery of Albert, blaming Charles for the unbearable pain she endured.

But not Beth. She had borne it all, whimpering a little or making small cries now and then, but never had she blamed him—indeed, she'd thanked him for remaining with her.

"What man deserves so precious a wife?" he asked aloud, stroking her damp hair. It was then he noticed her skin felt cool. He switched on the bedside lamp. She was pale—far too pale.

"Beth. Beth!" he called out, touching her shoulder.

No response. He shook her firmly, but her eyelids remained closed. He shook her again. "Beth! Wake up!"

Panic took hold, and Charles checked the bed. The sheets and waxed cotton liners were soaked with bright blood.

Gehlen had placed a handbell nearby, and Charles rang it over and over. "Nurse Reston!" he shouted. "Anthony! Anyone!"

The nurse had been on her way to the chamber, and she ran into the room. "Yes? Sir, what is it?"

The duke pointed to the blood-soaked bed. "She's bleeding!" he cried.

"You must leave, sir. Let us handle it."

"I am going nowhere! She's dying!"

Gehlen appeared in the entry. Seeing the situation, he began calling out orders, his voice remarkably calm. "Nurse, check that everything's prepared on the transfusion equipment and then fetch Dr. MacAlpin and Lord Aubrey. Charles, roll up your sleeves and lie down beside the duchess."

The duke did as ordered. "Is she going to die?"

"Not if we can replace the lost blood immediately. We'll likely need to use all three of you. I may require two pints apiece."

"Take it all. She cannot die."

"It won't come to that."

Michael Emerson arrived and began to prepare to help with the procedure. "I'll have Reston take blood from everyone in the house and perform the test. It looks as though we may need more than three donors."

The room became crowded with doctors and donors. Each man took his turn, offering life-giving tissue to the duchess's collapsing circulatory system.

Outside the windows, perched within a tall tree, two owls kept watch, heads bowing now and then. It took nearly an hour for a total of five brave men to offer their blood. Charles Sinclair, Paul Stuart, Henry MacAlpin—but also, as it turned out, Cornelius Baxter and a young footman named George Grimes, both also tested as compatible with the duchess's blood. Adele Stuart Sinclair, too, tested compatible, but neither her natural nor adoptive father would allow the adolescent to serve as a donor.

"No, darling," Sinclair told her. "I understand you want to help, but I cannot put you at risk. How else would I cope if your mother left us? I need you, Della. You must be my rock."

She'd hugged him and cried a little, insisting she could help by praying. Indeed, the rest of the Branham household joined together in groups. And the name of Elizabeth Sinclair rose up through the heavens and echoed in the ears of God.

For four long hours, the penitent family waited. Charles sat beside his wife, a bandage on his right arm, anxiously watching for any sign that she might improve. Gehlen had finally managed to stop the bleeding during that first, tense hour. A tiny bit of the second placenta had remained inside the new mother's womb, and detached itself just enough to tear the wealth of blood vessels there. Gehlen's expertise had found the cause, but without replacement of the lost blood, she would surely have died.

As the clock began to chime seven, Nurse Reston entered the chamber, carrying Georgianna in her arms. "We're all taking turns holding the children, sir. When not in their tented cots, Doctor thinks it helpful to keep them warm through human contact. I thought you might like to be next, my lord."

Charles wiped tears from his face. "Yes. Oh, yes, please." He took the pink-cheeked infant, cradling her close. "Hello, Georgie. Your mother's asleep and probably dreaming of you. You've the prettiest blue eyes, but I remember them as dark brown." He glanced up. "Nurse, will her eyes remain this colour?" he asked Reston, who was removing the transfusion equipment and freshening the duchess's clean sheets with scented powder.

"All babies are born with blue or grey eyes, sir, but the colour can change with time. We're not sure why. Dr. Gehlen insists it's exposure to light that does it. He's a brilliant man, so he might be right. Keep her head supported, sir."

"Yes, I know," he said, unable to stop looking at the smooth face. "She's staring at me. Can she see me yet?"

"Not likely, my lord."

Paul Stuart entered, carrying Robby in his arms. "Looks like you've been recruited as well. Apparently, we're all to take turns now and then cuddling them. The things I do for you, Cousin."

Charles smiled as he gazed at the earl. "You look quite natural with a baby, Paul. In just four months, you'll be holding your own son or daughter."

"I pray you're right," he answered wearily. "If Delia can hold on that long."

"Has she settled down?"

"Oh, yes. She's asleep. Henry's absolutely marvellous with her, Charles. It's God's mercy that both he and Gehlen are here. Almost as if it were planned."

"I suppose it was," the duke answered. Outside the owls' wings fluttered, and both their heads lifted up. The white owl moved closer to the window.

Georgianna began to cry, and Charles tried soothing her by singing an old lullaby. "Lullay, mine liking, my daughter, mine sweeting. Lullay, my dear heart, mine own dear darling."

Paul stepped closer, his arms carefully holding the young heir to the dukedoms. "I'd no idea you could sing. You're actually rather good, Charles."

The young duke laughed. "Adele calls it caterwauling. I suppose it is compared to my wife's voice."

"No, actually, it's quite good," the earl insisted, drawing close to that side of the bed. "See here, Robby appreciates it. He's smiling."

Aubrey bent low so Charles could see the curly-haired boy. His small lips were pulled up, and his cheeks puffed like tiny apples. The fair blue eyes blinked, and the black lashes fluttered like a pair of fans.

Sinclair's own eyes filled with tears. "What if she dies, Paul?"

"She won't die," his cousin promised. "The bleeding's stopped, and her face already looks rosier."

Georgianna reached up towards her father's face. The two men brought the twins close together, and Georgianna turned to look at her brother.

"She knows he's close," the earl said. "See?"

Then, a soft voice joined theirs. "You look quite natural holding a baby, Lord Aubrey," she said weakly.

Charles gasped, the unshed tears falling. "Beth?"

The duchess managed a faint smile. "Hello, Captain."

"My precious little one," he whispered in return.

"Hello, Georgie," the duchess said, her hands trying to touch the child in her husband's arms.

The baby's eyes widened, and her tiny hands spread out, the fingers stretched. "She's trying to find you," Sinclair told his wife. "Shall I put her in your arms? Are you strong enough?"

Beth shook her head. "I can't. Not yet. Is there water?"

Reston interrupted. "Sirs, if you'd take the children to the nursery and return them to their tented cots? The wet nurses can feed them. I'm sure Doctor will want to assess the duchess."

"Yes, of course," Aubrey answered. "Welcome back, Princess. Your own little prince says hello."

Beth's breathing was shallow, and she hadn't the strength to answer. The two men left, and Reston brought the duchess a sip of water. "Not too quickly. Any pain?"

"A little."

"You should sleep, if you're able. Dr. Gehlen may not wish to give you any pain medicine yet. My lady, I'm here should you need anything. Everyone's been praying for you."

Anthony and Emerson entered and began a slow examination of the duchess's condition. Below, in the main library where the family had gathered to pray, Charles reported the good news, and the group offered prayers of thanks. The pastor from the Branham church, who'd been at the hall since Sunday, led the family and staff in several hymns, and Adele sang a solo. Mrs. Stephens began to prepare a great feast in honour of the twins' birth, and soon the entire household was smiling and laughing.

When Charles returned to his wife's bedside, she was sitting up, wearing an apricot nightdress made from French silk and Austrian lace. Her dark hair had been brushed and braided across her right shoulder. Never had she looked more beautiful to her grateful husband.

"I'd marry you again just because of how you look now, little one," he said after kissing her. "Beth, you are the most beautiful woman in all creation."

She reached for his hand. "I love you, Captain. And I'd marry you again. And again. And again. I am still quite tired, though. I may need to sleep soon."

He kissed her hand, taking it twixt his own. "We nearly lost you. It's no wonder you're tired."

"Yes, Dr. Gehlen told me about that. I understand I now carry the bold blood of five, fine men in my veins. And some of that blood is yours. Shall my mathematics skill now improve?"

He laughed. "Perhaps, but I expect it was quite good already."

"Charles, you say you nearly lost me, but I think you did for a little while."

"What do you mean?"

"I had a vision. Or perhaps a dream. I'm not sure, but it was as real as you are now. I stood upon a hill, surrounded by eight trees. Two were willow, and the others oaks. Overhead, I could see flying machines, and these fired weapons against the trees. And then, I saw you. You emerged from amongst the trees, and you held a crown in your hand. When you looked up, the machines began to fire all the more, and it seemed to me they were angry. You raised your voice, and the machines vanished. Then, I saw the entire world shaking as though blown by a great tempest—or perhaps an earthquake. The trees remained rooted, never once faltering. And then you vanished. Afterwards, I felt myself flying, and I could see all of London, and then England, and then the entire world. All were rejoicing. And my flight took me higher, and I stood before God's throne. He told me that my time was not yet; that you needed me. That the trees must be born. And then, I heard a baby crying. I opened my eyes and saw you and Paul, holding our children."

"A dream," he said, though Sinclair knew Beth's dreams often held truth within them.

"No, Charles. I was really gone, but God sent me back to you. And I believe I know what the vision meant. The trees, I mean. If I must return for them to be born, then surely, the trees are our children."

"Eight children?" he asked, amazed. "Beth, I doubt that..."

"No, I'm sure of it! Do you remember that I've always said we'd have seven children. Henry told me that when he rescued me inside the Faerie's copse, the cottage was decorated with entwined hearts surrounding seven smaller hearts. You and I saw just two. Might the two be our twins, showing I was carrying them, but somehow the seven represent all our children?"

"All? But you dreamt of eight."

"Adele," Elizabeth said, smiling. "Two willows and six oaks. Two daughters and six sons. We have our two daughters now. Della and Georgianna. I only have to deliver you five more sons."

The duke sat back, considering her words. *It was what the angel had told him. Six sons and two daughters.* "I cannot say if your dream is a vision of our future or not, but if so, then we must allow God to reveal those sons in his time. For today, I'm content with Robby. Now, sleep, Mrs. Sinclair."

She yawned, moving down into the quilts. "Very well, Mr. Sinclair. I'll sleep. But once the twins are christened, and I'm fully recovered, you and I shall begin work on son number two."

He kissed her and switched off the lamp. "We'll discuss it then. Now, sleep."

She shut her eyes, and Charles remained until he was certain she slept. He called the nurse to keep watch, and then descended the stairs to join the others in the library.

You and your sons will change the world, Romanov had told him. Six sons.

The duke considered the idea of oaks and willows. Oaks are slow-growing, strong, proud trees. Willows were gentler, slender, and often took root by the water.

Eight children. Five to go. What miracles did God have in store for him and his little duchess? Only time would tell.

CHAPTER FIFTY-ONE

5th August, 1889 – London

Margaret Winstone nearly leapt out of her chair. "Frederick! Oh, my dear! It's an invitation from Charles and the duchess!"

Frederick Winstone had been enjoying a pipe and the morning paper, a time when his wife knew to keep quiet, and he nearly shot her an angry glance, but the import of her statement sank in before that glance surfaced onto his face.

"Charles?" he asked. "An invitation, you say? Well, let's see it."

The *Pall Mall Gazette* now proved most uninteresting, and it fell from the man's thin fingers as he reached for the elegantly engraved card. Putting on a pair of spectacles, the snobbish gentleman read aloud, "Her Grace, The Most Honourable Elizabeth Georgianna Victoria Regina Stuart Sinclair, the 12th Duchess of Branham and His Grace, The Most Honourable Commissioner Charles Robert Arthur Sinclair III, 1st Duke of Haimsbury, request your attendance at the christening of their twin children, The Most Honourable Charles Robert Arthur Sinclair IV, Marquess of Anjou, and Lady Elizabeth Georgianna Patricia Angela Sinclair, at Drummond Chapel. Ten o'clock. 11th August, 1889. Reception to follow at Drummond House, Westminster. RSVP to Haimsbury House."

Margaret walked to her husband's chair and peered over his shoulder. "We are going, aren't we, Frederick? Please, say we are. This is the event of the entire season, and I'd so love to see the babies!"

Winstone cleared his throat, tapping the invitation with his index finger. "Clearly, our presence means so much to Charles that he sent an engraved invitation. It would be rude to decline, my dear.

Yes, well yes, indeed. Perhaps, we should return the RSVP card personally. What do you think?"

"Oh, but would that be all right? I mean, they've only just arrived back in London, after all, and everyone's queuing to visit. Perhaps, we'd be in the way," she suggested, hoping her husband would overrule her.

Winstone stood, putting an arm round his wife. "My dear, that might apply to everyone else, but we're family, are we not? Did not the duchess send a birth announcement to us the very next day? Put on your coat, my dear. Let us take the morning air and enjoy a drive to Westminster."

ICI Headquarters – Queen Anne House
Charles Sinclair entered his office on the stroke of ten, surprised to find a claret red vase filled with a curious bouquet of flowers waiting for him. Returning to the hallway beyond his office suite, the duke called out to a man in a dark coat and grey trousers.

"Mr. Thick, are these flowers for me or my wife?"

The duke's secretary, Gerald Pennyweather, had stepped out to meet with Sir Reginald Parsons at the House of Lords, and the newly hired clerk, former Metropolitan Police Sergeant William Thick, left his small office and followed the short hallway to his superior's.

"Excuse me, sir? I had my head down working on the legal copies you requested. Did you call?"

"Yes. Flowers," the duke explained as he sat behind his large desk. "Who delivered them?"

"I didn't see, sir. The flowers were there when I arrived at eight. Shall I make enquiries?"

"No, don't bother. I take it Pennyweather is looking into the Wychwright matter for me?"

"Yes, sir. That's the document I'm copying, actually, my lord." Twenty-eight-year-old Thick had prematurely grey hair and cheerful blue eyes and a dark beard. He'd served in the Metropolitan Police for six years, one at H-Division as booking sergeant, and three as Sinclair's secretary at the Yard. Thick was childless and his wife Hannah worked as a nurse at the London Hospital. Impressed by the young man's work ethic, Charles had seconded him from the Yard as

Pennyweather's assistant and agency trainee several weeks earlier with a significant rise in pay.

"A strange selection of flowers," Sinclair mused, looking at the bouquet. "Fir branches? It's somewhat early to think of Christmas, don't you think? And these are the darkest roses I've ever seen. What's this one?"

Thick stepped closer, touching one of several green stems with bell-shaped flowers. "I've seen them before, sir, but I can't remember where. Perhaps, this will explain," he added, pointing to a small white envelope. "A card."

"Yes, I suppose it might." Charles removed the enclosure, attached with a black velvet ribbon. "Thank you, Thick. That's all for now."

The assistant left, closing the door as Sinclair sat at his desk, reading through the curious card:

Will contact you soon. Tick Tock.

Charles looked again at the enigmatic card, addressed using a typewriter to: Commissioner Sinclair, Duke of Haimsbury, Queen Anne House. "Tick Tock? Just what does that mean?" he mused aloud as Martin Kepelheim knocked on the door.

"Flowers?" the tailor asked. "Did I miss a special occasion?"

"None that I'm aware, and welcome back to London," the duke greeted his friend with a firm handshake. "Sit, Martin."

"Thank you. How fares our beautiful new mother?"

Charles beamed with pride. "More beautiful than ever, if that's possible. She's nearly recovered, and we plan to leave for our long-delayed wedding trip in just under a fortnight. And I'm pleased to say the twins are growing faster than Scottish thistle. How is everything at Branham?"

"Everyone is still talking about the twins, of course. And May's fête. Your performance on the tilt yard features prominently amongst the locals."

Sinclair laughed. "Yes, I imagine it does. And I'm very glad no one else noticed Wychwright's rifle. Whatever sudden wind blew him out to sea was a blessing indeed!"

"Yes, so it was. I doubt, however, that the wind was incidental or even natural. Divine intervention is not too much to consider."

"Our Lord is always with us, old friend. And Pembroke? Have you determined what happened at his home?"

"It eludes us still. Our Viscount Paynton's good father, Lord Salter, has returned to Kent, and he has taken up the case, you might say. The male statue remains locked inside your shed, of course. Thirteen pieces in all. Minus one very important part."

"Which is?" asked the duke.

"Ah, now that is personal, I suppose. Have you ever heard the legend of Osiris?"

"Only the basics. His brother Set killed him because, allegedly, Osiris had slept with Set's consort."

"Yes, some of the myths record that, but according to young Mr. Holloway, Egyptians had an aversion to recording negative events."

"Unlike the reporters of London."

The tailor smiled. "True. Seth told me that his research indicates a belief amongst the scribes that writing a matter could alter the future. That written words had the power to affect our reality."

Charles considered this for a moment. "Might that belief stem from an older legend, Martin? This story of Raziel's book?"

"I think it might. But it may explain why so little was written about these ancient gods and goddesses. Perhaps, our ancestors feared the power of writing."

"What does this have to do with the broken statue found in our lake?" asked Sinclair.

"Ah, well, we have thirteen pieces, which corresponds to one myth about Osiris: that Set divided his body into fourteen segments."

"Which implies we're missing a piece."

"Oh, yes, and it's quite obvious when you conduct an inventory. Your statue is missing its manhood."

Charles stared, the idea resonating in his mind. "Is it possible this private bit still lies beneath the lake?"

"No. Powers has drained Queen's Lake again, and he's recovered no regenerative organ."

"Regenerative," the duke echoed. "That is a telling word. Why do I feel as though we're in the middle of another of Redwing's long rituals?"

"Because, my friend, we are. Charles, it's unlikely these will stop. Why would they? Redwing's been conducting these rites since the dawn of man. Their earlier members called themselves by other names, of course, but the core spirits are the same. And with this internal war they're waging, I fear you and your family remain vulnerable." The tailor turned the crimson vase round to examine the bouquet. "Who sent you this?"

"The card has no signature."

"Charles, this is a warning. These are belladonna flowers. They are poisonous, and possibly the very plant used in your tea last year in Scotland."

The duke touched the violet bells. "Belladonna? Poison, yes, but doesn't the name also mean 'beautiful woman'?"

"Yes, yes, it does. And in floriography, or the language of flowers, it symbolises silence, death, or deception."

"Paul once mentioned using flowers to send messages. Apparently, they form part of his espionage toolkit. What do the fir branches mean? Not Christmas, I suppose."

Martin shook his head. "No. Actually, they mean 'time'. Put them together, we have time, deception or silence, and beautiful woman, possibly danger? Poison? Very strange."

Sinclair handed the tailor the small card. "This came with it."

"Oh, I believe the fir must indeed stand for time. Tick tock." Kepelheim reached into his coat pocket and withdrew a sheet of paper, folded into quarters. He handed it to his friend. "This may be related, and I fear it implies another spell. Or perhaps, another aspect of the one in progress."

Charles unfolded the letter. "Is this part of a diary?"

"A copy of one, yes. I have at last tracked down the family of Franz Meijer, the genius who built your two clocks. Jacob Meijer is the grandson. Also a clockmaker, but he despairs of fixing your clocks."

"Plural? Has the first one also quit?" asked Sinclair.

"I fear it has. In fact, according to Mr. Staunton, the jeweller whom our Aubrey asked to clean it, the clock stopped on the eleventh of June at three in the morning."

The duke grew quiet, his azure eyes moving back and forth as he tapped the sheet of paper. "Three, on the morning of the eleventh? Martin, that's when Beth nearly died. Why would that clock stop then?"

"It is yet another piece to this massive puzzle. Read the diary, Charles. Or rather the copy."

The duke examined the paper. It read:

10th June, 1860

This may be my final entry. Prince Aleksandr paid me a call four months ago and ordered me to produce one last clock for him. I have not written about this clock before now, but I must leave a confession for HIM. I pray HaShem will forgive me and that my son may never be visited by Koshmar or his evil brethren. He is a devil. A dragon who uses men for his own ends. I cannot undo what I have done, but I ask HaShem to protect the boy and his family.

The last clock is complete, and Koshmar collected it three days ago. The first two, 'Arthur's Victory' and 'Arthur's Defeat', were once my greatest triumphs. I laboured nearly a year on them. Never until now, did I realise their purpose was evil. When I watched my final clock begin to work, I knew the design Koshmar gave me was created in the pit. I have drawn it here, and I do not know where Koshmar has taken it. I asked if it were going to the boy.

"No," he say. "This one will sound but once. I shall call it 'Arthur's Return'. A rebirth to astonish the world."

I asked what he meant, and the demon laughed and asked me, "Do you know your Tanakh, old man? Isaiah 26:14. 'They are dead; they shall not live; they are deceased, they shall not live'. My friend and I intend to break that curse. Shatter it into tiny pieces."

"How?" I asked the creature.

"By breaking time itself with a beautiful machine made of flesh. Dead begetting dead, their blood bound up in intricate complications, and this clock—once baptised with the right kind of blood—will provide the ignition."

And so, I watch my own clocks as they tick tock, tick tock within my workshop. It is nearly dawn. My heart is slowing, and so are my clocks. Isaiah is open before me. Chapter twenty-four. Verse fourteen. The crafty devil is right. May HaShem keep his promise. May they never rise. And may their memory perish forever.

I ask my son to send this confession to the boy. His name is Char—.

"It stops," he told the tailor.

Martin sighed. "Yes, I asked young Jacob about that. His father said he couldn't deliver the diary to this boy, for the name was incomplete. Of course, it's obvious to us."

Sinclair felt unsettled, his thoughts turning through a dozen worries. "A third clock to undo God's promise? Martin, that's impossible."

"True, but let us remember what our Creator said when mankind sought to break the imprisoned Watchers from Tartarus by creating the portal of Babel. Our Bible tells us that God suggested a united mankind could accomplish anything."

"But we're not omnipotent, Martin. We have limits set by God."

"We do, but what if enough rebel angels inhabit mankind and teach them ancient secrets, what then? Charles, I do not believe this alleged machine could really undo God's promises, but it may deliver much evil to our world."

"Then it's our job to stop it."

"And if we cannot?" asked Kepelheim.

The duke smiled. "Remember the promise of Philippians, my friend. Chapter four, verse thirteen. 'I can do all things through Christ, who strengthens me.' I say, woe to any rebel angel who dares to come up against us. Not because of our strength, but because of His."

CHAPTER FIFTY-TWO
5 Fitzmaurice Place

"I'll have Sinclair's guts for garters!" shouted William Wychwright as he read the court summons. "How dare the banks threaten to take this house. It's been in my family for six generations!"

His idle friends, Sir Richard Treversham and Cecil Brandon, along with a third scoundrel sporting a neatly trimmed goatee and long dark hair, sat round a white wicker table, playing cards.

"Do put down the post, old boy," called Treversham. "Cecil's out, and it's your turn."

"My turn? I'll say it's my turn. MacAllen, can't you do something about this thorn in my flesh?"

Patrick MacAllen was a lanky man with considerable muscle and charm. He had the rugged good looks that caused impressionable women to hand over their inheritance, but in truth the earl had little regard for females. He preferred the reassuring company of men.

"Who's the thorn?" he asked.

"Sinclair. That damnable duke! And just how is he a duke, I ask you? The fellow's a jumped up policeman with questionable connexions to royalty. Duke of Twinsbury, they're calling him now in the press. His Royal Highness, the secret crown prince! Who is this man, really?"

MacAllen laughed, his cold grey eyes on the pile of shillings, sovereigns, and bank notes. "I've got men looking into it, never fear. Why's this thorn pricking you, old man?"

William rejoined his friends, turning up the hand to review his cards: a pair of eights, ace of hearts, knave of clubs, deuce of diamonds. Nothing that would win him the pot. He should fold, but instead the willful baronet threw the last of his pocket money into the centre of the table.

"I'll draw and see you, Treversham."

Brandon was dealer this round, and he took the top card of the deck and slid it across the table to Wychwright.

"Best of luck to you, Will."

The baron discarded the deuce, took the new card and slowly upturned it close to his face, greedily praying for a third eight but keeping his face passive, so as to not reveal any clues to his fellow players.

Another ace.

Wychwright's stomach turned, but his face showed no sign of turmoil. He now held aces and eights. *The dead man's hand.*

A large bird overflew their heads, crying out with the oddest sound anyone had ever heard. His friends looked upwards in unison. Using the distraction, Will skillfully withdrew a hidden ace from his left pocket and slipped it next to its two brothers.

"Looks like a lovely little triplet and a deuce kicker," he told his friends.

Treversham stared at Wychwright with a suspicious frown. "Strange you'd have an ace of diamonds, old boy. I was sure it was... Oh, never mind. Well done, Will," he concluded, adding his cards to the bottom of the deck without showing them. "Shall we play again?"

Patrick MacAllen also returned his hand to the pile of cards. "I'd never call a man a cheat. Not a friend, that is," he declared, making it clear he knew Wychwright had deceived them. "Money isn't everything, after all, now is it? So, tell me all about this thorn. Why does Haimsbury disturb you?"

Brandon laughed as he shuffled the deck. "Duke of Twinsbury," he muttered. "You have to admit, Will, it's rather good."

"Haimsbury, Twinsbury, the operative word here is '*bury*', and I should love to do that very thing to the man! Why does he disturb me, you ask? The jackanapes detective dared to handcuff me inside his little fiefdom on Pall Mall. Wretch of a man! He and Aubrey bring shame to the reputations of landed gentry."

"Landed?" laughed Brandon, ever reckless if not entirely foolish. "You may have been once, Will, but not for long."

Wychwright's face puffed into a fleshy field of red, and he flipped the table upside down, sending cards, Brandon's IOUs, coins, bank notes, and wine glasses onto the freshly clipped lawn. Joseph Avery, his latest butler, had been silently keeping watch from a window overlooking the terraced home's courtyard. Avery shrugged and opened a nearby closet, gathering up a broom, mop, and pail.

The four men moved into the small solarium, each taking a chair whilst Avery refreshed the courtyard, all the while deciding to quit and ask for his unpaid wages.

As they waited, talk turned to politics. "You're head of Special Branch, MacAllen, can't you use your position to investigate Haimsbury?" Wychwright asked, slowly finding a temporary calm.

"Hardly," the politician replied as Treversham perused the agony columns of the morning papers. "My appointment is rather tenuous just now. The only reason I'm not out on my aspirations is because I keep a secret regarding our Home Secretary's cousin. Matthews prefers that George's secrets don't get out."

Treversham peered over the edge of the *Times*. "I can imagine what that secret is. Say, did you see this? Your nemesis is having his spawn christened on Sunday."

"And why should I care about that?" asked Wychwright.

The black bird which had neatly distracted the poker players several minutes earlier soared past the French windows, startling Mr. Avery, who swatted at the attacker with his broom.

The baronet laughed at the spectacle. "Poor old fellow! Looks like a rusty knight against a feathered dragon!"

The butler ducked as a second aerial assault narrowly missed his face, but the bird managed to pluck several grey hairs from his balding head. Avery then threw down the broom and stormed off, leaving Wychwright's employ forthwith.

Will saw nothing, for his attention was riveted on the voice whispering inside his head.

"I think you've lost another butler, old boy," Treversham told him.

"Yes, so I have," Will muttered, glassy-eyed.

MacAllen seemed to be the only one who noticed their friend's odd behaviour. "Everything all right?"

The baron snapped out of his trance. "Never better. You say Haimsbury's having some ritual on Sunday? Chaps, I've a very good idea. A grand idea. Damn it all, a helluva an idea! Patrick, if you can bring me just a few simple items, we can be rid of this troublesome duke and all rest easier in our beds."

"If you still own a bed," Brandon joked.

"Oh, I'll own a bed all right. And if I can play this hand right, I may just control some of the finest beds in England."

CHAPTER FIFTY-THREE

11ᵗʰ August, 1889

Drummond chapel stood upon a small knoll overlooking the north gardens. Built in 1734, the cross-shaped limestone and brick building held five hundred in the sanctuary and aisles, with room for another thirty within an organ and choir loft, sitting over the transept. Two spiral staircases flanked the altar, representing man's ascent to heaven, and a great cross dominated the apse, that featured a quartet of stained-glass windows, arching upwards, filled with scenes from the gospels.

That Sunday morning, every pew was crowded with invited guests, family, and a few leading members of London's fifth estate, publishers rather than reporters. As Westminster's tower bells chimed the tenth hour, Dr. Edward MacPherson, the church's pastor and long-time member of the Stuart-Sinclair inner circle, addressed the full house.

"Good morning. May our Saviour's blessings be with everyone here. We are honoured today to welcome the newest members of the Stuart-Sinclair family into the family of God. We are of the Presbyterian faith. Therefore this christening does not impute salvation unto these two beautiful children, but rather charges parents and godparents, as well as all present here today, to provide guidance and God's wonderful love. This ceremony represents the baptism of water, to which even our Lord submitted, but one day, Christ will call to these precious children, and it is they who must answer, for each one of us is required to speak yes or no to the Spirit's invitation, renouncing all sin and accepting the free gift of life, which is in Christ's redemptive act, even the shedding of His blood."

Mac looked to the front rows of the congregation, where the Stuarts and Sinclairs sat. "Who brings a child for dedication to the Lord?"

Charles and Elizabeth stood. "We do. My wife and I."

James handed Robby to his nephew, and Paul handed Georgianna to Elizabeth. The proud parents brought their twins to the marble font, standing with their backs to the great transept balcony overhead.

Mac gazed into the congregation and asked, "And who stands ready to defend these children as godparents?"

Paul helped his wife to her feet, answering for them both. "My wife and I."

"Please, come forward," the pastor told them.

A few reporters and photographers had managed to infiltrate the sanctuary, and one began surreptitiously snapping pictures with a small Kodak. He was unceremoniously removed by one of the circle's many uniformed agents. A few in the back noticed the commotion, amused at the brash intruder's deserved treatment.

"May I have the eldest child?" MacPherson asked Duke Charles. Haimsbury gave his swaddled infant to his friend. The innocent babe was dressed in the christening gown his great-uncle James Stuart had worn in 1819, even then an historic garment, for it had been handed down for four generations prior to that. Kepelheim had even told Charles that the elaborate, ivory lace and satin gown had once adorned the infant body of King James VII (known as James II to the English).

"Charles Robert Arthur Sinclair IV, 15th Marquess of Anjou," MacPherson began, "you are descended from a long line of kings, queens, princes, and dukes. Your future influence upon our kingdom and our world may prove great, but no matter where life leads, may you always rest within our Saviour's loving hands." He looked to Charles and Beth. "Charles Robert Arthur Sinclair III, 1st Duke of Haimsbury and Elizabeth Georgianna Victoria Regina Stuart Sinclair, Duchess of Branham, do you both confess Jesus Christ as Lord and Saviour?"

"We do," answered both.

"Will you promise to teach your son to follow Christ each day of his life? Will you disciple him and teach him to turn from evil?"

"We will," the parents said in unison.

"And to Robby's godparents, will you promise to teach him to follow Christ each day of his life, and will you disciple him and help him to turn from evil?"

Cordelia appeared somewhat distracted. Her eyes often drifted upwards, as though following movement within the choir loft.

"Delia?" Paul asked.

"Is it time already?" she whispered.

"She and I both promise," he answered, squeezing her hand.

MacPherson had been warned that Lady Aubrey's mind sometimes wandered, and he moved on to the next phase of the ritual. "Lord Aubrey, should anything ever happen to either or both of this boy's parents, do you promise to act as substitute, either for one or both? Will you intervene as a mentor and father in Robby's life and lead him away from temptation?"

"I will."

MacPherson dipped a silver chalice in the shallow water of the font and poured it upon Robby's dark curls. "Charles Robert Arthur Sinclair, I now baptise you as a child of God, and I admonish your parents to teach you of Christ's sacrifice and resurrection, so that one day, when called, you will accept that blood sacrifice of your own free will. Infant baptism is symbolic, it does not confer salvation," he told the congregation. "Each of us must choose Christ or deny him. Both parents and godparents have sworn to teach Robby and disciple him, and therefore, we, too, as a congregation have witnessed their confession. May I have the second child?"

Charles took Robby and handed him to his uncle. He then took Georgie from Beth and passed the sweet-faced girl to Dr. MacPherson. With his great-grandson in his arms, James Stuart beamed with pride.

As the ceremony continued with Georgianna, Cordelia Stuart's light eyes kept rising to the upper regions of the sanctuary. She whispered to her husband, "Will's not real, is he, Paul?"

The earl drew her close. "No, darling. He's not real." Paul's heart grew heavy, for his wife's hallucinations of demonic entities with Will Wychwright's face had continued since June, growing evermore frequent. Seldom did a day pass now without one or two visions.

"I love you," he told her.

She smiled. "Yes, I know. Are there birds in here?"

Paul said nothing, but hearing Cordelia's continued questions, Charles glanced up. He turned round, motioning to Sir Thomas Galton, who was sitting in the second row. The baronet quietly left his pew and crossed back towards the main doors by way of the aisle. Once he reached the halfway mark, Galton turned to examine the altar area and choir loft, where the ranks of a great pipe organ rose to the peaked ceiling like metallic soldiers, spreading east to west.

Two large black birds skulked near the eastern ranks, whispering to one another.

Above it all, perched upon the longest, deep-throated pipe, he noticed a white owl.

Galton signalled to six other men, who'd been stationed throughout the sanctuary prior to the ceremony. Everyone moved to predetermined positions, for each understood the hand signal: Possible shooter above.

The following ten seconds passed thusly:

Charles signalled to MacPherson, who handed Georgianna to Paul. The earl then passed the baby to James, who in turn placed the girl inside her basinet. At the same time, James gave Robby to Martin, who performed the same service with the boy. By one second past Galton's initial movement, both babies were secured.

Next, Elizabeth pulled her cape up over her head, and Paul drew Cordelia's over hers. The countess asked, "Are we leaving now?"

James took both women in hand, and their husbands split apart, each to a different side of the church.

The Right Reverend Dr. Edward MacPherson then shouted to the congregation, "Everyone to the doors, please! We've just been told there's an explosive in the building!"

Everyone murmured, many starting towards the exits, assisted by inner circle operatives. Fearful for her adoptive father, Adele Stuart dashed towards Sinclair. "Come!"

Sinclair could see the glint of a rifle barrel now, and he pushed Della down to the floor.

Paul Stuart guided his wife and Elizabeth to a side door, where Arthur France led them into the safety of Drummond Park.

In the eighth second, the church organist, or rather the false musician who'd replaced him, turned round and shouted a command to another man at the railing. "Now, you fool!"

In quick succession, five shots pinged and echoed in the high rafters, and the white owl attacked the false organist.

Finally, in second number ten, the shooter leapt or perhaps was thrown from the railing and landed at Sinclair's feet.

The scene inside the church had transformed from a pleasant Sunday morning to utter chaos. The crush of titled attendees pushed their way through the main doors and into the park beyond. Coaches filled with passengers, but very few left the gravel park. Rather, the curious peers and businessmen kept watch on the doors, hoping to discover the reason for the madness.

Reporters who'd been denied entrance snapped photographs and scribbled quotes from anyone willing to offer one, whilst Galton's men ran from coach to coach reassuring the family's invited guests.

"Just a precaution," they told the panicked individuals. "Everything's fine now. If you'll just make your way back to Drummond House, we'll begin the reception."

Inside the church building, Charles examined the crushed body of the shooter, whilst Paul ran up the stairs into the loft to search for other men, finding one cowering near the western ranks. The earl nearly yanked off the man's arm as he dragged him back into the light. It was Cecil Brandon, young friend to William Wychwright. The terrified lay-about started to speak, but Aubrey's anger overwhelmed all curiosity at that point, and his fist landed on Cecil's jaw, instantly knocking the man out cold.

Sinclair called up to his cousin. "Who is it?"

"Brandon. He's not talking. Who've you got?"

Charles knelt beside the fallen man. His leg showed signs of compound fracture, and the left arm's angle had a most unnatural look to it.

"William," he answered. "We'll need a doctor."

By ten minutes past the initial hand signal to Galton, two physicians tended to the would-be assassins. Henry took Brandon, who'd regained consciousness but was spouting nonsense about ghosts; and Anthony Gehlen, who had assessed Wychwright's condition, determining two fractures of the right leg, a sprained left ankle, a broken left ulna, and a possible concussion. He could perceive no internal injuries. An A-Division police maria was despatched to convey both prisoners to hospital.

Sinclair made certain of his family's welfare within minutes of the arrest, reassuring his wife that all was well. "I'm sorry you had to go through that, Beth. We'd prayed William wouldn't try this, but you did very well."

"I knew God would protect us, Captain. And you would never allow any harm to come to us," she smiled.

The young duke kissed her. "It's all over. William will pay for his crimes. I've sent France to arrest Treversham as an accomplice. Even if he didn't participate, he likely was part of the planning. Wychwright and his gang will pay for all they've done to us and Cordelia. I promise. Now, go on back to the house. Paul and I will join you as soon as we've finished here."

Elizabeth obeyed, and Charles returned to the church. Ed MacPherson was removing his Geneva coat. "It's grown quite warm in here. And I do not think it only because of the August heat."

Sinclair smiled. "You played your part beautifully, Mac. No one realised you were baptising dolls, or that our wives wore bullet-proof Joseon vests beneath their dresses. It's a wonder that none of the shots came anywhere near us."

The clergyman managed a wan smile. "I'm very grateful they did not! But I'd thought Wychwright's reputation was as top marksman in Africa. I wonder why his aim proved so poor here?"

"God's intervention," Sinclair answered. "Prayers of righteous men effect much, and you and Grandfather prayed before we began."

"Once this is all done, I shall be happy to baptise the real babies. Let me finish changing, and I'll join you in a coach back to Drummond House."

"Good. Galton!" he called to the baronet.

Tom had been scouring the sanctuary in search of traces of spent bullets. "Yes, sir?"

"Find anything?"

"A few chips of wood, most likely fallen from the rafters overhead. It looks to me as though Wychwright's rifle sights were defective, praise the Lord!"

"We've much to praise him for this morning, Tom. I'll be outside in our coach. See you shortly."

Galton nodded, his head down as he continued to search.

Sinclair called up to Paul, who had been searching the loft. "Leave it! Let's go back to the house!"

The earl waved. "I'll be there in a minute. Go on without me. I'll walk."

Charles left the church and emerged into the bright sunshine. Most of the coaches and carriages had long since departed for the party at Drummond House, but two black landaus sat near the far turn. One bore the Haimsbury-Branham crest and was hitched to four dappled greys. The other was unmarked and hitched to four blacks. Charles headed towards the Haimsbury coach, but just before reaching it stopped. He'd felt sure he saw Adele talking with someone in the second landau.

"Della?" he called. "Adele!"

That's when he heard her scream.

The duke's boots bit into gravel as he ran to the mystery conveyance. The door opened before he got there, and he could see

Adele inside, a man's gloved hand on her mouth. Charles reached the coach, and then everything went dark.

Just as he arrived at the open door, a tall man who'd been hidden behind the black landau leapt out and placed a cloth soaked in chloroform upon the surprised duke's mouth. A second man dragged the unconscious peer into the coach, and before anyone noticed, the hooves of the midnight black horses threw up gravel, and the deceptive landau sped away.

The white owl watched the coach tear down Drummond Park drive and then vanish through an unseen portal. The owl elongated into its human form and then proceeded towards the main house.

At precisely thirty-one minutes past ten, Duke James's butler Booth answered the bell. "May I see your invitation, sir?" he asked the caller.

The tall man shook his head. "I have no invitation, Mr. Booth, but I come and go as I please. This day, I require an audience with your employer."

"I see, sir. Might I have your name, and I'll ask the duke if he wishes to speak to you."

"Certainly. Tell him Prince Anatole Romanov must speak with him and with all the inner circle. The next battle has begun."

THE REDWING SAGA CONTINUES
FALL OF 2020 WITH BOOK 7:

KING'S GAMBIT

ABOUT THE AUTHOR

Science, writing, opera, and geopolitics are just a few of the many 'hats' worn by Sharon K. Gilbert. She has been married to Sky-WatchTV host and fellow writer Derek P. Gilbert for nearly twenty years, and during that time, helped to raise a brilliant and beautiful stepdaughter, Nicole Gilbert.

The Gilberts have shared their talents and insights for over a decade with the pioneering Christian podcasts, *PID Radio, Gilbert House Fellowship,* and *View from the Bunker.* In addition to co-hosting SkyWatchTV's flagship interview program and *SciFriday* each week, Sharon also hosts *SkyWatch Women* and *SkyWatch Women One-on-One.* She and Derek speak several times each year at conferences, where they love to discuss news and prophecy with viewers, listeners, and readers.

Sharon's been following and studying Bible prophecy for over fifty years, and she often says that she's only scratched the surface. When not immersed in study, a writing project, or scouring the Internet for the latest science news, you can usually find her relaxing in the garden with their faithful hound, Sam T. Dachshund.

Learn more about Sharon and *The Redwing Saga* at her websites: www.sharonkgilbert.com and www.theredwingsaga.com

OTHER BOOKS BY SHARON K. GILBERT

- *Veneration: Unveiling the Ancient Realms of Demonic Kings and Satan's Battle Plan for Armageddon* (non-fiction, co-authored with Derek P. Gilbert)
- *Ebola and the Fourth Horseman of the Apocalypse* (non-fiction)
- *Blood Lies: Book One of The Redwing Saga* (fiction)
- *Blood Rites: Book Two of The Redwing Saga* (fiction)
- *The Blood Is the Life: Book Three of The Redwing Saga* (fiction)
- *Realms of Stone: Book Four of The Redwing Saga* (fiction)
- *Realms of Fire: Book Five of The Redwing Saga* (fiction)
- *Winds of Evil* (fiction)
- *Signs and Wonders* (fiction)
- *The Armageddon Strain* (fiction)

CONTRIBUTING AUTHOR
- *God's Ghostbusters* (non-fiction)
- *Blood on the Altar* (non-fiction)
- *Pandemonium's Engine* (non-fiction)
- *I Predict* (non-fiction)
- *When Once We Were a Nation* (non-fiction)
- *The Milieu: Welcome to the Transhuman Resistance*
- (non-fiction)